MONGOL STEEL

by

Chris Pinney

TELEMACHUS PRESS

Cover Designed by Telemachus Press, LLC

Cover Art:
Copyright © istockphoto/105069726/Thinkstock
Copyright © istockphoto/ 108545613/Thinkstock
Copyright © Zoonar/ 126538581/Thinkstock
Copyright © Dorling Kindersley RF/ 91284898/Thinkstock
Copyright © istockphoto/neotakezo/5959137

Published by Telemachus Press, LLC
http://www.telemachuspress.com

Visit the author website:
http://www.brazossteele.com

ISBN # 978-1-937698-05-8 (eBook)
ISBN # 978-1-937698-06-5 (paperback)

Version 2012.11.25

Printed in the United States of America

10 9 8 7 6 5 4 3 2 1

To Alexandra, Hunter, and Dakota

"Life is either a daring adventure or nothing"
– Helen Keller

Mongol Steel

PROLOGUE

The Far East 1227

THE PROCESSION APPEARED at dawn and snaked its way along a rocky path that separated a forest of pine from a shimmering floodplain. Over two hundred massive wooden carts, each powered by twenty oxen, lumbered forward like sauropods while men rushed up and down the line slopping lard onto axles to keep the wheels rotating smoothly. Companies of soldiers, sitting erect atop stubby-legged horses, flanked the carts on both sides. At the head of the procession, four statuesque men stood next to the driver of their royal cart, resplendent in robes of silk and leopard fur. The spacious domed felt tent mounted on the platform behind them shuddered with each bump along the path.

The column arrived at the base of a ravine that gently carved its way skyward between opposing slopes of pine and granite. Carpeted in luscious grass and a rainbow of wildflowers, the ravine was host to a shallow river that bubbled and churned down its center, connecting clear, icy mountain headwaters with the greedy floodplain below.

Without pause, the carts began their climb along the river's eastern bank. Three hundred meters into the ascent, the royal cart veered to one side and came to a halt next to a stretch of dry riverbed. In its center, soldiers and prisoners gathered around a rectangular hole in the earth marking the entrance to a vast subterranean tomb.

The second transport in line pulled up between the royal cart and the river bank. Under the keen eyes of the soldiers, prisoners removed the leather tarp from the cart and unloaded cargo into the hands of fellow captives who formed a human chain into the burial chamber. After the cart had been stripped clean of its contents, a new one moved in to take its place. The process repeated itself until all but the royal cart had been unloaded.

Soldiers now boarded the royal cart, entered the tent, and reemerged carrying an ivory sarcophagus and a throne of sold gold inlaid with diamonds. As the soldiers conveyed these items to the tomb, a royal elder raised his hands to the heavens and spoke to the warriors now lining both banks of the river. The warriors clashed their weapons together and sang in response to the speech.

Forty girls, all virgins of noble birth, were led forward with arms bound. Executioners slipped behind them and slit their throats. The innocents thrashed and struggled until their lifeblood had drained, then their corpses were placed with reverence into the chamber. Fifty captives were chosen at random and, together with a number of horses ushered into the earth with the dead virgins. The elder then gave the order to seal the chamber.

A team of oxen maneuvered a thick block of marble over the tomb's opening. The block dropped into place with a gritty "thud," forming a near-perfect seal. Workers then applied a waterproof mixture of pitch, sap, and sand to the edges to complete the seal and spread a generous layer of river rock and soil over the marble surface.

Within minutes, all evidence of the tomb's existence had vanished.

In his brief and tumultuous seventeen years of existence, Kuan had never known such treasure existed in this world. He could only wonder who commanded such wealth in life, and in death. It had taken two complete cycles of the sun to unload the treasure from the carts that crowded the valley and still a third to transfer it all into the tomb that descended deep beneath the riverbed. Now with his strength nearly sapped from sleep deprivation, Kuan wearily tossed another shovelful of dirt into the mouth of the trench that, together with a hastily fabricated dam, had so effectively diverted the river's flow around the gravesite. Beneath his tattered slate grey tunic, the chilled muscles in his body protested each movement. He glanced over at the group of prisoners now dismantling the dam. With their work near completion, Kuan paused to ponder his fate.

Malnutrition, forced marches, and the seemingly non-stop digging had transformed Kuan from a robust, one hundred and fifty pound teenager into ninety-five pounds of aching flesh and bone. Beneath a crown of matted hair, eyes that once sparkled with the excitement and vitality of youth were now simply pits of depression and despair.

"Keep shoveling," a voice whispered next to him. "Don't let them see you stop working."

"What's going to happen to us?" Kuan asked, resuming his work.

"Now that we've buried their leader and his riches, they're going to kill us," the voice answered him.

Kuan shot a panicked look at this friend. Jiang, the person behind the voice, wiped the dirt from his brow and methodically scanned his surroundings. Short, compact, and muscular, Jiang had borne the physical stress and malnourishment of the past days remarkably well.

Best friends since childhood, both young men grew up in Youhuaz on the banks of the Yellow River. The son of the emperor's most prized artisan, Kuan chose to follow in his father's footsteps and by the age of fifteen, had become a proficient metalworker and arms crafter. Jiang, on the other hand, had enlisted in the Emperor's Elite Guard. Whenever the two were together, they freely spoke of their dreams and hopes with one another, anxiously looking forward to the prosperous lives that lay ahead for the both of them. Then *they* came.

The barbarian horde swept down upon their city like a swarm of locusts. When the city finally capitulated, all surviving women, children, and men over the age of thirty, including Kuan's father, mother, and sister, were slaughtered. Only young and able-bodied males were spared, for reasons that Kuan now understood all too well.

"When I tell you, run as fast as you can to the forest," Jiang said, tossing a shovelful of dirt into the trench and nodding towards the tree line at the bottom of the ravine.

"But the soldiers," Kuan protested.

"Just do it and you might have a chance," Jiang replied.

Kuan saw a soldier approaching on horseback. It was the one they called Mengu. A loathsome creature, he sat atop a scruffy chestnut horse that had more battle scars on its body than did its rider. Two of Mengu's subordinates rode behind him.

From beneath his leather helmet, Mengu's merciless eyes locked onto the two boys. Fingering the thin, stringy mustache that hung low off of his pitted face, he reined in his horse next to Jiang.

"You slaves, no talking," Mengu ordered. Immediately and without warning, he prodded the point of his lance into Jiang's upper back. Jiang grunted and collapsed as a crimson stain fanned over his tunic. Kuan wanted desperately to help his friend, but he knew it would mean instant death if he tried.

"Get to your feet, dog!" Mengu shouted. Head bowed, Jiang struggled to his feet and resumed his work. Mengu watched him closely for any sign of defiance that would warrant immediate execution, but he found none.

Mengu spat at his victim. "When the time comes, I look forward to killing you myself," Then he and his men set off to terrorize other prisoners.

"Jiang," Kuan whispered.

"I'm fine," Jiang replied with a grimace. "Keep working."

The two continued to toss dirt into their stretch of trench, which now contained a thick coagulation of water and mud. Ten minutes later, the water behind the dam, its flow through the diversion channel seriously impeded, began overflowing its banks. Within moments, a sharp "crack" reverberated throughout the ravine. The impatient river, sensing a weak point in the barrier, burst through the timbers and surged violently downstream to reclaim its original course. Those workers unfortunate enough to be caught in the dry riverbed when the dam exploded were tossed up like straw by the torrent, then smashed against the rocky bottom of the river bed with lethal force.

Mengu and his men rounded up the prisoners and divided them into three groups. The barbarian ordered the first group forward and lined them up along a lower section of the trench that had yet to be filled in. Mounted soldiers with glinting sabers encircled the two remaining groups to prevent escape.

At Mengu's command, bowmen advanced and drew back their weapons. The hissing arrows hit their targets with sickening "whumps," knocking their victims into the muddy trench bottom. The remaining two groups of prisoners, hearing the awful sound and subsequent cries of their countrymen, fidgeted in terror, but were kept under tight control by their ring of captors. With well-placed arrows, the line of executioners dispatched the wounded still writhing in the pile below.

The second group of captives shuffled up to the edge under the point of steel. Several turned to run and were slashed down with swords. Mengu shouted out his order and a hail of arrows sent more bodies tumbling into the mass grave. This time, the executioners didn't bother with the wounded. Instead, Mengu ordered the final group forward.

Jiang and Kuan obeyed and walked to the lip of the trench, Kuan closed his eyes and wept. His legs shook. He did not want to die. Memories of his family and better times filled his head. His back muscles tensed as he imagined the arrow's initial impact and the excruciating pain. He held his breath and listened for the order that would end his life.

Instead of Mengu's voice, Kuan heard loud groaning next to him. It was Jiang. His friend had fallen to his knees and was now bent over at the waist, rocking back and forth. The murmurs among the line of doomed men steadily increased with each of Jiang's groans. The executioners aimed their arrows, awaiting Mengu's word to release them. The soldier who had his arrow trained on Jiang started to relax his finger for a smooth release. A fierce voice suddenly broke in. The finger froze in place, and the soldier lowered his bow.

"Do not kill this one," Mengu said. He reined his horse within a meter of the prostrate Jiang. "He is mine. I will kill this troublemaker myself."

Mengu drew his curved saber from its scabbard. Jiang remained doubled-over, groaning loudly. Mengu raised his sword high into the air, then leaned over in his saddle to deliver the fatal blow. Without warning, Jiang leapt to his feet and smashed a jagged rock into the eye of the barbarian's horse. The animal reared back in startled terror and pain.

The quick move caught the giant warrior off-guard. Mengu's foot slipped from its stirrup and he flew from his saddle. The wounded horse bolted through the line of soldiers congregated behind their leader, igniting a chain of panic among the other horses. Several of Mengu's men were thrown. Others dropped their weapons in attempt to regain control of their mounts, and still others released their arrows, cutting down a large swath of prisoners.

Jiang pounced on Mengu like a panther, slamming the rock into his face with crushing force. Mengu cried out in pain and shock, grabbing the remnants of his shattered face with his hands. With calculated precision, Jiang pulled a dagger from Mengu's belt and plunged it into its owner's neck.

"Run, Kuan," Jiang shouted.

The words jolted Kuan out of a terror-stricken paralysis. Seizing the opportunity, he darted through a gap that had formed between the confused soldiers.

An arrow struck Jiang in the left shoulder and knocked him backwards off of Mengu. With the weight removed from his chest, Mengu clutched his neck and thrashed violently. Soon, his movements ceased and his eyes, before so full of hatred and cruelty, became hollow with death.

Soldiers descended upon Jiang like a pack of hungry wolves. Jiang retrieved the dagger from Mengu's neck and rose to his feet. With his left arm dangling uselessly at his side, he bellowed in defiance, raised the dagger, and charged the soldier nearest to him. A flurry of arrows struck his chest and abdomen simultaneously, and Jiang's corpse, powered with left-over adrenalin, took four more steps before collapsing in a heap.

The panic spread. Prisoners scattered in all directions in a desperate bid for freedom. The furious horsemen bore down mercilessly upon them and the air reverberated with the terrifying whistles of the heavy iron-tipped arrows bearing down on their intended targets. Those captives who attempted to cross the river were quickly cut down, their blood staining the otherwise crystalline water. Still others attempted to clamber up the rocky slopes, but they too perished beneath hoof and steel.

Kuan's lungs were on fire. He had never run so fast in his life. He had to reach the forest. An arrow zipped past him, followed by a distant grunt of disgust from the archer who had missed him. Kuan turned to look. He spotted a soldier on horseback fifty meters away, bearing down on him while reloading his bow. Fortunately, the archer caught sight of two other prisoners nearer to him making a dash for the nearby rocks. He abruptly changed course and bore down upon the two hapless victims, not bothering to waste arrows on them but choosing instead to cut them down with his sword.

Kuan reached the forest edge and plunged in without slowing his pace. A thick blanket of pine needles cushioned his bare feet as he wove in and out of the trees, looking for someplace, anyplace, to hide. He spotted a low lying branch and with a forceful leap, grabbed on to it. Then, mustering what little strength he had left, he swung his leg over the branch and pulled himself into the tree. Loud crashes echoed throughout the forest. Horses. Kuan scrambled up the tree branch by branch. More screams. More shouts. Suddenly, horns sounded in the distance and the shouting ceased.

Kuan wedged himself between two branches thick with needles. Tears poured from his eyes. He thought of his family and of his friend Jiang. He buried his face in his tunic to muffle the sounds of his grief. Soon, both mental and physical exhaustion overtook him and he slipped into a deep, dreamless sleep, temporarily released from the horror he had just witnessed.

When he opened his eyes again, he was greeted by a fresh, morning sun. Pine sap stung the abrasions on his arms and his legs tingled. He cocked an ear in the direction of the ravine, listening for the sound of man or horse. He heard nothing, save for the faint bubbling of the river and the cries of a lone eagle patrolling the valley.

Both hunger and thirst gnawed at Kuan. Fearing enemies in the shadows below, he waited. Two hours passed before the cramps became unbearable. He had to move. He swung his legs them over the branch and started down the tree. He then dropped to the ground and crawled to the forest edge, ever alert for danger. The ravine was empty, it's once lush grass and wildflowers trampled into a thin mat. No bodies. No evidence of any struggle. The trench had been filled in completely, its surface brushed smooth.

Kuan rose and walked to the river bank. He crouched and scooped handfuls of icy water into his eager mouth. Something caught his eye. In the water in front of him, partially covered with sand. Two coins. Gold coins. They must have fallen from one of the massive chests he had seen carried into the burial chamber. He stuck his arm full-length into the river and retrieved them. The words inscribed on their surfaces were foreign.

He combed the river for more coins and for the marble slab that marked the tomb's entrance. He found neither. A new resolve swept over him. Others must be told of what happened here, so that the deaths of Jiang and his fellow countrymen could be avenged.

But first he had to eat.

Kuan surveyed the distant mountains and checked the position of the sun. Then, with the coins gripped tightly in hand, he set off in search of food and the land he called home.

CHAPTER 1

Neimenggu Province, Inner Mongolia.

DR. MARGARET TOWNSHEND seized the vial of diazepam from the metal instrument tray and thrust the needle into the vial's rubber top. She sucked up the contents into her syringe and threw the empty vial to the ground, then she sprinted to the rear of the tent. Her movements were awkward, encumbered by the protective gear she wore.

The patient, a villager in his mid-forties, fought violently to free himself from the nylon straps that restrained his wrists and ankles to the sides of an old army cot. Two wide-eyed nurses, also dressed in protective clothing, stood near the cot, stone-like, reluctant to get close to the man. Other patients lying in the nearby cots, too weak to move, could only shriek in fear at the spectacle taking place next to them.

"Quick, he's loosening his straps," Maggie yelled to her nurses. "Cinch them down, fast!"

She reached for the injection port on the IV line, but the man's struggle made it a moving target. Once again, she called for assistance. This time, the two nurses reluctantly obeyed, advancing at a snail's pace towards the patient. Maggie abandoned the syringe and reached for the wrist strap closest to her, bloodied from the struggle.

As she pulled it tight, the man turned his head and stared directly at her. A chill shot up and down Maggie's spine. She had never seen eyes so full of fury. It was as if she were staring into the portals of hell itself.

The possessed man emitted a throaty moan, then let out an ear-piercing scream. His torso arched upwards and remained suspended in air for a full five seconds before it came down. Maggie took two steps back. It saved her life.

The man's head lashed from side to side and spewed saliva like a salvo from a machine gun. Maggie ducked to avoid a direct hit, but the nurse standing next to her didn't and bore the full brunt of the onslaught. She stood frozen in time, too horrified to move, her arms held out to her sides as if she had just been crucified. Long viscous strands of body fluid dripped from her clothing, face mask, and goggles.

"I'll get his ankles," a voice with a thick German accent suddenly bellowed from behind Maggie. "Inject him!"

Dr. Klaus Braemer, a tall, stocky man who could have easily passed for an NFL offensive lineman, shoved the nurse to one side and grabbed hold of the left ankle strap. He cinched it down as hard as he could until it would go no more. Maggie retrieved her syringe off the floor as Braemer secured the right strap. The patient roared with fury. With a steady eye, Maggie caught the injection port, inserted the needle, and mercifully deposited the drug into the man's bloodstream. Within seconds, the contortions subsided and the tortured eyes rolled back in their sockets. A dollop of pink foam oozed out of the man's nose and mouth.

"Thanks," Maggie said with relief. "Your timing couldn't have been better."

"Don't mention it," Braemer replied. He nodded at the terrified group of nurses who had gathered nearby. Seeing him look their way, they abruptly turned away.

"Don't just stand there," he said with force. He motioned to the dripping nurse. "Get her to decontamination!"

Two nurses complied with his order, albeit reluctantly, and herded their unfortunate colleague towards the front of the tent.

Braemer turned to Maggie. "It looks as though we may have a mutiny on our hands in the very near future."

"Can you blame them?" Maggie said. She scanned the enormous blue U.N. canvas tent that served as the village's make-shift hospital. It was filled to capacity. Over a dozen hospital workers, all encumbered by protective gear, moved cautiously about the tent. Some tended to patients while others carried hand pressurized sprayers filled with phenol compounds, misting floors, walls, and contaminated bedding. The overpowering scent of the disinfectant, mixed with the smell of vomit and excrement, fouled the air.

Braemer approached Maggie. At fifty-six, he had been a World Health Organization medical director for over twenty years. Literally tens of thousands of Third World inhabitants owed their lives to Braemer and his international team of doctors, nurses, and aides, who, for the good of humanity, unselfishly put themselves at risk battling rogue outbreaks of Ebola, Marburg, smallpox, and other invisible murderers. He cared deeply for his medical staff and whenever the guiles of the enemy claimed a team member, he took it hard. In the three years she served on his team, Maggie never saw the man get flustered. But now those alpine-blue eyes behind the visor betrayed a sense of frustration and despair. Even with the enforcement of strict barrier nursing techniques and the use of protective gear impregnated with polymerized antimicrobials, the WHO team's casualty rate was alarming.

"We buried Gretchen Friedrich this morning," Braemer said. He lowered his head. "She was from Bonn. I know her father quite well."

"It's all a horrible nightmare," Maggie replied. "Like some Wes Craven movie."

She walked to the foot of her patient's cot and unhooked the medical record attached to it. The poor soul lay still, emitting a soft, crackly moan with every breath. Maggie recorded the sedative dose, then instructed a nurse to treat the abrasions on the man's wrists and arms.

"We should move him to critical care," Maggie said.

"No room," Braemer said. "We'll need to cordon off a new area at the back of the tent to accommodate the overflow."

He motioned to Maggie. "Right now, I need you to take a break and get some rest. I'll take over until McCafferty gets here."

Maggie smiled and rubbed her neck. "Thanks. I'll take you up on that."

She knew he was right. This enemy took no prisoners. One careless slip of the needle due to fatigue could prove fatal. Whatever it was they were fighting, it had no concept of forgiveness. Like most of her medical colleagues, Maggie learned to function on limited sleep. The key was to keep moving. Yet exhaustion shadowed her and she knew her usefulness to the team and to her patients waned with each passing hour without rest.

"Has Dr. Lin heard anything from the laboratory in Beijing?" she asked.

"Nothing yet," Braemer replied. "Hopefully before dawn."

"Be sure to disinfect yourself properly on the way out," he added.

Maggie started to leave, but then paused. "If you don't mind, I'm going to check on Dr. Hastings before I go."

"By all means do so," Braemer told her. "I checked on him an hour ago. Nothing has changed."

The medical director gave her a friendly wave and set off to make his rounds.

Dr. John Hastings lay prostrate on a faded olive drab army cot behind a thin curtain that marked the entrance to the hospital's critical care unit, a one-room, mud-brick hut nestled snugly against the backend of the hospital tent. His face was ashen, his lips pale, and his eyes, the scleras stained deep crimson, were recessed within their sockets. Maggie saw him force a smile when she slipped in through the curtain.

"It sounded like that guy out there didn't care too much for your bedside manner," he said in a hoarse croak.

Maggie approached his cot. She had worked with Hastings on several projects over the past three years. Although a romantic relationship never developed, the friendship they forged had blossomed with each passing year. When Braemer informed them that the team was being sent to Yushan, both figured it would be just another routine containment operation. Now he lay in bed, dying, and she felt totally helpless.

She took his wrist in her gloved hand and felt his pulse. It was irregular. She unbuttoned his shirt and placed the bell of her stethoscope on his chest. She didn't like what she heard.

"Are you feeling any better?" she asked.

Hastings licked his cracked, bloody lips. "Actually Doc, I feel like crap. The toramivir doesn't seem to be making a dent."

Maggie's face betrayed her frustration. Toramivir was among the latest breakthroughs in antiviral drug therapy. If it didn't work…

"Let's give it a little more time before we pass judgment," she recommended with feigned confidence.

Maggie gazed into his eyes. Any day now, the fragile life light they contained could be gone forever. She fought to hold back her tears.

"John, you're in the thick of this battle. What's your take on it?"

"It sure feels flu-like to me, only ten times worse. My lungs are burning and my head is pounding." He rubbed his throat. "I'm having a hard time swallowing."

He paused for a moment. "You know, it's almost as if…" A coughing fit cut him short. A tiny amount of blood-flecked saliva appeared at the corners of his mouth.

Once the attack subsided, Maggie pulled a tissue from her pocket and wiped his mouth. "It's almost as if 'what,' John?"

Hastings answered her in a whisper. Maggie's eyes widened in disbelief.

"There's no way," she said.

He tapped his finger on her arm. "Maggie, let's face it. It's only a matter of time before I'll be pushing up daisies next to those other poor souls in that sad excuse for a graveyard outside."

He attempted a laugh, but coughed instead. He took her gloved hand in his. Maggie felt his feeble attempt to squeeze it.

"Promise me you'll do two things for me," he said. "First, for God's sake, don't let me get like that patient of yours out there. When the time comes, don't spare the narcotics, if you know what I mean."

Maggie knew exactly what he meant. "John, you know I can't do that."

He ignored her and continued. "Secondly, when I die, I want you to harvest the samples needed to verify my theory."

Tears streamed from Maggie's eyes. "I can't. I'm not going to dissect you like some laboratory rat." She shook his arm. "Besides, you're not going to die. You fight this, you hear me?"

Hastings squeezed her hand again, this time with greater force. "You have to do it. Many lives are at stake. You've got to find out what this is and stop it." A tear formed in the corner of one eye and snaked down his cheek.

"Do it, Maggie," he pleaded. "Please. Before it's too late."

Chapter 2

JOHN MASTERS WORKED the keypad of his smartphone while he stood next to his car parked just outside a private terminal on a remote runway at Baltimore-Washington International Airport. The flight he waited for was an hour late due to bad weather. No matter. The delay afforded him time to respond to the pile of e-mails that greeted him upon arising this particular morning. Just like every morning for the past week.

As director of the United States Center for Biointelligence and Biocontainment, known by the acronym USCBB within Washington circles, Masters was responsible for investigating reports of emerging infectious diseases, as well as potential biological and chemical threats, both domestically and internationally. Earlier in the week, his agency caught wind of one such threat, although the intelligence at that time had been vague. But it sharpened as the week progressed and prompted Masters to call in his troops.

A retired army colonel in his early fifties, he appeared much younger than his age, a direct result of ceaseless efforts to stay in shape. A touch of grey did lighten his otherwise auburn hair, yet it only served to accentuate the blue in his eyes. As the wife of the

House Speaker was overheard saying at a recent Washington dinner party, the Director "aged quite well."

Masters exuded an administrative confidence devoid of conceit, a characteristic that earned him the respect of both his superiors and his subordinates. When it came time to lead, he did so by example, not by lip service. He got the job done and expected his people to do the same. Because of this mindset, the USCBB had managed to help thwart twenty-one major terrorist plots against U.S. interests both home and abroad since its inception, as well as assist in the containment of over a dozen infectious disease epidemics. In short, it was one federal agency that truly earned its funding. And it was about to be thrown on the hot seat once again.

The Gulfstream jet materialized out of the distant cloudbank like a tiny ghost and rapidly grew in size as it made its final approach. Masters rushed to finish his last message. He clipped the smartphone to his belt just as the wheels of the jet touched the pavement.

After a brief taxi, the jet pulled to a stop twenty-five meters from where Masters stood. The drone of the engines had yet to die away before the door opened and the co-pilot appeared. He lowered the stairwell and proceeded down the steps, followed closely by a much taller man toting a travel bag. The passenger's jeans were tightly-pressed, as was his white button-down shirt. Justin boots, buffed to a fine shine, complemented a head of sandy brown hair that lightly curled down to the brim of the collar. A pair of ocean-blue eyes, set firmly in a rugged face, locked on Masters when the man set foot on the tarmac. Masters met him halfway.

Dr. Brazos Steele was Masters' go-to guy, a key player in the USCBB organization. A seasoned veteran of the Army Veterinary Corps, Steele earned the reputation as one of the world's foremost experts on weaponized infectious diseases. He also earned the reputation among his troops as one bad-ass veterinarian, at least as far as his combat skills were concerned. For over three years, Masters and the USCBB collaborated with Steele's unit on numerous bioterrorism investigations within Europe and the Middle East. Needless to say, Masters was impressed with what he saw. Consequently, it came as no surprise that when Masters caught wind of Steele's retirement from the Corps, he offered him a top position within the USCBB. Steele balked at first, harboring a penchant more for travel and adventure than some boring Washington desk job. It wasn't until Masters explained his job duties more fully and sweetened the deal by allowing Steele to home base in Texas instead of Washington D.C. that his recruit agreed to join the team. It was a compromise that Masters would never regret.

"How was your flight?" Masters asked, extending a hand in greeting.

"Bumpy to say the least," Steele replied. "Glad I passed on that breakfast taco this morning."

Masters took Steele's bag. "We'd better get moving or they're liable to start without us. We'll pick up something for you along the way."

"No need," Steele replied. He patted his stomach. "I'm good until lunch."

Masters grinned. He knew the feeling. "So be it."

The two men were soon cruising northwest on Interstate 70 through dew-ladened farm country towards Frederick, Maryland. With no weekday traffic to contend with, the trip to Fort Deterick took only forty minutes. A loosely packed city of square brick buildings contained within a two hundred acre compound, Fort Deterick was home to the United States Army Medical Research Institute for Infectious Diseases, the backbone of the American biological research program. USAMRIID's job was to develop strategies, process information, and implement programs for the defense of the United States against biological threats worldwide, as well as aid in the diagnosis and identification of naturally-occurring pestilences that arose in those remote corners of the globe. It was also the premier Department of Defense facility designed for the study of the most lethal viral organisms found in nature.

A guard dressed in green camouflage fatigues checked the papers given to him by Masters. Satisfied, he handed them back and waved them through. After several turns, they rolled to a stop in front of a large building with the United States flag fluttering atop a pole next to the entryway. Masters parked the car and the two men entered the building. After signing in at the front desk, they took the elevator to the third floor.

The elevator opened into the spacious office of Colonel Marcus Breyling, acting commander of USAMRIID. Breyling's secretary showed Masters and Steele into an oak paneled conference room, where three men and one woman sat in chairs around a rectangular table that dominated the room. All conversation stopped when Steele and Masters entered. At the far end of the room, a man in military dress uniform stood up, placed his coffee cup on the table, and walked forward. Colonel Breyling was light-skinned African-American, broad and thin, with a semi-flat nose, strong, high cheek-bones, and Castilian brown eyes. He had buoyancy to his step and a coolness honed from a childhood spent in the suburbs of Detroit.

A graduate of West Point and veteran of both Iraq and Afghanistan, Breyling had been at the helm of USAMRIID for only a short time following the untimely death of its former commander, Colonel Robert Willett. Breyling inherited a loose organization in desperate need of new leadership and he struggled to provide just that. It hadn't been easy. It seemed as if every time progress churned forward, a new crisis would arise and threaten to bring it to a grinding halt. Now, true to form, another one reared its ugly head. Fortunately for Breyling, he had a staunch ally and friend to fall back on when the going got tough. His former Pentagon colleague, Colonel John Masters.

"Sorry to interrupt your weekend, Dr. Steele," Breyling said.

"Not a problem, sir," Steele replied. "It gave me a good excuse to blow off the lawn."

Breyling's secretary came back into the room and interrupted them. "Sir, the White House is on the line."

"Thank you, Judy. I'll take it in the outer office."

Breyling turned to Masters. "John, go ahead and introduce Dr. Steele to the room. I'll only be a moment." Then he left.

Masters led Steele to the table and gestured towards a distinguished looking man in a dark blue business suit and pale jonquil tie, who made his way towards Steele from the opposite end of the table. "Brazos, I believe you know the Secretary of State."

"Brazos, it's good to see you," the man said. He took Steele's hand in both of his. William Tyler was a longtime friend of the Steele family and had known the younger Steele when the latter was still in diapers. His long pleasant face displayed the warm smile that was his trademark in Washington. As a former congressman from South Carolina, he used that smile and his charismatic Southern drawl to advance his political career at a rapid pace.

"How is your father doing?" Tyler asked. "I've spoken to him once since your mother's funeral."

"My dad is doing great, Mr. Secretary," Steele said. "You know he's in Washington now. He spends most of his time digging up as many golf courses as he can."

Tyler patted Steele on the shoulder. "I'll have to give him a call when things settle down a bit." He chuckled. "And try to win back some of that money that I dropped to him on the last round we played together at Fairview."

"I'm sure he'd like that," Steele said.

Next, Masters introduced an attractive, middle-aged woman with wavy blond hair and intense blue eyes set behind a pair of sleek European wire-rimmed glasses.

"Dr. Klara Dietrich is the senior director of the World Health Organization's Disease Surveillance Program."

She acknowledged Steele with a friendly wave. In her conservative business suit, she could have passed for the CEO of a Fortune 500 company.

Masters continued. "And sitting next to Dr. Dietrich is Dan Win, director of the CIA's Bureau of Asian affairs."

The oriental Win was a graduate of Beijing University and Professor of Asian studies at UCLA. He looked to be about Steele's age. He wore round wire-rimmed reading glasses propped low on a wide nose. Despite his young age, his black hair showed flashes of winter white. He gave Steele a quick nod.

Breyling suddenly reentered the room, followed by his secretary holding a stack of manila folders in her arms. She distributed one to each attendee.

"Sorry for the delay," Breyling said.

"Everything okay at the Big House?" Tyler asked.

"The president requests a briefing in person after we finish up here," Breyling said. "He's been on the phone all morning with Russian President Molkov and Chinese Premier Deng."

Breyling motioned for Masters and Steele to take a seat, then sat down himself. "I want to thank everyone for meeting on such short notice, but this situation requires immediate attention." He turned to Masters. "John, why don't you take it from here?"

Masters obliged. "As you know, a 'heads up' went out ten days ago to WHO's Global Outbreak Alert and Response Network concerning an epidemic ravaging a village situated on the northernmost fringes of the Inner Mongolia Autonomous Region in northern China. From early reports, over eighty percent of the village's population had been affected and one hundred percent of those died."

"Good lord," Secretary Tyler said. "I didn't realize it was that bad. Why haven't we heard about this in the news?"

Breyling answered him. "To prevent panic, WHO has requested a temporary media blackout until more information is available."

"Dr. Dietrich, would you be so kind as to give us some background?" Masters requested.

Dietrich shifted in her chair and adjusted her glasses. When she spoke, she did so with a thick German accent. "WHO learned of the outbreak after a Chinese military unit on a routine border patrol reported seeing corpses, both humans and animals, lying in the streets of a desert village called Yushan. Thankfully, the unit chose to return to their headquarters and report the finding rather than venture into the village and risk exposure."

"After receiving this information," Dietrich continued, "we diverted twelve members of an international team of doctors and scientists, who were working at the time on a cholera outbreak in Shenyang, to Yushan. Their job was to initiate containment operations and to provide us with an epidemiological assessment until a secondary medical team could be deployed. As of yesterday, four members of the team have died and another member is ill. Unfortunately, the Chinese military has quarantined and sealed off the entire village. I can't get my secondary team in there."

Steele broke in. "Have they been able to test any samples from the village to find out what's causing this?"

Dietrich answered him. "Initial on-site tests of the soil, air, food, and water from the village all came back negative for known chemical, heavy metal, or biotoxin contamination, including mycotoxins, ricin, botulinum toxin, or Staph enterotoxin B. We don't suspect a food or water-borne illness since the medical team had their own supplies and no history of exposure to either the local food or water."

"What about tissue and blood samples?" Steele asked.

Dietrich shook her head. "They never made it to the lab. The Chinese wouldn't allow them out of Yushan. They're sending one of their scientists into the hot zone to test the samples on-site." She removed her glasses and set them on her folder. "This thing is hot and it's scaring a lot of people. Symptoms include cough, headache, fever, body aches, vomiting, diarrhea, pneumonia. Later on, patients complain of an intense burning sensation in their muscles. Within hours to days, a furious dementia sets in, followed by a progressive paralysis that ultimately kills the victim."

"If it is an infectious disease, it must be a new one," Steele said. "From what you've told me so far, the epidemiology doesn't match any organism I'm familiar with."

Steele then turned to face Breyling. "Colonel, I do have one question." He motioned at Win. "Why are the State Department and the CIA at this meeting?"

"I'm afraid this is where the plot thickens," Breyling replied. "Dr. Win, would you be so kind as to give us a brief political update on the region?"

Win sat up in his seat. "Ladies and gentlemen, as you well know, China has been under the gun from the United Nations for human rights violations in Taiwan, Tibet, and, most recently, Inner Mongolia. Tensions have been on the rise for several months with Inner Mongolia pushing for independence from China in order to reunify with her parent country to the north. Even though the majority of citizens within Inner Mongolia are Chinese, a group that calls itself the Inner Mongolia Liberation Front, or IMLF, has organized a network of fighters who have claimed responsibility for sporadic acts of violence against Chinese citizens and troops stationed there. In response to what they perceive as terrorism, the Chinese have started a measured troop build-up within the region."

Win took a quick sip of water, then continued. "As you can imagine, this has made the Mongolians to the north, and their Russian neighbors, very nervous. To add fuel to the fire, China has accused the Russians of supporting the IMLF. The Russians of course deny the accusation. In fact, it is Mongolia's new president, Vachirdorj Bagaryn, who has stirred up the forces within Inner Mongolia to push for political independence."

"It sounds to me like the bastard is trying to start a war with the Chinese," Tyler said.

"His motives are still unclear. But of more concern to us is Russia. You must understand that they still view Mongolia as a strategic geographic and political barrier against their old archenemy to the south. As a result, Russia issued a statement last week pledging military support in the event of a Chinese encroachment upon Mongolian soil."

"What does all of this have to do with Yushan?" Steele asked.

"Word has it that the Chinese want to pin the blame for the outbreak on the IMLF," Win replied.

"Mighty convenient for them, isn't it?" Steele said.

"Folks, in addition to a potential worldwide health threat that faces us, we're sitting on a political powder keg," Breyling said. "We need to find out what we're dealing with, and fast, before this blows up in everybody's face. And in order to do that, we need tissue samples."

Breyling glanced at Masters, who then turned to Steele. "Brazos, we want you to go to Yushan and get those samples for us. At the same time, we'd like you to track the source of this outbreak."

"But didn't you say Yushan is off-limits?" Steele asked.

"That's true," Breyling replied. "However, Secretary Tyler feels confident that he'll be able to cash in a few chips with his diplomatic friends in Beijing and get us in."

Breyling stood, an indication that the formal meeting was over. "All of you will find more information in the folders in front of you. Mind you that information is classified, so please treat it that way."

Breyling addressed Steele. "Colonel Masters will be in close touch with my office, so feel free to relay any messages to me through him. USAMRIID will keep the State Department and the CIA apprised of developments as they arise. Are there any questions before we adjourn for a quick lunch?"

No one responded. Breyling gathered his papers together. "Very well then, let's eat and get to work."

The meeting broke up. Steele remained seated, studying the file in front of him. Masters gripped his shoulder.

"You know it could get a little heated over there," Masters told him. "Are you sure you're up for it?"

"Looking forward to it," Steele replied. "Do you mind if I take Jeb along with me on this one?"

Masters nodded. "I've already made the arrangements."

Steele held up a finger. "One more question. What if Secretary of State Tyler can't open those doors for us?"

Masters grinned. "Then we'll have to come up with an alternate plan, won't we?"

"Great," Steele said in a satirical voice. "Maybe if I stick flowers into the gun barrels pointing at us and sing songs of peace, they'll let us pass."

"Whatever works," Masters said. "Don't worry. We'll get it figured out. In the meantime, I want you to remember one thing."

"Shoot," Steele said.

"Take the strictest precautions when handling any samples you obtain. We've dealt with some nasty stuff in the past, but I've got a bad feeling about this one."

Masters watched Dietrich and the rest of the group leave the room. Only Breyling's secretary lingered at the doorway. Masters' face grew dead serious.

"If this agent is as hot as I think it is," he said in a hushed voice, "we've got to do whatever it takes to keep it contained."

His eyes locked onto Steele's. "If this gets away from us, Brazos…then God help us all."

Chapter 3

THE BUZZ OF the alarm clock wrested Maggie from another dreamless sleep. She turned it off, then lay back against her pillow and forced her eyes to stay open. After several minutes, she mustered her strength, swung her legs over the edge of her bed, and stood up. She stretched her slender arms far above her body, letting them fall to her side. Time to mentally prepare. She had to. The last three days had been sheer hell. Seven more patients had died and ten more villagers were now exhibiting symptoms. The one bright spot: Hastings was still alive. Hanging on. Much longer than had any of the others. Maybe he'd be the first one to successfully fight off this thing. The mere thought of this brought a smile to Maggie's face.

Although she would never grace the cover of Cosmopolitan magazine, Maggie was attractive in her own unique way. A year shy of thirty, she had a home-town girl look about her, the type who could get away without make-up. Her five-foot, eight-inch body was lean and firm, the result of an active lifestyle. Although she spent much of her time outdoors, her facial skin remained smooth and tanned, a perfect backdrop for her beguiling eyes of amber.

Maggie was passionate about her work with the Canadian Medical Outreach Program (CMOP), a government program that assisted the World Health Organization by providing medical relief services throughout the world. The only child of a broken household, Maggie grew up in her mother's care, yet idolized her father, a member of Canada's Parliament. Although her father was willing and able to provide for his daughter's needs, Maggie chose to put herself through college and medical school without his assistance. Upon graduation, Maggie worked in a private family practice for two years before deciding that being cooped up inside an air-conditioned office, treating cuts and colds, was not exactly the life of contribution and adventure she had promised herself.

After applying for a position with the CMOP, she was readily accepted and soon ended up in parts of the world she never knew existed. Her first assignment baptized her into the world of highly lethal infectious diseases, serving in the frontline trenches during an Ebola outbreak in Zaire that claimed over twelve hundred lives. Although she was in constant battle with fear, she found the experience strangely exhilarating. She enjoyed working with Dr. Braemer and looked forward to each new assignment with eagerness and anticipation. She was living her dream yet that dream had turned into a nightmare.

Maggie nabbed a protein bar and a bottled water from her duffle bag and walked over to a grey and white, square fold-out card table that served as her work desk. She powered up her laptop, then sat and peeled the foil from her breakfast. Fifteen seconds later, a soft chime indicated that the remote satellite access had kicked in. After several clicks of the mouse, she accessed her e-mail. No new messages. Next, she logged on to CNN.com. Continued U.N. debate over the U.S./China policy. The season's first tropical depression brewing in the Caribbean. Another hockey strike on the horizon. Nothing concerning the outbreak. Strange. A humanitarian crisis of this magnitude, yet no news coverage?

She checked out the homepage of the *Toronto Sun Times* to catch up on happenings at home. Then she logged off and placed her computer into its case. She had three hours before her shift started. Plenty of time to visit with Dr. Lin.

She walked to her bed, where she undressed and slipped into a clean tan t-shirt, khaki shorts, and hiking boots. Underwear was optional in the field. One less item of clothing to clean. She brushed her teeth with a disposable toothbrush and a special no-rinse paste, then reached to the makeshift stack of white plastic boxes that served as her nightstand and retrieved a rubber band. She pulled her shoulder length brown hair behind her head, securing it in a ponytail. Her hair felt gritty, a gift from the ever-present wind that constantly whipped over the sand dunes dotting the southern-most rim of the Gobi desert. Hastings once quipped that air in northern China contained more sand than oxygen. At times he was right.

Maggie reached into her duffle and pulled out a disposable surgical mask. She stuffed it into her pants pocket and headed out the door.

Outside, the sun peeked timidly over the eastern horizon. The air felt unusually warm for late August, considering the fact that this region of the world could expect its first hard freeze by mid-September. A dry, thirsty wind sliced through the village and created tiny dust tornados that danced and skipped erratically across the ground before vanishing as suddenly as they appeared.

Snuggled in tranquil isolation between the graveled sands of the Gobi Desert and the green infinity of the Inner Mongolian grasslands, the tiny village of Yushan was once a key stopping point for sojourners and merchants along the legendary Silk Road. In the center of the village, a shallow depression ten meters in diameter and surrounded by a sparse scattering of poplar and pine trees was the only remaining evidence of the once fertile oasis that watered and nourished merchant caravans and roving bands of marauders seeking to relieve the former of their wealth and treasures.

As overland trade gave way to salt water and ships, the wealth of the village shriveled, as did its oasis centuries later. Now, the only water within fifty miles of the village came from a deep well located in the center of the dry oasis bed. And Yushan itself, once the bustling overland trade center, had degenerated into a motley collection of desiccated wooden shacks and mud huts, with livestock pens constructed from dried camel dung wedged between them. During the long, frigid winters, these same bricks would be burned for fuel by their owners.

On the northern border of the village, two parallel lines of green poplars and bristly pines, backed by a three meter high reed fence, stood guard against the encroachment of the ominous sand dunes that towered over the community like tidal waves frozen in time. The lone road in Yushan, a well-trodden dirt and gravel path, entered the village from due east, looping around the dry oasis bed before leaving the same way it came.

Maggie panned the tiny village with her eyes and listened for sounds of life. The problem was, there wasn't any. The silence was unnerving. No birds singing. No livestock bellowing or bleating. No villagers talking or singing. On any given morning, Yushan would be bustling with herdsmen on horseback coaxing their sheep, goats, and camels out to the grassy steppes, while children played and women gathered water and prepared meals for the day. Yushan was now a ghost town, with residents either too afraid or too sick to venture into the street. Maggie wondered if this is what the streets and back alleys of Europe looked like during the Great Plague when a third of the world's population went on to meet their Maker. Somehow, this had to be it.

The smell in the place was unnerving as well. All along the village perimeter, heaping piles of livestock - a medley of horses, goats, sheep, and camels - smoldered and crackled in the wind, the carbonized remnants of the village's economy. Many succumbed to the same disease as the villagers, but most were shot by the Chinese troops and incinerated to prevent spread of the pestilence. Unfortunately, many untended carcasses still remained scattered throughout the village and fouled the air with the putrid stench of decomposition.

Maggie walked eastward. Her eyes locked on a pair of portable guardhouses two hundred meters in the distance situated on either side of the road with wooden barricades placed across the road between them. A formidable five foot high, double layer of thick razor wire fanned out in a wide perimeter around the entire village like a hangman's noose. The Chinese commander in charge of the small garrison warned Braemer that if any person attempted to leave the village without authorization, he or she would be shot on sight. So far, no one had been granted that authorization. Braemer and his superiors in Geneva lodged a complaint to Beijing, claiming that such arrangements only served to impede relief efforts and were, in fact, nothing short of imprisonment. But the Chinese officials turned a deaf ear. They weren't in the mood to be told what to do.

As Maggie approached the guardhouses, the soldiers there caught sight of her and started to talk among themselves. She felt uneasy and quickened her pace. She veered off the road to her right and wove her way through the grape-like cluster of beige tents that served as living quarters for the medical aid workers, then ducked behind a neat row of six Land Rovers and two Hummers, all white with blue WHO acronyms splashed across their doors. Not far off, she could hear the dull drone of the portable generator that supplied electricity to the camp. Dr. Lin's laboratory was located next to that generator.

A pathologist from the Institute of Epidemic Prevention at Beijing University, Dr. Xu Lin, arrived in camp from the capital two days ago to aid in the identification of the mystery killer. Unlike her country's belligerent politicians, she was friendly and courteous, with an attractive personality and positive attitude. Maggie connected with her almost immediately.

Maggie arrived at an expansive tent with a sign that read ACCESS RESTRICTED, written in both English and Chinese, slung across the top of the entrance. Next to the wording, a crudely drawn stick picture of a man with a thick "X" slashed through it reinforced the warning.

"Knock, knock. Anybody home?" Maggie said outside the entryway.

"C'mon in," a voice from inside said in oriental accented English. "Just be sure to gown up."

Maggie ducked through the tent flap and entered a small ante-room. Pressed against one of the canvas walls, a free-standing set of shelves housed fresh protective clothing, plus a red metal biohazard container for discarding used protective gear.

Maggie unclipped the phone attached to her waistband and placed it on a shelf. Then she sat down in a nearby plastic chair and put on a gown, hat, mask, goggles and booties. After snapping on a double layer of latex gloves, she pushed the thick transparent plastic curtain that separated the changing room from the laboratory to one side and entered the lab.

Dr. Lin stood in front of a metal table with her back to Maggie. With her right arm bent ever so carefully at the elbow, she coaxed a drop of fluid from the end of a 25 gauge needle into a port on a hand-held machine that looked like a palm-top personal digital assistant. A plethora of equipment, including centrifuges, a refrigerator, microscope, CBC and blood chemistry machines, several metal racks containing vacutainer tubes full of fluid samples, and a laptop computer all competed for limited table space within the lab. An incubator for growing cultures sat beneath one of the tables, along with two liquid nitrogen tanks for preserving tissue samples. Next to the table, a portable sink drained into a spacious biohazard container. On a set of teal-colored stackable bins crammed into the corner of the lab, a portable radio played a number from Handel's *Escape from Egypt*.

Lin didn't bother to look up. "Did you have a good night's sleep?" she asked as she placed another drop of sample into her machine. The lab coat she wore over her protective clothing swallowed up her short, petite frame. It was bleached white, the preferred hue for those who worked in laboratories handling hazardous materials, as accidental spills and spatters could be easily detected and quickly neutralized.

"I was out before I hit the pillow," Maggie said. "I needed it."

Although she was only thirty-two-years-old, Lin's straight black hair was streaked with grey. She had a young face, fair skin, raven-like eyes, and a perpetual smile that warmed everyone she met. Although hidden by her mask, Maggie knew it was there.

"Anything new to report?" Maggie continued.

"Actually, I'm glad you came by," Lin said. "I do have something."

Lin placed her hand-held device on the table next to her laptop computer, then tossed the syringe she held into a nearby hazardous waster container. "I've identified a virus common to all of the samples I've tested." She opened her laptop and waved for Maggie to approach. "But come look at this."

With gloved hands, Lin took hold of the laptop's USB cord and plugged it into the handheld. She pushed a green button on the latter. The machine chattered, clicked, and emitted a loud beep. Lin pecked the computer's keypad.

"What is that?" Maggie asked. She pointed to the handheld.

"A portable biosensor designed to run polymerase chain reaction (PCR) assays," Lin said. "It will amplify any viral DNA or RNA in the sample, then cross reference it against any number of viruses and their serotypes." Lin popped open a compartment and ejected a minidisk. She held it up for Maggie to see. "It saves the findings on this." Lin put the disc back in. "I didn't find any DNA in the samples I tested last night, so we know we don't have that kind of virus. However, when I added the reverse transcriptase enzyme to the sample to make a complimentary DNA copy of any RNA that might be in the sample, I did get a hit. I was just repeating the process to verify my results when you arrived."

"And?" Maggie asked.

Lin nodded at her laptop's screen. "Watch this."

Within moments, three chimes sounded in quick succession and the screen came alive.

"Check this out," Lin said, pointing to a read-out that had popped up on the screen. "I tested both human and animal samples. It appears we have high levels of the influenza virus in both blood and saliva, especially in those patients with advanced disease."

Maggie cocked her head like a curious puppy. "Influenza? Don't tell me this is an outbreak of influenza. Since when does the influenza virus cause patients to become mentally deranged and bite other people?"

"I know, it's strange," Lin replied. "But the fact is antigen keeps showing up in the samples. It's even detectable in the blood of three villagers with no clinical signs. This virus appears to contain a genetic sequence similar to the H5N1 strain of highly pathogenic avian influenza isolated in Hong Kong."

Maggie remembered the epidemiology course in her third year of medical school that taught her about the influenza virus, yet it focused more on the origins of the disease rather than its treatment and prevention. One fact was certain: She had never seen a case of influenza look like this.

"Most influenza outbreaks originate in China, don't they?" she asked Lin.

"They do. Southern China to be exact, where humans and a variety of flu-susceptible animals, especially pigs and ducks, live in close contact with one another. The swine and human flu varieties are believed to have derived their genes from the avian influenza virus."

Lin scrolled down the screen to scan the computerized profile of their foe. She continued. "Pigs are considered the major 'mixing vessel' for influenza viruses and play host to a variety of strains, including swine, avian, and human. Once in the pig, these strains can mix and exchange their RNA, producing new strains that can be passed directly to humans or be picked up by ducks and other migratory birds, which then carry it to all parts of the globe. Lakes and rivers along migratory pathways can literally teem with influenza virus excreted in their droppings."

"I've never heard of a strain so lethal to so many species at one time," Maggie said.

"Neither have I," Lin said. "And there's something else unusual in this case."

"Like what?"

Lin pointed to the screen. "Look at this. The sequencing on every sample that I've tested so far is incomplete."

Maggie looked at the screen, then turned to her. "What do you mean?"

"It appears that only about thirty percent of the viral genetic sequence is that of H5N1," Lin said.

"So what about the other seventy percent?"

Lin shrugged her shoulders. "I'm not sure. It doesn't match up with any other known strain of flu virus on the biosensor's information chip. Or any other virus on the chip for that matter."

"That's strange," Maggie said.

"Very," Lin replied. "I haven't heard from my lab in Beijing on the profile I sent, but hopefully by this evening we'll have some new information. In the meantime, guess what?"

"What?" Maggie replied with a surge of curiosity.

"I was able to track down the index case," Lin said excitedly. "Well, sort of."

Maggie's eyes lit up. Since the team arrived in Yushan, they had been unable to obtain any information regarding the origin of the epidemic within the village. Most of the villagers tightened their lips when questioned about the subject. Whether a medical team made up exclusively of foreigners caused them to clam up, or something else completely different, Maggie didn't know. It was strange. But this was a stroke of luck.

"That's fantastic," Maggie said with excitement. "How did you do that?"

Lin put the laptop in stand-by mode. "Last night when I was in the hospital tent, a teenage boy in the critical care ward told me that several weeks ago, he and his grandfather, the village elder, were visited by an American wearing a hat and vest and carrying a black box with a nose that he would point at everyone he saw.

Maggie cocked her head. "A black box with a nose?"

"A camera," Lin replied. "The man was a journalist. He told the boy's grandfather that he was in Outer Mongolia for Naadam celebrations and slipped across the border to do a story on the Chinese oppression of the Inner Mongolian people for a magazine.

"What magazine? Maggie asked.

"He didn't say. The boy had a baseball cap with him in the tent. He said the man gave it to him. I'm not too familiar with your American baseball, but I think it was a New York Yankees cap. Anyways, the boy told me that two days after arriving, the man became very violent and attacked a village woman. Bit her on the neck. When some of her neighbors tried to subdue him, he attacked them as well. They ended up clubbing the American in the head and killing him. Fearing a Chinese government reprisal against the village if they ever found out, the boy's grandfather had them bury the body and belongings far out in the desert."

"I guess they forgot to bury the hat," Maggie added. "Does Dr. Braemer know about this?"

"Not yet," Lin said. "I didn't see him in the tent last night."

"We'd better let him know," Maggie said. "I'd like to talk to this boy myself. Can you take a break?"

"Sure," Lin said. She carefully removed the disposable sample well from the biosensor and discarded it along with three sample tubes into the biohazard container. She placed the sensor into an ultraviolet sterilization tray parked next to the entrance to the dressing area. Then Lin picked up a pressurized sprayer next to the table and misted the room with disinfectant.

"Arms up," Lin instructed Maggie. Maggie lifted her arms and Lin sprayed her down with disinfectant. Maggie did the same for Lin. Then, both women hustled to the changing area and shed their protection.

"I'll meet you there," Maggie told Lin. "I need to stop by my tent."

With that, Maggie hurried off, anxious to find more answers.

Chapter 4

MAGGIE TOSSED HER used protective gear into a makeshift incinerator fashioned from a rusty fifty-five gallon drum and ducked into the decontamination room that adjoined the hospital tent. She put on a fresh pair of coveralls from the shelf, then donned a pair of knee-high rubber boots, surgical cap, protective goggles, ultrafilter mask, and two pairs of gloves. A tedious routine to say the least, but a necessary one.

Many of Maggie's colleagues accused her of being paranoid when working around infectious disease. Yet if they thought a cavalier attitude towards a deadly unseen adversary was some noble sign of faith or bravery, she saw it only as sheer stupidity. Infectious diseases such as the one they were up against in Yushan showed no favoritism and killed without remorse. Hastings and a number of other WHO workers found this out the hard way.

Maggie entered the main room of the hospital and saw Braemer bent over one of the nearby cots, listening to a patient's chest. After he finished his exam, Braemer recorded his notes on the patient's chart. He nodded when he saw Maggie approach.

"Get some sleep?" he asked.

"Yes, I did, thank you."

Somewhere outside, the rattle of gunfire could be heard.

Braemer looped his stethoscope around his neck and collapsed into a nearby chair. "What the hell are they doing out there?"

"Probably shooting at stray dogs. I spotted a couple on my way over that had wandered into the village, no doubt looking for food.

"Well, it's upsetting the patients," Braemer said with directed anger. "They need to cease and desist." Maggie noticed that the director's cheeks and forehead were flushed.

She walked to his chair and placed a gloved hand on his forehead. She could feel the heat through her latex gloves.

"Dr. Braemer, you're burning up," she said. "How long have you been feverish?"

"I'm fine," he replied to her. "Just a combination of stress and exhaustion, I'm sure."

"Did Dr. Lin tell you?" Maggie asked.

"Tell me what?"

"We think we've identified the index case."

"Really?" Braemer replied with interest.

Maggie nodded. "A journalist from the States apparently brought the disease to Yushan."

"From where?" Braemer asked.

"Somewhere in Outer Mongolia," she replied.

"Have you notified Geneva yet?"

"Not yet. I knew you needed some relief, so I got over here as soon as I could."

Braemer took a deep breath and rose to his feet. "No problem. I'll call them as soon as I get to my tent."

"How is Dr. Hastings doing this morning?" Maggie asked.

The look on Braemer's face ripped her heart right out of her chest. "Maggie," he said solemnly. "John died during the night."

A sledgehammer to the face couldn't have hit her any harder. She felt light on her feet and her eyes started to glisten. Braemer saw that she was shaken. He stepped forward to support her.

"Where did they take his body?" she asked. Her speech was broken.

"To the block house. They've probably already buried him."

Maggie looked at Braemer with anxiety. "John asked that I perform an autopsy on him if he died. He told me he wanted me to collect samples…"

"I know," Braemer interrupted her. "He asked me to do the same. It's been taken care of."

Deep down, Maggie felt an intense sense of relief at not having to perform such an unwelcome deed. "Was the end violent like the rest of them?" Maggie asked with some hesitation.

Braemer shook his head. "Actually, a generalized paralysis set in quite rapidly. He died from respiratory failure."

Maggie closed her eyes and looked skyward. "Thank you."

Braemer motioned to a metal hospital cart parked next to the tent's entrance. "The samples are over there."

"Thank you, Dr. Braemer," Maggie replied, fighting off depression. She put her hand on his shoulder. "It's your turn for some shut-eye."

Braemer cracked a subdued smile. "That sounds wonderful." He then retrieved a chart from a nearby cot. "I just have a few items to tend to before I go."

Maggie excused herself and walked to the metal cart that housed the samples from Hastings. She took a deep breath to collect herself, then she removed a chilled aluminum canister about the size and shape of a Churchill cigar. This piece of equipment represented the latest in technology involving the preservation and protection of sensitive organic samples collected in the field where timely access to a laboratory was not readily available. Equipped with a solar-operated cooling system that maintained both frozen and refrigerated conditions within two distinct leak proof internal cells, the unit also had a compact lithium battery backup system.

Maggie slipped the canister into the pocket of her coveralls. Out of the corner of her eye, she glimpsed Lin at the far end of the tent, kneeling beside a cot occupied by a girl no more than eight-years-old. Maggie made her way over to her.

"How's she doing?" she asked.

Lin looked up at Maggie and her eyes narrowed from the smile beneath her mask. "She seems to be holding her own. I'm going to check her viral count today. Compare it to yesterday. Perhaps we can learn more about the virus' replication pattern."

Maggie looked around the room for the teenage boy. "Where is our Yankees fan?"

Lin's silence answered her question.

"Did he..." Maggie said.

"At 4 a.m. this morning," Lin said with uncharacteristic gloom in her voice.

Maggie couldn't talk. First John. Now the boy. The strain was becoming unbearable.

Lin removed an alcohol wipe and vacutainer set from a Ziploc bag, prepped the girl's arm, and drew a blood sample. After Lin finished, the girl started to cough. The spell lasted fifteen seconds.

The youngster's plight jolted Maggie from her growing sense of impotence. She removed a penlight from her front pocket and shined it in the girl's eyes. The scleras were tinged with blood and the pupils barely responded to the light. The girl struggled to swallow. Maggie retrieved a tongue depressor from a nearby supply cart and opened the girl's mouth. The back of the throat was red and swollen, and a pool of saliva formed near both tonsillar crypts. Maggie then listened to her chest. The lungs were moist and raspy. She pressed her fingers on the girl's abdomen to search for areas of tenderness. They weren't too hard to find.

The chatter of more gunfire outside reverberated throughout the tent. Several patients screamed and wailed at the sound. Maggie looked across the room and saw Braemer slam his otoscope down on a cot, then storm out through the decontamination room.

"I think Dr. Braemer is going to have a heart-to-heart with our soldier boys," Maggie said.

"It won't do any good," Lin said. "They won't listen to him." She finished labeling her sample tubes.

Maggie scribbled a few notes on the girl's medical record. Again, she heard gunfire, this time much closer than before and coming from several directions.

That's weird. She turned to Lin. "I think I'll take a look."

Maggie took two steps towards the decontamination room and suddenly saw Braemer stagger into the hospital treatment area. His protective gear was gone and a crimson stain fanned out across his tan safari shirt just above the belt line.

He forced his right arm into the air and croaked "get out" before collapsing to the floor. Maggie missed what he said, but she could hear the screams of two nurses standing next to Braemer's lifeless form. Designed for disease containment, the hospital tent had one way in and out, and that was through the decontamination room. Hospital staff workers and those patients who could still move rushed towards the exit like a tsunami. The machine gun fire began again, this time from within the decontamination room itself. Maggie and Lin watched in horror as bodies were blown back into the ward like chaff in the wind.

Seconds later, a lone figure wearing goggles and mask and dressed head to toe in desert camo, stepped over a heap of fresh corpses and into the main room of the hospital. He swept his

Kalashnikov from side to side and sprayed the first four rows of cots with bullets. Patients and hospital personnel were transformed into bloody, coarse-ground lumps of flesh. Two workers rushed the gunman head-on, but were dispatched without mercy by a burst of gunfire.

Suddenly, the sides of the hospital tent were hit with enfilading fire. Hundreds of slugs ripped the canvas walls to shreds. The wails and cries of the terrified and the wounded blended with the gunfire, producing a dark melodic song of death.

Maggie and Lin stood frozen in terror at the scene unfolding before them. The deadly mayhem had yet to reach the back of the tent, but it was on its way. Several of the doctors and nurses near Maggie panicked and fled towards the exit. They were summarily mowed down.

Maggie's survival instincts kicked in. She turned to Lin, who stood dazed and motionless, her lower jaw dropped in disbelief. Maggie grabbed Lin by the arm and said "follow me" to others nearby. She pulled Lin behind her like a rag doll and made for the isolation ward at the rear of the hospital. Two nurses decided to join them. Maggie ripped open the curtain that separated the ward from the main hospital. The group weaved their way through the cots over to the farthest wall. Maggie snatched a bottle of dexamethasone from a nearby cart and hurled it to the floor, then picked up a jagged piece of glass and stabbed it through the canvas. In a matter of seconds, she created a slit big enough to crawl through.

"Quick, through here," Maggie said. She pushed Lin through the opening and waved for the two nurses to follow her. A flurry of lead vaporized the curtain. Several bullets thudded into the back of one of the nurses. She flopped to the ground. The other nurse stared at Maggie with tragic eyes, hands clasped around the front of her neck, her mouth in motion but producing no sound. Bright red blood spurted out between her fingers from the hole just below her chin.

She wobbled on her feet for a moment, then finally let out a gurgled moan and crumbled to the floor. Maggie wasted no time and dove through the slit in the canvas.

A bullet caught her in mid-air.

Chapter 5

MAGGIE CRASHED TO the ground outside the tent. A tidal wave of pain washed over her body and lapped at her brain. She clutched her thigh.

"I've been shot," she cried.

Lin seized her by the arm and helped her to her feet. Maggie pointed to the makeshift morgue, which happened to be the village's one room schoolhouse, fifty meters ahead. "Over there!"

With Lin serving as a crutch, the two stumbled over to the building and ducked inside. Maggie slammed the door behind them. Except for the sliver of light that poked in through the top edge of the doorframe, the interior loomed dark and ominous. Both doctors struggled to the back of the room and slumped to the dirt floor with their backs against the wall. A horrible stench ripened the air. Maggie noted the vague outline of three body bags stacked like cordwood against the wall next to her. She grimaced in pain. Her leg throbbed like an overworked generator. The lower left side of her coveralls felt tacky.

Lin trembled uncontrollably. She gripped Maggie's arm. "What is going on?" she cried, her eyes desperate for an answer.

"I don't know," Maggie said with frustration. Maggie shook Lin's hand loose and crawled to the door. She cracked it open. Four men in desert tan kicked open the door of a house across the street directly opposite the schoolhouse and tossed in a grenade. A muffled, fiery explosion was followed by the inward collapse of all four walls. Satisfied with their work, the killers moved on to the house next to it and repeated the carnage. Farther down the street, huts were doused with petrol and set afire. Those unfortunate inhabitants attempting to escape a fiery death were shot in their tracks. The grey smoke from the fires swirled and spread like a thick blanket over the village.

Maggie returned to Lin's side. "I need to get to my phone. I left it in the dressing room of your lab. We might be able to call for help." Maggie knew she was grasping at straws, but she had to try.

She unzipped her coveralls. "Let's get out of these."

Lin reluctantly followed her lead and both women shed their protective gear. Maggie removed the sample container from the pocket of her coveralls and transferred it into a pocket of her blood-soaked shorts. Then she unbuttoned her shorts and pulled them down partway. Gritting her teeth, she probed the bruised, oozing wound beneath her left buttock. Lin removed her grizzled t-shirt and handed it to Maggie.

"Here," she said, dressed in only a pair of navy shorts and a white sport bra. "Use this as a compress."

Maggie accepted it with gratitude. She bit her lip and affixed the garment over the wound.

"Can you run?" Lin asked.

"I'll make it," Maggie replied. She summoned her strength and took hold of Lin's hand. They looked out the doorway together. It appeared that the coast was clear.

Maggie released Lin's hand. "Let's go."

They crept out of the building and slid along the north wall. The heat from the flames consuming the hospital tent warmed their exposed flesh. The gunfire moved to the west end of the village. Reaching the end of the wall, Maggie cocked her head and listened for activity, but she heard nothing. She peered around the wall. Nothing.

The two of them dashed across the village grounds, using trees, livestock pens, and burned-out buildings for cover. At one point, their path nearly led them right into a group of the assassins torching a storage barn, but they managed to hide before being spotted.

After what seemed like an eternity, Maggie and Lin arrived at the WHO camp. Strangely enough, none of the tents had been sacked or burned, although Maggie could see that many were riddled with bullet holes. No doubt the occupants within them were as well. Except for one vehicle with its two front tires shredded, the row of SUVs was unharmed. Maggie assumed the vehicles, as well as the camp's inventory, were spared for plunder.

She motioned to Lin. "I need you to get to the Land Rover, the one with the number five on the hood. The keys are in it. The door combination is three-two-seven-eight-six. Can you remember that?"

The look on Lin's face told Maggie she didn't want to be left alone. Maggie placed her hand on Lin's arm for reassurance. Lin closed her eyes and repeated the combination over and over. "Three-two-seven-eight-six," she said one final time. "I think I've got it."

"I'll meet you there in two minutes," Maggie said. She limped across the road and laced her way between the rows of tents until she finally arrived at Lin's laboratory. The hum of the generator was deafening, making it difficult for Maggie to listen for danger that might be close by. She ducked into the dressing room and seized the phone she had left on the shelf. Its battery was dead. She pitched it to the ground in disgust.

Maggie turned to leave, but happened to catch a glimpse of Lin's hand-held PCR unit beneath the ultraviolet sterilizer beyond the plastic barrier curtain. She dashed into the laboratory. Snatching up the unit, she removed the machine's mini disc and shoved it into the pocket holding the sample tube. She then hobbled back to rejoin Lin.

When she reached Land Rover Number Five, she found Lin in tears, pumping the gas pedal while turning the ignition switch. The truck's engine coughed, then died. Maggie slid into the passenger seat and looked up and down the street. They still had not been spotted.

"C'mon, Lin, let's go," she said.

"It won't start," Lin replied.

"Here, let me try," Maggie said. She slid under Lin and switched positions with her. Maggie turned the key. The engine sputtered. She tried again. More sputter. She tried again. It started.

Maggie shoved the transmission into gear and pressed the gas pedal. The Land Rover lurched forward, but the engine started to hack.

"Stay alive, baby," Maggie begged while she played with the pedal. The engine protested for several more seconds, but finally it leveled out.

"We're in business, Lin," Maggie said with much relief.

"Did you get your phone?"

"The battery was dead."

Lin slumped into her seat. "Where do we go?" she asked. "The road is blocked at the checkpoint and there's barbed wire all around us."

Maggie looked towards the checkpoint. Flames licked the interior of the transport truck that blocked the road. She saw dead soldiers lying next to their guardhouses. Several bodies hung from the open doors of yet another crippled truck. Caught by surprise by the marauding force, the Chinese troops had little chance to defend themselves.

Maggie scanned the perimeter fence and pointed south to an apparent gap in the barbed wire. "There! They must have cut through it to gain entrance into the village."

"This truck won't fit through that," Lin said.

Maggie's brows furrowed with determination. "We've got to try. Buckle up and hold on."

She jammed the accelerator to the floor. For a split second, all four wheels of the Land Rover spun in place, kicking dust and gravel in all directions. At last, they gained solid footing and propelled the vehicle forward. They plowed over three tents before hitting the straightaway towards the gap in the wire. Maggie could see the sunlight sparkle off of the razor wire that grew larger with each passing second. She watched the speedometer - 62 kph...88 kph...101 kph. Lin's eyes widened. The wire came closer and closer. Maggie steered for the center of the gap and tightened her grip on the wheel.

"Here we go," she said. "Hold on."

The SUV hit the breach in the wire barrier going 128 kph. The impact jerked both women forward, but their seat belts snapped them back in place like rubber bands. The Land Rover's forward momentum was crushed amidst a howl of scraping metal.

"C'mon, just a little farther," Maggie said, rocking in her seat as if she would be able to somehow push the truck forward. Suddenly, both right-side tires exploded and the vehicle surrendered to the wire's onslaught. It came to a halt, dangling from razor wire like a fly trapped in a spider's web.

Maggie and Lin unbuckled their seat belts and crawled out onto the roof of the Land Rover. There were shouts in the distance. Three assassins pointed at them and raced towards the Land Rover, their weapons spitting fire. Maggie and Lin plunged into the narrow gap in the wire and negotiated their way through the steel barbs that clawed mercilessly at their exposed skin.

They cleared the wire well ahead of their attackers and ran for the grassy plain stretched out in front of them. Maggie was weak from blood loss and barely able to keep pace with Lin.

"What do we do?" Lin gasped. "We have nowhere to go." The panic that seized her earlier gripped her again. "We're going to die," she added. Tears streamed down her face.

Machine guns spat in the distance. Clumps of grass and gravel danced about the women. The voices grew louder and Maggie detected the whine of an engine. She looked back and spotted a tan Hummer three-quarters of a kilometer to their right, apparently joining in the pursuit. Maggie knew further escape efforts were in vain. It would be a matter of seconds before she and Lin were overtaken. Her head started to spin, and the fire in her lungs now matched the fire in her thigh. It all seemed like some surreal dream.

Still, she refused to quit and called forth her last remaining strength to lead her forward. Lin, on the other hand, was out of breath and fell behind. She suddenly stopped and dropped to her knees.

"I can't go on," Lin said.

Two slugs zipped by close to Maggie's ear. "Get up!" Maggie said. But Lin didn't respond.

What little hope Maggie had left inside quickly dissipated. She couldn't leave Lin to face death alone. This was it then. She returned to Lin's side, knelt down, and cradled her in her arms.

The three assassins were no more than fifty meters away. Seeing their prey give up flight, they slowed to a walk. Maggie watched one of them remove his mask. His cold eyes glared at her without the slightest drip of feeling; eyes that would no doubt take extreme pleasure in killing at point-blank range.

The Hummer was still a tenth of a kilometer away, but rapidly approaching at an angle and showing no signs of slowing. A puff of smoke issued from the passenger side window. At the same instant, the unmasked assailant fell dead. Confused, his two companions turned to face the vehicle. One of them raised his machine gun to fire, yet his finger went limp on the trigger and he too dropped face-first to the ground. The last survivor of the trio emptied his clip at the approaching vehicle and turned to run. But it was too late. The Hummer was on him like a shark on chum and slammed into him at full speed. The body stuck to the grill for a moment, then disappeared beneath the tires.

The two women were still huddled together on their knees, numb with disbelief. The Hummer made a sliding U-turn and started towards them. It came to a screeching halt just meters away. The driver's door opened and a man with wavy hair stuffed beneath a baseball cap jumped out. He approached the two women and knelt beside them. Maggie had never seen eyes so blue...or eyes so welcome.

Brazos Steele reached out his hand. "You ladies need a ride?"

Chapter 6

"LET'S GET MOVING folks. Round two is about to begin."

The words didn't come out of Steele's mouth, but from his friend and partner, Jeb Walker, who emerged from the passenger seat of the Hummer and helped Lin to her feet. He, too, was a big man, even taller than Steele and outweighing him by about 30 pounds. The brown hair on his head was cropped ultra-short and overshadowed by the neatly-trimmed mustache and goatee. To those familiar with Southwestern ethos, he looked as though he were "right off the ranch." To those unfamiliar with it, the beefy Texan looked down-right formidable.

Jeb pointed out a Toyota pick-up truck to Steele. It was some distance away but headed their way. "I don't think they're bringing us refreshments," Jeb quipped.

The words had barely left his mouth when a machine gun mounted in the bed of the pick-up began to chatter.

Steele and Jeb quickly helped the two women into the back of the Hummer. The men then climbed in themselves and Steele punched the accelerator. The Hummer squealed off.

Steele glanced in his rearview at Maggie. "You must have really ticked somebody off."

"Who are you?" Maggie asked.

Steele tugged at the brim of his hat. "Brazos Steele at your service. The crack shot sitting next to me here is Jeb Walker."

Jeb tipped his "Army of One" cap at the two women. He then rotated the cap to face backwards on his head, leaned out his window, and emptied the clip of his SIG P-229 at the pick-up.

"Talk about a pair of knights in shining armor," Maggie said.

"We haven't reached the castle yet, my lady," Steele said. "Buckle up and keep your heads down." The two women readily complied.

"How bad are you hurt?" Steele asked Maggie.

Lin chimed in. "She's lost a lot of blood. We need to get her to a hospital."

"Where are you hit?"

"My thigh," Maggie replied. "I'll be okay. The bleeding has stopped. It just hurts like hell."

Steele could tell by the subtle slur of Maggie's voice and pale color that her Chinese friend was right. She had lost a significant amount of blood.

"Both of you are doctors?" Steele asked.

"That's right," Maggie replied. "Dr. Lin and I were in the hospital when the fighting broke out."

Steele kept a close eye on the activity in his side mirror. The armed vehicle continued to gain ground on them. "Who's trying to kill you?" he asked.

Maggie shook her head. "I wish you could tell us, because we don't have a clue."

Jeb leaned out his window and emptied another clip at the Toyota. It responded in turn with its machine gun. Bullets skipped and ricocheted off the passenger side door panels, forcing Jeb inside.

"All right, now I'm pissed!" he declared as he shoved another clip into his pistol.

Steele looked over and saw his friend's face red with anger.

"You hit?"

"No," Jeb said. "But this is getting very personal."

They've done it now, Steele mused. He had the distinct pleasure on a number of occasions to witness Jeb's wrath in action. And it wasn't pretty. It did, however, manage to extract them out of several tight scrapes during the time they spent together in college pursuing women and later in the Middle East pursuing terrorists. Fortunately, the army taught Jeb how to harness his anger, or at least discipline it to come forth only on command. Unfortunately for the bad guys in the Toyota, that command had just been issued.

Jeb stuck his entire upper body out of the window and discharged his pistol in a slow, methodical fashion. The Toyota truck swerved to dodge the shots, forcing its machine gunner to crouch and hold on tight to keep from being thrown. After depleting the clip, Jeb ducked back inside. Undaunted, the Toyota continued its chase.

"I think you scared them," Steele said.

"Yeah, right," Jeb grunted. "If we want to scare them, they need to hear you sing."

The Hummer bounced and barreled over the stubby landscape, distancing itself from the burning village. The Toyota stayed hot on their trail. Steele knew they couldn't outrun it. It was as if the Red Baron were clinging to his ass, biding his time before delivering the fatal burst. He looked in his rearview just in time to see Maggie clutch her thigh and double over in pain.

"Jeb, see if you can grab a clean dressing from the first aid kit for Dr. Townshend," he said. "And see if there is something in there for pain."

"You got it," Jeb replied. He placed his pistol on the seat next to him and retrieved the first aid box from the glove compartment.

Lin reached over the seat and took it. "Here, I'll do it."

A swarm of bullets peppered the driver side of the Hummer and shattered Steele's side mirror. Lin shrieked.

"Son of a bitch," Steele said. He pulled several splinters of mirror from his bloodied left cheek. "We're not going to outrun them in this."

Jeb unbuckled his seat belt and grabbed his pistol. He climbed over his seat and fell between Maggie and Lin. He then retrieved the last clip from his pocket. There were only four shells in it.

"Duck," he told the women. He aimed and pulled the trigger, shattering the rear windshield of the Hummer. Three shells left.

He dove into the far back and kicked out the mangled glass. A volley from the Toyota caused Steele to swerve to the left, which hurled all three of his passengers to the right. Maggie groaned.

"Sorry about that," Steele said.

"Just try to keep it steady," Jeb said. "I'm gonna take out that driver."

Resting one forearm across the other, Jeb took careful aim and pressed the trigger. The Toyota jerked to the left, then swerved back into position behind them. The driver, still very much alive, flashed Jeb an unflattering gesture with his hand. Two shells left.

Jeb sighted in again and shot. This time, a swarm of incoming lead deflected his bullet and ripped into the rear of the Hummer. Holes sprang up throughout the roof and back panels, but miraculously, Jeb remained unscathed. The Hummer was not so lucky. It lurched to the right, its rear tire blown. Steele regained control, but critical forward momentum was lost.

Jeb saw the Toyota's gunner frantically working on his weapon.

"Their machine gun is jammed," he said to Steele. "Quick, slow down."

Steele read his friend's mind. Now was the time to take out the driver. Unfortunately, if they failed to do so before the gunner unjammed his weapon, they'd be sitting ducks.

"Keep her as steady as you can, brother," Jeb said above the thump of the blown-out tire.

Steele backed the Hummer down and in his rearview, watched their enemy close the gap. He could see the face of the driver, a young man who couldn't have been any more than twenty-years-old, locked in fierce determination to give his gunner an easy target. Steele wasn't sure the driver knew that his machine gun was out of commission.

Maggie slouched lower in her seat. Lin sat upright with her head and shoulders propped against her door.

"Get down, Lin," Maggie cried.

Jeb sighted in his target with careful precision. The flat tire made it difficult to keep the barrel steady. One shell left. No margin for error. He fired.

The driver's face disappeared behind a white haze that engulfed the Toyota's windshield. The truck lurched ninety-degrees to the right, hurling the machine gunner through the air. It then flipped on its side, landing right on top of the unfortunate gunner, and commenced to roll. After six graceful pirouettes, it came to a standstill. For several moments, oily smoke billowed from the crushed engine compartment. Without warning, a bright orange fireball erupted from beneath the vehicle and billowed skyward. It then descended gracefully back to earth, engulfing both truck and driver in flames.

Steele watched the fireworks through his rearview mirror. "Not a bad shot."

"Nothing to it," Jeb replied.

Despite the cavalier comment, Steele knew that Jeb took no pleasure in taking another man's life. And neither did Steele. But when their own lives or the lives of innocent people were at stake, neither man would hesitate to do it. Exchanging light conversation after the fact was simply one way they cushioned the emotional baggage brought about by pulling a trigger.

Steele guided the crippled Hummer another kilometer and brought it to a stop. He unbuckled his seat belt and turned around to face the back seat. "Everybody in one piece?"

Maggie straightened up. "I think so," she said. Her face was pale and the jostling from the rough commute caused her thigh to hemorrhage once again.

Lin still leaned upright against her door. Maggie reached over and jostled her arm. Lin's eyes were fixed and glazed, her face ashen.

" Xu Lin!" Maggie's voice was panicked. She shook her friend's arm again. Lin wouldn't respond. Jeb reached over the back seat and placed his fingers on Lin's neck. There was no pulse. He glanced at Maggie, then at Steele.

Maggie reached over and pulled Lin towards her. The body flopped onto her lap like a rag doll. Lin's back was smeared with blood, with two gaping holes just below the strap of her sport bra. Two matching punctures defiled the upholstery of Lin's seat.

"Oh God, no," Maggie wailed. "No!"

Before Steele could react, she slumped over Lin's corpse and lapsed into unconsciousness.

Chapter 7

A BARE-CHESTED Vachirdorj Bagaryn stepped off the wrestling mat like a bull that just gored the matador. He snorted an order to a nearby servant, who hastily offered him a towel. Bagaryn wiped the sweat from his face and body, then towel-dried his coarse black hair. He shot a contemptuous look at the broken figure lying still in the center of the mat.

"Is this the best Mongolia has to offer?" he said, tossing the towel to the servant. "Get him out of here!"

Another attendant rushed up behind him and draped a gold-trimmed robe over Bagaryn's burly shoulders while two men in tan army uniforms descended on the mat and removed the prostrate figure by the arms.

The recreation room of the presidential palace was spacious and well-equipped, adorned with a medley of treadmills, elliptical trainers, resistance machines, and free weights that served to keep their owner in excellent physical condition. The mat sat in the center of the room, nestled between four massive marble pillars, sky blue in color that rose to a vast ceiling painted with powerful action scenes from Mongolia's glorious past. For all of its pleasantries, the room doubled as a death chamber for the handpicked opponents of Bagaryn, who loved to boast that he could kill any man with his bare hands. So far, the claim appeared to be a valid one.

A solid five-foot eleven-inches with enormous legs and a heavily muscled upper body, Bagaryn, even approaching sixty, still had a round, smooth, boyish face. Thick black eyebrows arched over even blacker eyes that radiated a cold ruthlessness from deep within their inner darkness. His skin was copper in color, a feature that made him popular among the common folk of his country, who viewed those with fair complexions as elitists and traitors to the traditional Mongolian nomadic way of life.

Bagaryn strutted to his breakfast table and picked up the morning newspaper as if the man he killed minutes before never existed. He harbored no guilt about ending a life, viewing his fellow human beings as mere tools to achieve his goals. A shamanist at heart, Bagaryn believed that he was predestined by Tengri, the chief spirit of all life, to restore Mongolia to her former greatness. In short, he saw himself as his country's next Genghis Khan.

His rise to power had been smooth and calculated. He attained hero status early in life as his country's premier wrestling champion, a sport whose popularity in Mongolia rivaled that of football in Europe and Latin America. Bagaryn held his title for five consecutive years, a feat that made his name famous throughout his country. After retiring at the top of his game, he attended the Moscow Military Institute and served in the Mongolian People's Army, rising quickly to the rank of lieutenant general, one of the youngest his country had known. When the great Soviet Revolution foundered, Bagaryn left the army and immersed himself in illegal drug trafficking across Mongolian soil between Kazakhstan and the new Russian Federation. It was a lucrative enterprise that made him a quick fortune.

Once Mongolia shed its own communist skin, it gave birth to dozens of political parties that all rushed to gain power footholds within the new political environment. Backed by his former "business" partners, Bagaryn founded the Mongolian People's Democratic Party (MPDP). With gifted oratory skills and a pre-established popularity among the people, he grew the MPDP into a political force to be reckoned with.

After years of planning and patiently biding his time, Bagaryn, with the help of Mongolian military leaders he commanded two dec-ades earlier, seized power in a bloodless coup. One month later, the Mongolian Republic was dissolved, a move that caught the rest of the world, including the United States, completely off-guard. By the time the United Nations had a chance to call together a special session to discuss the crisis, the new government was firmly entrenched and functional.

Bagaryn allowed the Great Hural, Mongolia's governing body, to remain intact, yet effectively rendered it powerless to influence policy. He expelled American military advisors from his country, and extended a hand to Mongolia's traditional ally to the north, Russia. Apart from the United States, which recognized the geographic sig-nificance of this land buffer between two superpowers, the remainder of the world viewed Mongolia as otherwise insignificant in the grand scheme of world politics, which left Bagaryn's regime to do as it wished. Little did they realize the consequences of this monumental mistake.

"Where is my breakfast?" Bagaryn demanded.

Six women dressed in colorful dels, the traditional wrap-around robes worn in Mongolia, responded with servings of fruits, breads, and meats. They placed them on the table before their employer. Without lifting his eyes, he reached out and grabbed a strip of dried mutton with his bare hands and dropped it to the floor next to his chair. A dog, some type of shepherd-wolf cross, scampered over and snatched it up, then lay down at his master's feet.

As Bagaryn took the last bite of his morning meal, a giant of a man dressed in a tan general's uniform and knee-high Russian jackboots approached the table and bowed. The tar-like eyes of General Munhgarad Tsogt that peered at Bagaryn served as portals into a soul that had condemned countless men, women, and children to their premature deaths. He stood almost seven feet, with a square face and features consistent with gigantism, a genetic anomaly known to occur infrequently among the Mongolian race.

Tsogt was Bagaryn's right hand man. A ruthless sadist, he had served as a junior officer under Bagaryn and eventually became a general in the new Mongolian Army during the last decade of the twentieth century. Bagaryn was duly impressed by his subordinate's intense loyalty and dog-like dedication, and maintained close ties with him after leaving the military. It was Tsogt whom Bagaryn called upon to convince a number of his fellow officers to raise arms against Mongolia's weak political machine.

In return for his help, the newly empowered Bagaryn appointed the general head of his elite Royal Guard, with the commander of the Mongolian People's Army, General Sukeyaan Natambaa, reporting directly to him. Tsogt didn't waste any time purging the People's Army of those officers he deemed to have questionable loyalties, and transformed the Royal Guard into his own personal tool of terror to extort his way to a lifestyle of perversity and excess. His cruelty was notorious, as was his pedophilia. On more than one occasion, Mongolian mothers were forced under the threat of reprisal to sit back and watch Tsogt claim their sons and daughters for his own personal play toys. Bagaryn knew of this evil vice, yet chose to ignore it in order to keep his general happy.

"Your eminence, the Russian Petrokov is here," Tsogt said in a deep, throaty voice.

Bagaryn took a sip of tea. "Send him in."

Tsogt signaled to two guards posted on either side of the room's main entrance. One stepped through the door, then reappeared with a thin man dressed in a sharp navy business suit. The man's face was streamline, sporting a narrow nose, icy blue eyes, and sunken cheeks. Beneath those cheeks, a vicious scar cut obliquely across the neck and disappeared beneath the man's tie, a gift from a Chechen rebel who failed to slice deep enough. Bagaryn had known Mikail Petrokov for over two decades. It was Petrokov's ties with Russian organized crime that helped Bagaryn complete his power play.

Petrokov approached Bagaryn's table with an air of confidence and a slight limp. The Mongolian leader wiped his mouth, then stood up and extended his hand to the Russian.

"Mikail, it is good to see you. Please sit and make yourself comfortable."

Bagaryn motioned to a servant, who pulled a chair out for Petrokov. "Would you like tea or coffee?" Bagaryn asked him.

"Coffee would be fine, "Petrokov replied. "Thank you, Vachir."

A servant materialized at his side with a cup in hand. Petrokov nodded a polite greeting to Tsogt but the latter did not acknowledge him. He was too preoccupied with Bagaryn's dog, which, out of its master's sight, kept baring his teeth at the general.

Petrokov pulled out a pack of cigarettes from his inner coat pocket. "May I?"

"Certainly," Bagaryn lied out of politeness. Deep-down, he detested the air of arrogance carried by Petrokov and his fellow countrymen, a conceit that grew out of the feelings of superiority adopted by the Russian people towards their neighbors to the south during decades of Soviet "supervision." But he was willing to play along. At least for a little while longer.

Bagaryn rose from the table and walked to a window to escape Petrokov's second-hand smoke. He gazed out over the courtyard of his compound as if in thought. Then he abruptly turned to the Russian.

"Our timetable has been moved up, Mikail," he said. "I will need delivery of the finished product in two weeks."

Petrokov leaned back in his chair. He crossed his legs and took an extended drag from his cigarette. "That may be difficult."

"Difficult or not, I must have it no later than the twenty-sixth," Bagaryn said. Smoke billowed out of Petrokov's nostrils. "Do you have it?" he asked. He glanced at Tsogt, then at Bagaryn.

"Not here," Bagaryn replied casually.

Petrokov's face flashed with anger. He dropped his coffee cup on the table. "We have upheld our part of the bargain. It is imperative that we get started before the first winter snow sets in."

Bagaryn smiled. "No need to worry, Mikail. It is waiting for you in a safe location. General Tsogt and his men will be happy to assist you in its retrieval."

Petrokov glanced at the general, who stood at attention with a face devoid of expression. He crushed his cigarette butt into the empty coffee cup, rising to his feet. "General Tsogt, when can you and your men be ready?"

Tsogt looked to Bagaryn for permission to answer and received it. "We can leave this evening," he told Petrokov.

"Very well," Petrokov said, rising to his feet. "If you will excuse me, I have some calls to make." Petrokov turned and abruptly left the room, followed by the guard who first escorted him in.

Once the door closed, Tsogt spoke up. "Your Excellency, we're not going to hand over the relic to that Russian slime, are we?"

Bagaryn sat down in his chair and plucked several grapes from the fruit bowl. He put one in his mouth. "We will let him do the work for us, dealing with him later as we see fit. It will look better to the Mongolian people if we do not associate ourselves with the search, only with the disposition."

"Ah yes," Tsogt replied with a comprehending smirk.

Bagaryn continued. "For now, we will give him the help that he needs."

"And the ones who escaped Yushan?" Tsogt asked. "Our spies have told us that they are still in Beijing. What would you like us to do with them?"

"We will have to address them later," Bagaryn said. "We have work to do." He stood up and walked to the window. The infinite expanse of blue sky in front of him hypnotized him. But only for a moment.

"Destiny is at hand, my dear general," he said. "In ten days…" Bagaryn paused to allow a wicked grin to spread across his face, "…the dragon will be cast to her knees."

Chapter 8

"VISITING HOURS END in fifteen minutes, so please be brief." The shift doctor at Beijing University Medical Center spoke in broken English, addressing Steele and Jeb in a courteous yet stern tone. He waved at the two men to follow him down the hallway to the hospital's isolation ward.

"She regained consciousness late this afternoon," the doctor remarked without bothering to look back. Steele and Jeb both struggled to keep pace with him. "Your Dr. Townshend is one lucky woman. That bullet missed her femoral artery by millimeters."

He finally turned his head. "Too bad fate wasn't as kind to Dr. Lin. Do you have any idea what happened out there?"

"Not really," Steele lied. He wasn't about to release details to anybody without permission from Masters.

A pair of stern-looking policemen protected the entrance to the isolation ward. The doctor flashed his ID, then spoke to one of the guards. He gestured in the direction of Steele and Jeb. The guard nodded his head and allowed the three men to pass.

They entered a changing room through an automatic sliding glass door and donned protective clothing and face masks. They then went down another hallway and through another door into a cramped isolation room stuffed with a collection of monitors, metal carts, and IV poles equipped with fluid pumps. Steele detected the faint purr of the room's closed ventilation system, designed to cycle airborne pathogens through HEPA filters located at the top and bottom of each wall to prevent their inadvertent escape.

Maggie, arrayed in a standard issue hospital gown, lay awake in a hospital bed in the center of the room, her head propped up by two pillows. Her face was pale and her hair disheveled, but she appeared to be alert. A hunched-over nurse with a wrinkled face attached a needle to a vacutainer hub, swabbing her patient's arm with an alcohol wipe. Maggie winced and closed her eyes when the needle entered her arm. When she opened them, Steele and Jeb were at the foot of her bed. She smiled.

The doctor turned to Steele. "I'll leave you now. Again, please make your visit brief." He gave them an abbreviated bow and retreated.

Steele pulled up a chair next to Maggie's bed. He pulled down his mask. "Good to see you smiling," he said. "For a while there, I thought we might lose you."

"I feel as though I've fallen off the top of a ten-story building," Maggie complained. She held up her heavily bruised right arm. Her left forearm, equipped with a catheter that delivered a slow drip of fluids, electrolytes, and antibiotics, displayed its own medley of purple and violet blotches.

"I can empathize," Jeb said from across the room. He pushed up the sleeve of his gown. The upper third of his forearm exhibited similar discolorations. "These nurses wouldn't know what a vein looked like if it slapped them in the face."

"They've been drawing blood and checking all of us for viral antigen on a daily basis," Steele told Maggie. "So far, we've all passed the test."

Maggie looked around her sterile environment. "How long have I been here?"

"You've slipped in and out of consciousness for the past four days," Steele said.

"Four days!" she said. She sank into her pillow, the look on her face morose. She closed her eyes again and remained silent. Steele noticed that her respiratory rate increased. Either she was in physical pain or she was reliving the terrible nightmare in her mind. Steele guessed the latter.

"Have you been here the entire time?" she finally spoke in a subdued voice, her eyes still shut.

"Just down the hall," Steele replied. "Been cooped up in a room smaller than this with nothing to do but watch television. Jeb is already hooked on some Pakistani soap opera." Steele threw him a grin. "I had to pry him away from it just so we could come see you."

A tiny smile cracked the corners of Maggie's mouth. She opened her eyes. They were sad eyes filled with confusion and pain. To Steele, however, there was also something attractive, something intriguing about them. He just wished he could somehow erase the endless loop of horror he knew was haunting them. But that wasn't possible. That was a challenge she would have to cope with herself.

"Who are you guys?" she asked.

"Just a couple of friends sent in to help with your operation," Steele replied.

Maggie pointed to a glass of water on the stand next to her bed. "Could you..."

Steele had it in her hands before she could finish. She took a measured sip. Her lips were dry and cracked.

"Do you remember what happened in Yushan?" Steele asked her.

Maggie stared at the ceiling. "All those people," she lamented. "All of my friends...Lin."

Steele noticed her eyes starting to mist, so he spoke. "We weren't far from the village when we saw the flames and heard the shooting. We saw you and Dr. Lin running across the desert. We figured you were in trouble so we decided to help." Steele paused and looked over at Jeb. "I guess we didn't do a very good job of it."

"What do you mean?" Maggie replied. She wiped tears from her eyes and her face hardened. "If it wasn't for you, Lin and I would have been executed like rats."

She took a deep breath and regained her composure. "Did anybody else survive?"

"You're it. As I understand it, everything in the village was completely destroyed. They even dug up graves and burned the corpses."

"Who are 'they?'" Maggie asked.

"That's the million dollar question," Jeb said. "Whoever they were, they obviously wanted to wipe Yushan from the map. Perhaps the Chinese government was behind it."

"Possibly, but I doubt it," Steele replied. "Why would China kill its own soldiers and medical workers, not to mention foreign humanitarians? Talk about reaping an international backlash. Besides, the driver of that Toyota didn't look Chinese to me. I'm not quite sure what nationality he was."

"They could have been hired guns," Jeb theorized.

Maggie shook her head. "All I know is that one minute we're treating patients and the next minute we're running for our lives. It doesn't make sense. We were sent there to help those people. They didn't have a chance. First disease, then genocide."

Anxiety suddenly flooded Maggie's face. She lifted her head off her pillow. "The samples!"

Steele placed his hand on her arm. "Don't worry," he said. "We've got the canister and the disk. I called the American Embassy and had one of its staffers meet us at the outskirts of the city before we brought you to the hospital. I gave them to her for safe-keeping. I had a sneaking suspicion they might be confiscated if found."

"What are you planning to do with them?" Maggie asked.

"That's one reason Jeb and I wanted to come by to see you," Steele replied. "We sent them to the States for analysis."

"Thanks for asking," Maggie said irritably. She then lowered her eyes. "I'm sorry. I didn't mean anything by that. It's just all so frustrating."

"Any idea what might be crawling around in that canister?" Steele asked.

"So far, all we know is that it has the genetic make-up of an influenza virus," Maggie said. "At least in part."

Steele raised an eyebrow. "In part?"

"Only thirty percent of its genome sequence is H5N1."

"A chimera?" Steele asked.

Maggie nodded. "Could be."

Jeb confusion was apparent. "A 'what?'"

"A chimera," Steele repeated. "Comes from the Greek word 'chimaira,' which means 'she-goat.' In Greek mythology, it referred to a monster, half-man and half-animal."

Jeb rubbed his goatee. "She-goat, huh? Sounds like that girl from Lubbock you dated for those two weeks last March."

"Very funny," Steele replied. Judging by her smile, Maggie thought it was.

She finished the explanation. "In virology, the term is used to describe an organism that harbors a hybrid genome with genetic material from two or more different families of viruses."

"Why do I have the sudden urge to wash my hands again?" Jeb said.

Maggie flinched and squeezed her eyes shut.

"Are you okay?" Steele asked her.

"It'll pass." she replied, opening her eyes. "I could use a bit more pain medication though."

Jeb held up his arm. "I'll go find our nurse. Hold on." He left through the sliding door.

"I'll be fine." Maggie reassured Steele with a smile.

"I spoke to the Canadian embassy earlier today," Steele said. "They'll arrange to get you to Toronto as soon as you can travel."

The smile vanished. Maggie looked at him as though she were an athlete who had just been told to hit the bench.

"You're kidding me, right?" her voice rebelled. "I'm not leaving until I get some answers. Innocent people have been murdered and I want to know who is responsible."

Steele placed his hand on her arm. "I understand your anger and frustration, but it's not safe for you here. Keep in mind that whoever orchestrated the massacre at Yushan no doubt knows that you escaped. They may come looking to finish the job. There are guards posted outside your ward."

Maggie took a deep breath and lowered her voice. "Look, Dr. Steele…"

"Please," he said. "My friends call me Brazos."

She paused. "Look, Brazos, I appreciate your concern and everything you and your friend have done for me. I really do. But I'm a big girl. I can take care of myself from here."

The sliding doors opened and the old nurse walked into the room with Jeb on her heels. Steele quietly slipped his mask back on. The nurse checked Maggie's chart, then drew up a dose of pain medication and injected it into Maggie's IV line. Maggie's face relaxed as the drug hit home.

Jeb reached into the back pocket of his jeans beneath his gown and extracted a can of Skoal. He pulled his mask up and tucked a pinch of tobacco behind his lower lip. The nurse saw this. Her eyebrows furrowed and she chattered at him like an angry squirrel, pointing to the can in his hand.

Jeb shrugged his big shoulders at her, his lower lip pooched out like a bed roll. "What?"

Another flurry of admonishments, and then the nurse retrieved her vial of pain medication and marched out of the room.

"I don't think you're supposed to be doing that in here," said an amused Maggie in a slightly drug-slurred voice.

Jeb yanked his mask and snapped the straps. "We don't need these any more. It's obvious you're not contagious."

Steele followed suit. Maggie shifted in bed to ease the pressure on her injured thigh. "I may not be, but I bet you there are others out there that still are."

"What do you mean?" Steele asked.

"It didn't start in Yushan. The point of origin was somewhere in Outer Mongolia." Maggie then told them Lin's story about the western journalist.

"The American didn't show any clinical signs until three days after his arrival," she said. "Since the incubation period is around five days, and we allow a day for travel, he must have picked it a day or two before he left for Yushan. The question is: Where was he before he came to Yushan?"

Jeb searched in vain for a spit cup. Unable to find a cup in the room save for the one with Maggie's water in it, he requisitioned an emesis basin from a nearby table. "If this disease is wreaking havoc somewhere else," he spoke, "wouldn't we have heard about it?"

"If our journalist picked it up in some remote village, it could go unnoticed," Maggie replied. "You have to remember that hundreds of miles sometimes separate the people living in the Gobi desert."

"Thank goodness that guy didn't decide to visit Beijing," Jeb said.

"I shudder at the thought," Maggie replied.

Steele pointed at Jeb. "As I recall, you've got a friend who works for the *New York Times*, don't you?"

"Sure do," Jeb said. "Her name is Jennifer Beals."

"See if you can contact her and make some inquiries concerning this mystery journalist," Steele requested. "He seems to be the missing piece to our puzzle."

"Consider it done," Jeb said. He spit some tobacco juice into the basin.

She crinkled her nose and pointed at Jeb's spittoon. "By the way, that is a disgusting habit."

"I know. I'm going to quit. It's going to be my New Year's resolution."

"What do you mean?" Steele asked skeptically. "You've made that same resolution for the past five years. Last year, you didn't make it to half time of the Fiesta Bowl before blowing it."

"That's because you ran out of chips. It was the only way I could curb my munchies."

Their exchange was abruptly cut short as the doctor and Jeb's nurse nemesis reentered the room. She glared disapprovingly at Jeb. Jeb responded by unloading a wad of tobacco juice into the basin.

The doctor spoke. "Time is up, gentlemen. Dr. Townshend needs to rest." He scribbled a few treatment notes on Maggie's chart. The nurse ordered Steele to his feet while she adjusted Maggie's IV fluid pump.

Maggie reached out and took Steele's hand in hers. "Thank you again for saving my life." Exhaustion softened her tone.

"Don't mention it, Dr. Townshend," he replied.

"Please, my friends call me Maggie," she said. "In any event, I owe you one."

Steele grinned in turn. "I tell you what. You can buy me dinner sometime, when you're up to it."

"It's a deal," Maggie replied. "Have they told you when they plan to let me out of here?"

Steele nodded towards the doctor writing on her chart. "He said you should be back on your feet in four to five days. In the meantime, you need to get your strength back."

Jeb removed the tobacco from his lip and tossed it into the trash. He motioned at the old nurse. "I'm sure Atilla the Hunness here will see to that."

Maggie released Steele's hand. "Will I see you guys tomorrow?"

"Sure," Steele said. "They gave us our walking papers today. But we'll be holing up in a hotel across the street for the next couple of days. We'll come visit you."

Steele could tell from Maggie's expression that she was pleased. Despite her façade of self-sufficiency, she no doubt felt alone and vulnerable in her current state. It would be nice to have friendly faces nearby.

The men exchanged good-byes with her and started down the hallway towards the changing station.

"So what do you think?" Jeb asked.

"Want the truth?" Steele said. "I think we're in a world of trouble. Whatever this organism is, it wasn't made on the sixth day."

"What do you mean by that?"

"This chimera came from a laboratory, not from nature."

The two men arrived at the changing station. Steele stepped forward and activated the sliding door.

Jeb touched Steele on the shoulder. "Hold on a minute. If that's the case, then who made it?"

Steele turned. A determined smile filled his face. "I'm not sure, but you can bet we're going to find out."

Chapter 9

THE AZURE SKY slowly faded into the ashen grey of dusk as the sun dipped below the hills of the central Mongolian province of Arkhangai, located some four hundred kilometers west of the Mongolian capital of Ulaanbaatar. The golden spires of Damba Zuu Khiid, the fortress-like monastery located on the east bank of the Orhon River, glowed and sparkled under the sun's dying rays like burning embers. Built in the late sixteenth century, the monastery housed fifty- two devoted followers of Buddha. Its twenty foot high outer walls were adorned with one- hundred-and-eight evenly-spaced spired stupas, or pagodas, and enclosed seven temples of worship, each with coral red-tiled roofs that curved above the troop barracks interspersed between them.

To the outsider, Damba looked reminiscent of a medieval Oriental castle rather than a place of worship. It became Mongolia's oldest monastery by default after the magnificent Erdene Zuu Khiid, built on the ruins of the ancient Mongolian capital of Karakorum in the neighboring Ovorkhangai province, was converted into a palace residence for Bagaryn. Unlike the other monasteries in Mongolia, complete with visitation hours for tourists and expensive souvenir shops, Damba Zuu Khiid remained off-limits to the public, which only served to stoke the fires of mystery and reverence surrounding it.

Although General Tsogt had never set foot in Damba Zuu Khiid, he was intimately familiar with its floor plan, both above and below ground, thanks to a disgruntled ex-monk in his service. Surprise was crucial, for he knew the monks of Damba weren't about to let him just waltz in unopposed and take what he wanted. He timed his arrival at the monastery to coincide with the evening prayer. Fifteen of his best commandos, all trained in Russia and in top physical shape, were recruited to secure entrance into the monastery and to quash any resistance the monks might offer.

The general knew there could be no failure this time. After the fiasco in Yushan, Bagaryn turned a cool shoulder to him, holding him personally responsible for the mishap. Tsogt still wasn't sure how the American journalist slipped through his security net, but what he did know was that his leader would not tolerate any more screw-ups. The junior officer Tsogt put in charge of the Yushan mission paid for his failure with his life. But it wasn't enough.

Tsogt had only two fears in life. The first was dogs. As a boy, Tsogt had been attacked and almost killed by a pack of mongrels. As a result, the mere sight of a dog was enough to shake him up.

He also feared disappointing his leader. Over the years, he had been infected by Bagaryn's all-consuming vision of a revived Mongolian empire. And the Yushan debacle almost destroyed that vision. Now was his chance to slip back into his leader's good graces and reestablish Bagaryn's confidence in him.

The drumming of the rotors echoed off of the nearby hills and announced the approach of the three helicopters from the east. Tsogt wasn't concerned that the noise would raise an alarm among the inhabitants of Damba, for the flight path they took was well-worn and the monks were accustomed to aircraft passing overhead.

The pilot of the lead helicopter banked to the right and headed for a low hill situated about one mile north of the monastery. Cresting the hill, the helicopter descended out of sight and slowed to a hover, then touched down on a flat grassy plateau. The two other choppers followed suit. Tsogt and his men jumped out of the helicopters, fanned out, and started up the hill.

When they reached the top, Tsogt ordered his men to fall into two lines behind him and they began a brisk descent down the opposite slope. The monastery glowed in the distance below, and the men could hear its bells toll in unison, calling the faithful to prayer.

Dressed in black from head to toe, the commando party moved as mere shadows in the darkness. When they had made it just over halfway down the hill, Tsogt removed a slim flashlight from a sheath attached to his belt and turned it on. He took care to keep the beam pointed to the ground. At the same time, the man behind him struck a match and lit a cigarette.

Tsogt snapped his head around. "Put out that cigarette," he whispered sharply.

Petrokov took another puff, then grudgingly tossed the cigarette to the ground and extinguished it with the toe of his boot. Tsogt panned his flashlight to and fro until the beam came to rest on a small shaman shrine, a pyramid-shaped collection of stones, rock slabs, and pieces of wood. A lone wooden pole with colorful silk scarves affixed to it stuck out of the pile like a giant Dixie straw. Tsogt barked out an order for his men to dismantle the offering. Although tradition implied that doing so would invariably unleash a plethora of evil spirits on the participants, Tsogt's men complied with his order without hesitation. The only evil spirits most of them cared about were those found in bottles of cheap Russian vodka.

It took less than five minutes for them to tear down the shrine and uncover the steel trap door that lie beneath it. Tsogt's personal assistant, Lieutenant Aagii, a thin, fierce warrior-type with narrow eyes and a pock-marked face, stepped forward and pulled it open. Tsogt shined his light into a dark tunnel that extended into the earth. He then climbed through the opening and descended a lengthy flight of stairs. His men followed him single file with flashlights in hand. The interior of the passageway, with its walls, floor, and ceiling hewn out of dirt and granite supported by timber, smelled of rot but felt dry. Petrokov, a closet claustrophobic, started to hyperventilate, yet beat it back with a steady stream of self-talk. Other than his low-grade chatter, the column remained silent and flowed through the well-lit tunnel.

Fifteen minutes later, they arrived at the foot of yet another staircase, this one going up. Tsogt signaled his men to halt. He waved his lieutenant forward. Aagii followed him up the stairs until they came to a heavy wooden door reinforced with wide transverse steel bands. An elaborate carving of a dragon, its mouth agape and men-acing, curled around the door's steel latch and lock. Tsogt kept his light fixed on the beast while Aagii removed a pack from his waist and extracted several instruments. He then began to work on the lock.

Twenty seconds later, a loud click prompted a thumbs-up from Aagii. Tsogt stepped past him, pushed on the latch, and opened the heavy door ever so slightly. He peered carefully into the monastery's library. A lone kerosene lantern flickered atop a desk in the corner of the room; otherwise, the room was vacant. Tsogt pushed the door open wide and ordered his men forward. Tsogt repeated the drill at the library's exit door. The outer hallway was clear. With weapons in ready position, he and his men flooded the hallway and fanned out into a spacious courtyard. Three worship temples lined each side of the yard, while a faint chant complemented by a timed drumbeat echoed from the main temple that occupied the far end.

The group reached the arched entryway of the main temple, then re-formed into two lines and entered the building. Commandos spread out behind the massive golden support columns that lined the outer perimeter of the temple's central sanctum, advancing past an abundance of statues and colorful prayer wheels. They kept their weapons trained on the holy men in the room the entire time.

The monks of Damba never knew they had company. With shaven-heads and wine-colored robes, they knelt with eyes closed in front of an altar occupied by a seven meter tall, five ton bronze statue of Sakyamuni, the original Buddha famous to history. Gilded with gold, adorned with precious gems, and clothed in fabric spun from gold and silk thread, the deity sat cross-legged on a lotus-flowered throne and glared menacingly at his tiny followers to remind them of their earthly insignificance. The sixty-seven year-old Holy Lama of Damba, Kyankumar, knelt in front, prayer book in hand, leading a chant. This continued undisturbed for another two minutes before several monks opened their eyes and saw the soldiers around them.

The mantras ebbed as more and more monks became aware of the intruders. Kyankumar kept up his morose song and rocked back and forth with eyes closed, as if oblivious to the new presence. But soon he stopped and rose to his feet to face the giant figure in the shadow of the entryway.

"What is the meaning of this intrusion?" Kyankumar asked with authority. "You have interrupted our holy prayers."

"I have come on behalf of His Excellency to retrieve the sacred relic of Temujin," Tsogt replied. His cold eyes burned through Kyankumar's. "You will release it to me immediately."

"We have no such relic here," the lama replied. His face betrayed a glint of concern. "How did you get into the monastery?"

"That doesn't matter," Tsogt said "You will show me to the sacred relic, or I will instruct my men to open fire."

An audible murmur spread among the kneeling mass of monks. A sacred relic in their midst? No one had heard of this.

"Show me to the relic," Tsogt repeated.

Kyankumar stepped towards Tsogt, his arms wrapped tightly around his prayer book. "We harbor no such relic on these premises. This is a temple of worship. We are..."

A deafening volley of bullets interrupted him. Eleven monks collapsed face first to the floor while an equal number of wounded shrieked and cried out in agony. Their arms groped the stunned survivors, pleading for help. Kyankumar dropped the prayer book and rushed to the aid of a nearby monk whose eviscerated body barely clung to life.

Two of Tsogt's men rushed up behind the old lama and wrestled him to his feet. Tsogt pressed forward until he was face to face with him.

"You are wasting my time," Tsogt said. "I will ask again only once. Where is the relic? Tell me, or the rest of your faithful will die."

"I do not know."

A wicked backhand caught Kyankumar across the cheek. Blood streamed from his lower lip. A groan of protest arose from the surviving monks huddled close together. They resumed their prayers, although now they were prayers of death.

Tsogt reached to his waist, unsnapped the flap of his leather holster, and withdrew his Grach MP443 9mm pistol. He raised the barrel into the air.

"Silence!" he said.

The monks ignored him and continued their prayers.

He fired off two warning rounds. The wounded ceiling above sprinkled the monks with debris. The room quieted.

"Who knows where the sacred relic is stored?" Tsogt asked. "Rest assured that your life will be spared if you cooperate."

Again the monks did not respond. Disgusted, Tsogt holstered his pistol and walked to the temple entrance. Aagii and Petrokov followed him.

"Bring him with us," he said over his shoulder. Kyankumar, still reeling from Tsogt's backhand blow, offered little resistance. Once in the open air of the courtyard, Tsogt nodded to his lieutenant. Aagii re-entered the temple. Moments later, gunfire erupted. It continued until the screams died away.

"Why have you done this?" Kyankumar moaned. "This is a holy place and you have defiled it."

Tsogt tossed his head back and laughed. Aagii stepped forward and drove the butt of his AK-47 into the prisoner's stomach. Kyankumar collapsed to the ground. Tsogt placed a dusty boot on his chest. "You are not to speak unless it is to tell me where the relic is located."

They dragged Kyankumar to his private office next to the main temple and threw him down into a chair. They then secured his hands and legs with rope. The lama's face was pale and his breathing labored. Petrokov approached Tsogt.

"Do you think he knows where it is?" Petrokov asked.

"He knows," Tsogt replied. "And he knows that we will take this place apart if we have to. However, it will save time if he will tell us where it is."

"Do you mind if I spend a moment with him alone," Petrokov asked. "I think I may be able to persuade him to cooperate."

Tsogt hesitated for a moment, but then agreed to Petrokov's request. The general knew that his own impatience with Kyankumar would only lead to the man's premature death and the loss of valuable time. He motioned to Aagii and his men to follow him out of the room.

Oh General, just one more thing," Petrokov mentioned with a casual coolness. "May I borrow your knife?"

Chapter 10

TSOGT AND AAGII waited outside the office door, unmoved by the horrific screams and groans that resonated from within the room. Suddenly, the sounds of torture stopped. Moments later, the door opened. Petrokov walked out, wiping his hands with a piece of Kyankumar's robe. He smiled at Tsogt.

"He talked," Petrokov said proudly. After all, it took him a mere sixteen minutes to extract the information they sought.

Tsogt glanced into the room over Petrokov's shoulder. Kyankumar sat with his head slumped over, his robe torn almost completely off and his sagging body horribly mutilated.

"Is he dead?" Tsogt asked indifferently.

"He still hasn't met Buddha in person," Petrokov replied. He wiped the blood from the blade of Tsogt's knife with the same piece of robe. "I wanted to make sure that the information he gave me was correct before we send him on his way."

"Where did he say the relic was?" Tsogt asked.

"In a vault beneath one of the stupas." Petrokov handed the knife to its owner.

"This monastery contains over a hundred stupas," Tsogt said. "Did you think to ask which stupa he meant?"

Petrokov shook his head. "He passed out before he could elaborate. However, he did mutter 'Gomba' several times before he lost consciousness, whatever that means."

"Gomba is the name of a popular Buddhist god," Tsogt said.

Aagii chimed in. "General, the stupas will contain statues dedicated to their gods."

Tsogt turned to him. "Have the men search them at once. If my memory serves me, the image stands erect and clutches a sword with both hands. Start with the south wall."

Aagii saluted, then left.

"Why the south wall?" Petrokov asked Tsogt.

"Our ancestors believed the doorway to eternal life faces south, so that direction has special meaning to the Mongolian people. It made sense that relics of our past would be placed in such a location."

"Makes sense," Petrokov replied. He snapped his fingers. "One more thing. Kyankumar mentioned something about Bagaryn having betrayed him. What did he mean by that?"

Tsogt's face remained expressionless. "The mere mumblings of a dying man."

Petrokov didn't like the answer. He started to speak, but Tsogt interrupted him.

"Come, we've been here too long. It's time to claim what we came for and leave." Without saying another word, Tsogt turned and walked to the courtyard.

Aagii and his men quickly found the stupa they were looking for. As Tsogt predicted, it was indeed built into the midsection of the south wall. Aagii sent a soldier to notify the general, and Tsogt and Petrokov hurried to the site.

Tsogt entered the pagoda with Petrokov and Aagii right behind him. They found it empty except for a three-meter tall statue of a fierce-looking deity in the center of the room. The interior was cramped, unable to accommodate more than seven bodies at once, including Gomba's.

Petrokov scanned the vacant interior with disgust. There was no relic. He checked the seams in the floor and walls. All were intact and original.

Petrokov was furious. "There's nothing in here. The old man lied." He paced the floor. "I will make him pay dearly for this."

Tsogt ignored Petrokov's outburst and walked methodically around the statue. He turned to Aagii. "Have the men bring me some rope."

Aagii left and Tsogt continued to inspect the statue, or more specifically, at its base. Less than a minute later, four men, each with ropes in hand, entered the stupa.

"Pull it down," Tsogt ordered.

Each man tossed his rope over the statue as if lassoing a calf. They then gathered together in a tight group and pulled. The statue didn't budge. Tsogt and Petrokov joined them and tried again. This time, the base creaked and a light puff of dust rose into the air.

"Again," Tsogt ordered. Everyone leaned back and tugged in unison. The statue started to inch away from its resting spot.

"There!" Petrokov said. He released the rope and knelt next to a wooden hatch that occupied the space where the statue's base had once been. Petrokov stuck his fingers into a recessed handle. He pulled, but it wouldn't open. Tsogt requisitioned a Kalashnikov and stepped towards the hatch. Petrokov backed away and shielded his head. Tsogt angled a short burst of gunfire at the hatch, which left a jagged piece of wood dangling from a single iron hinge. Tsogt kicked the splinter free with his boot.

Tsogt ordered everyone except Petrokov out of the stupa. He then wiggled his large frame through the opening and disappeared down a flight of stairs. With some reluctance, Petrokov followed him. The stairway descended a good fifteen meters and ended in a spacious chamber hewn out of solid rock. The air was dry and cool against Petrokov's face, helping to counteract the sweat caused by a blend of excitement and claustrophobia.

A domed white silk tent with a slender neck and cone-shaped spiral top sat in the center of the chamber affixed to a rose granite platform. Ornamental oil lamps hung from support poles on each side of the tent's entryway.

Tsogt waved his flashlight back and forth over the structure. "The White Ordon of Damba."

"What the hell is an 'Ordon?'" Petrokov asked.

"The Ordon are the resting places for the most sacred relics from the old kingdom. Their construction was commissioned during the reign of the Khan Kublai."

"This one sure doesn't show its age," Petrokov said.

"It has been maintained by Kyankumar and his monks," Tsogt said. He shined his light around the walls of the chamber. "There's another entrance into this space somewhere around here."

"How many are there?" Petrokov asked. "Ordon, I mean."

"At least fifty, maybe more," Tsogt said. "The majority rest within the borders of the occupied country to the south."

"You mean Inner Mongolia," Petrokov said.

"I mean the occupied country to the south," an irritated Tsogt said. "The Chinese are nothing more than squatters. Their time to leave has come."

Petrokov didn't reply, but laughed inwardly. Who was going to expel them? Bagaryn and his whopping 500,000 man army?

"After you, General," Petrokov said. He waved his arm in front of Tsogt like a maitre d' showing a dinner guest to his table. Tsogt, unamused, brushed past him and entered the Ordon.

The interior walls were covered in golden cloth with a wide emerald brim. An oblong silver box sat on a wooden stand in the center of the tent.

Tsogt opened the box and lifted out a leather-bound book, along with a purple silk pouch. He gave the book to Petrokov, dumping the contents of the pouch into his hand.

Saliva pooled within Petrokov's mouth as he inspected the two gold coins in Tsogt's outstretched palm. The Russian reverently opened the book in his own hands. He could hardly contain his excitement. The writing was in Italian, but Petrokov needed no translation. All of the years of searching were finally over. He closed his eyes and spoke a few words of thanks to a deity he didn't even believe in. Then he opened his eyes again and ran his finger along the author's name at the bottom of the page. The ink was faded, but the name was unmistakable.

It read "Marco Polo."

Chapter 11

STEELE SAT ON the edge of the bed and tied the laces of his running shoes. It was 4:30 a.m. The news he just received from Maryland was disturbing. Very disturbing. He figured a good jog would help clear his mind and give him time to think. He needed time to think. There were too many unanswered questions. Too many pieces. And now with this development…

Steele jogged for over an hour. It seemed like minutes to him. Much to his surprise, Jeb was waiting in the hotel lobby with a cup of coffee in each hand when he returned.

"Here, I brought you one." He gave one of the cups to Steele.

"Thanks," the latter replied. Steele blew on the contents, then took a sip. "What are you doing up so early?"

"I thought you might like to know that my friend at the Times called me. She's identified our mystery journalist. His name was James Fielder. Freelance writer on assignment in Mongolia. He was doing a piece for National Geographic Magazine and came up missing two weeks ago."

"Do we know where he was prior to Yushan?" Steele asked.

"The magazine received an e-mail from him on the 31st. He was at the International Hotel in Ulaanbaatar. Said he was to be moving on to Dogan, wherever that is. After that, nothing."

Steele was ecstatic. "It's a start. I'll get a hold of Masters right away and arrange a trip to Mongolia."

"Great. When do we leave?"

"Actually, I need you to stay here and watch over Dr. Townshend until she gets released. I thought about it long and hard. She's right, you know."

"What do you mean?" Jeb asked.

"We're gonna need her help," Steele said. His voice grew deadly serious.

"She's the only person alive who has first hand field experience with this bug. Once she's out of the hospital, I want you two to come join me in Mongolia."

Jeb gave Steele a wary look. "Spit it out, Steele. Do you know something I don't?"

Steele glanced over at the hotel clerk behind the front counter. "Let's talk up in the room."

The two of them made their way upstairs to Steele's room. Jeb shut the door behind them.

"I spoke with Masters a couple hours ago," Steele began. "They've discovered the source of our virus. It appears we have the Russians to thank for our little friend."

"The Russians!" Jeb said. He pounded the wall with his fist. "Should've known those assholes were behind it. How did Masters find out?"

"From a scientist named Poplikov. He owns a biotechnology company that holds several large defense contracts."

Jeb snapped his fingers. "Yuri Poplikov? I know that name. Didn't he write a best-selling book last year about twenty-first century bioweaponry?"

"That's him."

"I read that book," Jeb said. "Some scary shit in there."

"Poplikov told Masters that Russian scientists had been trying to harness the power of the influenza virus for over eighty years. Apparently they created three hybrids before the Soviet Union went tits up and two more during Putin's tenure. Poplikov is pretty sure our organism is one of those chimeras."

"What were they doing with it in Yushan?" Jeb asked.

"The Russian government claims innocence," Steele said.

Jeb laughed. "So what's new?" He paused, sipped his coffee. "How do we know this guy's information is credible?"

Steele didn't answer right away. He walked to the window and studied the early morning skyline.

"Jeremy Frank was on the line with Masters this morning," he finally spoke. "He's chief scientist at USAMRIID's BSL-4. His people identified the chimera's mystery genome. It matched a description Poplikov gave to Masters."

"And?" Jeb asked with anticipation.

"You're not going to believe it."

Jeb walked up behind him. "For God's sake, try me."

Steele turned and looked his friend directly in the eyes. "Jeb, those people in Yushan didn't die of influenza." He wiped the perspiration from his face with the sleeve of his sweatshirt.

"So what got 'em?" Jeb asked.

"Rabies," Steele replied. "They died of rabies."

Chapter 12

URI KOMVICH'S STEEL blue eyes narrowed. He took a calculated drag from his cigarette, then mashed it in a butt-ladened ash-
tray on his desk next to a bronze bust of General Georgi Zhukov,
hero of Stalingrad. Petrokov sat across from him, sunk low in a plush
maroon leather chair. He despised that chair, knowing full-well that
its sole purpose was to provide Komvich a dominant position over
its occupant. Not that Komvich needed any psychological advantage.
As a former general and current leader of Russia's most prominent
crime family, he earned a fearsome reputation for his iron-fisted leadership, particularly his unforgiving soul. Komvich viewed himself as
subordinate to no one, Russian President Molkov included.

The crime boss was an imposing figure. His double chin and size
46 waistline, the by-product of years of extravagant living at the
expense of decency, were tempered by a black Kiton business suit
and custom-made blue power tie.

"So Mikail, I trust your trip was successful?" Komvich asked.
His causal tone belied his intent to intimidate.

Petrokov nodded. "I have the book and the map."

He leaned and reached into his brief case. He pulled out the
book taken from the monastery.

Komvich didn't respond, but Petrokov noted a faint smile on the crime boss's otherwise stalwart face. It had been over thirty years since the Soviet military machine, strapped for cash and desperately looking for any potential sources of revenue, requested that Komvich, then the commander of the Russian garrison stationed in Ulaanbaatar, organize an expedition to search for the fabled treasure of Genghis Khan. Not wanting to waste time on such a ridiculous order, Komvich dumped it on the nearest subordinate he could find. Needless to say, Petrokov was that subordinate.

At first, Petrokov was irritated about his new assignment and only with reluctance set out to gather information to aid him in this seemingly-impossible task. But as the facts started to flow, his apathy morphed into a healthy curiosity, and then later, after three unsuccessful yet adventurous expeditions to find the treasure, into a magnificent obsession. Petrokov even went so far as to convince his commanding officer that a treasure did indeed exist and that it was only a matter of time before it would be found. It was a dream that prompted Komvich to fund Petrokov's expeditions even after the general transitioned into his life of crime.

A decade passed and by that time the honeymoon was over. Komvich grew increasingly impatient with each successive failure by Petrokov to find the Khan's tomb. Needless to say, the latter, knowing that another failed expedition could literally be his last, was much relieved when his old friend Vachir Bagaryn informed him that a definitive record of the burial site existed. Now he had that record in hand and with it, the good graces of Yuri Komvich once again.

"May I see that?" the individual seated next to Petrokov asked. He held out a smooth, well-manicured hand. Nicholas Ustimovich, the CFO of Komvich's crime empire, was a short man with a thin face, a sharp nose, and darting brown eyes. The color of his suit matched that of his boss, yet his maroon tie was much more subdued. His black dress shoes, polished to a blemish-free shine, reflected his obsessive attention to detail.

Petrokov handed him the book. Ustimovich opened it and turned the fragile pages, handling it as one would a delicate work of art. However, it was apparent that the woman seated next to Ustimovich wasn't so easily impressed by this important piece of history.

Olga Pushkarev, a top level information officer for the Russian Federal Security Service, sat with legs crossed and glared at Petrokov with cool, piercing blue eyes set behind a pair of fashionable wire-rimmed glasses with small oval lenses. To Petrokov, she was the mother bitch of bitches. He often kidded with his colleagues that she carried around more testosterone than a male bull elephant. If she did, there wasn't any outward evidence of such. She was an attractive woman in her forties, long-bodied with a blue pin-striped suit that hugged her well-proportioned feminine contours. Her black hair was pulled back tightly in a bun, emphasizing her high cheekbones and full-lips. These two features appealed to Komvich, who slept with her on a regular basis.

Ustimovich closed the book and looked at Komvich. "This book is no doubt worth a fortune in itself."

"Screw the book." Komvich said. "I want the treasure." He looked at Petrokov. "When will your next expedition leave?"

"We are gathering men and supplies," Petrokov said. "But I'm low on cash. I'll need more funds."

Komvich sat back and grinned sardonically. "Mikail, you go through money faster than you go through whores." He turned to Ustimovich. "See that he gets what he needs."

"President Bagaryn demands payment by next Wednesday," Petrokov said.

"Hold on a minute," Pushkarev broke in. "How do you even know this book is legitimate?" She leaned forward and placed a hand on Komvich's desk. "Don't you think we should get some type of verification before we give anything to Bagaryn and…" She paused and looked with disdain at Petrokov, "…before you start dishing out more money to this man?"

Petrokov experienced a surge of anger, yet managed to suppress it.

"You think I'm lying?" Petrokov challenged her. He reached into his pant pocket and pulled out one of the two gold coins that Tsogt found in the Ordon. Petrokov slid the coin across the desk towards Komvich.

Komvich's brows lifted. He picked up the coin "What is this?"

"A sign of things to come. That coin is just an infinitesimal part of the treasure that awaits us."

Komvich held the coin up to one eye and examined its inscription like a jeweler would the facets of a diamond. Then he grinned. "Where did you get this?"

"From Bagaryn," Petrokov said. "I've already checked its authenticity with a team of numismatics experts who work for the Moscow Museum of History. They've dated it back to the thirteenth century. They were quite concerned to say the least."

"Why is that?" Ustimovich asked.

"They thought I had stolen it. From what they told me, there are only three such coins known to be in existence. Two of them are in the Chinese National Museum in Beijing and the third is in the hands of a private collector. They even went so far as to contact the Beijing museum officials and inquire as to the status of the coins in their care. Needless to say, nothing was missing."

"Did they ask you where you got it from?" Ustimovich asked.

Petrokov nodded. "I told them that I inherited the coin from my grandfather and wanted to get it appraised."

"And did they?" Ustimovich said.

Petrokov jutted out his chin and nonchalantly rubbed the scar on his neck. "Not officially, but they offered me two-hundred thousand US dollars for it. I figured they were low-balling me. I could probably fetch more on E-bay. And I told them that, too."

Petrokov smiled when he saw the astounded look on the faces of Ustimovich and Pushkarev. Only Komvich appeared unaffected by the declaration.

The crime boss studied the coin for several seconds, then looked Petrokov in the eye. "I'm pleased that you didn't decide to take them up on their offer, Mikail. You know how important loyalty is to me."

Komvich slid the coin across his desk at Petrokov. "Here, you hold onto this," he told him. "I just suggest you keep it stored someplace else besides your pants."

Although Petrokov showed no outward reaction to Komvich's sudden show of generosity, inside he screamed with elation. He could already feel the warm sands of those Havana beaches against his skin, his Swiss Bank account filled with more money than he could ever spend in a hundred lifetimes.

He took the coin and put it into his briefcase, while Ustimovich and Pushkarev stared in utter disbelief at his sudden windfall. Pushkarev turned to Komvich with a look of silent protest.

Komvich read her mind. "Patience, my dear. There's more, much more, where that came from." Still upset at being usurped by Petrokov, she slumped in her chair with a pout on her face.

Ustimovich spoke up. "General Komvich, let's assume the book is legitimate. Do you think the Mongolian president is just going to step aside and allow you to plunder a national treasure?"

"He damn well better," Komvich barked. The general rubbed one side of the band of short grey hair that circled his bald crown. "We put his ass into power. We can take him out just as easily if he refuses to cooperate."

"President Bagaryn is getting what he wants," Petrokov broke in. "He won't give us any trouble."

"That's just it," Pushkarev said. "What exactly does your friend want with the weapon?"

Petrokov shifted in his chair. "He told me he wanted it in his military arsenal to provide some defensive leverage against the Chinese."

"Is that all he wants it for?" Pushkarev asked cynically. "Is that why the crazy idiot tested it out on his own people?"

"He wanted confirmation of its efficacy."

"We told him it worked," she replied. "We gave him all of the scientific data that he needed."

Petrokov shook his head. "Yeah, on monkeys." He paused. "If I was him, I would have wanted to test it as well. It shouldn't have been a big deal. Someone just screwed up."

A heavy silence descended upon the room. Everyone present knew that Pushkarev had been placed in charge of the team of scientists responsible for testing the chimera's effectiveness; as a result, the blame for the Yushan debacle rested directly with her. It fell on Komvich's own security force and Tsogt's commandos to mop up her mess.

The irritated look on Komvich's face told Petrokov he had just crossed the line. She must be incredible in bed for Komvich to allow her to live after that type of mistake. Petrokov figured that it was in his best interest to change the subject, and fast.

"General Komvich, what should I tell President Bagaryn regarding the delivery of the agent?"

"You tell him it will be delivered to him next week."

"Who will be taking it to him?" Ustimovich asked.

Komvich gestured towards Petrokov. "Why, Mikail will."

Petrokov's stomach dipped south. After hearing about the test mishap, the last thing he wanted was to get within a hundred miles of that viral bullshit. He suspected it was payback for the remark aimed at Komvich's bitch mistress. Unfortunately, there wasn't much Petrokov could do about it now. He was in no position to argue with Komvich.

"I still think it's a bad idea," Pushkarev said.

Petrokov suddenly found himself in agreement with her.

"There is no cause for concern," Komvich replied. "I've already taken care of matters."

"What do you mean?" Pushkarev asked.

Komvich drummed his desk with his fingers. "I arranged to have the virus chemically inactivated. This next batch will be rendered harmless before Bagaryn gets his fat little hands on it."

Petrokov breathed a subliminal sigh of relief. He watched Komvich lean back in his chair, wiping a piece of lint from his lapel. The old general was truly a paradox. Here was a man who wouldn't hesitate to order the wholesale assassination of men, women, and children if he deemed it to his advantage to do so. Yet here he was, going out of his way to protect humanity from his own weapon of mass destruction. Perhaps it was an old soldier's sense of duty. Komvich knew the power of the weapon and the consequences of an uncontrolled release. Oh well, it didn't matter to Petrokov anyway. He was just happy that he didn't have to carry around a lethal virus on his person.

"What happens when Bagaryn finds out?" Ustimovich asked.

Komvich lit another cigarette. "Not to worry." A crafty smile crept across his face and he blew a heavy stream of smoke from his nostrils. "By the time he does find out, the grave of Mongolia's national hero will be just another empty hole in the ground."

Chapter 13

THE POWDER BLUE MIAT 737 lurched to a halt at the end of the airstrip, then taxied to the terminal at Ulaanbaatar International Airport. A mobile stairway approached along with two attendants who ushered the passengers from the tarmac through an open door leading to customs. Steele was surprised to see the terminal so abuzz with activity. Mongolian soldiers occupied most of the chairs and spare floor space, while at the sole ticket counter, a sea of outbound travelers besieged two stone-faced agents, sparring for boarding passes for the next outbound flight.

Steele spotted a man dressed in a dark pewter business suit standing in front of the airport gift shop. Next to him, a young Mongolian woman held a sign with Steele's name on it. She was uniquely attractive, with long black hair accenting a pair of obsidian eyes, a gentle nose, and smooth, milky white skin. Steele's eyes met hers and he started in their direction. The woman promptly nudged the man beside her.

"Dr. Sangidansranjav?" Steele asked. He tried not to butcher the pronunciation too much.

The man's face broke into a giant smile. "It's a tough one, isn't it?" He extended his hand. "You must be Dr. Steele."

Steele sat his bags down and returned the handshake. "It's a pleasure."

"My Western friends call me Enkee. Please, feel free to do so yourself."

Forty-one-years-old with bronze skin and an angular wind-creased face framed by a head of bristly black hair, Dr. Enkee Sangidansranjav was the director of Mongolia's Health Ministry. Dark bushy eyebrows flanked a Roman-like nose, and his pleasant pecan-colored eyes made Steele feel instantly at ease. His English was excellent, having learned it while in medical school at Moscow University.

Enkee turned to the woman next to him. "This is Ms. Erdene Gungagarad."

"Ms. Gungagarad," Steele repeated. He extended his hand and bowed his head. "Did I pronounce that correctly?"

Her handshake was firm. "You did very well, Dr. Steele," she said. "Mongolian names can be tricky for Westerners. Please call me Gunga."

"Gunga works at the Ministry of Interior," Enkee said. "They have been so kind to loan her to us to be your personal driver and translator while you are here."

"It is my job to see that all your needs are taken care of," Gunga added. The corners of her mouth turned up ever so slightly and she took his bags. "Did you check any luggage?"

"No," Steele replied. "I prefer to travel light."

"Very good. Please follow me." Gunga turned and started for the exit.

"After you," Enkee said. He waved Steele on in front of him.

The two men followed Gunga out to a maroon Mercedes double-parked in front of the terminal's main entrance.

"The WHO office updated me on the Yushan epidemic," Enkee said. He clicked his seat belt on. "I must tell you Dr. Steele, it is alarming to think that such an organism could be loose in my country."

"We appreciate the Mongolian government's cooperation in this matter."

"Do they have any idea what type of organism it is?" Enkee asked.

Steele glanced up and saw Gunga watching him through the rearview. She smiled and looked away, then merged the car into the airport traffic. Steele knew he had to lie and it made him uncomfortable. Here was Mongolia's Chief Health Minister and he couldn't even tell him the identity of the potential bioengineered time bomb ticking away within his country's borders. Yet both Masters and Dietrich insisted that all information be kept under wraps until more facts on the virus could be gathered. Dietrich simply informed Enkee that an as-of-yet unidentified respiratory virus may have strayed into the country within the lungs of a photojournalist. The reason for Steele's trip was to visit the man's last known location and screen for the presence of the virus there.

"They're still working on it," Steele replied. He quickly changed the subject. "How far is Dogan from Ulaanbaatar?"

"It's about a ten hour drive south of here," Enkee said. "I've been there once, about five years ago. Not much there. It's a small settlement with a population of anywhere from thirty-five to seventy-five, depending on the season. It serves as a convenient water stop for herders crossing the Gobi."

Steele shifted in his seat. "Has your office received any reports of unusual illnesses from that area or for that matter, anywhere else within the past ninety days?"

"None," Enkee replied. "We did have a Chinese tourist admitted to the State Hospital here in Ulaanbaatar with clinical signs of severe viral upper respiratory disease. As it turned out, he was diagnosed with AIDS-related pneumonia."

Enkee continued. "After Dr. Dietrich notified me that the man may have been in Dogan, I contacted officials at the hospitals in Sajn Sand and Erenhot, the two towns closest to Dogan. The doctors there reported nothing unusual has passed through their doors. The southern part of the Dornogov province where Dogan is located is sparsely populated, with very few attractions or facilities to lure tourists. Unfortunately, they have no phone lines or electricity, so direct communication with the settlement itself is impossible. However, Gunga has made arrangements to drive us there tomorrow."

"Excellent," Steele replied. He glanced out the window and admired the green, undulant topography for which Mongolia was so famous. Soon, the hills gave way to the urban outskirts of Ulaanbaatar, home to over a third of Mongolia's population. The Mercedes crossed the Tuul River and sped along Genghis Khan Avenue, past Nairamdal Park and into the heart of the city. Gunga weaved through the traffic and potholes as if she were competing in a downhill ski event. The car turned east and careened past high rise apartments, skeletons of unfinished factory buildings, columned government buildings, and statues of communist and military leaders that stood frozen in time, pouting over their failed twentieth century experiment.

Steele saw an impressive convoy of olive brown military trucks rumble past them going the opposite direction. Their canvas-covered beds were packed with troops and several towed pieces of Russian artillery behind them.

"What's with the troop build-up?" Steele asked. "The airport, too. It was packed with soldiers."

"President Bagaryn has ordered a limited mobilization in response to the latest Chinese troop movements within Inner Mongolia," Enkee said. He shook his head. "I'm not quite sure what he's thinking."

Enkee paused to allow Gunga time to agree with him, but she remained silent. He continued without her endorsement. "At any rate, not a smart move in my book."

Minutes later, Gunga slowed the car and without bothering to signal, turned into a broad, lengthy horseshoe-shaped drive. A collection of six-storied apartment buildings lined both arms of the horseshoe, while in its center, a treeless park, complete with a dried-up concrete fountain, basketball court, and haphazard arrangement of wooden benches and seats, served as the community hang-out when the day's work was done. North of the park, an old Soviet armory sat abandoned behind a barbed wire fence, its collection of tanks, fighting vehicles, and artillery pieces gathering rust. It was a lonely end for what once represented the finest in Cold War muscle.

Gunga drove past a line of trucks and SUV's parked bumper to bumper along the outer curb of the drive. Unable to find a parking spot, she double-parked next to shiny new Land Rover.

"This reminds me of downtown Manhattan," Steele mused.

"It's normally not this bad," Enkee said. "A group of Russians arrived in town this morning. They just happen to be staying in the apartment complex next to yours."

Enkee pointed to the building in front of them. "Your accommodations are in there, Dr. Steele."

Steele surveyed the building's exterior. Its paint was flaky and the grass-speckled sidewalk that led to the short flight of steps was chock-full of potholes deep enough to snap an ankle.

"The Health Ministry rents out several apartments to accommodate foreign visitors," Enkee continued. "This is one of them. We thought you'd be more comfortable here than in a hotel."

"I appreciate that, "Steele replied. He inspected the rectangular courtyard that separated the Russians' apartment building from his. Several men in fur caps milled around in conversation, while two others worked to get a fire started on a grill.

Steele followed Enkee up the three flights of stairs to the front door of his unit. While Enkee searched for the correct key on his key ring, a door across the hall cracked open and the faces of an elderly man and woman appeared.

"Sain bainuu," Enkee greeted them.

The old man smiled and opened his door all the way. "Sain bainaa, Enkee Sangidansranjav."

Enkee introduced Steele to his neighbors. Both the man and wife were thin and frail. His back was bent from years of factory labor, while her face was extremely dry and wrinkled.

"Chinbat and his wife are the self-appointed hall monitors of this floor. Every time we have guests stay in the apartment, they take it upon themselves to watch over them like they were their own."

"That's mighty nice of them," Steele said.

"If you need something," Enkee continued, "don't hesitate to knock on their door. They can't speak English, but they're pretty good at figuring out what you're trying to tell them."

The elderly couple smiled, bobbed their heads several times, and retreated to their home. Enkee finally found the key he was looking for and opened the door to the guest apartment. He placed Steele's luggage on a worn brown leather couch situated in a tiny living room.

"There are drinks and food in the refrigerator," Enkee said, pointing to the apartment's even tinier kitchen. He beckoned Steele to follow him down a narrow hallway. "The bedroom is there," he said, motioning to a doorway at the far end. He then turned right and flipped on the bathroom light. He pointed out the two buckets filled with water beneath the bathroom sink.

"Water and electricity in the capital city can be quite unpredictable. That's your emergency water supply." Enkee smiled. "Just like home, right Dr. Steele?"

Steele chuckled. For him, it brought back fond memories…of deer camp in South Texas.

With the tour of the apartment complete, Enkee walked to the front door. "I'll leave you so you can rest up. If you feel like eating out tonight, I know a good restaurant that will introduce you to some authentic Mongolian cuisine."

"Thank you for the offer, Dr. Enkee, but I think I might call it a day if you don't mind. I have some work I need to catch up on."

"I completely understand," Enkee nodded graciously. "Gunga and I will be by in the morning at six o'clock to pick you up." He shook Steele's hand and left.

Steele moved his bags to the bedroom, then returned to the living room and turned on the television. After flipping past a cheesy Indian soap opera and a Russian talk show, he found, much to his delight, the familiar faces and voices of Fox News. He retrieved a Diet Coke from the refrigerator, fixed a sandwich, and returned to the couch to watch a summary of the day's news, weather, and sports. Mention was made about a special session of Congress addressing military tensions in the Far East, yet nothing about the troop movements Steele witnessed on the way in.

It was just past midnight when Steele awoke to the voice of the news anchor and to the sounds of revelry outside his apartment. Having fallen asleep on the couch, he was surprised to discover his soda still locked in his right hand. Luckily, none had spilled. He turned off the television and went to bed. He closed his eyes, but the obnoxious noise outside didn't allow them to stay closed for long. Half-annoyed and half-curious, he got up and walked to the window.

Russians from next-door packed the courtyard below him, most of them drunk on vodka. They sang a medley of out-of-tune ballads that Steele figured were either drinking songs or sacred anthems of the Motherland. For a brief instant, he felt like telling them to pipe down, but decided it would be a futile gesture. He was about to return to bed when he caught a glimpse of two men at a picnic table near the courtyard grill.

One of them was rather tall and thin and wore a black overcoat with a matching fur cap. The other man was his opposite; a short, burly individual with a bald head snuggled beneath a black stocking cap. Together, the two were studying a map spread out on the table before them. At one point, a group of revelers stumbled to the table with vodka bottles in hand and tried to join in, but the thin man chased them off. Steele noticed he walked with a limp.

Suddenly, he heard shouts directly beneath his window. He looked down to see two inebriated Russians waving at him, an invite for him to come join the festivities. Steele declined the offer with friendly gesture and retreated to his bed. He pulled his IPod from his travel bag and put on the headphones, hoping a little white noise from *Ocean Tranquility* would help drown out the party noise.

He lay in bed and thought about tomorrow's trip to Dogan. What would they find? Hopefully a sleepy little village with healthy inhabitants. But what if that wasn't the case? What if the chimera was there? What the hell would he do then? Steele's mind raced through a myriad of scenarios for another thirty minutes. Finally, like a welcome guest, fatigue stepped in and coaxed him into a deep, much-needed sleep.

Chapter 14

THE ROLLING WAVES of green carpet morphed into a tawny desert platform as Enkee's Russian-built AvtoVAZ jeep and its passengers bounced along a set of shallow tire tracks worn into the earth. Stunted, tough little bushes and diminutive, wind-thrashed trees intermingled with the scant blades of desert grass and clung tenaciously to the desiccated soil, extracting whatever nourishment they could find. To the left, a herd of antelope matched the jeep's speed against the brilliant blue horizon, as if refusing to allow this intruder to beat them to some unseen finish line.

It had been over four hours since they left Ulaanbaatar and Steele slept most of the way. But now he was wide awake and his ass hurt. Unfortunately, they still had three hundred kilometers to go before they reached Dogan. Just the thought caused him to shift several times in his seat.

"What is the matter Dr. Steele, you don't care for Russian automotive engineering?" Gunga asked.

With the mid-morning sun firmly implanted in the sky, she had removed her sweater, revealing a sleeveless khaki blouse. Her petite arms were firm and toned, like those of an athlete. The top two buttons on her shirt were undone, as was the fourth. There was no bra in sight. Steele wasn't sure if she left her shirt that way intentionally or by mistake, but either way, he wasn't about to open his mouth.

"I'd pay top dollar for a stadium seat about now," he replied to her. He turned to Enkee. "I wanted to ask you. What are the Russians next door doing in Ulaanbaatar?"

"Grave robbers," Gunga said.

"Treasure hunters, Dr. Steele," Enkee clarified.

"Really?" Steele replied. "And what treasure is that?"

"The treasure of the Great Khan,"

"You're talking about Genghis Khan?"

Enkee nodded. "Over the past twenty years, there have been no less than thirty expeditions - Russian, Japanese, American, you name it - into the Khentii aimag, just east of here. His tomb, and the treasure it contains, is supposedly located somewhere in that region."

"And the Mongolian government allows them to do it?" Steele asked.

"The Mongolian people resent these searches," Enkee replied. "Genghis Khan represents our national identity. To some, he is seen as a god. His grave was to remain untouched forever. The idea of foreigners disturbing his resting place is unthinkable."

"So why do they allow the searches to continue?" Steele asked.

Enkee rubbed his thumb and index finger together. "Money, Dr. Steele. These people pay a lot of money just for the opportunity."

"That figures," Steele said. "Do you think they will ever find the site?"

"I doubt it," Enkee replied. "Its location has remained a mystery for eight hundred years. Even with the latest in exploration technology, all efforts to find it have failed. Genghis Khan was born somewhere in the Khentii province and according to Mongolian tradition, he was buried near his birthplace. That's where the majority of these expeditions have taken place. In reality though, his grave could be just about anywhere in the country. I suppose that deep down the government officials who authorize these expeditions know the chances of locating it are remote, so why turn down the money?"

"True," Steele nodded. "Still, you have to wonder what would happen if they do find it."

The conversation ended for several minutes as Enkee checked his GPS coordinates. Steele then turned to Gunga. "Did you grow up in Ulaanbaatar?"

"Actually, I'm originally from the Inner Mongolia Autonomous Region," she told him.

"How did you end up in Ulaanbaatar?"

"My father brought me here ten years ago." Steele heard her voice crack. "You see, Dr. Steele, my mother was murdered by the Chinese government."

"I'm sorry, Gunga," Steele said. He groped for a seatbelt that wasn't there. Plan B. So much for the small talk. Change the damn subject altogether.

Thankfully, the subject changed itself. Three specks in the distance caught everyone's attention. Within minutes, the distinct silhouettes of two men and a van appeared. It was a rusty white Volkswagen variety, similar to the classic hippie vans of the sixties. It faced into the wind with its hood propped open. One young man, wearing a baseball cap and dressed in a woolen sport coat and jeans, leaned against the passenger door. His older travel companion, wearing an emerald green del and a chocolate fedora, knelt in front of an impressive pile of rocks, wood, and bottles.

Gunga swung the jeep off of the path and slowed to minimize the dust cloud kicked up by the tires. The younger man watched with indifference. The left side of his face was disfigured. A plum-colored scar replaced part of a missing cheek.

As the jeep crept past, the older man rose to his feet. He began a chant and tossed pebbles on the pile.

Steele turned around in his seat to watch. "What's he doing?" he asked Gunga.

"He's making an offering to the spirits that inhabit this place. The mound you see back there is called an ovoo. It is a shrine to the shamanistic gods. You'll find them all over the country."

Gunga stuck her arm out the window and waved at the two men. The one in the fedora ignored the gesture and continued his worship, but the young man acknowledged her. Gunga punched the accelerator and the two men and their van disappeared behind a billow of Gobi dust.

Steele thought it odd. Not so much that two men were worshipping a pile of rocks in the middle of nowhere. No, that wasn't it. It was the way the stranger acknowledged Gunga. He had given her a "thumbs up."

Like he knew her.

Chapter 15

THE SUN SHIMMERED low in the western sky. In the distance, a pair of impressive hills rose and fell like humps on a camel's back. Enkee toyed with his hand-held GPS unit, then leaned through the front bucket seats of the jeep.

"Dogan should be just on the other side of those," he said, pointing to the landmarks. Seventy minutes later, those same hills were well behind them.

"Gunga, slow down." Enkee said

"What's up?" asked Steele.

Enkee didn't answer him, but punched the buttons of the GPS. It responded with a series of blips and chimes. Enkee surveyed the desert panorama, then turned and checked the twin landmarks. He fiddled with the device once again. Steele sensed something was wrong.

"Are we lost?"

"It's not here," Enkee replied.

Steele's eyes lit up. "What isn't here?"

"Dogan. It's not here."

"Are you sure the GPS is working properly?"

Enkee shook his head. "There's nothing wrong with the GPS."

Steele became uneasy. "Are you saying Dogan has disappeared?"

Enkee looked bewildered. "It appears that way."

"That's nonsense," Gunga broke in. "They probably decided to pack up and move west before the first winter snows hit."

"Dogan is a permanent community," Enkee said. "They don't migrate with the seasons."

"They obviously changed their minds," she said.

"I don't think so," Enkee said. "Something is not right. Gunga, make a wide circle around this area here."

Gunga did as Enkee asked, but they found nothing. No tracks, no discarded objects, no remnants of civilization. It was as if the Gobi desert had opened up and swallowed up Dogan. After fifteen minutes of fruitless circling, Enkee asked Gunga to stop.

"It'll be dark in a couple hours," he said, the frustration obvious in his voice. "Unfortunately, we didn't pack for an overnight stay. Better start back for Ulaanbaatar."

He reached over the seat and placed his hand on Steele's shoulder. "I'm sorry, Dr. Steele. I don't know what's going on. Once we get to the city, we'll launch an investigation right away. If the inhabitants of Dogan did relocate for some reason, we need to find out where and make sure they aren't packing your virus with them."

Steele didn't hear him. His eyes were fixed on a spot a hundred meters to the right of the jeep. "Gunga, drive over there."

"See something?" Enkee asked.

Steele nodded. It was barely discernible. But it was there.

"I noticed it earlier," he said, "but didn't think anything of it."

Gunga drove slowly in the direction indicated by Steele. "Stop here."

Steele jumped out of the jeep and knelt beside a subtle bulge in the otherwise flat desert floor. It looked like a well-worn pitcher's mound.

Enkee climbed out of the jeep and joined him at his side. "What do you make of it?"

"I'm not sure," Steele replied. "Did you bring a shovel?"

Enkee nodded affirmatively. He put a hand on Enkee's back. "Let's find out."

They retrieved the shovel and took turns digging. Enkee was hard at it when the shovel scraped against wood.

"What'cha got?" Steele asked.

Enkee cleared away more sand and gravel. "I think it's a well cover."

"Could it belong to Dogan?" Steele asked.

"Possibly," Enkee replied.

Steele stepped forward and took over shovel duty. In no time he uncovered a round wooden panel two meters in diameter.

"It's a well cover, all right," Enkee said.

Steele let the shovel fall to the ground. "Why would the people of Dogan bury their well before they left?"

Gunga propped her forearms against the steering wheel and spoke through the open passenger door. "Perhaps it dried up."

"I doubt that," Enkee said. "The wells in this region are quite deep and fed by a network of underground aquifers."

Gunga started the jeep and shouted over the engine noise. "Regardless of what happened, unless we want to spend the night out here, we'd better start back."

"We will, Gunga," Steele replied. "Just hang tight for a minute." He turned to Enkee. "Do you smell that?"

Enkee crinkled his nose. "I do."

Steele took a knee and slid the cover to one side, revealing a gaping hole in the earth. He was met with a blast of decay that nearly made him vomit. Steele shoved his hand over his nose and mouth and peered into the well. It was dark and he couldn't see a thing.

"There's a flashlight in my bag," Steele told Enkee in a muffled voice.

Enkee retrieved the light. Steele clicked it on and shined it down the well. The sight was ghastly. A new rush of nausea hit him. He leaned to one side and vomited. Steele was never one to be easily shaken, but this time, he had been caught off guard.

Enkee took the flashlight from his hand and looked for himself. His face paled. He handed the light back to Steele.

Enkee was right. The well wasn't dry. There was still plenty of water.

And bodies. Lots of bodies.

Chapter 16

"THIS REMINDS ME of back home in Deets," Steele said as he eased into a quiet corner booth of the Moravia Restaurant, located one mile north of the American Embassy in downtown Ulaanbaatar. The man across from him, dressed like a weekend golfer in a pair of stone poplin slacks and a cashmere sweater, laughed and motioned to a waiter behind the bar. Ambassador Paul Wheaton flashed a white-toothed smile at Steele, creating a prominent dimple beneath each of his friendly brown eyes. Steele guessed Wheaton couldn't be older than thirty-five, yet the man's mannerisms and speech exuded the confidence and experience of someone much older.

A native of Rochester, New York and a Harvard graduate, Wheaton had been in Mongolia for six years, first serving as an economic advisor for the World Relief Organization and then later as the joint services director of the Asian International Economic Aid Council. He immediately fell in love with the people and their land, eventually marrying the daughter of a prominent Mongolian legislator and subsequently tapping into his father-in-law's connections to lobby for education and economic reform within the country. Washington recognized his unique position and later offered him the ambassadorship to Mongolia. Whereas most diplomatic appointments meant lives filled with luxuries and splendid dinner parties, this particular appointment failed to come with such grandiose perks and was looked upon by other aspiring career diplomats as nothing short of self-imposed exile. But Wheaton truly cared for the country and its welfare and accepted the appointment with much appreciation and zeal, which made him one of the youngest persons to serve the State Department in such a capacity.

"I knew you'd like it here," Wheaton said. "The restaurant was built by a wealthy Czech outfitter to cater to his European clients. It's only open from June to September.

"I'm sure you're wondering why we're here and not at the embassy," Wheaton continued. "We found out last week that our illustrious embassy building has more bugs in it than an Amazon rain forest. Our people uncovered one just last week in the bathroom, of all places."

Steele grinned. "That's getting kinda personal, isn't it?"

"You can say that again," Wheaton said. "Fortunately, half of the listening devices didn't work. They must have picked them up cheap at an FSB garage sale."

Wheaton glanced around at the nearly empty restaurant. "As you can see, there's no shortage of privacy around here."

The waiter behind the bar, a skinny, bony-faced man dressed in black slacks and a traditional Czech vest embroidered with gold and indigo designs, scurried to their table. He fluffed his puffy shirt sleeves, adjusted his tie, snapping to attention. Clipped to his vest was a button with the Czech greeting "Jak se mas."

"Good evening, Mr. Ambassador," he said in barely recognizable English. "May I get you something from the bar?"

Wheaton held up two fingers. "Jargal, please bring us two Budvars."

"Very good, sir," The waiter replied. "Would you like menus?"

"No need," Wheaton replied. He smiled at Steele. "If Dr. Steele will trust me, we'll have the roast pork and dumplings."

"Sounds good to me,' Steele said.

The waiter promptly returned balancing a tray containing two frosty mugs of beer. He plopped two leather coasters down on the table and placed the drinks on top of them. "Here you are, sir."

Wheaton pointed at a dark-suited gentleman sitting by himself three booths down. "And be sure to put that man's food and drink on my tab as well." The waiter bowed and left.

Steele motioned towards the lone diner. "Your driver?"

"And bodyguard," Wheaton replied. "It's an unfortunate necessity these days if you're an American living in a foreign land."

Wheaten lifted his beer mug into the air. "Cheers, Dr. Steele. To the United States of America."

Steele raised his mug. "To the United States."

The two mugs met mid-table with a "clink."

Wheaton took a drink of his beer, then placed it on the table. "My office told me your phone call sounded urgent. What can I help you with?"

Steele leaned forward and lowered his voice. "I'm in Mongolia on behalf of the Defense Department investigating a potential biological threat to the region."

The ambassador raised his eyebrows. "Biological threat?" he repeated, his concern evident.

Aware of Wheaton's security clearance, Steele gave him a brief run-down of the events of the past ten days, including the trip to Dogan. Wheaton listened intently, absolutely stunned by Steele's story.

"A well full of bodies?" he said.

"Someone murdered Dogan's inhabitants and then bent over backwards to hide the evidence," Steele replied. "Just like Yushan."

"And you're sure there's a connection?" Wheaton asked.

"I collected tissue samples from the bodies in the well," Steele said. "Ten to one we'll find our bug."

"This otherwise peaceful country seems to be embroiled in a slew of killings lately," Wheaton said.

"Why do you say that?"

"I heard this morning that there was a shooting at the Damba Zuu Khiid monastery, located to the west of here. Apparently, a number of monks were murdered, including the Holy Lama. Reports are still sketchy to say the least."

"Wow," Steele replied. "That's brutal."

"Very," Wheaton said. "So what did you end up doing with the bodies? In Dogan, I mean."

"Dr. Sangidansranjav has sent his people out to quarantine the area," Steele replied. "We're not moving the remains until we hear from the lab. My partner arrives tomorrow from Beijing. He's going to personally escort the samples to the States."

Steele picked up a coaster and tapped it reflectively on the table. "This may sound crazy, but I believe Dogan was used as a biological test site."

Wheaton took a sip of his beer and wiped the foam from his lips with a napkin. "Yushan, too?"

Steele shook his head. "No. Yushan was an accident. Started by an American journalist whom we know was in Dogan for a week prior to Yushan. Somehow he slipped through Yushan with the virus in tow. When they learned of the subsequent outbreak there, they had no choice but to slip a goon squad across the border and mop up their mess."

Wheaton raised his eyebrows. "That's some theory, Dr. Steele. Who is 'they?'"

"That I couldn't tell you." Steele leaned forward. "What about this IMLF outfit I've heard about? Could they have somehow gotten their hands on the chimera?"

"Anything's possible, I guess," Wheaton replied. "But it sounds as though from what you've described, these operations were well-organized and well-coordinated. That pretty much rules out the IMLF. As far as Al Qaeda is concerned, they have a presence on the western edge of Kazakhstan, but not here. They won't find much support for their radical Islamic agenda in this country."

The conversation stopped when the waiter approached with their food. He placed a generous portion of steaming dumplings and chunks of tender pork in front of Steele. Steele leaned over his plate and savored the aroma. "If this tastes as good as it smells, I may have to order seconds."

After the waiter left, Steele continued. "Is there a way you could arrange a meeting with President Bagaryn? Maybe he can help us. Besides, I think he needs to know what is going on in his own country."

"That may be a tall order, Dr. Steele," Wheaton said. "I'm not the most popular person with the president these days." He took a bite of his food.

"Why is that?" Steele asked.

Wheaton finished chewing and explained. "Six months ago, Bagaryn expelled three of my staff from the country. Claimed they were spies."

"What's the deal?" Steele said. "I thought the U.S. enjoyed good relationships with Mongolia. Didn't they provide soldiers to the coalition to help out our own troops in Iraq? Now they bug our embassy and expel our personnel?"

"Unfortunately, that relationship has cooled. And those coalition troops you mentioned? Bagaryn pulled them soon after he seized power. As you can imagine, the Administration has not been too pleased with the Mongolian president. In July, they took it upon themselves to slip several CIA operatives into the country without anybody's knowledge. I didn't know anything about it until a rumor of their presence surfaced and Bagaryn caught wind of it. Of course, I was accused of orchestrating the move and bore the brunt of Bagaryn's wrath. Frankly, I'm surprised he hasn't kicked me out of the country already."

"What would covert CIA operatives be doing in Mongolia?" Steele asked.

"Most likely aiding the opposition force."

Steele cocked his head. "Opposition force?"

"Yes," Wheaton replied. "It's led by several ex-military officers who went into hiding when Bagaryn seized control. They saw him then, and see him now, as a threat to world peace, a view shared by Washington. Their group would love nothing more than to see Bagaryn's government tossed out and replaced by a democratic, more U.S. friendly administration."

Steele stared at the dumpling stuck in his fork.

Wheaton took note. "Is there something wrong with your food?"

Steele looked up and smiled at him. "No, no. Not at all. I just had a thought."

"What's that?" Wheaton said.

"Maybe we're fishing at the wrong hole," Steele said.

"What do you mean?"

"Maybe Bagaryn himself is somehow involved in all of this?"

Wheaton laughed. "The man is egotistical and a bit eccentric, but unleashing a bioweapon on his own people seems like a stretch even for him."

"Unfortunately, it's not so far-fetched," Steele replied. "Sadaam, Stalin, Hitler. The list doesn't stop there. Dr. Sangidansranjav told me Bagaryn has aspirations of restoring Mongolia to the position of power it once held centuries ago."

Wheaton bobbed his head and smiled. "It's a great concept to capture the imagination and votes of the people, but it's nothing but a fantasy."

"Even so, Ambassador, if a belligerent leader of a third world country wanted to boost his military might, he'd turn to biological weapons. It's the poor man's alternative to spending millions of dollars on a nuclear arsenal. And at one point he would have to test the effectiveness of those weapons."

Wheaton paused to digest Steele's remark. Then he dropped his fork to his plate and the smile disappeared. "That son-of-a-bitch!"

Wheaton's outburst startled Steele.

"Kuanin," the ambassador said.

"Excuse me?" Steele replied.

"The Kuanin. They're one of several minority groups in Mongolia. Number about five thousand. They're descendents of the first group of Manchus to invade Mongolia in the 1700's."

Steele was still perplexed.

Wheaton clarified. "The major ethnic group in Mongolia is the Khalkh, who make up close to ninety percent of the population. Bagaryn is a Khalkh himself, as are all those he has appointed to his government. He has been criticized on numerous occasions by the United States and the international community for his blatant campaign to tax and suppress the various minority ethnic groups within the country, especially the Kuanin people. Bagaryn harbors a special animosity towards them because of their Chinese ancestry."

"I still don't follow," Steele admitted.

"Dogan."

"Don't tell me."

"Yes, Dr. Steele," Wheaton continued. "Dogan is, or should I say was, a Kuanin settlement." Wheaton's face grew pale.

Steele, on the other hand, was flushed with energy. He had no idea his meeting with the ambassador would bear so much fruit. But every answer brought forth new questions.

"It sounds as though we have a lot to talk about with the president," Steele said. "Do you think you'll be able to get that meeting?"

"Prime Minister Magaarad should be able to help me. He and Bagaryn keep an open dialogue going. In fact, Magaarad is at Bagaryn's palace in Karakorum as we speak. When he returns, I'll see what I can do."

Steele's mind raced. He brought his hand to his chin and leaned back in the booth. "Bagaryn is friendly with the Russians, is he not?"

Wheaton drained the last bit of his beer. "Russia views Mongolia as an important buffer between her and China, yet I do know that Russian President Molkov personally can't stand Bagaryn. Luckily, the Russian ambassador here in Ulaanbaatar has good rapport with the president, so he's able to act as an effective buffer between the two leaders."

Steele was curious. "What does Molkov have against him?"

"He's not used to dealing with someone more conceited than himself. He also frowns upon the company Bagaryn keeps."

"What do you mean by that?" Steele asked.

"One member of Bagaryn's inner circle is a countryman of Molkov's named Mikail Petrokov. From what the State Department tells me, he's not a very savory character. Years ago, Petrokov was sent to Mongolia by his then commander General Yuri Komvich to act a military advisor to our one and only Lt. General Vachirdorj Bagaryn."

Steele held up a hand. "Komvich. I've heard that name before. Isn't he connected to the Russian mob?"

"He is," Wheaton replied. "Komvich organized one of Russia's most powerful crime syndicates and oversaw a redistribution of Russian property on a scale unprecedented in history. Apparently Petrokov and several of Komvich's former junior officers helped him do it. Many feel that the Russian mob played a key role in Bagaryn's rise to power."

"What would the Russian mafia want with Mongolia?" Steele asked.

"Prostitution, drugs, smuggling, extortion, vodka, mining operations in the Gobi...the list goes on."

"Hmm," Steele murmured.

"What are you thinking," Wheaton asked.

"The Russian mafia is big into arms-dealing, are they not?" Steele said.

Wheaton nodded. "No doubt about it." He paused, then grinned. "I think I can see where you're going with this."

"Do you know where Petrokov is now?" Steele asked.

"I couldn't tell you exactly, but he comes to Ulaanbaatar quite often. If not on business, then on pleasure. He has an eccentric hobby."

Steele's curiosity was aroused. "Hobby?"

"Hunting for lost treasure."

Like a sudden north wind, Wheaton's words blew away the haze that shrouded the mystery in Steele's mind. The pieces of the puzzle were finally beginning to fit together, and Steele didn't like the picture they formed.

"Let me guess," Steele said. "He's looking for the tomb of Genghis Khan."

Wheaton's eyebrows arched with surprise. "Why yes, Dr. Steele. How did you know that?"

"It seems that the subject comes up everywhere I turn these days. In fact, a good number of Petrokov's treasure hunting buddies set up camp in the apartment building across from mine."

"You know they claim that the Khan's grave contains billions worth of treasure," Wheaton said.

Steele pushed his residual meat and dumplings to one side. "That may be the case, but I have a sneaking suspicion that it holds the key to something much more valuable than treasure."

"Really," Wheaton said. He signaled for the waiter to bring the check. "And what might that be?"

Steele grinned from ear to ear. "The answer we've been looking for."

Chapter 17

PRIME MINISTER SUKHAAR Magaarad sat on the edge of an enormous emerald leather chair in the foyer of Bagaryn's office in the presidential palace at Karakorum doing everything he could to compose himself before his meeting with the Mongolian president. He was not looking forward to it.

Ever since Bagaryn seized power, the animosity between him and former leaders of the country had smoldered. Instead of exiling or imprisoning his opposition, Bagaryn held out a conciliatory hand to them through Magaarad, the prime minister of the government he overthrew. A puppet government materialized with the sole purpose of carrying out Bagaryn's mandates. At first, Bagaryn actually invited Parliament's input on political and economic matters that involved the state. Yet in the past few years, Magaarad and his peers noticed that Bagaryn distanced himself from them. Increased political tensions with China and unsettling rumors of presidential involvement with Russian organized crime were all hot topics at Parliament's most recent session. As appointed head of the "government," Magaarad assured his colleagues that he would make the trip to Karakorum and speak to the president directly. He would insist Bagaryn address these issues in person to the Great Hural.

In his late fifties, Magaarad was a handsome man with a head full of well-groomed black hair with no hint of gray. Dressed in a standard issue politician's blue suit, he carried himself with confidence and charisma that overshadowed his otherwise small stature. In fact, among his countrymen, his popularity was second only to Bagaryn's. Yet today he felt his confidence slip.

The president's secretary typed at her desk in front of a computer monitor. She wore a matching black skirt and blouse, which contrasted with her milky-soft skin. Her lengthy raven hair was pulled back in a bun and her doe-like eyes and fair facial complexion were complemented by a light layer of make-up. Magaarad watched her work. She was very young, no more than twenty-years-old. No doubt one of Bagaryn's many mistresses.

He deplored Bagaryn's vain assertions that he shared the same family tree with the Golden Clan of Genghis Khan. Bagaryn's attempts to emulate the famous leader repulsed him even further. It was as if the president truly believed he was the actual reincarnation of the Mongol strongman, and thereby determined to prove as such to the world.

Thankfully, despite his sexual lasciviousness, Bagaryn had yet to produce an apparent heir. Magaarad laughed inwardly at the thought. He doubted that Bagaryn would ever admit he was sterile. No, he would continue to use and discard his concubines like napkins, ever affixing the blame on them for his reproductive deficiencies.

Magaarad's thoughts were interrupted by the sound of the buzzer on the secretary's desk. She picked up her phone, then put it to her shoulder.

"The president will see you now."

Magaarad winced when he stood up. His knees had given him fits for years and he knew that his arthritis would eventually sideline him unless he succumbed to surgery. Perhaps next year, he reasoned.

The prime minister followed the young secretary through a door into Bagaryn's office. Then she bowed and left the room, shutting the door behind her.

The president stood behind his desk. He stepped forward and shook Magaarad's hand.

"My friend, it is good to see you again," Bagaryn said, his voice devoid of sincerity.

"Thank you for meeting with me on such short notice, Mr. President." Magaarad's tone was cordial yet carried with it a touch of contempt. He looked around the spacious office. "This is the first time I've been to your new palace. Quite impressive."

The comment was not without hidden meaning and Bagaryn knew it. The legality of using public funds and manpower to build a new presidential palace had been a hot topic of debate among law-makers, a debate that infuriated Bagaryn. He used the occasion to take down the names of those who opposed his building plans, with Magaarad topping the list. In the end, Bagaryn got his way, in a large part due to his adoring public who rose up and supported their hero, pressuring their elected officials to pass the building appropriation measure.

Bagaryn simply smiled at Magaarad and sat down. "Not as impressive as the original built by Genghis and his sons, but it will have to do."

He motioned to a leather chair in front of his desk that matched the one in the foyer. Magaarad took a seat. He studied the enormous map on the wall behind Bagaryn. It was a map of the ancient Mongol kingdom, spreading from the Pacific Ocean to the frontiers of East-ern Europe.

Bagaryn flashed Magaarad an inquisitive look. "So what are these pressing matters you needed to meet with me about so urgently?"

"My colleagues in Parliament are concerned about the deteriora-tion of our diplomatic relations with China and of your support of the IMLF. You do realize that China wants the United Nations to classify them as a terrorist organization?

Bagaryn shifted in his seat impatiently. "I am aware of that, Prime Minister. Is that all?"

Bagaryn's indifference agitated Magaarad. "That seems to be plenty," he said. "If we continue to provoke China, she will have no choice but to declare hostile actions against our country. And you and I know we cannot resist her."

"You give the Chinese more credit than they deserve," Bagaryn said.

Magaarad couldn't believe his ears. He shifted forward in his seat. "What are you talking about? Their armed forces outnumber ours a thousand to one. I don't see where we have any leverage whatsoever."

"You forget about our friends to the north," Bagaryn said.

Magaarad shot him an incredulous look. "Who? Russia? It took us seventy years to get them out of our country, and now you want them back?"

Bagaryn leaned back in his chair. "My dear Prime Minister rest assured that I have everything under control. My Russian contacts…"

"You mean your Russian mafia friends," Magaarad said. "And what do you have to say about the reports that you purchased weapons from Russian arms dealers?"

Bagaryn glared at him coldly.

"Well, are those reports true?" Magaarad said. He wasn't about to let Bagaryn evade the question.

"Who told you this?" Bagaryn asked.

"We have credible sources who desire to remain anonymous, Mr. President. You have been seen in the company of Yuri Petrokov on a number of occasions. His connection with criminal elements in Moscow is well-known."

"My relationship with Yuri Petrokov is no secret," Bagaryn said, his voice bellicose. "Our friendship goes back a long way. As far as his business goes, they are of no concern to me. Nor to you." Bagaryn raised his index finger and pointed it at Magaarad. "And rest assured, Mr. Prime Minister, that your 'credible sources' will be uncovered and dealt with accordingly. I will not tolerate traitors to my authority."

"Is that a threat, Mr. President?"

Bagaryn sneered. "You can take it any way you want. I only allowed you and your friends to retain your government posts as a goodwill gesture in order to afford a smooth transition of government. Do not forget. I rule Mongolia, and those not with me are against me."

Magaarad's anger caused him to tremble. He took a deep breath, speaking slowly and carefully.

"You made a promise to the Mongolian people to hold free elections within a year of your coming to power. It's been two years, and not one local election has been held."

Bagaryn stood up. "What the Mongolian people need is a leader to restore them to their former greatness, not to coddle them and yield to their democratic aspirations."

A soft knock on the door suspended the ever-building tension in the room. Bagaryn's secretary entered and walked over to him.

"I apologize for disturbing your meeting, Your Excellency, but the e-mail you were expecting just arrived." She handed him a hard copy.

Your Excellency? Magaarad thought. Spare me.

Bagaryn examined the paper the girl gave him. His frown once again turned into a smile.

"Also, Your Excellency, General Tsogt is outside."

Bagaryn motioned to her. "Send him in."

Bile scalded Magaarad's throat. Tsogt, the psychopath. He should be in prison, not advising the president.

The secretary left, and with choreographed precision, the Mongolian general entered the room arrayed in full military dress. Magaarad arose to shake the hand of the man he despised, yet Tsogt walked right past him without a crumb of acknowledgment and went straight over to Bagaryn.

"Mr. President, we still have plenty of vaccine left over from the test. It should be enough to get us by," Tsogt said in his deep guttural voice.

Bagaryn dropped into his chair and clapped his hands together with excitement. "Excellent." He pointed to the hardcopy of the e-mail he received. "Petrokov will deliver the package tomorrow. Our timetable is set."

Tsogt continued. "Are we still going to hand over the relic to him?"

Magaarad watched the two men and tried to comprehend their conversation. When he finally spoke, his voice cracked with anger. "What vaccine? What relic?"

Bagaryn acted nonchalant. "Why, the relic we borrowed from the monks at Damba Zuu Khiid."

A chill shot through Magaarad's spine. His eyes widened. "You! You were responsible for the murders at Damba Zuu Khiid."

Bagaryn grinned and nodded to his general. "An unfortunate incident, but one that could not be avoided. It was necessary for our plans to move forward."

"And what plans are those?" Magaarad said.

"Sit, Prime Minister," Bagaryn replied. He nodded at Tsogt. The general placed his hands on Magaarad's shoulders and shoved him back into his seat. Outrage welled up inside of the prime minister, but he remained seated. He knew he wouldn't win a struggle against the giant towering over the back of his chair. For the first time since he arrived, fear became his predominant emotion.

"Mr. Prime Minister," Bagaryn said. "As of this moment, consider Parliament officially dissolved."

Magaarad began to speak but Bagaryn's hand shot up. "I'm afraid your services are no longer needed."

Magaarad looked at him uneasily. "You can't do that."

"On the contrary, I can do anything I want," Bagaryn replied. "The Chinese will find that out soon enough."

Magaarad was dizzy with fear and outrage. "The Chinese? What are you talking about?"

"In one week, we will reclaim our land to the south from the Chinese, the first step in the revival of the great Mongol Empire."

Magaarad sat absolutely stunned. "You're mad, Bagaryn! Do think the United Nations will allow you to do this? American Ambassador Wheaton himself will…"

Bagaryn interrupted him. "The American Ambassador is no longer a concern of ours."

Magaarad couldn't speak through the lump in his throat. It was the way Bagaryn had said it.

The latter looked at Tsogt. "Remind me when this is all over that we must crack down on crime in the streets of our capital."

The general smiled smugly.

Magaarad's rage broke through his fear. "I demand to know what is going on."

Bagaryn pounded his fist on his desk. "You will demand nothing, Mr. Prime Minister." He walked to the large window behind the desk and stared out over the palace courtyard. Then he turned to face Magaarad. "I believe our meeting is over."

Magaarad remained silent for a few moments and allowed the enormity of Bagaryn's grand design to sink in. He finally spoke.

"What you are proposing will lead to World War III. When the United Nations finds out about your plans, they will take immediate action to step in and stop you."

"I doubt very seriously if it will come to that," Bagaryn replied with confidence. "And besides, how would they find out about my plans? Other than me, General Tsogt, and his commanders, you are the only one who knows about them."

"You're insane," Magaarad said. He failed to grasp the implication of Bagaryn's last statement.

"Perhaps. But we'll let history decide, won't we?"

Realizing the futility of further discussion, Magaarad stood up as if to leave. This time, Tsogt didn't make a move to restrain him. With barely-contained contempt, Magaarad declared, "I'm leaving."

"I don't think that would be appropriate," Bagaryn said. He motioned to two of his personal body guards who appeared in his office. They marched up to Magaarad and grabbed him by the arms.

"What is the meaning of this?" Magaarad said. "Unhand me at once."

Bagaryn didn't answer him. He pushed a button on his desk.

Within moments, four additional guards entered the room lugging an enormous carpet. They dropped it to the floor behind Magaarad and unrolled it. The prime minister struggled to free himself, but couldn't. They flung him to the carpet and pinned him down while two men rolled him up in the thick fabric like a spider wrapping its prey. When they finished, the only parts of the prime minister's body visible were his hands and feet jutting out opposite ends of the carpet. The guards secured their package with rope, then carried it and its contents from the room.

Bagaryn opened the French doors behind his desk and stepped out onto a balcony that overlooked the palace courtyard. General Tsogt joined him. The six guards and their heavy load soon emerged in the courtyard below. They maneuvered to the middle of the yard and irreverently tossed their load to the ground.

Six riders appeared at the end of the yard and lined their horses up in single file facing the lump of fabric that lay twenty-five meters in front.

"Too bad the Prime Minister couldn't have joined up with us," Bagaryn said with sadistic amusement. "He would have seen that my vision for Mongolia is nothing short of glorious."

"Yes, it is too bad, isn't it?" Tsogt replied. His typically expressionless face broke into a sinister smile.

"To the New Mongolia, General Tsogt," Bagaryn said, raising his arm in the air as if proposing a toast. Then he let it fall.

Within his claustrophobic confines, Magaarad struggled for air. It was as if a giant boa constrictor was squeezing the life from him. He screamed in terror at the realization of his fate, yet it came only as a muffled murmur to those outside of his woven coffin. He heard the thunderous sounds of hoof beats and the ground shook beneath him. Suddenly, his legs and pelvis exploded when the first of the horses hit the rug. The pain was excruciating and he screamed for mercy. A single hoof found its mark and answered his plea, popping his skull like a water balloon and shoving the prime minister into the outstretched arms of Death.

Chapter 18

STEELE THANKED AMBASSADOR Wheaton for a very enlightening lunch and hailed a taxi to take him to his apartment. From the back seat of the cab, he placed a phone call to Dan Win. Steele was riding on a hunch and needed information. He figured Win was the man to contact.

The U-shaped drive of his apartment complex appeared just up ahead. Steele tapped the driver on the shoulder to slow down. Instead, the driver sped up, cut across two lanes of busy traffic and turned into the drive doing 90kph. Then and only then did he use his brakes. The tires screeched in agony and the vehicle slowed to a crawl. Steele's boisterous Russian neighbors, busy loading boxes of equipment and food into their SUV's, momentarily stopped to see what all the noise was about. Two exceptionally large specimens next to a Land Rover scrutinized the taxi that crept past them. Steele acknowledged them with a nod. They didn't return the gesture.

Steele paid the driver and bounded up the steps to his apartment. He inserted his key into the door. It was already open.

He took a big step back. Steele knew he locked that door before leaving. His nerves tingled and his body tensed as every instinct screamed a warning. With muscles taut and ready for action, he eased open the door just enough to slip an arm through. He felt along the wall until he found the light switch, then flipped it on and swung the door open all the way.

The apartment's interior looked as though it had been hit by a scud missile. Twice. The couch was ripped open, with contents thrown everywhere, and the television pushed off its base and smashed. The cupboards and drawers were emptied, and in some cases, ripped from their hinges. Steele entered the room like a whitetail buck sensing danger, his eyes and ears alert for trouble. He heard noise coming from the bedroom.

"Whoever you are, you'd better get the hell outta here right now!" he said in a bellicose voice.

He heard a grunt behind him, but before he could turn, Steele received a fiery blow to his lower back that sent him sprawling face first to the floor. A hefty man with a wooden bat in hand stood over him in triumph. Another man emerged from the bedroom and took up position opposite him. This one wore an evil grin on his youthful face, a face devoid of its left cheek. Steele recognized him immediately. The ovoo worshipper from Dogan. The young man yanked Steele to his feet by the collar.

"Where are the samples?" he demanded in English. Steele spit in his face. The batter stepped forward and rammed the end of his weapon into Steele's abdomen. The air rushed out of Steele's lungs. He doubled over and collapsed to the floor.

"Where are the samples?" the young man repeated.

Steele remained silent, partly because he had no air left in his lungs and partly because he wasn't about to tell these goons a damn thing. He relaxed his body and focused on regaining his breath.

The man raised his bat to strike Steele again, but he seemed to freeze in mid-air. The bat then clattered to the ground. Steele looked up and saw why. Chinbat stood in the doorway of the apartment. And he was angry. The old man waved the barrel of a rusty shotgun at the two assailants, who backed up and stood at attention with their arms raised high in the air.

Chinbat shuffled into the room and helped Steele to his feet. With an air of authority, Steele's guardian shouted at the two men and motioned to the door with the gun barrel. The trespassers refused to comply. Figuring that both Chinbat and his gun were older than the earth's core and could probably do little to stop them, the two men decided to rush the old man.

The blast from the shotgun knocked Chinbat backwards against the wall and sent a barrage of ceiling plaster and wood on the heads of the two men. With their courage literally shot, they scrambled for the door, stumbling over each other along the way like two stooges. The elder marksman scurried after them with his weapon in hand. He stopped at the top of the stairs and ripped off a flurry of admonishments. Chinbat's wife added her two cents worth from across the hall.

Steele was still spitting plaster dust when Chinbat and his wife reappeared in his apartment. Chinbat grinned like a dog with tetanus. He hobbled over to Steele, leaned the ancient firearm against the wall, and wiped plaster dust from Steele's clothes.

Suddenly, footsteps resonated from the bottom of the hall stairwell. Steele grabbed Chinbat's shotgun and rushed out into the hallway. The footsteps grew louder and faster. Steele felt for the gun's safety. There wasn't one. A head popped into view on the stairs. Steele heaved a deep sigh of relief and lowered the gun. It was Gunga.

She ran up the last of the stairs. "Dr. Steele, are you hurt?"

"I'm fine," Steele replied. He rubbed the snow from his hair. "Just a bit plastered."

Steele handed the gun to the old man with an appreciative nod.

"I was outside when I heard an explosion," Gunga said. "Two men almost ran over me on the front steps. What happened?"

"I caught them rifling through my room," Steele replied. He rubbed his stomach. "One of them was the young dude we saw on our way to Dogan."

Gunga turned to Chinbat and his wife and thanked them for their Samaritan act. Chinbat smiled and spouted off something Steele couldn't understand.

Steele turned to Gunga for help. "What did he say?"

"He said that he was glad you weren't seriously hurt. He apologizes for the actions of those men. They do not represent the citizens of his country."

Steele reached out and shook Chinbat's hand. Chinbat spoke again and pointed a bony finger towards the gaping defect in the apartment's ceiling.

"He also apologizes for your ceiling," Gunga translated.

Steele laughed. "You tell him that's one repair job I'll be happy to pay for myself."

Chapter 19

GUNGA ESCORTED CHINBAT and his wife to their apartment. Steele, in the meantime, picked up several chunks of plaster from the floor and stacked them in the hallway.

"I wasn't expecting to see you here," he told her when she returned.

"You left your book in the jeep," she said. She pulled a paperback from her purse and handed it to him. "I just wanted to return it."

"Thank you," he replied. "I wondered where that went."

Gunga walked to a chair that had been knocked on its side. She righted it and patted the seat. "Why don't you sit down? You could use a break."

Steele took her up on the offer.

"Would you like a drink?" she asked.

"As in?" Steele asked.

"Let me see what Enkee tucked away in the cupboard for you. He mentioned he always makes it a point to stock some liquor for his foreign guests."

She disappeared into the kitchen. Steele heard several doors open and slam close again. Moments later, Gunga returned with two bottles in hand.

"The kitchen is a mess. They ransacked it. These are the only ones that survived the storm." She held up the bottles. "Genghis Vodka or..." She paused to read the label on the other bottle. She didn't need to because Steele recognized it immediately.

"Jack Daniels!" he said. "Bless your heart. I didn't even know it was in there. Remind me to commend Enkee for his taste in spirits."

"How would you like yours?"

"Over ice," Steele said.

"Coming right up."

Gunga withdrew to the kitchen. Steele heard the freezer door open and the sound of ice cubes hitting a glass. Within moments, she returned with two drinks in hand. She handed one of them to Steele. He took a sip. It slid gently down his throat. A bit off-taste. Probably the ice. But, oh, did it taste good.

Gunga put her glass down and went to the kitchen.

"Chinbat sure showed up in the nick of time," Steele said. He took another sip of his drink. "I was about to put a major hurt on those fellows."

Steele heard Gunga laugh and turn on a faucet. The water cut off and she returned with a wet washcloth.

"Of course you were" she said with a smirk. She placed the hot washcloth on the back of his neck. The moist heat penetrated deep into his aching muscles.

Steele laughed, then gripped his side in pain.

"Anything broken?" Gunga asked.

"Just my pride. After all, an eighty-seven year-old man had to step in and save me."

She knelt beside Steele's chair. Her perfume smelled of spice.

Gunga dabbed several abrasions on his face with the cloth. "What do you think they were looking for?"

"The Dogan samples," he replied.

She drew back. "They didn't get them, did they?"

"They're still safe and sound," Steele said. He stood, now light-headed. He walked to the bathroom. Gunga followed him. Steele lifted the top off of the toilet tank. Inside, tucked into a bed of ice, was a compact vinyl cooler.

"Interesting hiding place," Gunga said.

Steele slid the porcelain top back on the tank. "Works great for beer too, just in case you run out of space in your fridge. That is, unless you need to flush."

"What were you planning to do with the samples?" Gunga asked.

"They're going back to the United States with a friend."

"And if they test positive for your organism, what then?"

Steele's knees buckled. He reached out and grabbed the bath-room sink for support.

"What's wrong?" Gunga asked with a flair of concern in her voice.

Steele forced a smile. "Nothing. I'll be fine." He closed his eyes. His world was spinning.

Gunga took his arm. "Here, you need to lie down for awhile." She led him to his bedroom.

Steele glanced at his watch. "Actually, I need to make a call to my friend in Beijing," he slurred.

Gunga shook her head. "You can do that in a little while. Right now, lie down and rest." She pushed him onto the bed and fluffed the pillow beneath his head.

Steele didn't protest. He was exhausted.

"What time do your friends arrive tomorrow?" she asked.

"Eleven a.m. You'll drive me to pick them up?"

Gunga didn't respond. Through heavy eyelids, Steele could see her staring at him like a pathologist analyzing a fresh cadaver.

"Stay put," she finally spoke. "I'll be right back." She then ducked out of the room.

Steele wasn't going anywhere. Something wasn't right. The world inside his head became more jumbled with each passing moment. He didn't feel nauseous, but a numb sensation began to creep into his body. First his face, then his arms. He tried to move, to sit up in bed, but his body wouldn't listen. Several minutes later, he heard noise at his bedroom door. With great effort he turned his head to look.

Gunga stood in the doorway, completely naked, with one hand propped up high against the doorframe while the other held the vinyl sample bag. Her skin was creamy white, her breasts round and tight, highlighting an upper body that tapered into a firm, muscular stomach, then blossomed out once again into a well-proportioned set of hips and thighs. To Steele's taste in women, her body was as close to perfect as they came. Perfect that was, except for the rough, pitted scar, shaped like a half-moon, emblazoned into the skin of her left thigh.

He tried to speak, to ask her what she was doing, but couldn't get the words out of his mouth.

Gunga held up the case. "Don't worry, Dr. Steele. I'll take good care of these samples."

She walked over to the bed and placed the case on the nightstand. She undressed Steele, then climbed on top of him. The scent of her perfume, stirred by her movements, overwhelmed his senses.

Steele dipped in and out of consciousness. The drug Gunga put into his drink absorbed into his bloodstream quickly. He fought to clear his head, to maintain consciousness, yet he knew it was a battle he was going to lose. There was to be no resistance; she had him at her complete mercy.

Gunga's slow measured movements evolved into violent spasms of lust. Steele's world was spinning like a cyclone. His body was numb to all sensation, save for an intense pressure within. It rose like molten mercury, climbing higher and higher and higher. At last, the floodgates opened in a storm of light and then slowly, very slowly, Steele slipped off into the nigrescent void.

Chapter 20

"TELL ME AGAIN just who are we supposed to be meeting with?" Maggie asked.

Jeb settled up with the cab driver. "He's a professor of antiquities at the University. Brazos wanted us to meet with him before we left for Ulaanbaatar. Supposedly he's one of the top experts on Mongolian history. We're meeting him at a park near here."

Standing on the sidewalk opposite the southeast entrance to Beijing University, Jeb seemed to survey his surroundings in an attempt to decipher the directions the professor gave him over the phone.

The cab ride took ten minutes longer than expected and they were running late. Early morning Beijing bristled with activity. A cacophony of horns from both cars and bikes greeted those who had yet to leave their homes and apartments.

"Follow me," Jeb said. He set off down the sidewalk at a quick pace, dodging the human traffic in his way. Maggie struggled to keep up with him. Her leg throbbed, yet she wasn't about to complain.

"Why do we need a history lesson on Genghis Khan at 6 a.m.?" Maggie asked. She jerked to one side to avoid a head-on collision with a hurried Chinese businessman.

Jeb glanced over his shoulder. "This is the only time the professor could meet with us. It actually works out well. It gives us plenty of time to get to the hotel and pack up before we fly out."

"You didn't answer my question," Maggie said.

"Brazos seems to think there is a connection between Yushan and the old Mongol warlord."

"You gotta be kidding me," Maggie said. "I didn't know his men wore ski masks when they went around conquering the world."

Jeb shrugged. "Don't look at me. We're just here to gather information."

They crossed over into a small city park, one of many in Beijing that served as quaint and heavily wooded escapes from the bustling sprawl of the surrounding civilization. A wide pathway led them into the heart of the grounds.

Arriving at an impressive marble monument that commemorated the People's Revolution, Maggie caught a glimpse of a man walking towards them at a brisk pace. He was short in stature, rounded at the shoulders, and wore a battleship grey sweat suit with a towel thrown over one shoulder, plus sneakers that matched the wild, white thicket of hair on his head. His face was dry and worn, yet his eyes sparkled with the enthusiasm of a teenager.

The man approached Jeb with his hand extended. "You must be Mr. Walker," the man said in pristine English. He shook Jeb's hand and bowed. "I am Professor Lao Zhu."

Jeb introduced Maggie.

"We didn't mean to interrupt your morning work-out," she said.

"I was just cooling down when you arrived," Zhu said. He dabbed his brow with his towel and then pointed to a park bench tucked away in a wooded cul-de-sac nearby. "Shall we have a seat?"

"We appreciate your fitting us into your schedule this morning," Jeb said, following Zhu to the bench.

"Anything to help out Dr. Win," Zhu replied. "Bright fellow. Former student of mine, you know? He told me that you are interested in Genghis Khan, or should I say, the mystery surrounding his burial. Tell me, Mr. Walker, what do you already know about Genghis Khan?"

"Aside from being one tough hombre who sported a cool mustache and killed lots of people, not much," Jeb replied.

Zhu proceeded to share his knowledge pertaining to the famous Mongolian leader. Both Jeb and Maggie listened with fascination as the story unfolded. Maggie's eyes grew large when Zhu mentioned the immense treasure purportedly entombed with Genghis Khan.

"Do you really think such a treasure really exists?" she asked.

"In museums around the world, there is a huge deficit of cultural artifacts from China dating from the late twelfth and early thirteenth century, the time period in which Genghis and his offspring raped and pillaged this country. If this wealth was buried with him, then that would explain this shortfall."

"It seems strange that no one has a clue as to where this guy's grave is located, considering he once ruled the world," Jeb said.

"According to Mongolian legend, all those individuals who prepared the burial chamber were put to death in order to keep the tomb's location anonymous. Even the soldiers who attended the ceremony were slaughtered days later by the Khan's family to ensure complete confidentiality. The grandson of Genghis Khan, Kublai Khan, took it one step further and handpicked a small group of men from twelve prominent families and marked them with the seal of the empire. Known as the Darkhad, Kublai entrusted them with the secret of the tomb's location, with the mandate that they protect it for all eternity. Unfortunately, with the fall of the Yuan Dynasty in the mid-1300's, the fate of the Darkhad became a mystery in itself."

"Do you think any of them live today?" Maggie asked.

"Very doubtful. Even if some of their descendents managed to survive into the twentieth century, they were no doubt eliminated by the communist purges. Both Stalin and Mao viewed Genghis worship as a direct threat to political harmony and used all of their resources to eliminate everything connected with his memory."

"Why would Kublai Khan entrust the family secret to a third party?" Jeb asked.

Zhu smiled. "Actually, I personally believe his hand was forced. It is possible that the famous explorer and close friend of Kublai Khan, Marco Polo, found out about the treasure."

Maggie raised her hand like a schoolgirl, then spoke. "I remember reading his book *The Travels* in my college literature class, but I don't remember him ever making mention of such a treasure."

"You are correct, Dr. Townshend," Zhu said. "That information wasn't mentioned in his most famous book, the one you are familiar with."

Maggie shot him a quizzical look. "Are you implying that he wrote other books?"

Zhu nodded. "In 1530, a rogue historian of the Italian Renaissance named Adolpho Giberti claimed in his writings that Polo penned a second book years after his famous work swept through Europe yet this subsequent book was never published. In it, according to Giberti, Polo described 'the greatest treasure the world has ever seen' and gave detailed instructions as to its whereabouts."

"I never heard of that," Maggie said.

"Not many have," Zhu said. "If you recall in his *Travels*, Polo claimed he left China because the Great Khan himself asked him to escort a Mongol princess to Persia, where she was to marry a man called Arghun. But according to Giberti, Polo fabricated that story to cover-up the real reason for leaving."

"And what was that?" Jeb asked.

"Polo supposedly learned of the tomb's location from a survivor of the original burial procession."

"I thought they killed everybody associated with the funeral?" Maggie asked.

"One man apparently escaped judgment, at least initially. Poor fellow. Spent a lifetime trying to convince people of his story. No one would believe him. No one, that is, except Kublai Khan. When the Khan found out about the man and his tale, he had him boiled alive. The entire population of the man's village was put to death as well. According to Mongol law, Polo should have been executed, too. But because of their close friendship and mutual trust, Kublai allowed Polo to swear an oath of silence and bid him to leave the kingdom."

"Why would Polo break his oath by writing that second book?" Maggie asked.

"You must remember, Dr. Townshend, that Polo was a businessman at heart and that his world revolved around monetary profit," Zhu said. "With the death of his old friend Kublai Khan and the subsequent disintegration of the Mongol empire, I'm sure he saw no reason to take such a lucrative secret with him to the grave. According to Giberti, before Polo died, he gave the sole copy of his literary sequel to one Pietro Savelli, a merchant apprentice of Polo's. Historical records confirm that Savelli led an expedition to the Far East in 1331. One can only speculate that the goal of the trip was to find the treasure."

"Obviously he failed," Jeb said.

"The expedition was ambushed and every member murdered before it reached Chinese soil," Zhu said. "Giberti blames the Darkhad."

"And the book?" Maggie asked.

"Disappeared. Proponents of the tale believe it was either destroyed on the spot or taken back to Mongolia by the Darkhad.

Some feel that it was tucked away for safekeeping, along with other relics and artifacts from the Genghis era, deep within one of the many Buddhist monasteries within Mongolia's borders during the sixteenth and seventeenth centuries. If so, it was no doubt destroyed during the Stalinist purges of the last century."

Maggie was absolutely mesmerized by the professor's tale. "This is all unbelievable."

Zhu turned to face Jeb. "Mr. Walker, you never told me. Where does your interest in the treasure lie? You aren't planning to look for it yourself, are you?"

"No, not at all," Jeb replied. "We're just gathering information for a friend of ours who happens to enjoy these types of historical mysteries."

Zhu smiled. "That's good, because Mongolian legend has it that if the final resting place of the Great Khan should ever be disturbed, the world and all we know of it, shall come to an end."

"Lovely," Jeb replied sarcastically.

"I don't think we have anything to worry about," Zhu added.

"You don't think his tomb will ever be found?" Maggie asked.

Zhu shook his head. "Man has searched for that tomb for over eight hundred years and hasn't even uncovered one clue as to its whereabouts."

He looked Maggie in the eyes, a look that exuded certainty. "No, Dr. Townshend, you can rest assured that this is one event that will never happen in your lifetime, or in the lifetimes of your children's children's children."

Chapter 21

A FLURRY OF frost and ice blurred the bright row of spotlights designed to illuminate a landing pad tucked deep amidst a sea of fir and poplar. Still, the bronze helicopter descended confidently out of the frozen night sky. The instant its wheels hit solid ground, the pilot cut the switch. Two beefy guards on the landing pad approached the side door of the aircraft. Arrayed in matching overcoats and berets, they moved forward cautiously, keeping their semi-automatic rifles slung over their shoulders and their heads well away from the dying blades. Within moments, the door opened and unfolded into a set of stairs. Mikail Petrokov appeared in the doorway with a briefcase in hand. The two guards fell into position on either side of Petrokov at the base of the stairway and escorted him up a well-lit walkway to the front entrance of a sprawling six acre, two-story, white-brick laboratory and office complex home to the Brevost Corporation.

Located 250 km northeast of Irkutsk, tucked away near the western shore of Lake Baikal, the complex was built by the Russians for the production of pharmaceuticals, and, far less publicized, for biological and chemical weapons research. The government later sold the facility to the Brevost brothers, who used it to manufacture nutraceutical and herbal supplements. The Biosafety level 4 research laboratory, located at the rear of the complex, was subsequently shut down.

A decade later, poor management and a shaky economy pushed the company and the two brothers towards bankruptcy. Desperate for working capital, Gregor Brevost turned to Yuri Komvich, who loaned them the money they needed to continue operations in return for a 33 percent share in their company. It wasn't long before Gregor's brother mysteriously disappeared while on a business trip to Moscow, an event made extremely suspect a week later by Gregor's abrupt decision to sell out to Komvich for a fraction of the company's worth.

Komvich retained the company name and the supplemental business as a front for his new operation, which involved the manufacture of cheap imitation drugs that could be sold at a hefty profit on the worldwide black market. At the same time, he recognized the enormous profits that could be realized through the purchase and resale of chemical and biological weapons to third world countries. In secret, he cleaned and reopened the biosafety laboratory and hired a team of unemployed scientists to serve as his own personal weapons experts.

Petrokov was greeted in a spacious reception area by a thin man just slightly shorter than himself, dressed in faded jeans and a full length lab coat with black ink stains on the breast pocket.

"Mr. Petrokov, I expected you earlier in the evening," he said with a hesitant smile on his face.

The man's hair was greasy and haphazardly combed to one side. By the thick film of gritty plaque wedged between the edges of his teeth, Petrokov figured he hadn't bothered to use a toothbrush in years.

Dr. Grigory Stavlova had been hired by Komvich to oversee the scientific activity within the BSL-4 laboratory, the majority of which took place after normal business hours. The freedom and lack of direct company supervision that came with his after-hours position well-suited the introverted biochemist. He rarely stepped foot into the lab he was supposed to be managing, preferring to delegate the hazardous work to his younger scientists who submitted hourly activity reports to him. This freed him up to sit in his office for most of his shift and pursue his true passion, downloading pornography off the Internet. He had been doing just that when Petrokov's helicopter arrived.

"Weather delay," Petrokov replied with indifference. He figured Stavlova didn't have to know that his late start was actually due to a last minute liaison with a Moscow stripper.

"Do you have the package?" Petrokov continued.

"It's in my office," Stavlova said. He pointed to a nearby elevator. "Please follow me."

Stavlova shooed the guards away, then led Petrokov to the elevator and to his office, which overlooked the main production floor of the pharmaceutical operation. Through a one-way glass panel that extended the entire length of one wall, Petrokov could look down and observe the crew of thirty workers put the finishing touches on the day's production.

Stavlova retrieved a metal canister, no bigger than an aerosol breath freshener, from his top desk drawer.

He thrust it towards Petrokov. "Here it is."

His sudden movement caused Petrokov to jump backwards.

Stavlova laughed. "Don't worry, my friend. It's been neutralized."

Petrokov was not amused. "Are you sure of that?"

"We've been conducting serialized tests with the inactivated agent on a colony of monkeys for the past two weeks. I'm happy to report that all of our furry cousins are alive, well, and disease-free."

Petrokov reluctantly took the container. He studied the cap affixed to one end of it.

"The container is equipped with its own built-in detonator located beneath that cap," Stavlova said proudly.

He reached into his pocket and extracted a tiny radio transmitter. "This transmitter can be used to activate it," he said as he handed it to Petrokov. "Once activated, the detonator punches a hole in the canister and releases the pressurized air inside. Of course, that's not all that will be released."

Stavlova leaned towards Petrokov and lowered his voice. "I still can't believe they tested the active form of this organism on those people in Mongolia. Talk about opening Pandora's Box."

His fetid breath made Petrokov wince. "I'll be sure to relay your feelings to Mr. Komvich and Ms. Pushkarev," Petrokov remarked. He was amazed at the scientist's blatant disrespect and insolence. Who did this worm think he was?

Stavlova didn't catch the innuendo. "In my opinion, we should torch the entire lot. I don't understand why Mr. Komvich wants to keep this stuff around. It's too dangerous. There are plenty of other agents we can weaponize and control much easier. If Molkov's agents ever found out what we had in our vault back there, we'd all be swinging from the gallows."

Petrokov narrowed his eyes and gave the scientist a once-over. "Why would they ever find out?"

The ominous look melted Stavlova, who seemed to suddenly remember who he was talking to. He attempted to soften his position. "I'm just saying this particular agent is just too hot to handle safely." Stavlova removed his lab coat. "Here, take a look at this."

He rolled up the left sleeve of his shirt. The skin of his upper arm was pitted with a big, ugly scar in the shape of a half-moon. He rubbed the roughed surface. "That's just from the vaccine."

Petrokov shrugged unsympathetically and walked to the office door. "I must be going."

Stavlova sheepishly nodded his head and put his lab coat on. He then escorted Petrokov and the container to the lobby. The two guards reappeared out of the shadows. One of them held the door open for Petrokov. Petrokov turned to Stavlova one final time.

"Oh, and just a suggestion," he said as he waggled his finger at the scientist. "Do what you are paid to do and keep your opinions to yourself. It's not healthy to question the intentions of Mr. Komvich."

Petrokov turned and disappeared through the doorway. Stavlova stood alone and cowed like a child reprimanded by a mean-spirited schoolteacher.

Stavlova had his head on his desk, an open bottle of cheap vodka next to him and a porn flick spinning in the DVD drive on his computer, when the phone wrenched him from his sleep. He looked at his watch. It was 4 a.m. The phone rang again and he picked it up.

The voice on the other end sounded troubled. And scared. It belonged to Stavlova's chief technician from the BSL-4 lab, the same man Stavlova put in charge of generating the batch of inactivated agent per Mr. Komvich's request.

"Sir, I need you to come to the lab right away. We have a problem."

"Take care of it yourself," Stavlova snapped at him, still groggy from the vodka and still seething at the way Petrokov treated him earlier. "I'm busy."

The technician hesitated. "It's the primates."

"What about them?"

"They're dying."

The adrenaline surge within Stavlova's body sobered him in an instant. "What are you talking about?"

"I've got monkeys from A Group exhibiting signs of infection."

Stavlova swallowed hard. He struggled to remain calm. "When was that group inoculated with the inactivated virus?" he asked.

"Fifteen days ago," came the reply.

"Have you collected blood yet?"

An uneasy pause ensued on the other end. "No sir, not yet," the technician finally said. "I did draw samples from B Group. They were inoculated ten days ago."

"And?" Stavlova said.

"We've identified active viral replication in at least one monkey out of that group."

Stavlova could feel and taste the bile rise in his throat. This can't be happening. He jerked up from his desk, knocking his computer's laser mouse to the floor. "So what are you saying?" he asked.

"It appears that the inactivation process failed," was the reply. "It only served to extend the incubation period of the virus."

Stavlova was numb. He knew that he had delegated one too many times and his neglect caught up with him. His scientists screwed up big time. And he knew he would be held personally responsible. Stavlova leaned over his desk, snatched the vodka bottle, and took a hearty swig.

"And that's not all sir," the voice on the phone continued. "It appears that the virus may have undergone a genetic mutation."

"What the hell do you mean?" Stavlova said. He almost lost his grip on the vodka bottle.

"Two of the monkeys in A Group and the infected monkey in B Group were controls."

The silence over the phone line was cruel. The controls had been vaccinated against the virus prior to exposure. To date, the vaccine proved to be 100% effective in exposure trials. Stavlova knew that this new twist meant only one thing. The efforts to inactivate the virus must have prompted a mutation or an antigenic drift that rendered the vaccine ineffective.

He subconsciously rubbed his scarred arm.

"Dr. Stavlova, whatever you do, don't let them have the sample we prepared for them," his technician pleaded.

"Too late," Stavlova replied with resignation in his voice. "It went out earlier last night."

"We need to let Mr. Komvich know right away."

"I'll take care of that," Stavlova said. "You make certain those monkeys are destroyed. All of them. And while you're at it, destroy every viral culture we have in stock."

"But sir," the voice said. "From what I understand, that decision can only be made by Mr. Komvich."

Stavlova slammed the vodka bottle to his desk, which caused alcohol to jump out from its spout. "Now you listen to me," Stavlova said in a voice cracked from stress. "Mr. Komvich has given me full authority to make such decisions in the event of an imminent threat. I'd call this an imminent threat, wouldn't you?"

The technician didn't answer him. Stavlova wasn't sure if the man believed the lie or not.

Stavlova took a deep breath and lowered his voice. "I will take full responsibility," he said with faked calmness. "Now get it done, no delay."

"Yes sir," his technician submitted. "Right away." Then a "click."

Stavlova hung up his phone and slumped into his chair, emotionally drained. He rummaged through his top desk drawer looking for a cigarette, but could only find one crumpled package emptied of its contents long ago.

His mind churned. This was not good, not good at all. If Komvich found out he screwed up, he was a dead man walking. If the chimera was released, the government would eventually trace it back to him. When they did, he would no doubt be shot as a co-conspirator. No, his best chance was to disappear, quickly and quietly.

He had relatives in the Ukraine. Now was an opportune time to revive those old family ties. The money he tucked away over the years from stealing and re-selling corporate inventory to unauthorized third parties would allow him to live comfortably for at least a decade.

His course of action decided, Stavlova mustered a surge of energy and jumped out of his chair. He rushed to his office closet and there, pulled out two storage bins full of office supplies and dumped the contents to the floor. Stavlova then emptied his desk drawers and file cabinet into the bins, stuffing the overflow into the white plastic bag that had lined his trash can. He stacked the bins on top of each other, hoisted the entire load to his chest, and struggled out through the doorway of his office.

Less than four minutes later he returned to his office, out of breath. He hustled over to his computer and punched the eject button on the DVD player. Retrieving his pornography from the tray, he stuffed the disc into the pocket of his lab coat. Then he turned and was out the door once again.

This time it was for good.

Chapter 22

THE NAVY BLUE Cressida bullied its way between two bulky army transports parked in front of the main terminal at Ulaanbaatar International Airport. Steele climbed out of the backseat and handed the driver a US$50 bill.

"Stick around. I'll be about ten to fifteen minutes," he said to the driver. With his head pounding, it hurt to talk. The driver inspected the likeness of Ulysses S. Grant. A broad smile came to his face, excited by this unexpected windfall. He nodded to Steele.

Steele entered the airport and made his way to the international arrival gate. His head throbbed with each step, and his eyes felt as though they would explode at any moment. He lamented the fact that the two ibuprofen he took forty minutes ago were unable to beat back the pain. His memory was a blur. He remembered Gunga in his room, but after that, he couldn't be certain. But there was one thing he was sure of. He had slept for over thirty hours and when he finally woke up his samples and his laptop were gone.

Steele called Gunga's cell phone several times, but was answered each time by a rapid busy signal. He tried her office, but the secretary there reported that she had yet to check in this morning. Steele then called Enkee and told him about the missing samples. Enkee mentioned that Gunga was scheduled to pick him up at 7:30 the prior morning for an important meeting, but she was a no-show and he assigned two of his assistants to track her down to make sure she was all right. But they had no luck in doing so. Steele couldn't fathom a reason why Gunga took the samples. But right now it hurt like hell to think.

Out of the terminal window, Steele saw a steady stream of people approach from across the runway tarmac. Jeb led the pack, with Maggie right behind him. His friend, towering above the Asian passengers that followed him, was difficult to miss.

Steele greeted them on the other side of the customs checkpoint and the three walked to the baggage claim.

"Good flight?" Steele asked.

"I'm just glad we're on the ground in one piece," Jeb said. "That plane creaked more than my left knee."

Maggie pointed to the uniformed presence throughout the terminal. "What's going on?"

"Troop mobilization," Steele replied. "Mongolia's president has decided he wants to play army with his neighbors to the south."

Maggie nodded. "No wonder the custom officials were being butts to the Chinese passengers traveling with us. I saw them detain several of them."

"Butts?" Jeb replied with an amused look on his face.

Maggie pushed his shoulder. "You know what I mean."

Jeb looked Steele up and down. "If you don't mind my saying so buddy, you look as though you just escaped from the county morgue."

Steele bit back a laugh. No laughing allowed until the ibuprofen kicked in.

"Rough night," he replied to Jeb. "I think I got hold of some bad shrimp."

"This far from the coast, I'd say so," Jeb said.

"How did your meeting with Professor Zhu go?" Steele asked.

"It was great," Maggie said. "What a charming gentleman."

"I guess you could say we're now full-fledged experts on Marco Polo and his barbarian friends," Jeb added. He puffed out his chest in a feigned show of intellectual superiority. "What exactly is it that you need to know?"

Maggie motioned towards an abused brown suitcase and a blue duffel with a white WHO acronym stitched on its side entering the luggage carousel. One end was smudged with airplane grease. "Here come our bags."

Steele retrieved their luggage. "Let's get going," he said. "We can talk on our way into the city."

Outside, Steele looked around but found no signs of his prepaid taxi driver. A middle-aged man wearing a white shirt with a pocket-full of pens and a worn brown fedora stuffed on top of a bronzed, puckered face, pulled his silver 2002 Honda Accord to the curb in front of them. He leaned across the front seat and waved at Steele with one hand through the open passenger window. The other hand gripped a sandwich.

"You need ride to city. I take you," he offered in butchered English. His somber eyes begged them to accept his offer. Steele couldn't help but notice that those eyes were set as close together as he had ever seen. Any closer and they could share an eyebrow.

The man popped the trunk from the inside, then set his sandwich on the seat beside him. He hopped out of the idling automobile and hurried around to the curb.

"Where's the car that was here?" Steele asked him.

"He leave. Tell me take you. He tell me where you stay. I take you there." The man smiled, then bent over and picked up the two bags, depositing them into the trunk of the car.

"How much are you going to cost?" Steele asked, perturbed at being duped by the other driver.

"Ten American dollar."

Steele pulled out his money clip and extracted two fives. He handed them to the new driver. "Here," he said. "Payment in advance."

The man took the money with a curt bow and opened the front door for Maggie. Jeb and Steele took up positions in the backseat. The interior of the car reeked of mutton and chronic perspiration.

With passengers secured, the driver ran around the front of the car and climbed behind the wheel. He tossed the remains of his sandwich out his window, then sped off on a course to the city.

"So what did the professor say about the treasure?" Steele asked anxiously.

For the next ten minutes Jeb and Maggie took turns telling him. Steele remained quiet the entire time and mentally constructed the puzzle from the pieces they threw at him. It all fit. Polo's lost book, the Darkhad, the Savelli expedition, Giberti's claims, the monasteries. Steele recalled what Wheaton mentioned about the Damba Zuu Khiid monastery. Was there a connection? There had to be.

"The bottom line," Jeb concluded, "is that Professor Zhu doubts the tomb and its treasure will ever be found."

"He's wrong," Steele said.

There was a moment of thick silence in the car.

Maggie leaned her chin over the seat's headrest. "Why do you say that?"

Steele caught the cycloptic stare of the driver in the rearview mirror.

"I'll tell you later," he said. The driver quickly shifted his eyes back to the road and slowed for an approaching stop sign. The Honda turned right at the intersection and started south towards the mountains.

Steele leaned forward in his seat and tapped the driver lightly on the shoulder.

"Isn't the city back the other way?"

The driver swung his hand in a wide arc in front of him. "Short-cut to your apartment," he said with a grin.

"This is gorgeous country," Maggie said. "I'd love to see it in the springtime with all of the wildflowers in bloom."

Steele's satellite phone suddenly came to life. He removed it from his belt and took the call.

"It looks a lot like Montana to me," Jeb observed.

Maggie nodded. "National Geographic had a fantastic pictorial on Mongolia not too long ago. They have some beautiful lakes northwest of here towards the border with Russia."

"Maybe when the dust settles around here, we can sneak off for a few days and drown a few night crawlers, eh Brazos?" Jeb asked.

Steele didn't acknowledge him. In fact, Steele hadn't said a word since he answered his phone. His eyes were fixed on the road ahead. Cyclops watched him through the mirror. The face that looked at Steele was no longer innocent and cordial, but cold and serious.

Suddenly, Steele spotted them. Two specks on the side of the road that soon morphed into shiny black sedans. One was a Mercedes E55 AMG. The other was a Lexus. Several men were leaning against the front hoods, arms in the air. Maggie saw them, too.

"Look," she said to the driver. "They are waving us down. Maybe they're in trouble."

"We've got company," Steele spoke into his phone. "We'll meet you there." Then he ended the call.

"Meet who?" Jeb asked. "What company?"

Steele handed his phone to Jeb. "Here. Hold this and keep your head down."

Before Jeb could ask why, Steele leapt over the front seat and landed between the driver and Maggie. He lunged across the startled driver's lap and pulled the door handle with one hand and unbuckled

Cyclops' seatbelt with the other. The Honda swerved violently. Cyclops steered with his knees and tried to push Steele off his lap.

Maggie braced herself against the front dashboard, a "not again" look on her face, while Jeb clung tightly to the hand rest above his door, rolling with the Honda's gyrations. Steele suddenly fell over Maggie's lap and pressed his feet against the driver's right hip.

"Grab the wheel," he said to Maggie. Before she could answer, Steele said to Cyclops, "Sorry friend, but this is where you get off." He kicked as hard as he could. Cyclops squealed and his door popped open. He tumbled out of the car, pens flying everywhere. He hit the pavement, rolling and bouncing like an empty beer can tossed from the window of a pick-up.

For a split second, the Honda was driverless. Maggie let out a horrified gasp and groped for the wheel. But Steele's hand was on it first, and he slid behind it to take control. He jerked the wheel to the left and sent the Honda into a 180 degree slide. Then he downshifted and punched the accelerator. The tires screeched and clawed at the pavement for several seconds before achieving a solid grip. The car then jettisoned northward towards the city.

Armed men swarmed out of the two sedans like fire ants. Gunfire erupted. Bullets ripped into the right rear panel of the Honda and knocked out the taillight. Tufts of asphalt and grass erupted on all sides.

"Please make sure your tray tables are up and your seatbelts are securely fastened," Steele said as he snapped his in place.

"Now you tell us," Jeb said. He rubbed the top of his head. "I feel like I just went over Niagara without a barrel."

"Sorry," Steele said. He glanced in the mirror. He saw the welcoming party scramble to their cars. They had been caught off-guard, which translated into an excellent head start for Steele. But he knew the Honda's whiny V-6 engine was no match for the powerful

24 valve engines behind them. Logic dictated that the gap would be closed rapidly and that they didn't stand a chance. But Steele had never been the type to give up just because of logic.

"Do you mind me asking what the hell is going on?" Jeb asked.

"Ambassador Wheaton was murdered last night."

Maggie adjusted her shoulder strap. "My God. By who?"

"Bagaryn and his henchmen."

"The Mongolian president?" Jeb asked.

"The one and only," Steele replied. "The heat must have gotten to him. He killed those people in Yushan and Dogan, and now he wants us dead."

Jeb leaned over the seat. "What heat?"

"Our chimera. There is mounting evidence that Bagaryn may be the one throwing it around."

"You gotta be shittin' me, Steele," Jeb said.

"I wish I was," Steele said. "The way he's talking trash and strutting around like a mini-Mussolini, he's up to something. And it can't be good."

"How did he get his hands on it?" Maggie asked.

"From the Russian mob." Steele looked in his side mirror. The sedans had closed the gap. "I think he traded the treasure for it."

Maggie looked confused. "You mean the Khan's treasure?"

"Si," Steele replied. "The information Professor Zhu provided you confirmed my suspicions. I think Bagaryn knew exactly where Polo's book was located. In a monastery outside of Ulaanbaatar. I bet you he traded that book to the Russians for the chimera."

"This is crazy," Maggie said. "What does he want from us?"

"He knows we know."

She shook her head. "He can't just go around murdering foreign ambassadors and expect to get away with it."

Steele let out a stifled laugh. "Evidently he thinks he can. And our asses are next on his hit list."

"Speaking of asses, those cars are fixing to crawl right up ours," Jeb said, staring out the back window. The vehicles were less than two hundred meters to the rear and bearing down on them at a rapid rate.

Jeb leaned forward against the front seat. "What are we going to do, oh wise one?"

Steele hit the dashboard with the palm of his hand. "The first order of business would be to give this piece of shit a tune-up."

"I'll be sure to keep my eyes peeled for a Lube and Tune," Jeb said. "But until then, what's the plan?"

"The plan is to link up with Dr. Enkee. He's the one who just called and told me that the ambassador had been murdered and that the bad guys were after us. We're to meet him at the Zakh."

"The what?" Jeb asked.

"It's a big ass open air market not far from where I stayed. Always packed with people. Enkee figured it would be safest to link up someplace where there was a crowd."

Their conversation was interrupted by a burst of gunfire that peppered the rear end of the Honda and punched a line of neat black holes along the trunk. Inside the car, it sounded like corn popping.

"They're right behind us," Maggie said, her voice a near-scream.

Steele remained calm and focused on the road in front of him. He sorted through the options in his mind. "You wouldn't have your gun handy, would you?" he asked Jeb.

"In the trunk with my luggage. Where is yours?"

"Back at the apartment."

They both looked at Maggie.

"No, I don't have a gun," she replied sharply.

"A knife? Nail file? Pepper spray? Anything?" Jeb asked.

Maggie grabbed a left-over pen from Cyclops that was lying on the seat. "Will this do?" she remarked with sarcasm.

"Hold on," Steele said. He whipped the Honda into the passing lane to zip by a slow moving short-bed truck. The two sedans followed his lead and stayed on his tail like a pair of heat-seeking missiles. Fortunately, traffic on the road was light.

The Mercedes in the lead suddenly dropped back while the Lexus whipped over into the passing lane and accelerated until it was side by side with the Honda. A tinted rear passenger window directly across from Jeb's window descended slowly. A rough, solid face with dark sunglasses leered with belligerence at Jeb. Jeb shot him the bird.

Steele swerved towards the car to test the mettle of the driver. The Lexus veered away to avoid a collision. Steele deduced that either the driver was inexperienced or else he owned the car. The Lexus recovered, then sped ahead until it was six car lengths in front of the Honda. Suddenly, an object flew out of the passenger window of the Lexus.

"Grenade!" Steele yelled as he jerked the steering wheel. The besieged Honda followed his command and shot off to the grass. It balanced on two wheels for a split second before crashing back down on all fours. A thunderous orange flash caved in the Honda's rear window and ripped off part of the rear bumper and trunk lid. Steele gripped the steering wheel and braced for a rear end blow-out, but incredibly it never came. He looked over his right shoulder and noticed the shredded remains of luggage and clothing fluttering through the air like confetti.

"I hope you packed a change of underwear in your jeans pocket," Steele said.

"Son of a bitch," Jeb said as he watched the Mercedes and the Lexus take turns running over the remains of his suitcase. "My toothbrush!"

"Serves you right for flipping him off."

"I didn't like the way he looked at me," Jeb replied. He shoved the remains of the shattered back window to one side.

Maggie shook her head in disgust. "If you two don't mind, we have two cars behind us driven by people who want to kill us."

"Yes, that's true. But we do have one advantage," Steele said calmly.

"Oh really?" Maggie replied. "And just what might that be?"

Steele glanced back and gave Jeb the thumbs up.

It was Jeb who answered her. "Our good doctor here owns every *Dukes of Hazzard* episode known to man."

Chapter 23

STEELE STEERED HIS wounded car to the paved road and pushed it harder than ever. Both the Lexus and the Mercedes fell in line behind him, but they didn't stay there for long. The Mercedes swerved into the passing lane and overtook the Lexus. It was the break Steele hoped for, but the timing had to be just right.

At the exact moment the Mercedes came up alongside the Lexus, Steele veered off the road again and kicked up a puff of dirt and gravel. Then he hit his brakes. Both vehicles, not anticipating Steele's move, continued forward neck and neck at full speed and sealed the gap with the Honda. When the two cars were right next to him, Steele swerved towards the Lexus, which was wedged between Steele's car and the Mercedes. The driver of the Lexus acted just like Steele expected him to and jerked his car to the left to avoid a collision. When he did, the side of his vehicle caught the edge of the Mercedes' front bumper. The shriek of crunching metal followed and the Mercedes driver lost control. The car veered off the road and plowed through the grass, spinning like a tightly wound top. At the same time, the impact knocked the hood of the Mercedes loose. It flapped up and over the car's roof and crashed to the asphalt. The startled Mercedes driver slammed on his brakes and skidded sideways down the shoulder of the road.

"Nice move," Jeb stated. "Uncle Jessie would be proud of you."

"Thanks," Steele replied. He eased across the shoulder to the pavement. "I had a feeling that driver was a chicken-shit."

Steele glanced over at Maggie. Her eyes were wide, staring straight ahead, while both hands clutched her door handle. He detected a faint smile on her face. She looked as though she were riding in the front wagon of the world's fastest rollercoaster. Steele understood the feeling well. When you stare danger and death in the face, it can be both frightening and exhilarating at the same time. Steele had been there many times. To him, it wasn't how long you lived, but how you lived. Neil Young sang it best: It's better to burn out than it is to rust.

Both Steele and Maggie looked over their shoulders at the same time. The two sedans had shaken their dust and resumed the chase.

"Persistent buggers, aren't they?" Steele said. "Well, hold on. We're almost to the city."

He remained calm, his hands relaxed on the wheel. The Honda sailed over the crest of another hill and began a rapid descent down the opposite side. Ahead of them lay an urban panorama, complete with a motley collection of industrial smokestacks that belched out filthy phlegm into the soft blue firmament above.

Both sedans closed to within one hundred and fifty meters. The Mercedes dove over the top of the hill. It slammed to the pavement on the downhill slope, spraying the Lexus behind it with sparks.

Steele demanded more and more from the little Honda. It shook and grumbled in response to his commands. The steering wheel started to wobble. Steele tightened his grip. He knew that the old girl was liable to collapse and die at any moment, like a trail horse pushed too far. But it was a risk they had to take.

Steele and his passengers reached the city limits ten seconds before their pursuers did, flying across the Tuul River traveling north, past Naadam Stadium. Steele didn't bother to downshift when they closed in on Enkh Taivny Avenue, but laid on his horn and bolted through the intersection. The Lexus followed, while the hoodless Mercedes slid into a turn and peeled off down the eastbound lane of Enkh Taivny.

Both Steele and the Lexus executed sharp rights at the Mongolian Museum of Natural History. The road dead ended at Sukhbaatar Square, the city's main public gathering place and the site where ninety years prior, the hero of Mongolia's revolution, Damdiny Sukhbaatar, declared his country's independence from China. Steele honked, jumped a low curb, and proceeded into the heart of the square with the Lexus on his tail. People scattered like pigeons as the two cars plowed through row after row of displays and tables set up by local vendors hawking their wares to tourists and locals alike. Steele looked in his mirror just in time to see the Lexus make a move to pass on his right. One of its occupants leaned out a passenger window with a Kalashnikov in hand.

Maggie pointed straight ahead. "Look out!"

Out of nowhere, the black Mercedes materialized in front on a dead-end collision course. Steele had about four seconds to react before he and his passengers became stains on the pavement. He jerked the steering wheel with two seconds to spare. The Honda propelled to the left. The Mercedes and its Japanese counterpart swerved to miss each other, but clipped one another's sides. The Mercedes ricocheted towards the steps of the Parliament House at the north end of the Square and skated to a stop in front of the building. The Lexus wasn't so lucky. The gunman was ejected from his seat and exploded on the pavement. The sedan continued on, out of control. It shot across the Square with the force of a rocket-propelled grenade, narrowly missing several terrified pedestrians. Seconds later, it smacked head first into a massive bronze statue of Sukhbaatar perched proudly upon his horse. At impact, the hoodless engine compartment collapsed and overwhelmed the interior airbags, pulverizing the car's occupants. The backend of the Lexus flipped into the air along with a shower of glass, metal, and flesh. The mangled chassis twirled like a baton, then bounced to the pavement and burst into flames. Remarkably, the statue held its ground through the carnage and remained upright, although left with only a thin, ragged stalk of its former pedestal on which to balance.

Steele didn't slow down to watch the fireworks, but continued across the Square and hurdled to the opposite curb onto Enkh Taivny Avenue. Dodging the oncoming westbound traffic, he managed his way over to the eastbound lanes and then pushed the Honda as hard as it would go.

They had to make it to the Zakh. It was their only hope. Steele knew the Mercedes survived the encounter and would no doubt continue its pursuit. The Honda shook and groaned with each increase in rpm. Quite frankly, Steele couldn't believe the old crate made it this far. It wouldn't surprise him one bit if she began breaking apart like a piece of space debris skipping along the Earth's outer atmosphere.

"Here he comes," Jeb said. He pointed at the Mercedes weaving in and out of the line of cars to the rear. A covey of bullets suddenly ripped into the back of the Honda. The right rear tire detonated and pieces of rubber flew everywhere. Steele fought against the pull of the naked rim, yet kept his foot on the pedal.

"Hold on." Steele downshifted and slung the car into a controlled skid to the right. The exposed rim scraped the pavement and emitted a shrill whine along with a shower of sparks.

The front tires pawed frantically at the asphalt. When they finally did grab hold, the car rocketed up and over the concrete curb, and with a loud, bone-crunching 'thump,' landed on a sloping dusty dirt road leading into the inner bowels of a slum-like neighborhood that sprawled out for miles like a spring mushroom patch. The Mercedes overshot the turn-off, and with a wail of its brakes, skidded to a stop and backed-up recklessly, causing the oncoming traffic to swerve towards the sidewalks and medians.

The continuous line of shoulder-high wood fencing on either side of the dirt road made Steele feel as though he were a rat in a maze. The Honda rushed down the hillside with the tireless rim kicking up massive clouds of dust. Steele kept his eye on the shiny metal rooftop of the Zakh pavilion in the distance. Both Jeb and Maggie kept their mouths clamped and left Steele to concentrate on the task of finding his way through the labyrinth. Meanwhile, a plethora of new bullets stitched the back of the Honda. The Mercedes was now on their bumper. Like a drunk behind the wheel, Steele weaved his car back and forth, kicking up even more dust to obstruct their assailant's line of fire.

Up ahead, the road made a hairpin turn to the right. With the Mercedes stuck to his ass, Steele waited until the last possible moment, then yanked the wheel sharply into the turn. The lightweight Honda slid sideways and bounced off of the wood fence like a tennis ball, landing back on the dirt road. The driver of the Mercedes, his vision obstructed by dust, missed the turn completely and crashed through the fence going 100 kph.

Steele punched the pedal to the floor. The Japanese car sounded like a rattlesnake in the throes of death. Smoke belched from the tailpipe, and the engine compartment emitted a shrill, ominous whine.

"Come on girl," he said. "Just a bit farther."

"Are you talking to me or to the car?" Maggie asked. "I feel like a pinball with a target painted on my butt. Why is it that whenever you and Jeb get together, bullets start to fly?"

Jeb plucked a sliver of rear windshield from his arm. "It just means we're popular."

"She's right, you know." Steele grinned over his shoulder at Jeb. "You do have a tendency to bring out the worst in people."

"Me!" Jeb said. "Who offended the waitress in Austin and prompted her to dump the chicken fried steak on your head?"

"You did," Steele said.

Jeb paused for a moment. "You know, I think you're right about that one."

"Excuse me," Maggie said, "but the dashboard of this wreck is lighting up like a Christmas tree."

Steele glanced at the panel. The engine light, oil light, and fuel light all glowed various shades of red. Not good. Just a little bit farther. The Zakh had to be within a stone's throw.

It was. After circling around a bank of twenty rust-colored cargo containers, the road in front of the Honda blossomed into a gigantic parking lot jam-packed with humans. Steele braked to avoid plowing into the crowd.

"What does this Dr. Enkee look like?" Jeb asked.

Steele waved an arm at the mass of humanity in front of the car. "Like them."

Steele sat staring at the crowd. "Come to think of it, he never did tell me where to meet him. I hope he plans to find us."

"Good luck," Maggie said.

Steele looked in his mirror. The Mercedes was nowhere to be seen. He steered the Honda through the crowd at a crawl, honking politely to part the sea of shoppers in front of him. They eventually reached the edge of the Zakh's covered pavilion. It was then that the Honda sputtered, coughed, and in a gigantic puff of sooty smoke, gave up the ghost.

"I'm afraid she's had it," Steele said. He patted the dashboard as if saying goodbye to a beloved pet. "Jeb, would you like to say a few words."

"Yeah," he replied. "Your driving sucks."

"Oh, and don't look now," Jeb added, motioning towards the black Mercedes that finally made its appearance at the parking lot entrance, its front grill a tangled mass of metal and wood. "It looks as though our friends are determined to get their shopping done."

The three of them forsook the Honda and ducked into the pavilion. The driver of the Mercedes, spotting the Honda's smoke, hit the accelerator and mowed down several pedestrians in his path. This senseless act enraged other market patrons nearby, who descended on the Mercedes like a horde of locusts, pounding the sides of the car with their fists. Three men reached through the broken driver's side window and extracted the driver, then beat him senseless. His accomplice fired his machine gun into the crowd, but he too was yanked from the car and disarmed. He quickly disappeared into the mouth of the awaiting mob.

While the crowd doled out their vigilante justice, Steele, Maggie, and Jeb crossed through the pavilion and emerged on the other side. A wave of relief poured over Steele as he saw the familiar red jeep parked across the street just outside the Zakh's rear exit.

"It's him," Steele said. He waved his arms in broad arcs to catch Enkee's attention.

The jeep's engine roared to life. The three sprinted across the rear parking lot and through the exit. Steele held Maggie's hand to ensure her lame leg didn't hold her back. Enkee helped her into the jeep. Steele jumped into the front seat.

"Boy, are we glad to see you," Steele said, fastening his seat belt.

"Likewise," Enkee replied. "I saw your trail of dust and smoke coming down the hill. When I heard the commotion within the parking lot, I figured you would be coming this way and drove around here to meet you."

He turned to Jeb and Maggie. "Welcome to our fair city. Now, if you don't mind, say goodbye to our fair city because we're getting the hell out of here."

Chapter 24

"I HAD JUST met with the quarantine and recovery team when I learned of the ambassador's murder," Enkee said. He took shallow breaths and his voice was thick with emotion. "Five minutes later, I receive a call from a friend of mine who works in the Ministry of Defense telling me my life was in danger and that I should leave the city immediately. He mentioned you as well. That's when I called you."

"And just in time I might add," Steele replied. "Thirty seconds later and the three of us would have been mere checkmarks on somebody's to-do list. Remind me to send a thank-you note to your friend."

Enkee passed a pair of motorcyclists. "The Minister of Foreign Affairs issued a statement that pinned Ambassador Wheaton's murder on a disgruntled Chinese expatriate. The government has since issued an order to deport all Chinese nationals living in Outer Mongolia."

"That's bullshit," Steele said. "I had lunch with the ambassador yesterday. He was going to apply the thumbscrews to Bagaryn over Yushan and Dogan."

"Bagaryn?" Enkee asked. "What do you mean?"

Steele revealed his hypothesis to Enkee, including the probable link to the Russian treasure hunters.

Enkee mumbled to himself. "The Damba Zuu Khiid Monastery. Of course!"

He swerved around a huge pothole, then seized a two-way radio off the dash. He fiddled with the buttons with one hand and put the radio to his ear. Someone answered and Enkee spoke in his native tongue. Steele caught the reference to Damba Zuu Khiid on more than one occasion. But why? What was going on?

"Killing a United States ambassador," Maggie whispered to Steele, trying not to disturb Enkee's phone conversation. "Not a very smart move."

Steele shook his head in agreement. "I think Bagaryn is just crazy enough not to care. That said, he must be planning a major move very soon."

"Like what?" Jeb asked.

"I don't know. But we better find out fast."

"We need to get word to Masters and alert the cavalry," Jeb said.

"My thoughts exactly," Steele said. "I'll see if I can borrow Enkee's phone. I left mine in the Honda."

Enkee finished his call and tossed the radio on the car dash.

"Dr. Enkee, you wouldn't happen to have your satellite phone handy?" Steele asked.

Enkee groped between the seats and found his phone. He handed it to Steele. "The battery is about spent. It may not work."

Steele pressed in a number. After several tense seconds, the call connected. Five rings later, it was answered.

"Maria, this is Brazos. Get Colonel Masters on the phone for me. Tell him it's an emergency."

Masters' secretary put him on hold. Steele glanced over his shoulder at Jeb and nodded reassuringly. Then he heard the dreaded beep of a dying battery.

"Hold on baby, just a few more minutes." Steele shook the phone as if attempting to extract the last bit of battery power. After what seemed like an eternity, Masters' voice sounded on the other end.

"Brazos, where the hell are you?" the familiar voice asked.

"Colonel, I'm glad I could get through to you…" Another beep, then static.

"Colonel, can you hear me?" Steele repeated it twice before Masters' voice returned. "The situation out here is deteriorating fast. We are going to need…" Steele didn't get the chance to finish his sentence. Three more warning beeps sounded in rapid succession, and then the phone went dead.

"I don't believe this," Steele said. He pumped the phone's power button in a futile attempt to resurrect the call.

Enkee looked at him apologetically. "Sorry. I was afraid that was going to happen."

Steele slumped in his seat and took several deep breaths. He peered out his window. High above, two Mongolian fighter jets screamed south towards the Chinese border. Steele knew it was a race against the clock and that every second counted. But at the same time, he was helpless to act, so there was no point wallowing in anxiety.

"Where are we going?" Maggie asked no one in particular.

"To the country," Enkee said. "To meet up with some friends. They're expecting us."

The jeep passed by an abandoned airstrip, once a bustling base for the Soviet Air Force decades ago, now nothing more than an empty, grass-infested concrete eyesore. Soon afterwards, Ulaanbaatar's urban topography faded away and grassy pasture land took its place. Five kilometers beyond the city limits, traffic started to back up.

"What's going on?" Steele asked.

"Toll booth," Enkee replied. He decelerated to a slow creep behind a battered, grey Toyota minivan.

Steele inspected the road behind them. Jeb did the same. Thankfully, there were no black luxury sedans to be seen.

"The Soviets took it upon themselves to construct checkpoints along several major roadways leading in and out of the city," Enkee said. "After they left the country, these were converted into tollbooths. They provide a lucrative source of cash flow for the local city government."

Steele couldn't remember the last time he saw toll booth attendants with semiautomatic weapons. "You must have a problem here with people driving off without paying," he quipped.

"Let me do the talking," Enkee said. "Chat among yourselves and ignore them if they ask you anything."

"You got it," Jeb replied.

A pair of soldiers questioned each vehicle that stopped at the booth, but kept the line moving quickly. At last, one of the soldiers, an underfed fellow in an oversized, olive brown uniform, waved Enkee forward. Enkee pulled up and rolled down his window. The other soldier, a taller version of his partner, wandered over to the jeep's passenger door.

The first soldier bent over and looked past Enkee at the other passengers in the jeep. Jeb and Maggie were locked in a heated debate over who won the War of 1812. The soldier observed the argument for several moments, then turned to Enkee and questioned him. In his most convincing voice, Enkee explained that the three westerners in his car were volunteers working with the Ministry of Health and that they were on their way to the Dornod province to provide medical assistance to several outlying communities near the town of Choibalsan. He reached into his shirt pocket and produced a government identification card with a 50 Euro bank note pressed tightly to it. The soldier casually slipped the note into his pocket while examining Enkee's card.

"What do you mean the Canadians kicked our butts and burned Washington to boot?" Jeb shouted from the backseat.

Maggie sat with her arms crossed, her face victorious.

"Canada wasn't even a country in 1812," Jeb said. He motioned to the soldier. "Tell her, will ya? It was the British who burned Washington."

A confused look descended over the soldier's face. He looked at Enkee for some sort of explanation or translation. Enkee just smiled and shrugged.

The line of vehicles behind them was growing and the next car in line revved his engine impatiently. The soldier stepped back from Enkee's window and unslung his gun. Steele tensed and readied himself. But the soldier simply moved the weapon to the opposite shoulder and motioned to his partner to raise the gate. He then waved the jeep through.

All four in the jeep heaved a collective sigh of relief upon seeing the open road unfold in front.

"That was close," Maggie said.

Steele nodded. "For a moment there, I thought he was going to make us get out." He turned to Enkee. "Nice little trick with the Euro and the ID card."

Enkee didn't respond. He appeared to be deep in thought.

"What's on your mind?" Steele asked.

"I was just wondering?" Enkee said.

"Wondering what?"

Enkee glanced over at Steele, then through the rearview mirror at his two other passengers. "Who did win the War of 1812?"

Chapter 25

IT WAS EARLY evening by the time the jeep arrived at the edge of a narrow meadow tucked neatly between two impressive boulder-strewn ridges. On the east bank of a bubbling stream that sliced the meadow in half, three sizable mushroom-shaped tents, also known as gers, huddled around an enormous cooking fire. It was the first sign of life Steele had seen since they left the city.

Two men on horseback rode out to meet them. The larger of the two men wore a maroon del trimmed in gold. He had a rugged, weathered face with dark bristly eyebrows similar to Enkee's, yet unlike Enkee's closely-trimmed mane, this man wore his coal black hair down to the shoulders.

The other rider was a teenager of sixteen with a short, plump body tucked into a pair of dark jeans and a stonewashed denim shirt with both sleeves rolled up. He sported a tattoo on his left forearm identical to Enkee's. His face was round and pudgy, with the down of youth on his chin and a crown of unruly black hair stuffed beneath a yellow Los Angeles Lakers cap.

Enkee parked the jeep next to the stream and introduced the men to Steele and the others.

"This is Tsek and his younger brother, Munke. They are close friends of mine."

Munke flashed a smile at Maggie, revealing a gold-capped front tooth.

On the far bank, a slender woman shuffled various pots and pans over the fire while two small children, a boy and a girl, frolicked in and out of the gers, playing tag, using the woman as home base. They abruptly stopped their game when they saw the strangers and bolted towards the stream. Two enormous brown dogs took off after them. The woman shelled out a reprimand that prompted one of the dogs to skid to a halt and retreat to her side with ears tucked.

Tsek and Munke led their guests on foot across the stream on a flimsy pontoon bridge fashioned out of old, discarded wooden pallets. Tsek's children were there to greet them. Both surveyed the strangers with curious, owl-like eyes, then ran to Enkee and wrapped themselves around his leg. Enkee feigned injury and fell, dragging the children with him. He pinned the boy to the ground and tickled him.

"Tulum," Tsek said. "Help Munke take care of the horses."

Enkee released the boy. He hopped to his feet and threw another play punch at Enkee, then scurried to join his uncle.

Meanwhile, the dog that had accompanied the children eyed the three strangers like fresh porterhouse steaks. He stepped forward with head lowered and emitted a deep, contemptuous growl. His mane bristled with aggression and the upper lip twitched northward on either side, exposing extraordinarily long canine teeth. Steele rarely succumbed to intimidation by a dog regardless of its size, but this one was a definite exception.

Tsek barked a command and the dog backed off. He retreated to Tsek's side, but never took his eyes off of Steele the entire time.

"Please excuse the dog," Tsek said. "His name is Gobi, like our famous desert. If you don't look him in the eye, he won't bother you."

Jeb let out a deep sigh of relief. "I'll be sure to remember that."

The woman joined them. Tsek introduced his wife, Arhigee, to his guests. She was in her early thirties, attractive, with doe-like eyes accented by high cheekbones and smooth brown skin. Dressed in her pale jonquil sweatshirt and blue jeans, she looked like a country girl right out of America's heartland.

"Dr. Townshend, I'm sure you would like to freshen up before dinner," Arhigee said.

Maggie brushed the dust from her shirt and jeans. "That would be wonderful, thank you."

Arhigee took Maggie by the hand. "Come. You may use our ger."

"I'm going to get firewood for the woodpile," Tsek said to Enkee, inadvertently pushing back the sleeve of his del. There it was again.

Steele watched him leave, then turned to Enkee.

"Can I ask you a question?"

"By all means," Enkee replied.

"Your tattoo. Tsek and Munke have the same one."

"I like the design," Jeb added. He gave Steele a clever glance. "I don't think you'll find that one in Ozzy's Tattoo Shack on Sixth Street."

Enkee rolled up his sleeve and traced the outline of his tattoo with his index finger.

"My friends and I share similar tastes in art." Enkee turned to Jeb. "Do you have any tattoos, Mr. Walker?"

"Can't say that I do," Jeb said. He poked an elbow at Steele. "But the Steeleman here does, right Brazos?"

Steele didn't reply, but looked straight at the ground.

"And it ain't no eagle," Jeb said. "He'd show it to you, but it wouldn't be proper with women and children around and all that."

"I understand," Enkee replied with a grin. "Some things are better left to the imagination."

Chapter 26

AFTER WASHING UP in the stream, Steele and Jeb returned to camp and sat on wooden benches situated around the fire. Tsek, Enkee, and the others soon joined them. Munke attempted to sample the evening's dinner straight out of the pot, but received a slap on the arm, courtesy of Arhigee's spoon. Maggie showed up bright and refreshed. Steele slid over on his bench to make room for her, hoping she would take him up on the offer. She did.

He felt like a nervous schoolboy sitting next to the prettiest girl in the class. It wasn't just her physical allure that attracted him. There was something genuine about Maggie, something natural, original. They were qualities that he had not encountered in a woman for a long, long time. He also admired her toughness, a character trait that no doubt prevented Jeb from attempting to charm the good doctor into his notorious web of romance.

Arhigee ladled generous portions of soup into metal bowls and instructed the children to pass them out. Enkee placed his bowl to his nose and inhaled. "Mutton and Arhigee's homemade noodles," he said. "You're in for a treat, Dr. Steele."

Steele sampled his portion. The broth was salty, the noodles thick and chewy, and the mutton, well, muttony. But it tasted wonderful and would definitely merit seconds. Jeb obviously agreed. He worked his bowl like a Labrador after a long day's hunt.

Maggie's eyes suddenly widened. "Don't look, Jeb, but you've got company."

Jeb glanced over his shoulder. Gobi had snuck up behind him and now gazed with salivatory admiration at Jeb's dinner. Jeb reached into his bowl and extracted a piece of boiled mutton with several noodles dangling from it. He held it over his shoulder as a peace offering, taking care to avoid eye contact with the dog. Gobi sniffed at it suspiciously, then accepted the gift. He sat down next to Jeb and, with tail at full wag, begged for more. Steele couldn't help but laugh. It appeared Jeb made a new friend.

The healthy appetites gathered around the fire limited the conversation. Afterwards, Steele thanked Arhigee for a wonderful meal. Arhigee beckoned her kids to gather the plates and utensils and take them to the stream to wash. Maggie stood to help, but Arhigee insisted she sit. Tsek had Munke fetch the horses.

Steele rubbed his full stomach. "So what's the plan?" he asked Enkee.

"For starters, Tsek and I are going to ride to get help," Enkee replied. "Then we'll figure out what do next."

"You're not taking the jeep?" Steele asked.

"Too slow in this part of the country," Enkee replied. "Besides, it's low on fuel."

Munke returned with the horses. He handed one to his brother and one to Enkee.

"Do you want one of us to go with you?" Steele asked.

"There's no need for you to do that, Dr. Steele," Tsek said. "In fact, I'd like you and your friends to stay and watch over the camp while we're gone. Munke will stay behind as well, but..." Tsek paused and grinned at his baby brother, "...he is still young and needs supervision himself."

Munke squeaked out a muffled protest to his brother. He glanced at Maggie, a look of humiliation on his pudgy face. Maggie returned a warm smile designed to soften the blow to his ego.

"We should return by morning," Enkee said. He tossed a saddlebag across the rear of his horse and motioned to Steele. "I'll be sure to bring back a phone that works."

Steele nodded appreciatively. "Anything you need us to do around here while you're gone?"

"Get some rest," Tsek said to him. "There will be enough to do when we return."

Tsek and Enkee mounted up. Tsek kissed Arhigee and waved goodbye to his children. Then, with Gobi hot on their heels, the two men cantered off into the darkness.

Chapter 27

"I'M GOING FOR a walk." Steele said. "Anyone care to join me?"

Maggie raised her hand as if she were in a classroom. "I'll go."

"Jeb?" Steele asked his friend. Steele was just being polite. Now that Maggie wanted to go, deep down he hoped Jeb would decline the offer.

"No thanks. I'll pass," Jeb said, much to Steele's silent delight. "I promised Tulum a wrestling match."

"Hold on just a minute, you two," Arhigee said. She walked to her ger and returned with two woolen blankets and a flashlight.

"Here, take these with you," she said, handing them blankets. "You'll need them."

Arhigee glanced up at the full moon and handed Steele the flashlight. "This, you probably won't need, but take it just in case." She pointed to the tree line in the distance behind camp. "There's a path through the woods you can follow to the top of the ridge. With the moon shining like it is, you'll be able to get a nice view of the surrounding countryside."

"Thank you, Arhigee," Steele replied. "We won't stay out too long."

The stars filled the night sky like silver glitter in a pool of black ink, and as Arhigee predicted, the full moon offered more than enough light to illuminate the way. Steele and Maggie approached the tree line; the scent of pine, sharpened by the falling temperature, freshened the already pure night air. They found Arhigee's path and followed its undulant course up the ridge. When they finally broke through the trees at the top, they paused for a moment to catch their breath, and then climbed atop a mammoth boulder in order to get a better view of the surrounding terrain. Majestic hilltops and sweeping valleys spread out for miles in all directions, like waves in a great geological ocean. Far below them, Steele could make out the tiny glow of the fire, as well as the silver glint of starlight upon the surface of the stream next to the camp.

"Do you mind if we find a place to sit," Maggie asked. "My leg is starting to ache a bit."

"By all means," Steele replied. He looked around, and then pointed to a broad slice of earth wedged between two large boulders that fanned out right to the brim of a steep drop-off. "Over there."

Steele walked to it and spread one of the blankets on the ground.

"Madame," Steele said waving his arm towards the blanket as if playing restaurant maître d´. "Your seat awaits you."

Maggie bowed before kneeling on the blanket. "Why thank you, sir,"

Steele draped the other blanket over her shoulders and sat down beside her. He zipped his jacket up to his neck and drew in a deep breath of the cool night air, then gazed up at the heavens. Maggie's eyes followed his.

"Beautiful, isn't it?" Maggie said softly.

Steele nodded. "Reminds me of the Texas Hill Country."

"I've never been to Texas," Maggie said. She wrapped the blanket tighter. "I can only imagine what it's like."

"Ever been country-western dancing?"

"I can't say that I have."

"Well, I'll tell you what. When our work is done here, you need to come to Deets and I'll teach you."

"I'd like that," she replied. "Very much."

There was an awkward silence for several moments, reminiscent of two high school kids on a first date. Then Maggie spoke.

"Is Deets where you're from originally?"

Steele shook his head. "No. I was an Army brat. My father moved us around a lot. We were living in San Antonio when he retired."

"Do your parents still live there?"

"After my mother died..."

Maggie interrupted him. "I'm sorry."

"No need. She had a good, full life." Steele paused to let a series of pleasant past memories flash momentarily across the picture screen in his mind, and then he spoke again. "After she died, my father moved to Washington D.C. to be near my sister. She's a trial lawyer there. I always loved the Hill Country of Texas. That's how I ended up in Deets."

Steele turned the attention to Maggie. "What about you? Are you originally from Toronto?"

She nodded. "I was born there, but I spent my early years in Ottawa. My father is a member of Parliament. Has been for the past fourteen years. After he and my mum divorced, I moved to Toronto with her."

"And that's where you attended medical school?"

"University of Toronto. I eventually became involved with the Canadian Medical Outreach Program and went on to work with the World Health Organization and their Rapid Response Unit. That's how I ended up in Yushan."

Both paused to admire the dazzling night sky. Two dead stars raced neck and neck towards the far end of the horizon, crossing the line in a photo finish.

"What do you think he's gonna do?" Maggie asked.

Steele looked over at her. "Who?"

"Bagaryn. Do you think he's actually going to attack China?"

"In my book, he already has," Steele replied. "And I have a sick feeling he is going to do it again. Somehow, we have to stop him."

Maggie dropped her head. "But how? It's all so overwhelming. This is a job for the United Nations, not us. What can we do?"

Steele reached over and squeezed her hand. "Everything will work out for the best, Maggie. It always does."

She looked at him with soft, tear-filled eyes. He released his grip on her hand but she held on. Steele drew her close and gently pressed his lips to hers. He withdrew ever so slightly, but she followed after him. The blanket around her fell away. Steele pulled her warm body tightly against his. Their breathing synchronized and heightened with each passing moment. At last, they sank to the ground as one and surrendered to the fires of passion, fires that would serve to insulate both of them against the chilly night air.

Chapter 28

STEELE RAN AS fast as he could, but try as he may, he couldn't reach her. He could hear the frantic calls for help, the pleas for mercy, but he kept losing ground. Her voice faded, as if moving away. The landscape around him burst into streaks of orange, blue, and red like some funky abstract painting. In the shimmering metallic sky above, a giant eagle extended its talons and swooped towards him. The wings thumped louder and louder. Again, a distant plea for help. He ran faster. The eagle drew closer. Its wings beat with a deafening roar. Suddenly, the bird's talons pierced the skin of his back, penetrating deeper, ever deeper…

Steele awoke with a start, his face drenched with sweat. A dream. A bad dream. He sighed. Nothing more wonderful than to wake up from a bad dream. Maggie stirred beneath the blanket next to him. He took another deep breath to settle his nerves. Then he heard it again. The wings.

The sound reverberated throughout the valley. Steele jumped to his feet and wrested Maggie from her slumber. He reached the ledge just in time to see the olive drab helicopter, its rotors spinning at half speed, perched on the outskirts of the camp. Armed men flowed from its belly. Steele heard several gunshots, followed by the screams of familiar voices.

Maggie propped herself up on one elbow, still half asleep. "What's happening, Brazos?"

Steele rushed to her side. "Trouble. We've got visitors."

She sat up and struggled to get her boots on. All of a sudden, the air hummed once again, first very faintly, and then with growing intensity.

She looked at Steele. "That sounds like a…"

Steele tackled her mid-sentence, taking her down hard. Another chopper, this one tan in color, buzzed low overhead and disappeared over the rocky ledge. Steele recognized the chubby body and slender tail of the Russian made MI-8T, the splitting image of an obese dragonfly. The throaty whistle of its twin Klimov turbo shaft engines and five-bladed rotor was unmistakable. It made a wide sweeping turn across the valley, then flew back and descended next to the tree line. Its downdraft pounded the grass below it into submission. Five men jumped from the chopper's side door and disappeared into the woods. The machine rose into the air again and went on to join its counterpart at the camp.

Steele scrambled to his feet. "They're coming for us. You have to get out of here."

"What about you?"

"Jeb is down there. I've gotta help him."

Voices arose from the wooded path. Steele looked around for an alternate escape route. They were trapped. There was only one way down and at the moment that way was occupied. Less than a minute later, five of Tsogt's Royal Guards emerged from the woods. They pointed their rifles at Steele and Maggie.

Steele raised his arms in the air. "I guess we'll go together."

One of the soldiers stepped towards Maggie with an unhappy look on his face.

Steele nudged Maggie on the shoulder. "I think they want you to put your hands up."

She quickly complied.

The soldiers patted down their prisoners. They bound their hands with plastic ties and led them down the path. Emerging from the woods at the base of the ridge, Steele heard shouts and cheers off in the distance. As they reached camp, he saw why.

Jeb, his face cut and bruised, stood like a wounded gladiator at the bank of the stream. He held a substantial piece of the pontoon bridge in his hand, goading a crowd of armed men to come and get him. Munke was on his knees behind him, his shoulder bloodied from a bullet wound. Three inert figures, including one with his face crushed beyond recognition, lay sprawled on the ground in front of Jeb.

Prompted by his peers, one particularly bulky soldier let out a wild yell, threw down his gun, and charged Jeb. Jeb let him close to within three feet and swung his wooden club. The impact spun the soldier like a twister. Blood sprayed from his nostrils and he fell to the ground. Jeb advanced and struck him again, this time in the back. He prepared to deliver a lethal blow to the head. But before he could do so, another soldier rammed Jeb from behind and drove him to the dirt. Jeb's weapon flew from his hand. Both men jumped to their feet simultaneously, but Jeb reacted first. He nailed his assailant with a well-placed fist to the jaw, knocking him into the water. Out of nowhere, another soldier tackled Jeb at the knees. Like flies on a ripe carcass, ten other men jumped in and descended on the big man, beating him while keeping his head underwater.

Steele opened his mouth in protest, but a rifle butt to the hip silenced him. Jeb struggled to lift his head out of the water in a desperate search for air, but his face was pushed down harder against the jagged river rocks. He thrashed in a final attempt to free himself, but couldn't. The struggle waned and Jeb's muscles relaxed as his body prepared to concede to death.

"Enough!" a voice shouted from the bank of the stream. It was Tsogt. "Bring him to me."

The soldier whose nose Jeb had broken yanked Jeb's head out of the water by the hair and he, along with four others, dragged him out of the stream and threw him down on the bank. Jeb lay motionless on his back, his face covered with blood that oozed from multiple facial lacerations. Tsogt stepped forward and used his boot to shove Jeb onto his side. The big body shuddered and coughed, spewing water out of its saturated lungs.

Four men hoisted Jeb by the arms and propped him up in front of Tsogt. Tsogt grabbed Jeb's hair, pulled his head back, and looked him in the eyes. An evil grin spread across the general's face. He unsnapped his holster and withdrew his pistol.

"Before I kill you, I want you to tell me where the others are," Tsogt growled. "Tell me, and I promise you a quick death."

Jeb mumbled unintelligibly.

Tsogt let his head fall. "We'll give him a few minutes to gather his senses." He walked to Arhigee and squeezed her chin with his hand.

"Perhaps this one can provide us with the information we need," he said with a chilling edge to his voice. Munke struggled with the men restraining him and shouted Mongolian imprecations at Tsogt. Tsogt nodded to one of the guards, who slammed the butt of his rifle into the wound on Munke's shoulder. The defiant words were replaced by shrieks of pain.

The soldiers marched the new prisoners to Tsogt. One of them shoved Maggie to the ground in front of the general's feet. Tsogt stepped over her and circled Steele. Steele stood as still as a concrete statue. Tsogt stopped in front of his face.

"Dr. Steele, I do hope you forgive us for interrupting your fun with the good doctor," Tsogt said.

"How did you find this place?" Steele said.

"A simple transponder planted inside of Dr. Sangidansranjav's jeep allowed us to follow your trail."

Tsogt gestured at Jeb. "Your friend there is having trouble with speech at the moment. Perhaps you could tell me the whereabouts of Dr. Sangidansranjav and his friend."

"Sure," Steele replied with a straight face. "I overheard them say they were going to Wal-Mart to pick you up some breath mints."

Tsogt drew his pistol and pressed the barrel against Steele's forehead.

"Enough of your cocky American attitude," he said. "Tell me where he is or I will be forced to see if your lady friend will be more cooperative."

"Why should we tell you anything?" Steele said. "You're going to kill us anyway."

Tsogt appeared to ruminate on Steele's remark. A sinister smile formed on his face. "You're right, Dr. Steele. You're absolutely right."

Then he calmly pulled the trigger.

Chapter 29

THERE WAS NO explosion, no spatter of bone and blood, only a resounding "click." Steele didn't flinch when the hammer came down on the empty chamber. Inside, though, he fought a growing numbness. Tsogt's Russian-roulette had flustered him, but he wasn't about to let the son-of-a-bitch know it.

In a flash, Tsogt flipped his pistol around in his hand and swiped the butt across Steele's face. For a brief moment, Steele's world went as black as deep space and he lost his footing.

Tsogt towered over him for a moment in victory. He re-holstered his pistol and approached Maggie. Looking her up and down as if he were a seasoned buyer at a Saharan slave auction, Tsogt abruptly pulled her to her feet by her hair. Maggie cried out in pain.

His vacant black eyes locked on hers. "Save your squeals for my men." He shoved her into the eager arms of his troopers.

Munke went ballistic. He kicked one guard in the shin and broke free from the other. He then let out a blood-curdling yell and charged at the soldiers detaining Maggie.

The ten meters or so he had to cover gave Tsogt ample time to draw his pistol and take aim. He waited until Munke was an arm's length away, then he pulled the trigger. This time there was a loud report, and Munke flew backwards and hit the ground with a grotesque "thud." A red fountain spewed from the powder-burned hole in the middle of his shirt, then dwindled into a steady, tapered flow that fanned out across the denim fabric.

Munke's lifeless eyes stared up at Maggie, as if apologizing for having let her down. Maggie stood with her mouth open, unable to utter a sound. Only when the screams and wails of Arhigee and the children began did she drop her head and sob uncontrollably.

Summoning his power of speech, Jeb shouted across at Tsogt, "You chicken-shit mother fucker. He was just a boy!"

A guard stepped forward and jammed the butt of his rifle into Jeb's stomach. Jeb's legs wobbled like those of a newborn foal, but his face remained defiant. The guard pointed his gun at Jeb's head.

"Go ahead, tough guy," Jeb sneered. "Shoot before I kick both your ass and Lurch's ass over there."

The guard's eyes begged for the order to shoot. Tsogt was about to issue it when he saw his personal assistant, Lieutenant Aagii, approach.

"General, we must get back," Aagii told Tsogt. "You have a meeting with His Excellency at his palace in Karakorum in three hours, remember?"

"You're right," Tsogt replied. "We're wasting time here. Gather the men and load up." He pointed at Arhigee and her children. "Bring them with us. Perhaps Colonel Tsek will surrender himself in exchange for their lives."

Tsogt motioned to Maggie and Steele. "Bring them as well."

"And the remaining prisoner?" Aagii asked, rubbing his chin.

"Kill him. The wolves will dispose of the bodies for us."

Tsogt nodded at the soldier pointing his gun at Jeb. "Make him suffer before you put a bullet in his head. Repayment for killing three of our men."

The soldier smiled beneath his purple swollen bulb of a nose.

Jeb spit at Tsogt, but missed him by meters.

"No. Please no," Arhigee pleaded with wet eyes. Tulum and his sister clung tightly to their mother's leg.

Tsogt turned to her. "Once I have some free time to get to know you and your two children better..." He paused to bend over and caress Tulum's head, the latter recoiling as he did. "I guarantee you'll forget all about them."

"You perverse bastard!" Maggie said.

Tsogt marched over and backhanded her across the face. She fell backwards with a grunt.

"You will speak only when spoken to," he snarled.

He repeated the warning to Arhigee and her children, then turned and walked to the tan helicopter. The soldiers ordered the prisoners to follow. Maggie complied reluctantly, but Steele refused to get to his feet. His mind raced. He had to do something. He couldn't just walk away and allow these criminals to kill Jeb. A Royal Guard poked a rifle barrel into his side, but Steele still didn't budge.

Two men forced Jeb to his knees. Steele struggled to free his hands, but couldn't. He watched Aagii circle behind his friend and draw his pistol. It was now or never. Steele slipped out of his guard's grasp and flopped down to the grass. He then lashed out with both legs, his feet connecting squarely with the guard's right knee. Tsogt's man cried out and fell to the ground. Steele sprang to his feet and raced straight for Aagii. Alerted by the commotion behind him, Aagii wheeled around only to see Steele bearing down on him like a mad rhino. He raised his pistol, squinted his narrow eyes, and shot.

Steele heard the bullet zip by within inches of his right ear. He left his feet and rammed his shoulder into Aagii's chest like a missile. The force of the blow knocked the pistol from the lieutenant's hand.

Aagii lay on his back, completely incapacitated. Steele had been stunned by the impact as well. Before he could gather his senses, a blunt object crashed into the back of his head. Steele's world flashed into a tailspin. He fought the heavy veil of unconsciousness that was oozing down over his eyes. It was a losing battle. Steele felt himself dragged over the grass, then hoisted and tossed haphazardly onto the tempered floor of the helicopter. He tried to move, tried to fight, but his body refused to obey. The drone of the engine increased. The rotors chugged faster and faster like a giant locomotive gaining speed.

Steele thought he heard the crackle of gunfire. Jeb. His mind screamed in protest, but then it suddenly let go and he plunged into an ink-like, sterile nothingness.

Chapter 30

THE LOOK ON the face of the soldier standing next to Jeb was one of utter bewilderment. The man dropped his gun, lifted his hands to his neck, and clamped them around the arrow that stuck out of it at a ninety degree angle. He emitted a strange gurgling noise, then collapsed to the ground, his lifeblood spurting out between his fingers and the arrow's shaft. Another would-be executioner lay flat behind Jeb. A neat hole glistened in the middle of his forehead. Still a third soldier stood frozen and wide-eyed nearby, inspecting the bloody, fleshy stump that had once been his right hand. Bullets chewed the ground behind him. He bent over to retrieve his pistol, but a bullet found its mark. He squawked and dropped.

It didn't take Jeb long to react to the sudden change in events. He scrambled to the woodpile next to Tsek's gear. He arrived just as the valley erupted in a shower of gunfire and a rain of arrows. Ghost-like figures scurried among the rocks on the northern ridge while Tsogt's men scrambled for cover like roaches surprised by light.

A volley of bullets smashed into the woodpile. Jeb pulled a five centimeter sliver of timber out of his forearm. He peered over the top to see a line of horsemen materialize at the base of the ridge.

Suddenly, one of Tsogt's fighters saw him and crashed over the top of the woodpile to get him. The upper third of the stack caved in and landed on top of Jeb.

With a lightning quick move, the soldier pulled a knife and thrust the blade at Jeb. Jeb grabbed the wrist with both hands and stopped the blade's descent just three centimeters from his chest. The soldier shifted his entire weight over the hilt and pressed. The blade crept closer and closer. Jeb's strength, already compromised by the earlier beating, ebbed further. He could only brace himself for the fatal sting; that burning pressure and suffocation brought about by the penetration of cold steel into the chest cavity.

But the blow never came. What did come was a vicious growl, a bloodcurdling scream, and one hundred and eighteen pounds of matted fur and exposed teeth that pounced on the back of Jeb's assailant and took a deep bite out of one shoulder, causing the knife to drop harmlessly to the ground. Gobi then sank his teeth into the soldier's neck. The crushing pressure forced the man's mouth open, but no sound came out. He reached an arm back and grabbed Gobi by the hair, but the dog thrashed his head violently from side to side, as if playing tug of war with a towel. A grotesque "snap" followed. Jeb felt the body on top of him go limp.

Jeb slid out from beneath the unfortunate soldier while Gobi held on. Finally, the dog released the body and sniffed his kill. With a hint of satisfaction on his face, he trotted over to Jeb and, with ears back, licked his hand as if nothing had happened.

Lieutenant Aagii was being loaded into the helicopter on a stretcher by two of his men when he heard the shots. He thought nothing of it at the time. His men had just carried out General Tsogt's orders. It wasn't until the intensity of gunfire increased that he realized something was terribly wrong. Clutching his ribcage, he sat up on the stretcher and peered out the side door of the helicopter. He was greeted by a scene of utter chaos.

The ground was littered with the bodies of his men. Those still alive huddled behind whatever cover they could find, engaged in a firefight with an enemy blended into the rocky slope of the ridge. Meanwhile, dark figures on horses poured from the woods. Three soldiers made a mad dash for the helicopter, but heated fire from the riders ultimately cut them down. A volley of bullets peppered the side of the chopper along with two arrows that thudded harmlessly off the steel siding.

Aagii staggered to his feet. He made his way forward to the cockpit. "Get us airborne, now!" he commanded the pilot. Once in the air, he knew he could easily change the course of the battle with a few quick passes of the machine's deadly 7.62mm machine guns.

The pilot punched the starter control. The big machine groaned to life. The five-bladed aluminum alloy rotor started to rotate. Aagii looked out from the cockpit window. With a growing fury, he watched his men throw down their weapons and surrender to the approaching horses.

Aagii hit the pilot on the shoulder with his fist. "Faster, faster!"

But the pilot and his fellow crewmen made a grave error in judgment. They shut their machine down completely after landing. Now, from a cold start, it would take at least sixty more seconds for the massive blades to achieve lift-off rotation.

Aagii saw at least ten horsemen break from the main group and start towards the aircraft. A series of bright flashes from their saddles were followed by the sound of ripping metal. The frantic pilots attempted to coax the big machine into the air. The increasing centrifugal force of the spinning rotors caused the helicopter to rock back and forth on its non-retractable landing gear. But it still had a long way to go.

Aagii scurried into the main cabin and grabbed an AK-47 from an arms rack mounted on the wall. He didn't bother to take careful aim. The gun spat viciously at the oncoming riders. The two horses in the lead caught the main brunt of Aagii's initial volley and pummeled to the ground along with their riders. The remaining group of horsemen broke formation and dispersed, circling around to the backside of the helicopter like Indians surrounding a wagon train. Aagii waited for them to reappear in the doorway, but they never did. He felt the MI-8 finally break away from the ground. It started a slow vertical ascent. He shouted to the pilot to hurry up the process when suddenly, a chorus of "pops" coincided with the appearance of multiple holes of light in the floor of the craft. Aagii's back exploded in a flash of fiery pain. He squealed, then collapsed to the floor, paralyzed from the bullet that had pulped his spinal cord. His machine gun dropped with him, bounced once, and tumbled out the door.

The pilot, hearing Aagii shout yet not understanding him, temporarily stopped the craft's ascent. Two grenades bounced in through the open door. They settled next to Aagii's flaccid body. Aagii's eyes widened and he wailed in helpless terror.

The grenades exploded simultaneously with a roar in a massive orange-white flash. The blast blew a hole in the belly of the MI-8 and sliced through the main rotor shaft. A gigantic fireball consumed the interior of the helicopter and its contents. Glowing like a hot ember, the machine fluttered in space momentarily, followed by the massive rotor apparatus disengaging and boomeranging into the rocky slope of the ridge. The leftover shell of the aircraft dropped to the earth like a piece of spent uranium. It shattered on impact, transforming into a burning cloud of metallic debris.

General Tsogt and his prisoners were twelve minutes into their flight when the distress call came in from the pilot of Aagii's helicopter. Unfortunately, the transmission abruptly cut off before the pilot could reveal the nature of the emergency. Tsogt flew into a rage, furious at the interruption to his trip to Karakorum. He couldn't imagine what prompted such a call. Other than having to deal with Steele's vain attempt to help his friend, Aagii's men seemed to have everything under control. Now this. He ordered his pilot to return to the camp.

Tsogt surveyed his prisoners through the cockpit door. Maggie sat next to the still-unconscious Steele with his head nestled in her lap. She stroked his sticky, blood-matted hair with her hand. Arhigee, her children huddled beside her, sat in the far corner of the helicopter, doing her best to ignore the crude sexual comments from the men next to her.

Tsogt seriously considered tossing all of the prisoners out the moving craft. He knew that Bagaryn would be angry at him for bringing them back alive, especially Steele and his doctor friend. But with the major events set in motion by the president, he figured it was probably prudent to keep a few hostages on hand as bargaining chips just in case.

Arriving at the edge of the meadow, they were greeted by a huge charcoal plume of smoke that billowed skyward from the mangled wreckage of Aagii's craft. The meadow was full of armed men and horses. In addition to the lifeless forms scattered about the landscape that once represented his crack assault unit, Tsogt saw the surviving members of his team herded into the corral with their hands clamped behind their heads.

"What in the…" Tsogt said.

The pilot backed off on the stick and put the machine into a hover. Tsogt and his flight crew remained speechless, unable to fully comprehend what they were witnessing.

The co-pilot broke the silence. "Shall we attack, General?"

"With what?" Tsogt snapped. The MI-8 helicopter they were in was equipped for the transport of troops, not for offensive action. Tsogt knew the lone machine gun mounted in the cabin would not be able to inflict serious damage without putting the helicopter itself at risk. And judging from the burning wreckage, he guessed the brigands below may even possess rocket propelled grenades. Tsogt cursed Bagaryn under his breath for plundering the national coffers of the country for his own personal use; money that could have been used to upgrade the military's machinery and weaponry, including the addition of several more MI-8 attack helicopters to the arsenal. As it was, well-over seventy-five percent of the equipment put at Tsogt's disposal was over thirty-years-old.

"We can do nothing here," Tsogt hissed, his eyes ablaze with wrath. "Return to Karakorum!"

Without hesitation, the pilot wheeled the metallic bird around one hundred and eighty degrees. Then, with a deafening whine, the nose dipped and the MI-8 sped away towards the western sky.

Chapter 31

JEB WATCHED THE helicopter turn and leave, then saw Tsek and Enkee approaching the woodpile on horseback. Gobi ran out to greet them. Both men reined their horses to a stop and jumped off. Enkee slid his lever-action Winchester 30/30 into a saddle holster.

"Boy, talk about timing," Jeb said.

Tsek looked for Arhigee and the children. Apprehension filled every line of his face.

"They took them," Jeb said to him. "They're still alive. He said he was going to use them to force you to surrender."

"Where's Munke?" Tsek asked.

Jeb motioned to one of Tsek's men leading a horse by the reins. Munke's lifeless body was draped over the saddle.

Tsek gazed upon his dead brother in disbelief. Gobi licked Munke's hand and whimpered.

Jeb's stomach churned. Not from the pain from his swollen face and bruised body, but from the knowledge that he and Brazos had let Tsek and the others down. They were entrusted to watch over the camp and they failed in their duty. Now Tsek's younger brother was dead and who knew what was going to happen to Arhigee and the children.

Jeb scraped some dried blood off his cheek with his fingernails. "I'm so sorry. I should have done more."

There was a moment of silence. When Tsek finally spoke, his face softened. He surveyed Jeb up and down.

"From the looks of you, Mr. Walker, you put up a commendable fight. Where are your friends?"

"The bastards took them, too," Jeb said.

Enkee walked up to Tsek and put his hand on his shoulder. "Don't worry, my friend. We'll get your family back."

"I know we will," Tsek replied with conviction.

Jeb limped closer to Enkee. "I do think I know where they took them."

"Where?" Tsek asked eagerly.

"The head honcho. A big goon about seven foot tall…"

"General Tsogt," Enkee said. He spit on the ground with contempt.

Jeb continued. "He mentioned something about having to be at a meeting in a place called 'Karaoke,' 'Quorum,' or something like that."

Enkee and Tsek looked at each other. "Karakorum," both said in unison.

Jeb snapped his fingers. "That's it. That's the place. How far is it from here?"

"A good eight hours hard ride," Tsek replied. He mounted his horse. "Are you coming with us, Mr. Walker?"

"You're damn right I am," Jeb said. "They've got my friends, too." He gently rubbed the knot over his right eyebrow. "Besides, I have a score to settle with that Tsogt fellow."

Tsek waved to a nearby rider on a mottled grey horse, a fierce-looking young Mongolian wearing a traditional dome-shaped loovuuz on his head and a bow and quiver slung across his back. Tsek instructed the rider to pick out six men to stay behind to care for the wounded and the dead. Then he was to gather the rest of the men together in preparation to ride on Karakorum. Jeb noticed a familiar sight on the man's forearm. It was that tattoo.

"Who are we going to send to intercept Petrokov?" Enkee asked Tsek.

"I have already made arrangements with Chugai and his men. They will be waiting for the Russians."

Jeb heard their exchange. A smile of comprehension crept across his face.

"What is it, Mr. Walker?" Enkee asked.

Jeb looked him straight in the eye. "You guys are Darkhad, aren't you?"

Tsek overheard the comment. "What do you mean, Mr. Walker?"

Jeb's eyes gloated with pride over his investigative prowess. "Your tattoos," he said. "I bet you if I checked the forearms of every man here, I'd find that same tattoo. It's the seal of the empire Professor Zhu mentioned, isn't it? You're sending this Chugai fellow and his men to intercept the Russians and prevent them from disturbing the burial site of Genghis Khan, am I right?"

A pause, then Jeb's smile grew even wider.

"What do you know about the Darkhad, Mr. Walker?" Tsek asked.

"Only that its members have one main mission in life, and that is to protect the sanctity of Genghis Khan's tomb. My professor friend also said that most historians believed that the Darkhad were all but wiped out during the communist purges of the twentieth century."

Tsek hesitated briefly. "Almost, but not quite."

Jeb clapped his hands together as if he had just yelled "bingo" in a crowded VFW Hall. "Then I am right. You are Darkhad."

Tsek glanced at Enkee and then sat up in his saddle. "You are correct, Mr. Walker. We are Guardians of the Ordon, or as you call us, Darkhad."

Jeb turned to Enkee. "You too, Doc?"

"Me too, Mr. Walker," Enkee said.

Jeb grinned. "This doesn't mean that you're gonna have to kill me, now that I know?"

Enkee flashed a broad smile. "Kill you? We were actually thinking of making you and your friends honorary members of our group."

"Tsek's great-grandfather was the leader of the Guardians during the early part of the last century," Enkee said. "He and other Darkhad were seized during the Stalinist purges and never heard from again."

Tsek picked up the story from there. "My grandfather, only a child at that time, and many others, sought refuge in the mountains of this region in order to escape a similar fate. During the time of my great-grandfather, our numbers exceeded five hundred. Now, there are less than a hundred of us. Dr. Enkee is the last of his family. With Munke gone, my son is the last of my family."

Jeb detected the slight crack in Tsek's voice.

"We have people monitor every expedition that is sent out to search for the grave of our great ancestor," Enkee said. "Fortunately, in all the decades of searching, none ever came within two hundred miles of it."

"What would you have done if one of those expeditions had gotten warm?" Jeb asked.

"We would have stopped them," Enkee said matter-of-factly.

"By whatever means necessary," Tsek added with a similar no-nonsense look on his face.

Jeb caught the implied meaning and nodded. "I get your drift."

"So do you have the book?" Jeb asked Enkee.

"The book, Mr. Walker?"

"Marco Polo's book."

Enkee's mouth betrayed his amusement. "Your professor friend told you of this?"

Jeb nodded affirmatively.

Tsek glanced over at Enkee. "It appears that word has been getting out about our little secret more than we thought."

He continued. "For over five hundred years, the book lay hidden within the walls of the Damba Zuu Khiid monastery west of the capital."

"That is, until a week ago," Enkee said.

Jeb remembered Enkee mentioning Damba Zuu Khiid soon after he picked them up at the Zakh. "What happened a week ago?"

"The Holy Lama of Damba Zuu Khiid was murdered along with all of his monks," Enkee said. "It seems the perpetrators wanted the book. And they got it."

"Who do you think did it?" Jeb asked.

"If Dr. Steele's theory is correct, then President Bagaryn is the one to be held responsible," Enkee replied.

Jeb looked confused. "But how would President Bagaryn have known that the book was at the Damba Zuu Khiid monastery? I thought the only ones who knew that were you and your fellow Darkhad."

The rider with the loovuuz galloped up and slid to a halt in front of Tsek's horse.

"Colonel, the men are ready," he told Tsek. The man then tossed a moistened cloth to Jeb.

Jeb thanked him and wiped the blood and dirt from his face. He shot Tsek a curious look. "So you're a colonel?"

"Yes, Mr. Walker," Enkee said. "Tsek is not only Darkhad, he is also a colonel in the Mongolian People's Army."

"You mean 'used to be,'" Tsek corrected him.

"In the days before Bagaryn," Enkee qualified. "My friend here is one of several former officers leading the opposition movement to Bagaryn's dictatorial regime. The movement has been gaining strength for years, despite multiple attempts by General Tsogt to infiltrate it and put an end to it. Needless to say, many of our colleagues have lost their lives for the cause within the walls of Tsogt's torture chambers."

"There are many officers within Bagaryn's current army, including General Natambaa, who feel the way we do about him, especially with the recent rapid deterioration in Chinese relations." Tsek added. "We have also received valuable aid and input from your country's own Central Intelligence Agency. The others and I feel our level of support inside Bagaryn's own government has finally reached sufficient strength to set the machinery of political change in motion."

Enkee nodded in agreement. "After Ambassador Wheaton's murder and our discovery at Dogan, I knew the time for action had come. That's why I contacted Tsek and made plans for us to link up with him at his family's remote hideaway." Enkee paused and his face became somber. "I now regret that I did. I'm afraid I'm the one responsible for his family's abduction and for Munke's death."

"Enough!" Tsek said to Enkee. "Nobody will shoulder the blame for this except Bagaryn and his band of thugs. Do you understand?"

Enkee remained silent and nodded dutifully.

"We are wasting time," Tsek stated. "It is time to ride."

One of Tsek's men handed the reins of a fallen comrade's horse to Jeb. Jeb stuck his foot into the circular steel stirrup and took a deep breath. He swung his leg over the top of the wooden saddle. The pain he felt was intense. He had been on the receiving end of many a beating in his time, but the one Tsogt's men gave him definitely ranked among the best. Still, he'd be damned if he'd let the aches and pains slow him down. Not when there was work to do. He reined his horse around to face Enkee.

"Dr. Enkee, you never did get the chance to answer my question. How did Bagaryn know where to look for the book?"

Tsek's horse flared its nostrils and pawed impatiently at the ground. "I'll answer that one, Mr. Walker," its rider said.

Tsek's eyes were aflame with revenge. He pushed up the sleeve of his del and pointed to his tattoo. "It just so happens that Bagaryn, our illustrious leader, carries the seal of the empire on his forearm as well."

Chapter 32

"MY CHIEF ENGINEER and his crew are examining potential dig sites as we speak," Petrokov said. He took a long draw from his cigarette. "I'm expecting to hear from him any time now."

"You are to contact me as soon as you have the site located," Bagaryn said. "You and your men are not to enter the tomb unless I am present, do you understand?"

Petrokov nodded. The excitement welled up inside of him. Finally, after all of these years of effort, the dream was about to be realized. In a matter of days, he would become one of the wealthiest men in the world. He could already feel the warm Havana sand caressing his back, the gentle ocean surf lapping the edge of his own private beach. A knock at the office door rudely interrupted his daydream and the massive frame of General Tsogt entered the room.

Bagaryn smiled and walked over to greet his general. "General Tsogt. I trust your operation went well?"

Tsogt avoided Bagaryn's eyes. "They were not at their camp when we arrived."

The smile on Bagaryn's face evaporated. "So they are still alive?"

"I left Lieutenant Aagii in charge. He and his men were ambushed."

"Ambushed?" Bagaryn bellowed.

"By Tsek. He had about a hundred or so men with him. Lieutenant Aagii was killed." Tsogt paused. "He was an incompetent fool anyway."

To Petrokov, Bagaryn's veins looked as though they were going to pop right out of his forehead and strangle his general. Yes, this was getting good.

"And where were you when all of this was taking place?" Bagaryn demanded from Tsogt.

"We were on our way back, Your Excellency. By the time we received the distress call from Lieutenant Aagii, it was too late. There was nothing I could do."

Bagaryn walked to the window behind his desk. "General Tsogt, your loyalty to me goes back a long way. The only reason I don't have you shot for incompetence is because of that loyalty. Your repeated failures over the past week have been a great disappointment to me."

Petrokov watched the entire scene with glee. The expression on Tsogt's face never wavered, and Petrokov couldn't help but wonder what was going through the head of that giant psychopath.

"I have his wife and children," Tsogt said.

Bagaryn spun around to face him. "You were under strict orders not to take any prisoners, were you not?" he said.

"He will come for them."

"No doubt he will, General." Bagaryn's tone was condescending. "What do you plan to do when he gets here?"

"He will not get this far. I have ordered General Natambaa to send a battalion of men to intercept them before they reach Ulaanbaatar."

"A battalion against a hundred men," Petrokov said. "A little overkill, don't you think?"

Tsogt scowled at Petrokov. The Russian just grinned.

"Have you spoken with your general recently?" Bagaryn's tone was sarcastic.

"What do you mean?" Tsogt replied.

"I have word that General Natambaa patently expressed his dissatisfaction to his officers concerning my order to mobilize the army."

"I was not aware of that," Tsogt said.

"Perhaps if you paid more attention to the activities of your subordinates, you would have known."

An uncomfortable pause followed.

Tsogt finally spoke. "Tsek and his men will be taken care of."

"Let's hope they are, General," Bagaryn replied, his temper still threatening. "I will tolerate no further failures, do you understand?"

Tsogt clicked his heels and bowed. "I understand."

Bagaryn seemed satisfied that his point had been made.

"There is one more item, Your Excellency," Tsogt said.

"What is it?"

"The American and the Canadian doctor. I thought you might like to question them."

"I have no need for them," Bagaryn said. "They've troubled us enough. Eliminate them."

Bagaryn turned to Petrokov and spoke in a much friendlier voice. "Mikail, I would like you to stay for dinner with me and my daughter."

Petrokov held up his hands. "I need to get back to make final preparations for the expedition's departure."

"But I insist," Bagaryn said. "We will have you back in plenty of time."

Petrokov knew he'd piss off Bagaryn if he refused. He relented. "Thank you, Vachir. I would be honored to dine with you and your daughter."

Petrokov looked at Tsogt to catch the general's reaction. He knew it drove Tsogt crazy whenever he called Bagaryn by his first name. And he wasn't about to miss his chance to get in an extra dig, especially now that such an apparent rift had formed between Bagaryn and Tsogt.

Bagaryn clasped his hands together. "Very well then." He pulled out a decanter of brandy and three glasses from the bottom drawer of his desk.

"General Tsogt, are the soldiers who will be accompanying Mr. Petrokov on his mission ready for departure?" Bagaryn asked.

"They are in the city, awaiting my orders."

"Good," Bagaryn replied. He filled the glasses, then looked at Tsogt. "You will stay behind until you are certain Tsek and the others have been eliminated. Then you may join the expedition yourself."

Petrokov's jaw dropped. "What soldiers?"

"For your protection, Mikail," Bagaryn said. "Nothing more."

"Protection?" Petrokov repeated. He stepped towards the desk. "That is not necessary. I am fully capable of providing my own security."

"Yes, yes," Bagaryn replied. "But even so, I insist. You never know what kind of trouble you may run into."

Bagaryn handed a glass of brandy to Petrokov.

Petrokov took it. He studied Bagaryn's eyes closely. He suddenly felt very uneasy about his host's intentions. Petrokov always knew that Bagaryn might try to double-cross him. His gut told him this was no time to take chances. He would have to keep his back covered at all times.

Bagaryn raised his glass for a toast.

"Gentlemen. To a strong, unified Mongolia."

"To our Mother Country," Tsogt added. He thrust his glass towards the ceiling, spilling some of its contents.

Petrokov faked a smile, nodded, and followed suit. He couldn't wait until all this was over and he had the treasure in his hands. The inescapable pounding of the surf and the taste of the salty ocean air flooded his imagination.

"To Havana," he said. Then he put his glass to his lips, threw his head back, and drained it dry.

Chapter 33

THE PRISON FACILITY located beneath the presidential palace at Karakorum was equipped with all the torture devices and interrogation equipment that a sadistic psycho like Tsogt could ask for. Compact holding cells lined a thin hallway that led into the main "interrogation" chamber. Most of the cells were empty due to Bagaryn's preference for killing his enemies outright rather than hassle with feeding them. Although no older than the palace itself, the facility had seen a flurry of activity in its short life, and the odors of death, decay, and human waste drifted throughout its recesses like omnipresent ghosts.

Steele's eyes fluttered open and focused on the concrete ceiling. The back of his shirt was soaked from the puddle of stale water accumulated on the floor. His head throbbed, his throat dry and scratchy. He tried his arms and legs. All four limbs seemed to work, albeit painfully.

Steele forced himself to his feet. He paced around his cell for a few moments to work out the stiffness and aches in his bones. Then he walked to the hefty metal door of this cell and peered through the barred window.

"You're alive," he heard a familiar voice say. The twin banks of fluorescent lights along the ceiling hummed and cast an eerie greenish glow on Maggie's face, which watched Steele from a cell across the hall.

"How's it going?" he asked.

"As good as can be expected, I guess."

Steele smiled. It was good to hear her voice. "Are Arhigee and the kids in there with you?"

"Yes," she replied. "The children are asleep. Finally."

Steele placed his hand on top of his head and palpated the dried mat of blood. "How long have I been out of it?"

"At least eight hours, maybe more," Maggie replied.

"And Jeb?" Steele had to ask, but he feared he knew what the answer would be.

Maggie sighed. "I don't know, Brazos. I never saw what happened to him."

Steele withdrew into his cell, a solemn expression on his face. He couldn't believe Jeb was dead. His friend was as close to indestructible as they came. In all the years they worked together, they had been in well over a dozen tight situations and always managed to either talk their way out or fight their way out without serious harm to either of them. So much for their winning streak. Steele couldn't help but feel that if he had been at the camp with Jeb when Tsogt arrived with his men… No, he knew full well it wouldn't have mattered if he had been there or not. What did matter was Maggie, Arhigee, and the children. He had to figure out a way to get them out of this mess.

A loud "clang" at the end of the hall, followed by an echo of footsteps, interrupted his thoughts. He heard the jingle of keys and the click of the door lock. The cell door swung open and soldiers appeared. The one in front waggled his AK-47 and ordered Steele to step out. They did the same to Maggie across the hall. The two prisoners were led to a pristine, brightly lit room filled with an assortment of strange-looking racks, complicated machinery, and wall stations. At first glance, it looked like a state-of-the art fitness center. But this was no weight room. The limb and neck shackles mounted on the walls and equipment were a testament to that. A rubber composite material covered the floor and walls, with multiple floor drains spaced strategically throughout the room. The room was obviously designed for easy clean-up.

Steele noted one particularly interesting piece of furniture in the center of the room. It was a steel recliner. In fact, it looked like a very uncomfortable dentist's chair. A metal funnel attached to a swivel sat perched atop the headrest. Steele had seen photos of a similar set-up in one of Sadaam's prisons in Baghdad. A friend of his told him what the Iraqi dictator used it for. He prayed his friend had lied.

The guards led Steele and Maggie over to a wall and secured their hands in shackles. Then they hung them up, arms high above their heads, and affixed the shackles to the wall. Maggie's toes barely touched the floor. Steele saw she was having a difficult time breathing.

After ten agonizing minutes, Steele heard more footsteps and voices in the hallway. Tsogt appeared in the room, followed closely by Bagaryn and, much to Steele's surprise, Gunga. She was dressed in a black leather jumpsuit. She flashed a sinister smile when she saw Steele.

Bagaryn strutted over to Steele like a hunter approaching wounded prey. He folded his arms and leaned back on his heels.

"So you are the infamous Dr. Steele," Bagaryn said. "I must say you are quite resilient. Too bad you and your friends must die."

"Let the women and children go, Bagaryn," Steele said. "They are of no use to you."

"And neither are you, Dr. Steele. You'd be dead already if some-one very close to me hadn't insisted upon seeing you one last time." Bagaryn motioned Gunga forward.

Steele looked at her with disgust. "You were working for them all along, weren't you?"

"It was my job to keep a close eye on you and Dr. Enkee. You were not expected to find the Dogan well."

"So you took it upon yourself to steal the samples?"

Gunga walked up and kissed him hard on his lips. "And I enjoyed every minute of it, too. I just wanted you to know that before you died."

"Who is this bitch, Brazos?" Maggie asked with disdain.

Gunga slapped her across the face. A welt quickly formed on Maggie's cheek.

"You won't act so disrespectful after these men finish with you," Gunga hissed. "I just hope they don't catch anything from you."

Maggie's eyes spit venom at her. But Gunga just smiled and returned to Bagaryn's side.

Bagaryn put his arm around her shoulders. "If you're done, my dear, then we'll be leaving."

Steele spoke up. "Do you actually believe China is going to allow you to attack them with a biological agent and not shove their military machine right up your ass?"

Bagaryn feigned a surprised look on his face. "Why Dr. Steele, I don't know what you are talking about?"

"Bullshit," Steele said. It was time to see if his theory was indeed fact. "We know all about your dealings with the Russian mob, your release of the virus in Yushan, the slaughter of your own people in Dogan."

Bagaryn kept a straight face, yet Steele could tell that he had hit a nerve.

"And we know all about your plan to release the chimera against China," Steele bluffed. It worked.

Bagaryn glanced at General Tsogt, then at Steele.

"And who would have told you about this supposed 'plan,' Dr. Steele?" he asked.

"Does it matter?" Steele replied with his best poker face. "What does matter is that the appropriate officials in the United States, Great Britain, and Russia have been notified and are preparing to take action as we speak."

Bagaryn rubbed his chin. "That's funny. I have yet to receive any feedback to that effect. In fact, just yesterday, we received yet another reassurance from the Russian ambassador that his country would come to our aid if China takes military action against us."

Steele knew his bluff had failed. A diabolical grin occupied Bagaryn's face. "Face it Dr. Steele. No one, besides you and your little band of do-gooders, has any concept of our intentions."

"Ambassador Wheaton was on to you. That's why you murdered him."

Bagaryn shook his head. "We were all saddened by the news of the ambassador's untimely death. The people responsible for this senseless act of violence will be found and punished."

Steele laughed. "You better come up with a better story than that before our State Department begins their investigation."

"Ambassador Wheaton was a very outspoken individual. He made many enemies in my country."

"That's a lie and you know it," Steele replied.

"Your ambassador liked to meddle into affairs that were of no concern to him. This must be an American character trait, no?"

"No concern?" Maggie said. "Are you kidding? Stopping some madman with a bioweapon from wiping out every man, woman, and child on earth is of no concern?"

Bagaryn smiled. "You forget, Dr. Steele. It was your country that developed the bioweapon in the first place."

"This isn't some wrestling match," Steele said. "What you are doing will trigger another world war."

"I've seen what this thing can do first hand," Maggie added. "You can't contain it."

"Our only desire is to defend our national interests," Bagaryn replied. "As an American, Dr. Steele, you of all people should understand what it means for a country to take preemptive action when a threat is perceived. China covets Mongolia's natural resources. Her people would like nothing better than to mine the rich mineral deposits that lie beneath the Gobi, as well as implement their large scale animal husbandry operations on our abundant steppes and empty our forests of timber to fuel their military and economic machine."

Steele responded. "You know as well as I do the United Nations would not allow them to threaten your national sovereignty."

"The Chinese have already reabsorbed Tibet, Macao, and Hong Kong. They attempted to seize Taiwan, but failed. Now their eyes have turned north. Mongolia has been subservient to other nations for centuries. No more. China may consider me punishment for the sins of her past."

"So you are planning a release," Maggie said.

Bagaryn didn't bother to reply. There was a distant "clang" of a steel door, followed by footsteps. Petrokov entered the room.

"I hate to break up this little social event, but I've got eighty men in Ulaanbaatar who are anxious to get underway," he said with mild irritation in his voice.

"You must be Petrokov," Steele stated. He recognized him from the courtyard party the night Steele arrived in Ulaanbaatar. "You supplied the chimera, didn't you?"

"Congratulations," Petrokov replied with a smirk. "I'll sign autographs later."

Steele's hands tingled in their restraints. He wiggled his fingers to get the blood flowing.

"Did the good president here tell you what he planned to use it for?" Steele asked.

Petrokov pulled out a cigarette and lit it. He snapped shut his lighter. "We have been assured that the weapon will be used solely for defensive purposes only."

"That's a bunch of crap," Steele said. "He's going to affect a laydown against China."

Petrokov looked at Bagaryn, who smiled at him and shook his head in denial. "Our American friend here has a vivid imagination," Bagaryn said. "We have no such intentions."

"Liar!" Maggie said. "You just told us…" Bagaryn cut her statement short with a vicious backhand to the face.

Steele's brows furrowed and he glared vengefully at Bagaryn.

Petrokov puffed his cigarette. "I see no reason for the president to authorize such an absurd action." There was a true lack of concern in the Russian's voice. He approached Maggie and stroked her hair. She jerked her head away.

"Leave her alone, you son-of-a-bitch," Steele demanded.

"Or what, Dr. Steele?" Petrokov replied. "You're going to kill me? As you can see, I'm trembling with fear."

"You ought to be," Steele said firmly.

Petrokov grabbed Maggie by the chin. He jerked her head around to face him. "It's a shame I can't stick around so that we can get to know each other better, my dear, but more pressing matters call."

Petrokov let go of her and turned to Bagaryn. "I'll be waiting at the helicopter." He then left the room.

A junior officer approached Tsogt from behind and whispered in his ear. Tsogt excused himself from Bagaryn's company and followed the officer into the hall.

"Our Russian comrade is anxious to leave," Bagaryn said to Steele. "We mustn't keep him waiting."

Bagaryn motioned for Gunga to follow him. "Come, my dear. Let's leave the two doctors to enjoy their last few minutes on earth together."

"Just how are you planning to release the agent, Bagaryn?" Steele asked. He gambled that Bagaryn was too egomaniacal to ignore the question. His hunch was correct. Bagaryn stopped and turned in his tracks. His smile was devilish.

"Why should I bother telling you, Dr. Steele? You're a dead man."

"Because the Chinese are not going to let your men waltz into their country and release a weapon of mass destruction. Not with the troop build-up along the border."

Steele decided to stroke him. "You must have figured out a very ingenious way to do it, am I right?"

Tsogt re-entered the room before Bagaryn could answer. "Come, Your Excellency," he said. "You've wasted enough time with this dog."

"Is everything all right?" Bagaryn asked. "Has Natambaa reported in?

"Everything is fine," Tsogt replied, his face stoic. "I still have not received word from General Natambaa."

"Very well," Bagaryn said. "We will join you at the helicopter pad shortly."

"Yes, Your Excellency," Tsogt replied. Then he bowed and left. Four of his men followed him.

Bagaryn turned to Steele and picked up their previous conversation. "As far as our method is concerned, Dr. Steele, it is indeed quite ingenious. Actually, I have to credit it to Gunga. She came up with the idea. In fact, it is she who will personally deliver the weapon."

"Gunga?" Steele replied. That was par for the course. It figured Bagaryn would get her to do more of his dirty work. "She'll never get across the border."

"On the contrary," Bagaryn said. "I have issued an order to deport all Chinese nationals by train. Beijing knows this and has made arrangements to process the influx of their own citizens at the border."

"What does that have to do with Gunga?"

"I told you I was born in Inner Mongolia, did I not, Dr. Steele?" Gunga asked. "That makes me a Chinese citizen."

Bagaryn continued. "She will simply be one of many returning to her homeland, the same homeland that murdered her mother."

Steele was confused. He wasn't sure what Bagaryn meant by that. "Why are you helping these people?" he asked Gunga. "Don't you understand what they are doing?"

Gunga smiled and then, much to Steele's surprise, gave Bagaryn a big kiss on his fleshy cheek.

"I'm doing it, Dr. Steele, because my father asked me to do it."

Chapter 34

TSOGT LEANED BACK in Bagaryn's plush leather chair and swirled the contents in his glass. He looked through the office window at the green steppes splashed over the horizon above the outer walls of Karakorum and mulled his situation over in his mind. It was a dilemma he never dreamed he would have to face.

After seeing off Bagaryn and his entourage at the helicopter, Tsogt met again with his junior officer to confirm the news the man relayed to him in the palace's basement. And now, over a glass of his boss's expensive brandy, he contemplated his world, which happened to be collapsing all around him. The news his subordinate had brought wasn't good. In fact, it blindsided him. According to his intelligence sources, General Natambaa, to whom he had given direct orders to neutralize Tsek's rebel band, not only disobeyed those orders, but had thrown his hat in with the rebel leader. Tsogt knew that with the defection of General Natambaa, his grip on the Mongolian military was lost. And to make matters worse, Tsek's men were on a fast track to Karakorum with an escort of five hundred of Natambaa's best troops. The meager number of Royal Guards Tsogt had at his disposal within the walls of Karakorum was no match for the flood of guns that was approaching. Surrender was not an option

either. He was not about to be paraded around like a common criminal and held accountable for his many atrocities.

Tsogt drained his glass and filled it up again. He stared at a portrait of Bagaryn that hung on the wall next to the window. The president looked formidable and proud in his traditional Mongolian warrior outfit. Once Bagaryn found out about Natambaa's defection, he
would have Tsogt terminated. Not that it mattered though. He
doubted Bagaryn would ever get the chance to exact such a judgment. Tsogt figured that when Bagaryn's helicopter arrived in
Ulaanbaatar, he would be placed under immediate house arrest.

He knew there was only one feasible course of action left. The
despondent general removed his pistol from his holster and placed it
on the desk in front of him. He silently cursed Steele. He and his
friends had been nothing but thorns in his side ever since they
arrived on the scene in Yushan. He blamed them for his fall from
grace and he certainly planned to make them pay dearly for that. His
one regret was that he wouldn't be able to be on hand to watch.

Tsogt finished his second brandy, then pitched the glass across
the room. It shattered against the far wall. He picked up his pistol
and took aim.

The gun erupted in a firestorm. The blasts came in rapid succession until the clip gave out. When the dust finally settled, the once
proud portrait of Mongolia's leader lay mortally wounded on the
floor.

Chapter 35

STEELE AND MAGGIE had exchanged few words since Bagaryn's departure. Steele's mind raced fervently, wondering what the hell 007 would do in his situation. A determined optimist, he was confident something would pop into his head, that an opportunity would present itself. If so, it had better happen quickly. Time was running out.

The familiar clang of the prison door and echoed footsteps snapped the guards to attention. Tsogt entered the room, followed by his men.

"Bring the woman and her children to me," Tsogt barked at the prison guard closest to him.

The guard fumbled with the keys attached to his belt, then shot off down the hallway like a jackrabbit.

Tsogt sent for the garrison commander, then gathered the remaining prison guards and gave them their orders. Steele couldn't hear what he told them, but he knew it wasn't good. The guards were smiling.

Arhigee and her children entered the room. She held her daughter in her arms while Tulum positioned himself bravely between his mother and the guard. The soldiers with Tsogt enveloped them within their ranks.

"What are you going to do with them?" Maggie said.

"You needn't worry, Dr. Townshend," Tsogt said. His expression was altogether evil. "They will be well cared for."

The commandant of Karakorum's Royal Guard garrison arrived in the room out of breath and saluted Tsogt. "You sent for me, sir?"

"I have been recalled to Ulaanbaatar by President Bagaryn," he lied. "You and your men are to secure the palace until my return, do you understand?"

"And when will you be back, sir?"

"Three days, no more," Tsogt said.

"Very good, sir," the commandant replied. He saluted Tsogt, then left the room.

Tsogt approached Steele. "The time has come to say goodbye, Dr. Steele. I regret I won't be able to stay to watch you die, but I have other pressing matters to address. I have prepared a special torture for you though. It was used quite effectively by our medieval ancestors."

"I can hardly wait."

Tsogt walked to the steel chair in the center of the room. He placed his hand on the funnel. "Can you imagine, Dr. Steele, what it would feel like to have molten lead poured down your throat?"

Steele didn't bother to answer.

"I will tell you," Tsogt continued. "It burns the lining of the mouth, throat and esophagus as it slides its way down to the stomach. It also hardens quite rapidly, forming a perfect cast of your upper digestive tract. Done correctly in the hands of a professional, the airways are preserved so that the recipient can survive for hours, even days, in perfect agony. Of course, eating and drinking afterwards are out of the question."

Tsogt snapped his fingers. One of the guards, a wisp of a man with crooked teeth, round nose, and jaundiced eyes, scurried over to the general and stood at attention. He reminded Steele of an underfed dumpster rat.

"Batu here considers himself such a professional. I'm certain that he will make it a memorable experience for you, as he has for so many others. As a matter of fact, I guarantee it."

The guard twitched his nose and nodded his head in anticipation.

"We will now leave him to his work."

Tsogt started to leave, but then turned to Steele. "By the way, as an added bonus, I'm going to allow you to watch Dr. Townsend die first."

Steele gritted his teeth in anger. "You're a dead man, Tsogt."

"No, Dr. Steele," Tsogt replied with an indifferent grin. "You are the one who is dead."

He then waved to his men to follow him. They disappeared with Arhigee and the children.

Batu decided to waste no time. He ordered his fellow guards to unshackle Maggie. They grabbed her by the arms and legs and carried her to a table. Maggie kicked and thrashed the entire way. They threw her to the table and pinned her. One of the men wrestled with his belt.

Batu then retrieved two heavy bars of lead from a nearby shelf and placed them into a giant pitcher on a bench next to the steel chair. He hoisted the pitcher, affixed it to a hinge attached to the top of the funnel, and plugged the cord from the device into a nearby socket. Satisfied, he retrieved a bottle of vodka from a nearby table and drank while waiting for the lead to melt.

Several minutes later, Batu put the bottle down and told two of the guards to remove Steele's shackles. A third, nervous-looking character with black, beady eyes that darted back and forth across the room kept a gun trained on the prisoner's chest. Steele's arms were as heavy as lead weights. He clenched and unclenched his fists to work out the numbness. His arms tingled as if a zillion needles were tickling his flesh.

The guards led him to the steel chair and shoved him into it. Batu secured Steele's right wrist with a leather strap. Steele could feel the heat from the lead melting in the pitcher poised above his head.

Across the room, Maggie's aggressors managed to remove her pants and underwear, but were having a tough time prying her legs apart and keeping them apart. After a brief period of intense struggle, Maggie seemed to give up the fight and spread her legs in resignation. Both guards smiled in victory. The one controlling her legs released one of them to drop his trousers. It was a huge mistake.

Maggie kicked out her free leg and connected squarely with the man's groin. He bellowed in agony, dropping to the floor, clutching his smashed testicles.

It was the distraction Steele hoped for. When the man hit the floor, his beady-eyed comrade with the gun on Steele lowered his weapon and rushed to his aid. Batu, busy at work securing the restraint on Steele's left arm, yelled at him to stop. With lightning quick movement, Steele jerked his left arm straight up and landed the back of his fist on Batu's nose. A loud "crunch" was followed by a gush of blood, and Batu fell to the floor clutching his face. Without a second's hesitation, Steele reached over with his free hand and yanked the other guard down on top of him, then wrapped his arm around the man's neck like the coil of a snake. He reached for the man's holster.

Beady-eyes raised his rifle and fired at Steele, but hit the man on Steele's lap. Steele released the grip on the dead man's neck and pulled the pistol from the holster. He heard the click of Beady-eye's bolt action, but Steele was faster. His bullet knocked the rifle from the guard's hands and caused him to lose his balance. His head fell against the edge of one of Tsogt's torture racks. Steele aimed the pistol at the stunned guard who still held Maggie by the arms. He dropped him with a shot to the neck.

Maggie rolled off the table and crawled for cover. Batu struggled to his feet. Steele aimed his pistol and fired, but heard nothing but a hollow "click." He hurled his useless weapon at Batu, fighting to release the strap on his right wrist. Batu blew a clot from his broken nose and drew a knife from his belt. He lunged at Steele with blade outstretched, but Steele managed to free his wrist just in time to parry the thrust and knock Batu backwards with a shot to the jaw. Batu came at him again, but this time the toe of Steele's boot met Batu's arm in mid-air. The knife jettisoned from Batu's hand and clattered to the floor eight meters away.

Batu dove head first at Steele, but Steele juked him and Batu smacked face first into the back of the metal chair. He howled like a wounded coyote and fresh blood spewed from his grossly disfigured nose. Steele wasted no time. He reached up and pulled on the pitcher attached to the funnel, and a waterfall of molten lead poured down on top of Batu's head. Batu's mustard-colored eyes sizzled like fried egg yolks and vanished, replaced by two pools of glistening metallic fluid. The pungent smell of roasted flesh filled the room. Batu's body flopped to the floor and thrashed like a poisoned wasp in the final throes of death, hands digging at the layer of lead solidifying on the scalded surface of his face. With his airways choked off, the struggle was short-lived. Batu's body soon relaxed, skinless hands welded permanently to the death mask.

Steele heard movement behind him. He turned and found himself face to face with the barrel of a pistol aimed at his forehead. Behind it stood the guard who had tried to rape Maggie, his pants still around ankles, his free hand still clutching his damaged genitals. He cursed at Steele, but never got the chance to pull the trigger. The butt of a rifle collided with the back of the man's skull with a sickening "pop," and both he and his gun crumpled to the floor. Behind him stood Maggie, naked from the waist down, legs apart, with her shirt torn open. Her breasts glistened with sweat and heaved up and down from the massive doses of adrenaline coursing through her veins. In her hand, she gripped the barrel of the rifle she had used to deliver the knock-out punch.

She gloated over the inert body for several moments, then smiling fiercely at an exhausted Steele. "That'll teach the son-of-a-bitch to keep his pants on."

Chapter 36

STEELE PERFORMED A quick reconnaissance of the palace's parade ground, which was dimly lit by the night sky. It was vacant save for one soldier leading a horse to the stable located on the far side. Above them on the parapets, guards patrolled back and forth against the starry background. Maggie grappled with her pants and shoes. Steele removed his outer shirt and handed it to her.

"Let's go," he said.

He grabbed her hand and pulled her along the dark corridor that surrounded the grounds. They ducked behind a broad column to catch their breath and look for palace guards.

"What are we going to do?" Maggie whispered. "Something tells me they're not going to let us just walk out the front door of this place."

"That's assuming we can find the front door," he said.

Maggie pointed towards an archway at the southeast corner of the courtyard. "I think it's through there. I saw it when we flew in."

Steele looked in that direction. "We'd better get to it before the other sentries discover their friends cooling off in the basement."

Suddenly, voices sounded to their right in the corridor. Steele peered around the column. He spotted the glow of two cigarettes approaching.

"We've got guards," Steele whispered. "Stay low."

He took several deep breaths to prepare for the fight. It never came. The two guards meandered past the column, too lost in conversation to notice the shadows hunched low against the base. Before they disappeared, Steele saw one of them flick an unfinished cigarette into the grass. A plan pieced itself together. It was a long shot, but it was something.

"Sit tight," he told Maggie. He slipped out from the shadows and returned seconds later with the discarded cigarette dangling from his mouth.

"You've got it bad," she admonished. "Couldn't you have waited?"

Steele didn't answer her, but kept his eye on the parapet. When the guards passed from view, he grabbed her hand again and they ran across the parade ground to the stable. They pulled up next to the entrance and paused, then slipped inside. The interior was brightly lit. The lone soldier stood with his back to them at the far end of the stable. Steele handed Maggie his cigarette and signaled for her to stay put. With incredible stealth, he crept up behind the man and dropped him with a brutal chop to the neck.

Steele dragged the inert body into a stall, then picked up a shovel and dispatched the lights in the stable. He returned to Maggie's side.

"Stay low until I return."

Maggie motioned towards the stall containing the guard. "What about him?"

"He shouldn't be coming around any time soon," Steele replied. He handed her the shovel. "If for some reason he does, pop him with this."

"Gee thanks," Maggie said. "Where are you going?"

"Back to Tsogt's playpen," Steele said.

"What for?"

"You'll see. Whatever you do, Maggie, don't let that cigarette go out."

"I don't smoke," she said.

"I won't tell your parents."

Then, before she could say another word, he ran across the parade ground.

Eight minutes later, he returned. His sudden reappearance startled Maggie, who was hunched down next to the unconscious guard with shovel in hand.

"What is that?" Maggie asked, pointing to the bottle Steele held in his hand.

"Vodka," he said.

"Really, Brazos, you need to get a grip on your compulsive habits."

"I know," Steele replied. "But not now. Later."

He held the bottle up for Maggie to see. It was no ordinary bottle of vodka. In addition to the alcohol, it was stuffed full of 9 MM ammunition. A makeshift fuse made from a swath of Maggie's discarded shirt hung limply from the bottle's neck.

"What are you planning to do with that?" Maggie asked.

"Create one helluva diversion," Steele replied. He plucked the cigarette from Maggie's hand. It was nothing but a pathetic stub with only a fleck of ember clinging to life next to the filter. He sucked on it several times. Finally, the tip got its second wind and took on a fresh glow.

Steele removed a halter and reins from a wall hook. He handed them to Maggie and pointed to an ebony mare watching from the stall next to theirs.

"See if you can get these on that old girl," Steele said. "Do you know how to do it?"

"I've seen enough movies. I'll figure it out."

"Good," Steele said. He rushed to the stable entrance. "Because when I return, we're outta here."

Steele looked out at the parapet. No guards. He sprinted to the palace wall beneath the parapet, then took another deep drag from the cigarette. He removed it and held it against the fuse. Nothing happened. Steele puffed again on the butt, then tried again.

"C'mon baby," he said. No sooner had he said it than a tiny spark reached out from the cigarette and embedded itself into the cloth. The fuse ignited into a healthy flame that clawed towards the bottle. Steele grenade-tossed the bomb over the wall, then sprinted to the stable.

The cocktail barely cleared the parapet when it detonated with an ear-splitting boom, followed by a brilliant stream of fire that illuminated the landscape outside the palace wall. The bullets exploded en mass, spattering against the outer wall like a shotgun blast. To the guards on the parapet, it sounded as though a full frontal assault had been launched against their fortress. Several of them fired their weapons blindly in the direction of the sound.

Maggie was waiting with the haltered horse when Steele reappeared. Steele took the reins, then hopped on the horse and scooted forward along its bare back.

He reached out his arm. "Get on and hold on."

Maggie swung up behind him and wrapped her arms around his waist. Steele clamped his legs against the horse's ribcage and coaxed the animal towards the door.

The palace grounds buzzed with disorganized activity. Royal guards rushed to and fro along the parapets, shooting into the darkness. The gunshots eventually ceased and were replaced with voices and shouts. Steele watched his plan come to fruition before his eyes.

As predicted, troops poured out through the gate and fanned out into the darkness. Steele watched the guards stationed above the gate leave their posts and join their colleagues on the ground. It was time.

"Get up!" Steele said in the horse's ear while pounding its chest with his legs. The horse shot out of the stable and dashed beneath the archway and out through the open gate.

Steele held his breath. Had they been seen? He felt Maggie tighten her grip around his waist. Once he put some distance between them and the palace, the plan was to turn due north towards the Russian border. For all Steele knew, that could be a thousand miles away, but it was their only shot. He looked up at the constellations to get a sense of direction.

Bullets and red tracer lines zipped past his ear. So much for the plan. He glanced over his shoulder. Three separate sets of headlights appeared out of the main gate behind them and illuminated the dancing apparitions of at least a dozen horsemen thundering towards them at full gallop.

He cursed under his breath. No way were they going to make it. But anything was better than dying like an insect in that dungeon. A flurry of tracer bullets hissed by again and the headlights grew larger.

He felt Maggie release one of her arms from his waist. She rapped him on his shoulder and pointed straight ahead. "Brazos, look!"

A hundred meters ahead of them, a line of horse and riders flanked on each side by what looked to be two armoured fighting vehicles suddenly appeared and headed straight for them.

Steele brought the horse to a stop.

"We're trapped!" Maggie said.

A line of flashes erupted from the new threat, followed instantly by the crackle of gunfire. Steele slid off the horse and pulled Maggie with him.

"Stay down," he said as he shielded her from the fire.

Steele heard the rattle of large caliber machine guns, then saw one of the three trucks behind him burst into flames and smoke. The two vehicles next to it skidded to a halt, as did the horses around them. A sudden surge of hope enveloped Steele. He buried his head in Maggie's back.

"What's happening?" Maggie asked, her face pressed sideways in the grass.

Steele saw the remaining trucks and horses beating it back to the palace.

"You're not going to believe it, but I think we've just been rescued," he said.

"By whom?"

"I'm not sure, but we're about to find out. Here they come."

Steele recognized the armoured vehicles as the old seventies style, box-like American M113 Armoured Personnel Carriers, or APCs. One of them broke ranks and came towards them while the other three sped on with the riders towards the palace.

"I don't believe it," Steele said.

"What?" Maggie replied.

A familiar figure jutted through the rear hatch of the M113, his hand clutching a mounted 50 caliber machine gun. The fighting vehicle drove to within five meters of them and lurched to a stop.

"If you two lovebirds are finished rolling around in the grass together, we have work to do," Jeb said. He patted his weapon.

"Son of a bitch," Steele said. He jumped to his feet. "I thought you were toast."

Maggie bounced up and down with excitement. Jeb waved his arm over the M113 as if he were showcasing it on The Price is Right.

"Like it? It's not a Bradley, but it'll do."

"Where did you get that thing?" Steele asked.

"Compliments of General Natambaa. In case you haven't heard, his troops have turned on Bagaryn. Needless to say, our evil president is in some deep shit."

Without warning, the forward hatch on the APC opened and a Mongolian wearing an old-fashioned leather tanker's cap popped up like a jack-in-the-box. He was much shorter than Jeb, of medium build, with a roughened, weather-beaten face decorated at the bottom with a long, stringy mustache and cropped goatee, similar to those worn by his world-conquering ancestors. His russet-colored eyes glowed with enthusiasm, complemented by a magnanimous grin seemingly etched in permanent marker on his face.

"This is Nagi," Jeb introduced. "The best damn APC driver in the Mongolian People's Army."

Nagi responded with a snappy salute, which Steele cheerfully acknowledged.

"I must say, you look good behind that gun," Steele said to Jeb. "Just like old times."

"Don't get sentimental on me," Jeb replied. "We have work to do. How did you guys end up out here?"

Steele gave him a summary of the escape.

Jeb could only shake his head. "Who the hell do you think you are, MacGyver?"

The sound of hoof beats resonated behind them. It was Enkee and Tsek.

Enkee dismounted. "I'm glad to see the both of you in one piece."

Steele decided to forego a formal handshake and gave his Mongolian friend a hug. "Believe me, I am too."

"Have you seen my wife and children?" Tsek asked. His voice cracked with concern.

"Tsogt took them," Maggie said. "Where to, I don't know."

"Are they still in the palace?"

"Possibly," Steele said. "But we can't say for sure."

Tsek bent his head forward and took a deep, somber breath.

"They're still alive," Enkee said in an upbeat voice. "That's what counts."

Tsek forced a smile at Steele and Maggie. "You two look like you could use some warm clothes."

Maggie rubbed her arms. "That would be wonderful."

Tsek motioned to one of his men, who immediately rode to fetch the request.

"We've got to stop her," Steele told Enkee.

"Stop 'who'?" Enkee replied.

"Gunga," Steele clarified. "Did you know she was Bagaryn's daughter?"

The look of shock on Enkee's face told Steele he didn't.

"She's on her way to China with the chimera," he added.

"Say what?" Jeb replied.

"You heard me right," Steele said. "Bagaryn's daughter is planning an act of bioterrorism."

"How are we going to be able to find her, much less stop her?" Maggie asked. "China is huge. She could be anywhere."

Tsek, who listened quietly up to now, spoke up. "I think I know where she's going."

All eyes turned to him. Tsek looked at his watch. 11:30 p.m. "Tomorrow is the twenty-ninth. That means the first of October is two days away."

Enkee slammed his fist into the palm of his hand. "That's it!"

"What's it?" Jeb asked him.

"October 1st," Enkee said, his voice full of angst. "The anniversary of China's communist revolution. Citizens from every province in China are descending upon Beijing, specifically Tiananmen Square, as we speak."

"My God," Maggie gasped. "She's going to release it in Tiananmen Square."

"It makes sense," Steele reasoned. "What better place to release the virus? People from all parts of the country will be there. After the fireworks are over, they'll leave and take the virus home with them. Spread it throughout the entire damn country."

"We've got to get word out," Maggie said.

Enkee reached into his pocket and retrieved a satellite phone. He handed it to Steele. "Here's that phone I promised you. Fully charged, too. Better late than never."

"When did she leave?" Tsek asked.

"She went with Bagaryn and Petrokov to Ulaanbaatar about two hours ago," Steele said.

"She definitely won't be catching any flights to Beijing," Tsek said. "General Natambaa informed me earlier that Chinese fighters are patrolling the airspace above the border. All flights to the south have been cancelled."

"That leaves the train," Enkee said.

"Are they still running?" Steele asked.

"I think so," Enkee replied. "At least I haven't heard otherwise."

"Maggie and I gotta get to Beijing," Steele said. "Other than Dr. Enkee, we're the only ones who can identify Gunga. Is there a way we could link up with a train heading south?"

Tsek motioned to a second rider. A skinny little man in his sixties, dressed in a worn, coffee brown del and dusty leather knee-high boots rode up on a stubby steed that looked older than he was. The man's craggy face, ash-grey hair, and thick, rhinoceros-like skin all betrayed a hard life, yet the pleasant oat-colored eyes set above the tiny nose and mouth appeared to harbor no residual bitterness.

Tsek introduced him as Bambat. "Bambat will take you as far as Manmod. There's a train depot there."

Tsek glanced at his watch again. "There will be another train departing Ulaanbaatar in two and a half hours. If you ride fast, you should be able to reach Manmod and intercept it before it passes through there."

"How are we going to get on?" Maggie asked.

"Bambat will take care of that," Tsek replied with confidence. "How many soldiers does Bagaryn have defending the palace?"

"Around eighty," Steele replied. "No more than a hundred."

"Nothing but a light snack," Jeb said. He motioned to Nagi. "James, shall we?"

"You've got it, boss," Nagi replied in a congested accent. His leather head disappeared down the hatch like a turtle retreating into its shell.

Jeb threw Steele a half-assed salute. "Good luck, Brazos. Find that bitch and stop her."

"Trust me, that's the plan," Steele assured him. "You take care of yourself. Don't get too 'gung ho' on us and get yourself hurt."

"Wouldn't think of it," Jeb replied in a cavalier manner. Then he leaned over and banged on the forward hatch with his hand. The big diesel engine revved up, and the APC crawled backwards for several meters. Then it spewed out a cloud of dirty exhaust and rolled towards the palace.

A rider arrived with a pair of down jackets tucked beneath one arm. He handed them to Steele and Maggie, who didn't waste any time putting them on. Tsek gave Bambat a few final instructions. After exchanging good-byes and good-lucks with Steele and Maggie, both he and Enkee rode towards the palace to rejoin the others.

Bambat brought up an extra horse and a spare saddle. He waved his arm. "We go now. We ride."

Steele helped Maggie into her saddle on the new horse and secured the additional saddle to the black mare.

"Do you think we'll be able to stop her?" Maggie asked, her voice full of doubt.

Steele mounted and wheeled his horse around. The lines of his eyes and mouth hardened with resolve. Steele knew they had entered the fourth quarter of the game, and that the two minute warning was fast approaching. But this was one game he was not about to forfeit. Not now. Not ever. He smiled a smile designed to bring Maggie comfort and to infuse a much-needed hope.

"We *will* find her, Maggie. And we *will* stop her. Don't ask me how, but we're gonna do it."

Steele saw it. A faint look of determination reclaimed Maggie's face. The same determination that, up to now, had proven so disruptive to Bagaryn and his warped plans. It felt good to have such a woman at his side.

Maggie's brows softened and the corners of her lips lifted. "Well then, Dr. Steele, if you say we're going to do it..." She paused to coax her horse forward and nodded for the two men to follow her. "Then I guess we'd better do it."

Chapter 37

"WE'VE SEARCHED THE palace from top to bottom," Jeb said. He, Nagi, and several of Tsek's fighters had just entered Bagaryn's office where Tsek, Enkee, and the others gathered.

"There is no sign of your family, Colonel," Nagi informed Tsek, his trademark grin absent.

Jeb leaned his Kalashnikov against the wall and plopped on a nearby sofa. "Or General Tsogt for that matter."

A look of despair overtook Tsek's face. He slumped into Bagaryn's office chair. Deep down, he knew he was too late. The thought of what Tsogt would do to his wife and children made him dizzy and nauseous.

Tsogt's Royal Guards put up a stiff defense when Tsek and his men first arrived at the outskirts of the palace. But when Tsek delivered to the garrison commander an offer of amnesty if he and his men laid down their arms and surrendered, the commander complied with little reservation. After that same commander and his top officers refused to divulge the whereabouts of General Tsogt, Tsek sent out search parties to comb the palace in an effort to locate him, as well as Arhigee and the children. Much to his dismay, they were unsuccessful.

"We'll keep looking, Colonel," Nagi told Tsek. "We'll take the APCs and perform a perimeter search of the surrounding country-side."

Tsek could only numbly shake his head.

"There will be no need for that Colonel Tsek," a voice said from the direction of the office doorway. The man who spoke wore green and tan fatigues with the markings of a major in the Mongolian People's Army. He walked forward and saluted Tsek.

"Major Lodoi, from General Natambaa's Fifth Brigade in Khutag."

Jeb joined Enkee next to the desk.

"From where?" Jeb whispered.

"It's an army base to the north of here," Enkee said.

Major Lodoi continued. "My men were instructed to assist you in any way we can. From what I saw when we arrived, it appears as though you have everything here under control."

"It wasn't much of a fight, Major," Tsek said. He forced a smile "But we greatly appreciate your coming to our aid."

Lodoi returned the smile. "By the way, Colonel, I think you'll be happy to know we have found something that belongs to you."

The major motioned to a soldier in his command standing in the doorway, who in turn waved to someone outside the office. Curiosity temporarily tempered Tsek's grief. Tulum and his sister then burst through the doorway, shouting "Daddy, Daddy." Tsek knelt and they leapt into his arms, his neck enveloped with their hugs. Over Tulum's shoulder, Tsek saw Arhigee enter the room. She walked with a limp, yet smiled broadly at the sight of her husband. The tears streamed down her face. Tsek freed himself from the children and rushed to her, taking her into his arms. He fought back his own tears. Tulum, meanwhile, scampered over to Jeb, grabbed him by the leg, and tried to wrestle him to the floor.

Tsek spoke to Lodoi over his wife's shoulder. "Where did you find them?"

"General Tsogt and six of his men were trying to make it to the Russian border. We bumped into them quite accidentally while crossing the southern pass in the Hengiin Nuruu Mountains. General Natambaa issued specific orders to arrest General Tsogt on sight, so I must say it came as quite a pleasant surprise to run into him so soon after our departure." He nodded at one of his men by the door. "Fortunately, he and his men gave up without a fight. We found your wife and children tied up in the back of their transport."

General Tsogt, his hands bound, entered the room followed by four of Lodoi's men. His service cap was long gone and his usually pristine uniform was wrinkled and blotched with dirt and moisture. Tsek had Arhigee and the children escorted from the room. Arhigee spit in Tsogt's face as she passed by. Tsogt stepped towards her, but Nagi delivered a stern forearm to his back. The general stumbled forward. The edge of the desk broke his fall, the same desk he had sat behind just hours ago.

Tsek sat down. He looked with satisfaction at his new prisoner. How many lives would be spared now that this beast had been captured?

"General Tsogt," Tsek began, "you are under arrest on the charge of first degree murder and crimes against the People of Mongolia. Do you have anything to say for yourself, or would you prefer an attorney be present before you speak?" Tsek couldn't help but smile. He had been waiting years to utter those words.

Tsogt's face flushed with anger. "I demand you release me at once, you piece of dirt, or I will kill you myself!"

With his hands still secured behind his back, he started to circle the desk, but backpedaled when the growling started. Tsogt didn't need to be told what was coming next. Like a banshee from Hades,

Gobi lunged at him from behind the desk, teeth snapping and mouth frothing like steamed milk. Tsek yanked on the dog's leash and held him back.

"I apologize, General Tsogt," Tsek said. "I don't believe you and my friend here have been formally introduced. I must say, he certainly has a bone to pick with you. No pun intended."

"What are you talking about?" Tsogt replied defiantly.

"When you murdered my brother, you also murdered Gobi's best friend."

"That's the saddest story I have ever heard," Tsogt mocked.

Tsek gave Tsogt a razor sharp glance. He fought with all his might to suppress the urge to pull out his pistol and shoot Tsogt between the eyes. That would be too easy a death for this bloodthirsty psychopath. But still, the thought of Munke caused his blood to boil.

He handed Gobi's leash to Nagi, then fingered the flap of his holster. But it was Jeb who stepped in and inadvertently spared Tsogt's life.

"If I was you Lurch, I'd watch your mouth," Jeb advised. "You're not exactly among groupies here."

Tsogt looked at Jeb with disdain. "I should have killed you when I had the chance."

Jeb got right in his face. "Yes, you should have, but you didn't. Big mistake, you piece of shit."

"Too bad your friends weren't as lucky as you," Tsogt said. "I heard they begged for mercy before they died."

"Really," Jeb replied, looking around at the others in the room with a smile on his face. "I guess you haven't heard the news, have you?"

Tsogt's face still reeked of pugnacity, yet he didn't reply.

"It just so happens that at this very moment, my friends are on their way to Beijing to intercept Bagaryn's daughter." Jeb tapped his finger on his chin as if he were deep in thought. "I believe her name is Gunga, isn't it?"

To Tsek, the look on Tsogt's face was priceless. He knew the general had been planning to try to use that little piece of information as a bargaining chip if the need arose. Now it was as worthless as a saddle without stirrups.

Tsek rose from behind the desk and approached Tsogt. "I've had enough of you, General. Where is President Bagaryn?"

"I will tell you nothing," Tsogt hissed.

"You're not getting it, Lurch. Are you?" Jeb said. He turned to Tsek. "Let me have ten minutes alone with him…" he paused and grinned at Tsogt, "… and I'll have him talking like a parrot in no time."

Tsek ignored Jeb's request. "I will ask you again, General. Where is President Bagaryn?"

Tsogt didn't answer.

"Very well," Tsek said. He turned to his men. "Lock him up downstairs."

Four of Tsek's fighters escorted Tsogt from the room.

Tsogt shouted over his shoulder, "Rest assured, Colonel. I will not rest until your wife and your spawn lie rotting in sands of the Gobi. I will order my men to hunt both you and them down and exterminate all of you like insects."

"Get him out of here!" Tsek ordered.

"Your brother died like a dog, a coward like you," Tsogt said. The trail of insults faded away down the hallway as they took him away.

Jeb shook his head. "I sure hope you guys have an extra strong rope to keep his big ass from snapping it when he drops."

"The Mongolian people will decide his fate, Mr. Walker," Enkee said. "We can all rest assured that he will be held accountable for his crimes."

"It's time to tend to more important matters," Tsek said.

The men in the room gathered around Tsek. The latter pulled out a map and spread it on Bagaryn's desk.

"Major Lodoi will stay behind with his men and occupy the palace until reinforcements from General Natambaa arrive," Tsek said. He motioned at Enkee and Jeb. "We will intercept Petrokov's expedition."

After reviewing the detailed plan of action with those present, Tsek ordered his men to gather supplies from the palace storehouses and to wait for him at the front gate. The briefing adjourned and everyone left the room except for Tsek and Nagi. Nagi held on to Gobi's leash.

Tsek walked to the window and looked out over the palace courtyard. Tsogt's threats against his family still resonated in his ears. He knew they were true. His family would never be safe as long as Tsogt were alive. He couldn't take that chance. He wouldn't.

Nagi twisted one side of his mustache with his hand. "What would you like me to do with the dog?"

Tsek walked over to Gobi. He knelt down and stroked the dog's forehead. Gobi licked his arm.

"He looks hungry," he told Nagi. "Get him a bone to chew on."

The weathered warrior nodded and his grin grew to epic proportions. He saluted Tsek, then turned and led Gobi out of the room.

Outside the palace's front gate, Tsek's men sat atop their mounts, waiting for their leader. They didn't have to tarry long. Tsek appeared at the gate and drew in a breath of crisp air through his nostrils. He set his eyes upon his wife and daughter, standing nearby with their new bodyguards. Tulum brought him his horse. Tsek hugged his son and climbed atop his mount. He shouted for his men to follow, then galloped into the early morning darkness.

A faint sound escaped from the depths of the palace compound, mostly muffled by the chorus of departing hoof beats. However, several of Lodoi's men patrolling the palisades heard it and craned their heads in curiosity. The troops in the courtyard heard it, too. To some, it sounded like jackals fighting over a piece of meat. To others, it sounded like the screams of an operatic falsetto.

They were all wrong.

It was the sound a man being eviscerated by a dog.

Chapter 38

SECURITY AT THE Beijing Railway Station was tight. Gunga stepped on the platform with bag in hand and immediately immersed herself in a sea of anniversary pilgrims. Soldiers of the People's Liberation Army manned all exits and shuttled arriving passengers into one of eight lines in front of the immigration desk. It was the second immigration screen Gunga was forced to endure. The first one occurred in Erdene. She had no problems with the Chinese immigration authorities there and she expected none here as well. In fact, except for the trip's departure, everything had gone smoothly.

Her father wouldn't explain to her why he made the last minute changes to her travel plans, but she figured it had to do with the communiqué he received in flight on their way back from Karakorum. Instead of landing in Ulaanbaatar, where Gunga was to receive a final private briefing on her mission before boarding her train to China, her father diverted the helicopter south of the city to the remote army base at Nalajh. Petrokov drove to the city to join his men, while she and her father got into a black Toyota Landcruiser and shuttled westward across the steppes, during which time she received her final instructions and, most importantly, reviewed her escape plan. Thirty minutes later, they arrived at train tracks in the middle of nowhere. There, they waited an additional ninety minutes for the southbound train from Ulaanbaatar to appear. When it finally did, the men accompanying them flagged it down and much to the surprise of the passengers and crew, the president of Mongolia personally escorted her to her seat.

Standing in line, Gunga couldn't help but fidget. It was payback time. Payback for the oppression. Payback for her mother. Payback for the sake of payback. General Zhu Hong's day of reckoning.

Festivities were scheduled to begin in twenty-eight hours. The five day weather forecast for Beijing called for sunny skies, with few clouds and afternoon winds predicted at 15 to 20 kph. The sunny forecast wasn't the best news, since bioagents are susceptible to degradation from the sun's ultraviolet rays. Ideally, laydowns are best achieved when the skies are overcast, or at dusk, when a cool blanket of air settles in over a warmer layer of air lying close to the ground, a prime condition known to bioweaponeers as "inversion." Unfortunately, Gunga's weather forecast fit neither condition. The viral particles were coated with special polymers designed to protect them against solar degradation. As a result, the mid-afternoon laydown she planned should still be quite effective, especially since the crowds in the Square would be thick, the winds still brisk, and the sun well on its way to the west.

Following the release, she planned to drive north to the border village of Xangdin, avoiding the main roads that led to Erdene. There, a team of operatives sent by her father would penetrate the border, extract her, and escort her to Ulaanbaatar. Simple and straightforward.

After a ten minute wait, an immigration official motioned for Gunga to approach. With an innocent, relaxed smile, she handed him her papers. The official flipped through the documents and questioned her on her time spent in Mongolia. He then directed her to a partitioned cubicle beyond the immigration desk, where routine baggage searches and wand scans were performed on select passengers. Her heart raced. Bad luck. She hadn't expected to be singled out for routine screening.

Gunga placed her bag on a table in front of a tall, lanky officer, who opened it and filtered through its contents. A female security guard approached Gunga and pulled out her wand, then held it to Gunga's neck and scanned downwards. The wand emitted a shrill beep at Gunga's waist. The guard asked her to empty her pockets. The wand still protested. The woman eyed Gunga suspiciously, then called for her supervisor. A smartly dressed middle-aged man in a dark brown security suit approached them. The woman explained the situation to him, but Gunga interrupted her.

"My hip," she said in Chinese. She pointed at the area in question. "There's a metal plate attached to the bone. I fell from a horse as a child." She pulled a piece of paper from her pocket and handed it to the supervisor.

"Here's the medical record from the hospital in Shanghai where the surgery was performed," Gunga said. "I have to carry it with me whenever I travel." She smiled at the supervisor with a hint of seduction thrown in for good measure. "I set off metal detectors wherever I go."

The supervisor studied the medical record. Gunga was sure he could hear her heart pounding. Her make-up fought to conceal her sweat. She had to do something, and fast.

Gunga unbuttoned her pants and yanked them to her knees. Then she peeled down the left side of her underwear.

"Here's the scar," she said, pointing to the pitted skin defect on her thigh.

The supervisor saw more than the scar. His face blushed and he stammered. Not knowing what else to do, he abruptly folded the medical record and handed it to her.

"You are free to go," he said. "Thank you for your cooperation."

Gunga pulled her pants up and thanked him. It worked beauti-fully, the medical record, that is. Gunga vowed to personally com-mend the individual responsible for the forgery. The doctor's signa-ture on it was priceless. It did not belong to an actual doctor. Far from it. It was the signature of her father's personal chef.

She stuffed the document into her bag, then slung the bag over her shoulder and proceeded through the customs area. She noticed the supervisor still watching her. She continued walking with a calm air and displayed no hint of the anxiety that had risen to volcanic proportions. She didn't dare make eye contact. Did he suspect something? Or was he just horny? If need be, she would release the agent now. It would still wreak its havoc, even if this wasn't Tiananmen Square.

She reached the counter of the only rental car agency in the ter-minal. After providing the agent with a fake driver's license and sto-len credit card, she discreetly glanced over her shoulder. The supervi-sor was busy with a new passenger.

Gunga let out a deep sigh. Tengri and the gods had watched over her. Nothing would stop her now With her help, her father would join the ranks of the world's most powerful leaders. And most exciting of all, she would be by his side, the sole heir to a new Mongol dynasty, the sole heir to more wealth, power, and prestige than she could ever have imagined.

The drive from the train station to her hotel took less than ten minutes. She checked in under the same assumed name she used with the rental car agency, then took the elevator to her fifteenth floor room. She tossed her bag on the bed, walked to the window, and opened the curtains. Looking out across Jingshan Park below her, she could see the imperial ivory-yellow roofs of the Forbidden City tucked within its vermillion walls and surrounding moat, and beyond the City, the distant edge of Tiananmen Square. She returned to the bed and undressed. The plan was to grab a quick nap, then walk to the Square to check out the event's security structure. After that, she'd go shopping.

Gunga walked to the bathroom and turned on the shower. She removed the slim canister from between her legs and set it in the adjacent sink. Then she showered, totally indifferent to the fact that less than two meters away, billions of viral particles churned and vibrated within their metallic prison, waiting for their day of liberation, a day that would spell doom for a major portion of mankind.

Chapter 39

THE TRAIN TRIP to the Chinese border proved to be a test of endurance for Steele and Maggie. Not only was the ride rough, stuffy, and cramped, some brilliant voyager compounded the discomfort by opening a window next to the lavatory to let in fresh air. What he let in was an endless supply of Gobi dust, which coated the interior of the car and its occupants like a thin layer of spray paint. But Steele couldn't complain. Hey, at least they were on the train.

The horse ride from Karakorum took them just over three and one half hours, which put them into the station about the same time the train was scheduled to pass through. Steele was afraid they missed it. But Bambat assured them that no trains ran on schedule in Mongolia. He was right.

Steele tried to sleep, but his mind remained obstinate. Too much was happening. Way too much. The task that lay ahead of them was formidable. Time was running out. Gunga achieved a significant head start on them. How they were ever going to locate her amidst such a throng of people was anyone's guess. Masters predicted that over one million spectators were going to descend on Beijing for the festivities. It would be like trying to find a needle in a haystack. No, it would be more like trying to find the short straw in that haystack. Next to impossible. That is, if they even got to Beijing. How were they going to get across the border? They had no passports. Steele prayed his boss would be able to work his magic and pull the necessary political strings to get them into China.

The sun was halfway up in the eastern horizon when the train finally arrived in Zamyn-Uud. Within moments of detraining, Steele and Maggie were met by Mongolian border officials. Steele's heart sank, fearing that somehow Bagaryn caught wind of their intent and ordered their arrest. But this concern was relieved when the officials drove them to a border checkpoint, and without saying a word, released them to their Chinese counterparts across the yellow line. Steele smiled. He should have known his boss would come through for them.

The Chinese border guards escorted Steele and Maggie to a black Chevrolet Suburban parked nearby. An American dressed in a dark business suit and another man arrayed in the grey-green uniform of a Chinese officer stood next to the vehicle. The American reminded Steele of a fifty-year-old Chris Farley. The boyish face, planted atop a body that seemed as wide as it was tall, lit up when he saw Steele and Maggie approach. He smiled a toothy smile and held out a chubby hand.

"Dr. Steele. Dr. Townsend. Welcome back to China. I'm Bill Winger, chief of staff for Ambassador Malkland."

Winger turned to the man next to him. "This is General Fan Wuhang, vice chairman of the People's Central Security Council." Wuhang removed his cap, gave them a curt bow, then shook their hands. The Chinese general was a petite man in his early sixties, sporting a head of neatly groomed black hair that was either naturally or artificially resistant to graying. Beneath his round, wire-rimmed glasses, his eyes transmitted a confidence and strength that more than counteracted his slight physical stature. His English was exceptional, his voice friendly and charismatic.

"Any trouble getting across?" Winger asked.

"None whatsoever," Steele said. "In fact, it seemed too easy, considering…"

"Let's get on the road, shall we?" Winger suggested. "We can talk on the way."

Not wasting any more time, they piled into the Suburban and took off.

"I spoke with Colonel Masters earlier," Winger said as he adjusted his rearview mirror. "He told me what was going on. Frankly, it's damn hard to believe. A remote country with a standing army of a couple hundred thousand and no significant weapons systems to its name procures a bioweapon and sets out to release it on a major superpower. Go figure."

Keeping his eyes on the road, Winger reached to the floorboard and retrieved a can of cashews he kept stashed. He pried off the plastic lid and scooped a handful of nuts.

"General Wuhang is an expert on Mongolian politics," Winger said.

Wuhang turned and faced the backseat. "I am familiar with Bagaryn's weapons deals with the Russian mafia," he said. "But I must admit I was not aware that he had any children."

"Well, rest assured that he has at least one troubled child," Maggie said.

"I took it upon myself to do some further investigation. What I found was quite amazing. I'm embarrassed the intelligence failed to make it into Bagaryn's file."

"What intelligence is that, General?" Steele asked.

"As a young man, Bagaryn was invited by the Chinese government to participate in a Naadam wrestling exhibition held in the Inner Mongolian capital of Hohhot. You must remember that at the time, he was considered a famous sports celebrity in both Outer and Inner Mongolia. During the two weeks he was in China, he became romantically involved with a local woman, who ended up carrying his child. It is well-documented that he returned to Inner Mongolia at least four times during the next two years, presumably to visit the woman and the child."

"So I take it he ended up leaving her," Maggie concluded.

"Actually, Dr. Townshend, she died," Wuhang said.

Maggie's surprise was evident. "How did that happen?"

"It was about the same time Bagaryn was making his trips to China that the Inner Mongolian Liberation Front took root in Inner Mongolia, specifically in Hohhot. Some in government at that time believed Bagaryn was somehow linked to the origin of the movement. At any rate, the Chinese leaders acted swiftly to crush the IMLF before it could spread. Bagaryn's woman was found guilty by association and arrested along with hundreds of others. They were all sent to the infamous prison outside of Shenyang, where she was brutally beaten and raped by prison guards. She later died due to her injuries. No one knows what happened to the child."

"We do now," Maggie stated.

Steele shook his head. "That's some story."

Winger held the can of nuts aloft. "Nuts anyone?"

His passengers politely declined. Winger lowered the can and helped himself to more.

"I'm telling you, Dr. Steele…" Winger spoke through a wad of partially masticated cashews, "…it was like pulling teeth to get any of the Chinese higher-ups to believe the story. Luckily, Masters put me in touch with General Wuhang."

"I met Colonel Masters two years ago at a UN security summit," Wuhang added. "He certainly impressed me as a man who would not cry wolf unless there was good reason to do so."

"Your so-called leaders better get with the game," Steele said. "That wolf is fixing to shove a bioweapon right up their asses."

Maggie tapped Steele on the leg and mouthed for him to be quiet.

"Easy, Dr. Steele," Winger broke in. "General Wuhang is on our side. He came here to help."

Steele took several deep breaths. His face relaxed. He reached over and squeezed Maggie's hand.

"I apologize, General. It's just that in the past week, Dr. Townshend and I have been beaten, shot at, hung up on walls like cheap paintings, and threatened with lead margaritas. I guess I'm just a little edgy."

Wuhang smiled forgivingly. "I understand, Dr. Steele. And believe me, I am just as concerned as you are about this threat. I knew Bagaryn well enough to know that it was not beyond him to authorize such an act.

"How is Premier Deng reacting to Bagaryn's troop mobilization?" Maggie asked.

Wuhang took off his glasses and cleaned the lenses with a handkerchief. "He viewed the move by the Mongolian president as a simple bluff to gain concessions at the international bargaining table. He did not believe for a moment Bagaryn would attempt a conventional military strike at China. After all, it would be suicide."

"Excuse me General, but why are you talking in past tense?" Steele asked.

"I guess you haven't heard," Winger said. He honked his horn at a delivery truck he'd been tailgating for the last several minutes.

"Heard what?" Steele asked.

Winger whipped the Suburban into the passing lane and punched the accelerator. In a matter of seconds, the delivery truck was a mere memory in the rearview.

"Bagaryn has been deposed," Winger stated. "Happened early this morning. General Natambaa and his troops seized the government offices in Ulaanbaatar in a bloodless coup."

Steele pumped his arm. "That's the best news I've heard in a long time. I guess that would explain our smooth arrival."

"Natambaa has already sent out word for Mongolian troops to stand down. Emergency talks between Beijing and Ulaanbaatar are in the works. The two countries seem to be cooperating."

"Is Bagaryn in custody?" Steele asked.

Winger shook his head. "Unfortunately, he slipped out of the capital. Natambaa's men are searching for him. It's only a matter of time until he's captured."

Maggie looked at Steele. "Maybe Gunga didn't even make it to the train."

"That's one assumption we can't afford to make," Steele replied. He turned to Wuhang. "Were your people able to screen the passenger arrivals at the Beijing rail terminal?"

"In addition to the train you were on, two others have crossed into China from Mongolia in the past forty-eight hours," Wuhang said. "Unfortunately, the first one arrived before we could begin the screening process. If Bagaryn's daughter were on that train, then we would have no way of knowing it."

Steele swore under his breath, exasperated at the Chinese authorities who refused to believe the threat was real. Their skepticism allowed Gunga to slip into their country way too easily.

"What about the other train?" Steele asked.

"It arrived early this morning," Wuhang said. "We took photos of all female passengers on board and obtained a names list. They will be at my office when we arrive."

"Are you sure she even took the train?" Wilson asked.

Steele nodded. "I heard Bagaryn mention it."

Steele leaned towards Wuhang. "Is there a way we could speak to the customs officials on duty? Maybe they could help us."

"I have already done so, Dr. Steele," Wuhang replied. "They reported nothing too out of the ordinary. Several expired passports, illegal transport of contraband material, two passengers with criminal records trying to sneak into the country. One passenger set off the metal detector because of a plate in her hip."

"In 'her' hip?" Steele asked.

Wuhang nodded. "Yes, Dr. Steele. They did say the passenger in question was a woman."

"What train did she arrive on?"

"The second one, I believe."

"Did they say how old she is?"

"No, they didn't," Wuhang replied. "But we can certainly find out."

Wuhang removed a phone from the briefcase and punched in a number. Moments later, he spoke in rapid Mandarin Chinese to the voice on the other end. He shifted the phone to his chest. "I'm being connected to the customs officer on duty at the time." He put the phone back to his ear.

"Do you think it was Gunga?" Maggie asked Steele.

"Who knows? But any lead at this stage is worth a follow-up."

Wuhang spoke into his phone again. He sounded irritated. He put the phone to his chest again.

"I am speaking with the supervisor on duty at the time. He said the woman was in her late twenties or early thirties. She had appropriate medical documents to support her claim. He said she created quite a stir though."

"How so?" Steele asked.

"He said she pulled down her pants right there in the terminal and showed him the surgery scar."

There was a pause. Steele heard the alarm go off inside his head. "Ask him if the scar was pitted and shaped like the moon."

Wuhang shot Steele a dubious glance, but then complied with his request. Moments later, a curious look replaced the doubtful one, and he lowered the phone again.

"Yes it was, Dr. Steele. How would you have known that?"

Maggie leaned back and cast him a questioning eye. "Yes, how did you know that, Brazos?"

Steele ignored her. "That's our girl, General. Do they know where she was going or where she might be staying?"

Wuhang spoke to the supervisor. He relayed the man's answer. "He saw her go to the rental car counter."

"Bingo!" Winger said.

Maggie shook her head. "I'm sure she gave them false information at check-in."

"Perhaps," Winger replied. "But we can still get the license plate number on the rental car."

"What time do the ceremonies start tomorrow?" Steele asked.

"Nine a.m," Winger said. "They're expecting over five hundred thousand in and around the Square, with that number swelling as the day goes on."

"I take it, General Wuhang, that there's no chance at canceling the event?" Steele asked. He knew the answer in advance.

Wuhang hung up with the supervisor, then he smiled and shook his head. "I'm afraid it's too late for that. But I will have officers stationed throughout Tiananmen Square within the hour. I will need your help to generate a composite sketch of this woman that we can distribute to my people."

"Let's hope we can track down that rental car and find out where she's staying," Winger said.

"I'm sure she's staying as close to the Square as she can get," Wuhang added. "Driving in from an outlying location will be next to impossible twelve hours from now."

"How about it, Dr. Steele?" Winger asked. "Any ideas?"

Steele didn't answer immediately. Something tickled his memory. Something Gunga had mentioned on their trip to Dogan.

"General Wuhang, will Vice Premier Zhu Hong be at the ceremonies tomorrow?" he finally asked.

"He will be on the main grandstand with Premier Deng. Why do you ask?"

"Every villain has a character flaw that ultimately leads to his or her downfall," Steele said.

"Oh really?" Winger said. "And what is this woman's character flaw?"

"Revenge, Mr. Winger," Steele replied. "The insatiable desire for revenge."

Chapter 40

GUNGA STRODE BRISKLY through Jingshan Park, skirting the eastern wall of the Forbidden City. Her angst couldn't have been higher. She had slept through her alarm and a hotel afternoon wake-up call, turning her otherwise brief nap into a six hour slumber. She admonished herself the entire way. How could she have been so careless?

Tiananmen Square was already strewn with a colorful assortment of blankets, sleeping bags, and coolers, owned by squatters intent on securing prime seats for tomorrow's festivities. Gunga stopped for a moment and watched the Chinese troops drill in front of the Public Security Ministry. Meanwhile, in front of the Mao Zedong Memorial Hall in the center of the Square, work crews placed the final touches on a gigantic platform and grandstands from which the nation's top political and military leaders would, in less than eighteen hours, deliver rousing party speeches and observe the military might of the State parade before them. Temporary wire fencing surrounded the entire Hall to ensure its cadaverous occupant remained undisturbed by the celebrations.

Gunga cursed under her breath. That barrier was not supposed to be there. Her plan was to hide the viral canister within the ornate masonry of the tomb's exterior wall and thereby secure a centralized location from which to effect the release. She would have to change that plan. The thick security that surrounded the other buildings in close proximity to the Square, including the Great Hall of the People, the Agricultural Bank of China, and the Museum of the Chinese Revolution, made all of those sites impractical. And simply dropping the canister on the ground in the middle of the Square was out of the question, since the chances of it being discovered and inadvertently moved before she could escape and detonate it were too great.

And then there was the question of that escape. The bellman at her hotel informed her that the police planned to block off Dongchan'an Jie Avenue and other roadways leading to the Square beginning at midnight. Gunga would have no choice but to go on foot in the morning. It would be a good ten minute jaunt, and that was walking at a fast pace. That meant she would have to wait until she got to her rental car before she activated the detonator with the transmitter. Then the clock would start ticking. She would have ten minutes to drive as far away as possible. Not much margin for error. The vaccine scar on her hip gave her little solace. Vaccine or no vaccine, she knew accidental exposure to the high concentrations of the virus contained within the canister would be lethal.

She stood and mulled over her options. Overhead, a pair of fighter jets practiced their flyby for tomorrow. Gunga watched them disappear over the Beijing horizon. Something else in the sky caught her eye. Then another one. Then another. They were everywhere. A smile came to her face. That was it. The answer to her predicament.

Twenty meters from where Gunga stood, a young man stretched out atop a blanket reading a book, while his girlfriend stood next to him. She held a string in her hand. Gunga approached them, sporting her best smile.

"Excuse me," Gunga spoke to the girl in Mandarin Chinese. "I was wondering if you could help me?"

Gunga reached into her purse and extracted a thick wad of Yuan notes. The man on the blanket set his book aside and looked on wide-eyed as Gunga counted out the equivalent of $500 US. She pointed to the girl's garnet and maize-colored box kite fluttering high in the sky.

"I'd like to buy your kite."

Chapter 41

FLUFFY TUFTS OF snow were floating to earth when Petrokov's party reached the outer lip of the Zunulog, a broad flood-plain surrounded by the formidable jagged mountains of the Tsagaan Uul range. Impassable during the spring and early summer, when run-off from the mountain snow created an amorphous sheet of water over the entire surface, the plain was now a vast spider web of shallow rivers and streams that sliced it into multiple islands of grassy terrain.

Petrokov climbed out of his jeep and walked a short distance. He hopped over several tiny streams, frequently testing the integrity of the bare ground with his boots. It was exceptionally dry and firm, thanks to the crisp Siberian front that had rolled through a week ago and handed the region its first hard freeze of the season.

He pulled out his copy of Polo's map and compared its crude illustrations with the surrounding terrain. Petrokov didn't like what he saw. It was too generic. Floodplains and ridges like the ones in front of him were a dime a dozen in northern Mongolia. The drawing on the map could represent any one of them. But his chief engineer, Igor Vladochek, insisted that this was the location they were looking for.

Vladochek's optimism was founded on Geotopographical Integration Software Technology, or GIST, developed by the Russian military's Corps of Engineers, which he had employed to narrow the possible choices. After scanning Polo's map into his computer, along with maps obtained from the Museum of Natural History in Ulaanbaatar, some of them dating back as far as the late fourteenth century, he used the GIST software to merge the topographical information with detailed satellite photographs and modern geographical survey maps of northern Mongolia. After adding last minute information gleaned from Polo's written account, Vladochek commanded the software to merge it together. Much to his amazement, the software took a mere nine minutes to assimilate the data and to spit out a composite map of the region deemed to have common features with both the old and the new.

The results came as a complete surprise to Petrokov. He assumed, like those who sought the treasure before him, that the Khan's tomb lay somewhere in the Khentii region of eastern Mongolia, near the leader's birthplace. Now Vladochek's program claimed the likely site of the tomb was not east, but due north of Ulaanbaatar, in the upper reaches of the aimag of Selenge, close to the Russian border. It was a fantastic statement, and he wasn't sure he could trust the machine that made it. After all, computers were not foolproof. But Petrokov also knew he was running out of time. The euphoria he experienced earlier in Karakorum turned to anxiety. Within the next two to three weeks, the heavy snows would begin and the ground would freeze up as hard as spent uranium, making any attempts at excavation futile. He had two choices. It was either return to the Khentii region to use the map to manually search for key landmarks or take a chance on the computer's hypothesis. If the computer was wrong and they came up empty-handed, then another nine months would have to pass before they could resume their search. And that was time Petrokov knew he didn't have. Especially if the rumors Olga Pushkarev relayed to him over the phone less than an hour ago were indeed true.

Petrokov pulled out his radio. "Vladochek, do you read me?"

"Loud and clear, Mr. Petrokov," came the response.

"We have reached the floodplain and are ready to start across."

"The deepest stream shouldn't be more than a meter," Vladochek stated. "You won't have any trouble crossing."

"Where are you now?" Petrokov asked.

"About ten kilometers northwest of your position." Vladochek gave his GPS coordinates to Petrokov.

"Are you certain this is the area?" Petrokov asked.

"I'd bet my life on it," Vladochek said in a confident voice.

That you have, Petrokov felt like telling him. But instead, he put the handset to his mouth and spoke, "Very well then. Stay close to your radio."

Only one question remained: Would the heavy flatbed trucks be able to cross the plain without sinking up to their axles? Petrokov had a back-up plan in case they did. Prior to flying to Karakorum to meet with Bagaryn, he wisely made arrangements with Uri Komvich to have the necessary equipment airlifted in if ground efforts failed. As he surveyed the floodplain one last time, Petrokov was confident that those services would not be required.

Petrokov's mechanized expeditionary force consisted of several dump trucks, a fuel truck, and ten 18-wheel flatbed trailers, their backs ladened with backhoes, bulldozers, portable generators, light fixtures, lumber, and camp supplies. He waved for the first flatbed in line to drive forward. He then instructed the driver to start across. The massive vehicle moved out carefully across the open plain, wading across the streams and bumping over the tufts of terra firma that pocked the landscape. After a hundred meters or so, the truck stopped and the driver stuck his arm out of the cab window and gave the thumbs-up to Petrokov. Petrokov returned to his jeep and waved the rest of the convoy forward.

The convoy crept onward in single file across the lumpy terrain like a herd of lame pack mules. A pair of army trucks packed with the fifty Royal Guardsmen that Bagaryn had sent along for "protection" brought up the rear of the column. Petrokov knew full well that they had been sent with impure motives, yet he decided to tolerate their presence, at least for the time being.

The migration took just under two hours to cover five kilometers. But much to Petrokov's relief, all trucks and equipment made it across the plain without incident. Once they reached higher ground, Petrokov checked his GPS, then directed the column west on a course parallel to the mountain ridge. He sped ahead of the convoy and within minutes, the familiar outlines of Vladochek's two helicopters appeared in the distance. They had set down at the base of a broad ravine that wound its way lazily up the southern face of the mountain ridge. When Petrokov arrived, Vladochek was standing next to one of the helicopters with his engineers. He approached Petrokov's vehicle with an excited smile on his round face.

Petrokov remained in his jeep and stared blankly at the ravine. A thick copse of pine trees choked the center of it. And no sign of water. Anywhere.

"You idiots!" Petrokov exploded at Vladochek and his men. He waved his copy of Polo's map in the air. "Where is the water? This map clearly shows a river."

Igor Vladochek's smile vanished, but his excitement remained. "The computer…"

Petrokov cut him short. "You know where you can stick your computer! Now get your asses back into those choppers and continue your search. If we don't locate this gravesite before the first hard snow, it will be your balls on a stick."

Vladochek held up his hands, palms out. "Just a minute, Mr. Petrokov. I have something you need to see." He then dashed to the helicopter and ducked into the cockpit.

Petrokov climbed out of his jeep and glared icily at the three other engineers, who stood eyes to the ground, silent like reprimanded school children. Vladochek soon returned. In his hands he held a cardboard box filled with a wide multicolored assortment of smooth pebbles and stones.

"Impressive," Petrokov stated with sarcasm. "Unfortunately, I'm not paying you to collect rocks. I'm paying you to find a treasure."

Vladochek remained unfazed by his boss' belligerency. "We found a solid blanket of these stones beneath the ground surface in a number of random sites in the middle of those pine trees."

"And your point is?" Petrokov said.

"Dig three meters from the center on either side and you won't find them."

Petrokov reached into the box and pulled out a handful of rocks. He moved his thumb over their smooth, slick surfaces.

"You don't get surfaces that uniformly smooth without running water," Vladochek said. He pointed at the top of the mountainous ridge that stretched out in front. "Not only that, we found what appeared to be headwaters up there."

Vladochek pulled out his GIST map. With his finger, he traced an unnamed river shown coursing along the opposite side of the ridge. "They're feeding this river here."

Petrokov kept his eyes on the map. "What does that have to do with ours?"

Vladochek paused while the lead truck of the main column pulled to a stop behind Petrokov's jeep. He raised his voice above the noise of the big diesel engines.

"Those headwaters once fed our stream," he told Petrokov. "Someone dammed it up and redirected the flow of water. My men and I checked it out. You can see it as plain as day."

Petrokov kept silent and pondered the words of his foreman.

Vladochek continued. "Judging by the maturity of the trees in this ravine, it was probably done four, maybe five centuries ago."

The engineer next to Vladochek spoke. "But why would they do that? I thought they wanted the water to conceal the tomb. You don't think someone beat us to the punch and found it, do you?"

Vladochek's optimism took a quick dip, but then recovered. "I doubt that. My guess would be, if that group put in charge of protecting the site..." Vladochek paused and tapped his forehead with his index finger. "What was their name again, boss?"

"Darkhad," Petrokov said impatiently.

"Yes," Vladochek continued. "If the Darkhad knew the location of the tomb slipped out into the public domain through Polo's book, they may have altered the disguise by drying up the river and planting those trees." Vladochek pointed to the trees. "Look how uniformly spaced they appear to be. It doesn't look natural to me."

A sudden uneasiness gripped Petrokov. Vladochek was right. Petrokov failed to notice it when he first arrived, but now he did. The trees were arranged in a strangely uniform pattern, not haphazardly as one would expect to occur naturally. A twinge of bile irritated his throat. If true, the Darkhad may have gone one step further and relocated the tomb altogether. If so, then the map and Polo's book were nothing but historical garbage and he was back at square one.

Petrokov contemplated the scenario for a moment, then shook his head and dismissed it. "This is bullshit," he said. "This isn't even the right location. We're wasting our time here."

"At least allow us to run a scan of the area," Vladochek said.

Petrokov checked his watch. It read 4:18 p.m. "How long will that take?"

"If we start immediately, we can have it done in a few hours," Vladochek said. The excitement returned to his voice. "I've already laid out a search grid."

Petrokov surveyed the ravine once again. He then turned to Vladochek. "You and your men have three hours."

Vladochek ordered his men to retrieve the GPR, or ground probing radar, unit from the back of one of the trucks. The unit was designed to serve as a high tech depth finder, similar to those used by ocean-going vessels. But this one was to be used on land. Linked to a series of antennas, the GPR unit pulsed radar waves deep into the earth and plotted the returning echoes on a computer screen, providing a remarkably detailed image of the subsurface topography. If the Khan's crypt lay within Vladochek's search grid, the GPR unit would find it.

As Vladochek and his men disappeared into the pines with their antenna probes in hand, Petrokov ordered his men to set up a temporary camp. Most had not slept in the last twenty-four hours. But that didn't bother Petrokov. In fact, if Vladochek came back empty-handed, which Petrokov fully expected him to, then Petrokov vowed that this would be the last sleep these men would have in a long, long time, at least until he stood face to face with the centuries-old remains of a certain Mongol leader.

Two hours after Vladochek first left to perform his area scan, he burst into Petrokov's tent without warning. Petrokov was reading Polo's book for the fourth time, an assortment of maps spread on a card table in front of him. Vladochek tossed a computer printout on top of one of the maps.

"We found it," he said. "We found the son-of-a-bitch."

"What are you talking about?" Petrokov said, angry at Vladochek's abrupt entry.

"Look at this," Vladochek said. He pointed a stubby, dirt-ladened finger at his printout. "The unit picked up this density variation right in the center of our search grid, only about a third of the way up the ravine." Vladochek then rubbed his bald head as if summoning a genie from a magic lamp.

Petrokov eyed the printout. "It's probably nothing more than a subterranean cave or cavern," he said. "They're all over this part of the country."

"It could be," Vladochek admitted, "but take a look again." Vladochek traced the outline on the printout with his finger.

The light in Petrokov's eyes flickered to life when he realized what Vladochek was pointing out. The printout certainly indicated that the cave or chamber or whatever it was had a distinct rectangular shape to it, a geometric feat Mother Nature rarely accomplished on her own. Petrokov was stupefied. Could it be...?

"Mr. Petrokov, that's no cave," Vladochek said. His face beamed with vindication. "Whatever it is, it was definitely man-made."

Petrokov remained composed. He reached into his vest pocket and retrieved a cigarette. "How deep below the surface is it?" he asked.

"Twelve meters."

Petrokov lit his cigarette and inhaled. He inspected the GPR results again. He then turned to Vladochek and exhaled a stream of smoke.

"Well, why are you standing around?" he said. He snatched up the printout and shoved it into his foreman's chest. "It's getting dark. Order the men to start digging."

The first order of business for Vladochek was to fire up the portable generators and to erect floodlights along the sides of the ravine. To accomplish this, he enlisted Tsogt's Royal Guard to haul the heavy lighting equipment up the ravine by hand. With the soldiers effectively distracted, Petrokov ordered his own hand-picked security force to disperse and establish a wide security perimeter around the ravine.

The workers unloaded the heavy machinery from the backs of the trailers and refueled their tanks. Vladochek then deployed a good-sized force armed with chain saws and axes to begin the clearing work. They split up and cleared a path on both sides of the ravine wide enough for the trucks and equipment to pass. Then, at the site pointed out by Vladochek and his engineers, they attacked the piney copse from each perimeter, felling trees and cutting the trunks into movable sections. Bulldozers and backhoes followed behind them and plowed up the stumps, dragged off timber, and pushed away the undergrowth.

With the worksite lit up like a twenty-four hour driving range, the job continued well into the early morning hours without a single break. At 3:55 a.m., the two work parties met at the center of the bald copse and felled the last of the trees. The heavy machines spent another two hours clearing the area and smoothing the ground beneath them. At 6:20 a.m., with dawn glowing over the eastern horizon, Valdochek sent for Petrokov.

Seeing his boss approach, Vladochek gulped down the remaining coffee in his Styrofoam cup. "We're ready to begin the dig, Mr. Petrokov."

"Excellent," Petrokov replied. He walked over and stood next to one of the red flags that marked the edge of the proposed dig site. "You and your men did an exceptional job clearing the area."

"They worked hard," Vladochek replied, surprised at the rare compliment. "They're as anxious as we are to see what's under there."

Petrokov looked around. "Where are Tsogt's soldiers?"

Vladochek looked around. "I'm not sure. I haven't seen them since they installed the lights. Unfortunately, I haven't had time to play babysitter." He turned to Petrokov. "Did General Tsogt ever show up?"

"No, he didn't," Petrokov replied. "And I don't think he's going to."

"Why do you say that?"

Petrokov took a drag from his cigarette. "Just a hunch."

Vladochek gave him a queer look. "What about his men? Do you think they're planning something?"

Petrokov tossed the cigarette to the ground. "Rest assured that if they try to interfere with my operation…" He paused while he took the toe of his boot and mashed the glowing butt deep into the ground. "…they will join their Great Khan in his eternal kingdom."

Chapter 42

THE BACKHOES PICKED furiously at the earth like buz-
zards feeding on week-old carrion. Vladochek led the frenzy. His
machine roared and vomited curly grey-black smoke with each new
assault. One and a half meters beneath the surface, the buckets
scraped against loose rock. Soon, the rocky bottom that Vladochek
determined belonged to their lost mountain stream took form before
Petrokov's eyes. The backhoes continued to chip away at the stony
surface, scooping up bucketfuls of rocks and depositing them on a
dump pile created at the northern end of the dig site. The bulldozers
joined in and scraped away layer after layer of loose rock.

Petrokov was the first to spot it. He waved at Vladochek to
catch his attention, then he leaped into the pit, landing directly in the
path of one of the dozers. Luckily for Petrokov, the driver saw him
and hit the brakes. The blade of the machine came to within a meter
of Petrokov's waist before it came to a stop. But the Russian didn't
notice. He dropped to his knees and brushed the ground in front of
him. With each pass of his trembling hands, his eyes grew larger and
larger until finally, he sat back on his haunches and stared trance-like
at the white marble slab in front of him. He didn't notice that the
sounds of the machines around him had died and that his men

gathered around him. Nor did he acknowledge Vladochek when the foreman knelt beside him and helped clear the dirt from the outer seams of the marble block.

"What do you think, boss?" Vladochek said in a hushed tone. His eyes never left the slab.

Petrokov rose to his feet and brushed the dirt from his pant legs. He then turned to his foreman and smiled.

"I think I need to take a piss."

Chapter 43

TRY AS THEY might, Vladochek's men could not penetrate the seal of the marble lid with their picks and shovels. The goal was to lift it off in one piece. After several more attempts, Petrokov stepped in.

"This is bullshit," he said. "Just break through the damn thing."

Vladochek requisitioned a backhoe and maneuvered it into position. He raised the hydraulic arm high into the air and then, like the strike of a scorpion, he plunged the bucket down on the slab. The bucket bounced off with a loud "thud." Vladochek repeated the routine and this time, he wounded his adversary, as evidenced by the hairline fracture that snaked obliquely across the slab's surface. Vladochek went for the kill and the bucket hit home a third time. The slab shuddered for a brief instant. Then it suddenly caved in and chunks of marble tumbled into the dark hole they had shielded for so long. Vladochek used the bucket to chip away at the edges until the last vestiges of the lid were gone. Petrokov stepped forward and scanned the marble stairway that descended into the darkness. He placed a foot on the top step, testing it for stability.

"Someone get me a flashlight," Petrokov ordered.

Onlookers scurried in all directions at his request. Moments later, it was Vladochek who appeared with two flashlights. He handed one to Petrokov. The Russian flipped it on and aimed the beam down the stairs. A look of astonishment flashed across his face. He took a step backwards and bumped into Vladochek.

"What is it, boss?" Vladochek asked.

Petrokov stepped to the hole again, this time with Vladochek right behind him, and shined the light back down. The two eye sockets and toothy grin that greeted them belonged to one of a dozen skeletons splayed out across the steps for what appeared to be the entire length of the descent. Petrokov reached down and picked up the skull.

"What the …" Vladochek said. His curious men started to gather around.

Petrokov contemplated the skull in his hand for several seconds, like Hamlet pondering the fate of poor old Yorick.

Vladocheck spoke. "Buried alive, weren't they?"

Petrokov didn't answer. He tossed the skull to one side and kicked the headless skeleton out of his way. The individual pieces bounced and clattered down the steps to an awaiting pile of bones at the bottom.

The stairwell was tight. Petrokov backed his way down, clinging to steps above him. He turned every few steps and pointed his light down the shaft to track his progress. The air hitting him in the face from below was dry, chilly, and ancient-smelling, the odor of bygone glory. Any twinges of claustrophobia that Petrokov may have experienced were quickly displaced by feelings of elation that increased with every step. Random adrenalin-fueled thoughts tore through his brain. Would there even be a treasure? What if it were all a myth? What if all he found were a coffin and some dust? The knot in his stomach tightened. No way. There was a treasure, and he had found it. He knew it. He was about to become one of the wealthiest men on earth.

Bill Gates or Vladimir Bukhorov wouldn't be able to hold a candle next to him.

Reaching the bottom of the stairway, he crunched his way through a short vestibule towards an open archway carved out of subterranean rock and supported by ancient resin-coated beams made from larch wood. There were bones everywhere. He heard Vladochek shout from the top of the stairs, "Boss, are you okay down there?"

"I'm fine," Petrokov said. He flashed his light through the archway, then his jaw suddenly dropped and he stood paralyzed with awe. He realized that he grossly underestimated the size of the recovery operation. It took him a moment to gather his breath. When he finally did, it was barely enough to fuel his voice.

"Tell the men to assemble the crates."

"What was that?" Vladochek's voice replied.

"Assemble the crates," Petrokov bellowed.

It was more magnificent than he had imagined. The main burial chamber, fifty meters long and thirty meters wide, was remarkably preserved. The interior was completely dry, with no sign of water damage anywhere. The ancient engineers did a remarkable construction job. The floor was patterned out of white polished limestone, whereas blocks of pale blue marble, all tightly keyed with one another, formed the roof and walls like a vast expanse of cloudless sky that stretched from horizon to horizon over snow-covered steppes. Thick marble pillars five meters tall, twenty of them in all, provided ceiling support throughout the chamber.

The room was stuffed wall to wall with the plunder and wealth of a by-gone age: statues and sculptures molded and carved from solid bronze, gold, jade and ivory; weaponry and armour forged out of bronze, steel, and precious metals; gilded furniture pieces ornately encrusted with diamonds and other precious gems; and a virtual sea of resin-preserved cedar chests brimming with gold coins, magnificent jewelry, sparkling ornaments, and a rainbow of loose diamonds, emeralds, rubies, and sapphires.

Petrokov scooped up a handful of coins from one of the chests. He let them cascade through his fingers. The imprint on the coins was unmistakable. It was the same as those coins taken from the Damba Zuu Khiid.

Just when Petrokov thought his life couldn't get any better than this, it did. At the far end of the chamber, his flashlight illuminated yet another archway, much smaller than the previous one. Petrokov hastily weaved his way through the treasure and shined his light through the new opening. It was a vault, about one fourth the size of the main chamber. Inside to the left lay the skeletal remains of six horses, all neatly aligned one next to another, their detached skulls dangling over them from leather straps affixed to bronze rings attached to the walls. Stacks of bones lined the right wall of the vault as well. But these didn't belong to horses. Judging by pelvic anatomy, Petrokov surmised that they must have once belonged to healthy young girls. And judging by the bony arms bound by decayed leather, they were no doubt victims of sacrifice.

But Petrokov's eyes didn't linger long on the skeletal remains in the vault nor did he mourn their fates. His eyes focused on the ivory sarcophagus mounted on jade blocks. A ring of golden standards surrounded it, their pointed ends devoid of the royal pennants that had long since gone the way of their owner's flesh. And positioned at the head of the sarcophagus was a throne fashioned from solid gold, its fat arms and legs generously inlaid with diamonds of countless shapes and sizes.

Petrokov nearly choked. Never mind the stuff in the main chamber. He knew the face value of what he was looking at was staggering. Add in antiquity value, and one ran the risk of running out of space for zeros on the calculator. The European and Asian black markets were going to have a field day with this. Petrokov was thankful he was just the middle-man. Let Komvich worry about unloading the bulk of the find. Petrokov would be more than happy with the hefty percentage coming to him in cash. Of course, he would have to keep a few souvenirs for himself. A well-deserved bonus for his twenty-five years of service. Komvich wouldn't miss it.

Petrokov's thoughts were interrupted by noise in the main chamber. A luminescent glow appeared through the archway behind him and cast his shadow on the wall behind the sarcophagus. Vladochek entered with a fluorescent work light and an orange extension cord connected to a portable generator on the surface. The foreman approached Petrokov almost as if he were in a trance.

"Unbelievable," Vladochek said. He held his light over his head for a better look.

"Quite," Petrokov replied. It was the only word he could force out. He reached into his pocket and pulled out a cigarette.

Vladochek nodded towards the sarcophagus. "So the big man is in there, huh? Not so big and bad now, is he?"

Petrokov lit his cigarette. "You have to give the man some credit," he said. "He did know how to kill. I admire that."

Vladochek looked around. "A lot of good his wealth is doing him now."

Petrokov approached the coffin and scanned every inch of it with his flashlight. He slid his hand over the lid, over the intricate patterns carved into the lid.

"He had his time," Petrokov said. "Now it's ours."

Petrokov stepped over to the throne and sat on it.

"Perfect fit, don't you think?" he said to Vladochek. The cigarette in his mouth danced to his every word.

"Hold on," Petrokov said. He looked over one arm of the royal chair. "What's this?"

He reached down and retrieved a long, curved scabbard lying next to the throne. It was crafted out of gold and studded with brilliant diamonds, as was the hilt that protruded from it. Petrokov drew the sword and examined the blade. The steel was pitted with rust, but was in otherwise excellent condition.

He pointed the tip of the blade at Vladochek, then waved the sword as if challenging him to a fencing duel.

"Don't just stand there gawking like a teenage girl," Petrokov said. "Get the men down here and start loading."

Vladochek turned to leave.

"Just one more thing," Petrokov said. His eyes were cold and narrow. He flicked his cigarette to the floor. "If I catch you or any of your men trying to steal a single piece of this treasure..." He paused and patted the diamond encrusted hilt. "...I will personally ram this magnificent piece of history right through your gut."

Chapter 44

IT WAS A blustery fall day in Beijing, with the temperature at 58 degrees Fahrenheit. By eight a.m., crowds had filtered into Tiananmen Square and filled the gaps left by the revelers who braved the cold night on the hard pavement under the stars. Automobile traffic had been halted and the police presence, both civilian and military, was even thicker than the evening before. High atop the Great Hall and the other government buildings that surrounded the Square, sharpshooters secured their positions.

Steele and Maggie rose at 4:30 a.m to meet with General Wuhang and go over their plan one more time. It was agreed that Steele would join a sniper on top of the Mao Zedong Memorial Hall in the middle of Tiananmen Square, while Maggie would remain on the ground and filter through the multitude accompanied by some of Wuhang's men, all armed with a composite sketch of Gunga's face.

Now, perched atop Mao's final resting place, Steele sipped on a rancid cup of coffee and peered into the crowd with his binoculars. What he saw was a diverse mixture of people from every generation and walk-of-life; founding grey-haired revolutionaries and rural peasants decked out in traditional Mao work jackets and pants; accomplished businessmen and struggling entrepreneurs who bolster their fragile capitalistic self-images with casual business attire and chic warm-up suits; students emulating the latest fashion styles of their adolescent American and European contemporaries. Despite their outward differences, every person there seemed to share a common vision of a China no longer isolated from the world, but an active participant in the social, political, and economic destiny of mankind.

Steele knew the Chinese were a proud people, loyal to their unique style of government and reveling in a new economic prosperity rapidly becoming the envy of the West. In the eyes of the average Chinese citizen, they had the best of all worlds – a proletarian government, a strong economy, and an army both strong and efficient. Ten years ago, few Americans believed that the Chinese military establishment would ever rival that of the United States. After all, it was a well-known fact that communist regimes could never outspend capitalist societies when it came to weapons of war, as the collapse of Russian communism so amply illustrated. However, what the West hadn't counted on was a capitalistic economy to fuel a communist-style arms build-up, an economy that provided the constant flow of money necessary to forge and shape armed forces that would soon become second to none.

How this sleeping superpower would respond militarily to a state-sponsored terrorist attack on her own soil was anybody's guess. Regardless of what it might be Steele knew it wouldn't be immediate. It couldn't be, as the Chinese government would have their hands full responding to the health care crisis exploding within their borders.

Steele couldn't shake off the horrifying implications if Gunga succeeded with her release. The cloud of biodust would disperse in seconds. The same breeze that massaged Steele's face would keep the ultra light viral particles suspended in the atmosphere for an extended period of time. Invisible, odorless, tasteless, their victims wouldn't even know they had been exposed. For at least seven to ten days, that is. Then the general mayhem would ensue.

With each case that turned up, the pyre of confusion, fear, and panic would burn ever greater and eventually consume the entire country. Hospitals and health care facilities across China would be slammed with victims and quickly overwhelmed. Many nurses and doctors would no doubt walk off the job for fear of contracting the mysterious illness, leaving patients to die violent and lonely deaths. With the morgues and overflow holding facilities brimming with corpses, bodies would be left to decompose in the streets and homes, spawning a plethora of secondary epidemics. Neighbor would turn against neighbor. Livestock would be purged without discretion, depriving millions of their only sources of income. The fluid economy would congeal as workers elected to stay home rather than risk exposure at the workplace. Communication systems and public works would be overwhelmed. Chaos would reign.

And it wouldn't stop there. Even if human traffic into and out of the country was restricted, the virus could still hitch a ride aboard one of the millions of migratory birds leaving China every fall and emigrate to all fours corners of the earth…

Steele dumped the remaining coffee from his cup. This was no time to dwell on the consequences of failure. Time to get focused. She was out there somewhere and damnit, he was going to find her.

Chapter 45

WHAT TOOK THE ancients days to fill took Petrokov and his crew just hours to plunder. The tomb's vestibule was cleared of its bony remains. Wooden crates, hammered together on the surface and stuffed with white polystyrene packing material, were mounted on skids and hauled into the crypt. Once inside the main chamber,they were packed tightly with loose treasure and cedar chests, and then sealed with a lid. Workers marked each crate with spray paint according to its contents before muscling the finished product to the stairwell. Because each fully loaded crate weighed hundreds of pounds, chains had to be affixed to the skids and each container winched up the steps using a bulldozer. Once outside, a backhoe transferred them to the back of a flatbed or dump truck. This process was repeated until all available trucks overflowed with Petrokov's homemade wooden crates.

Both the Khan's sarcophagus and the throne were too large to fit into individual crates and had to be hauled up the stairwell by hand with considerable difficulty. The throne was just seeing its first taste of daylight in over seven hundred years when Vladochek approached Petrokov. Petrokov held an oversized black canvas bag stuffed full with artifacts for his own personal collection. The diamond-studded hilt of his new sword poked out of the zipper at one end.

"We have no more wood for crates," Vladochek stated. "There's still a ton of treasure down there. What do we do?"

"Leave it," Petrokov replied with a crooked grin. "We have enough here to last several lifetimes."

Vladochek pointed to the sarcophagus and throne. "What about those? We're out of room on the trucks."

Petrokov walked to the jeep parked next to one of the dump trucks and tossed the bag on the passenger seat. He turned to Vladochek.

"Find room for those," Petrokov told him. "Remove some of the crates if necessary." Petrokov then paused, his eyes fixed on the coffin.

Petrokov snapped his fingers. "Wait," he stated. "I have an idea. Have your men unload several of those crates and transfer the contents into the sarcophagus. That will give us additional room."

Vladochek looked perplexed. "How are they going to do that?"

Petrokov glared irritably at his foreman. "Well, for starters, you open it. Then you dump whatever bones and dust you find in there on the ground and replace it with the good stuff."

Vladochek balked, a horrified look on his face. "But boss..."

"But what?" Petrokov asked.

Vladochek didn't reply, but stared at the ground pensively. Petrokov was irritated that his otherwise dependable foreman suffered from a social conscience.

"Do you think I give a damn about the dried up remains of some has-been barbarian?"

Vladochek said.

Petrokov cut him off. "Are you questioning me, Igor?"

"No, sir," Vladochek replied sheepishly.

"Then do it."

Petrokov climbed behind the wheel of his jeep. "I'm going to my tent. Have someone come get me when the vehicles are ready to move out."

Petrokov had driven half way back to his tent when he decided to stop and call Rudi Komvich with the good news. He retrieved the phone from the dash and dialed Komvich's number. A gunshot from high up the ravine interrupted him. Another one followed it, then came the rattle of automatic weapons fire.

"What the…" he said. He tossed the phone down and removed his pistol from its holster. He did a quick clip check, then turned the jeep around and started up the hill, ignoring Komvich's inquiring voice that bellowed from the seat beside him.

He spotted a host of intruders clad in green and tan uniforms at the dig site gathering up his men and marching them at gunpoint into the crypt. Tsogt's missing soldiers. They were back, and with reinforcements.

"Damnit!" Petrokov said. Where was his security force? Perhaps they were just waiting for the right time to pounce. He wasn't going to wait around to find out.

Petrokov slammed the brakes and jammed the jeep into reverse. The chatter of machine guns brought him to a sliding stop. Soldiers converged from all sides. He was trapped.

The Russian clasped his hands behind his head and climbed out of the jeep. Soldiers closed ranks around him and escorted him up the hill to the gravesite.

Bagaryn stood like a conceited gamecock in front of the Khan's ornate coffin, flanked by body guards and personally directing the roundup of Petrokov's men. In front of him, reclined in a spreading pool of blood, was Vladochek, his head all but gone.

Bagaryn's men brought Petrokov forward. They forced him to his knees next to Vladochek's body. Petrokov felt the blood of his foreman wick up the leg of his pants.

Bagaryn walked up. "My dear Mikail, I do apologize for having to intrude so forcefully, but I thought we agreed that you would refrain from entering the tomb until I arrived?"

Petrokov maintained his cool. He looked past Bagaryn at the tree line behind him. No sign of his men. He then gave Bagaryn a blistering look. "You're one to talk, Vachir. You planned a double-cross from the start."

"Just protecting my country's national interests, that's all."

Bagaryn nodded at Vladochek's corpse. "Your man was about to desecrate the remains of our ancestral father." He glared knowingly at Petrokov. "I'm sure he acted on his own initiative and not on your orders, am I correct?"

"Spare me your patriotic bullshit, Bagaryn. You want the treasure to enrich your own personal bank account, nothing more." Petrokov grinned. "I imagine you'll need it now that you're out of a job."

Petrokov noticed his remark seemed to catch Bagaryn's men off-guard. The furtive glances exchanged between them told Petrokov that this was news to them. He decided to shove the knife in further. "I bet they're offering a sizable reward for your capture, too."

"You have a very active imagination," Bagaryn replied loud enough so that his soldiers could hear. "If you are referring to the uprising by Colonel Tsek's band of rebels, General Tsogt and his forces have taken matters under control. The uprising has been crushed and Colonel Tsek has been killed." He stepped over and glared into Petrokov's eyes. "I am still in full control of this country."

Petrokov wasn't about to let the subject die. He knew he had cast doubt into the minds of Bagaryn's men. If his troops could be convinced that they were taking orders from some has-been, they would be less likely to put up a fight against Petrokov's men when they did finally arrive.

He sneered at Bagaryn. "I don't believe you. Tsogt was supposed to meet up with us after he had taken those matters you spoke of under his control." Petrokov looked around using exaggerated head gestures. "I sure don't see him anywhere around," he said. "What does that tell you?"

"Just a minor delay, I assure you," Bagaryn replied calmly. His men seemed to believe him.

Petrokov grinned and continued. "You do realize that at this very moment, you and your men are surrounded."

Bagaryn let out a hearty belly laugh. "Please Mikail, you sound like a cheap American Western." He withdrew his knife and ran his finger along the blade. He motioned towards the rocky slopes on either side of the ravine. "No doubt you are referring to your little security force."

A sinking feeling bored its way into Petrokov's gut. His eyes darted back and forth across the ravine for signs of his security force. He saw none. In fact, thinking back, he hadn't seen or had any radio contact with them since he first sent them out. He had been too engrossed by the treasure to even notice.

Bagaryn turned the sinking feeling into a five hundred pound anchor. "Unfortunately for you and your crew, they will not be coming to your aid. You must promise to forward my condolences to their families."

Petrokov cursed inwardly. How could he have been so careless? Tsogt's men must have seen him deploy his security force and eliminated them before slipping out to act as guides for Bagaryn. Petrokov could kick himself for allowing them to live for even a second after they left Ulaanbaatar. Anger replaced his former confidence. Suddenly, being at the mercy of Bagaryn didn't sit well with him at all.

"We had a deal, Bagaryn."

"As of now my, friend, all deals are off," Bagaryn replied.

"Fuck you, Vachir," Petrokov replied. He rose to his feet, but was shoved down by the soldiers guarding him.

Petrokov protested. "Half of this treasure is rightfully mine."

"Oh, I fully intend to give you a portion of the treasure." He pointed to the stairway that led into the crypt. "Whatever is left down there is yours. You and your men can divide it up among yourselves."

Petrokov glanced at the tomb's entrance. He felt a tinge of relief that caused a smile to slowly return to his face. But the relief and the smile both vaporized when he looked up and saw fourteen of Bagaryn's men dragging a large slab of flat rock down from the western slope of the ravine with the help of one of Petrokov's backhoes. Petrokov's eyes widened in fear. He knew exactly what Bagaryn's warped mind had in store for him.

"You can't do that to me, Vachir," he said, his voice breaking.

An evil grin spread across Bagaryn's face. "You should be honored, Mikail. How many men get the chance to be buried alive in a tomb once reserved for royalty? Don't worry, though. With the limited air supply, your suffering shouldn't last more than four days at the most. Just be sure you don't fight among yourselves over the treasure. You'll use up the air faster."

Bagaryn nodded at the man guarding Petrokov, who then pulled Petrokov to his feet. Petrokov's legs were like jelly, which forced the guards to hold him up by his armpits.

"Vachir, we're friends," Petrokov pleaded one final time.

Bagaryn nodded "Yes, Mikail, we are, but even friends must someday say goodbye. And that time for us has now come."

At his signal, the soldiers dragged Petrokov kicking and cursing to the crypt. They lifted him by the arms and legs and prepared to toss him down the steps. But then they stopped. They dropped Petrokov to the dirt and turned their heads along with everyone else.

Petrokov scrambled to his feet and listened to the noise coming from the bottom of the ravine. It was a low-pitched clatter that grew louder with each passing second. Bagaryn opened his mouth to speak when, suddenly, a massive explosion rocked a thicket of trees to his right. Everyone dove belatedly to the ground, shielding themselves from the shower of dirt, rocks, and wood fragments.

The blast came from an AT-3 SAGGER missile, fired from a Russian-built BMP-2 Infantry Fighting Vehicle that arrived at the base of the ravine, its characteristic flat hull, sloping side armor, and stubby gun turret giving it the appearance of some reptilian reject from the Jurassic Period. Accompanying it were three other BMPs and a US M113 fighting vehicle. The M113 plowed right over one of Vladochek's helicopters parked at the base of the hill, then moved on to Petrokov's tent. It ground it and its contents into unrecognizable pulp beneath its tracks.

Mounted cavalry and a swarm of ground troops poured in behind the armor, then fanned out to await the order to advance. The vehicles came to stop and a lone rider on a chestnut mare galloped ahead of the group, stopping one hundred meters downhill from Bagaryn and the others. Bagaryn recognized him instantly.

Tsek shouted at the top of his voice, ordering everyone to lay down their weapons and surrender. Bagaryn snatched an AK-47 from the hands of one of his soldiers and took aim at Tsek. The machine gun spat and Tsek's horse took three rounds in the chest. The animal reared, flipped backwards, and ejected its rider. The retaliatory crackle of rifles and the steady staccato of machine gun fire generated a deafening roar within the ravine. Tsek, appearing shaken but unhurt, darted for cover.

Bagaryn's men sought their own shelters behind the trucks, heavy equipment, and nearby trees. Petrokov crawled like a lizard over to the Khan's coffin and hunkered behind it. His men, still sequestered within the tomb, opted to stay put. It was an unfortunate decision. One of Bagaryn's officers, fearing the Russians would seize the opportunity to join the fight against them, lobbed two grenades through the crypt's opening. Petrokov heard the muffled "plop plop" of the grenades, then saw a rolling plume of white smoke emerge from the tomb.

Another SAGGER missile screamed uphill and hammered a fuel truck. It ignited the contents into a bright orange fireball that tossed the truck like a ball and vaporized the five men behind it. Bagaryn's men responded and launched two rocket-propelled grenades at the lead BMP. The first missed its mark but the second hit the turret dead on and knocked it off. The concussion obliterated the crew inside.

Petrokov dove over the top of the sarcophagus and landed on the ground next to Vladochek's corpse. He flipped open Vladochek's side holster and withdrew the pistol, then scurried on all fours back to safety behind the coffin. He ejected the pistol's clip. It was full. He shoved it into the gun.

He knew exactly who would get the first bullet. Unfortunately, Bagaryn was nowhere to be seen. Petrokov scanned the battlefield but came up empty-handed. However, he spotted the officer who used the grenade on his men no more than ten meters away. Petrokov took aim and shot. A thin trickle of blood appeared on the man's temple. Within seconds, the trickle turned into a torrent, and the body slumped to the ground.

Chapter 46

THE EARTH EXPLODED six meters in front of the M113. Jeb was pelted in the face and upper body by an inverted pyramid of debris.

"Shit," he roared. He ducked through his hatch and tapped Nagi on the shoulder. "Hard left and get to those trees. We've got RPG launchers in front of us."

Nagi reacted instantly and threw the M113 into a jolting turn. Another ear-splitting blast lifted the hind end of the M113 and threw Jeb into Nagi, slamming his driver's head against the operator console. Lung-searing black smoke rapidly consumed the M113's interior. Jeb's ears were abuzz and his throat was on fire, but he managed to shove Nagi's limp frame through the open driver's hatch above him. Jeb climbed out and coughed up some gritty funk from his lungs. He checked Nagi's pulse. Much to Jeb's relief, it was strong. The flames licking the tail end of the M113 grew bolder, and the craft's metal surface heated up like a hotplate.

Jeb heard the scream of another RPG round approach. He flattened out on top of Nagi. The grenade whizzed overhead and exploded well-beyond the M113. Jeb looked to see where it came from. Seventy-five meters up the ravine, he spotted two individuals, one of them with an RPG launcher balanced on his shoulder. They both stepped out from behind a clump of trees; the gunner dropped to his knees and aimed the weapon at the burning M113. With cat-like reflexes, Jeb rolled off of Nagi, swung the fifty caliber gun around, and squeezed the trigger.

"Have a taste of this, you son-of-a-bitch!" he shouted over the firestorm.

Jeb's gun spit a continuous stream of lead. The fifty caliber slugs shredded everything in their path like a massive weedwacker. The enemy, and the clump of trees for that matter, disappeared behind a cloud of destruction. Spent shell casings pinged and clattered against the surface of the M113 like hail until the last bullet passed through the gun's chamber and the weapon went silent.

A deathly quiet permeated the ravine, as if all other fighting ceased in order to witness this one granddaddy of a firefight. When the cloud of debris finally floated back to earth, there was no sign of Bagaryn's grenadier except a few shreds of uniform here and there. Everything else was pulverized into oblivion.

The reprieve from fight was short-lived. Several bullets pinged off the side of the M113. One buzzed just past Jeb's ear, missing him by inches. Jeb heaved Nagi over his shoulder and abandoned ship.

He made it to cover behind several boulders lining the perimeter of the ravine. Jeb lowered Nagi to the ground and propped him against a rock. The tank driver was semiconscious, mumbling inco-herently. Jeb patted him on the shoulder, then rushed to the battle-field to find a weapon.

Chapter 47

HOURS PASSED AND still no sign of Gunga. The parade was in full procession. Military leaders and dignitaries adorned the grandstands and saluted the columns of man and machine that paraded past them. Bands blared out haughty marching music amidst a sea of tiny red flags that rocked back and forth in the hands of the exuberant assembly, while across the sky above Tiananmen Square, colorful streamers and kites of all shapes and sizes vied for dominant position.

Steele checked in with Maggie on his radio and then with Wuhang. So far, nothing on all ends. The sun sparkled high in the sky and Steele slipped on a pair of sunglasses. He chugged another pint of bottled water, then raised the binoculars to his eyes scanning the Square for the umpteenth time.

Try as he may, he couldn't keep the negativity at bay. It was crazy to believe that Gunga had yet to release the virus; in fact, she likely did so hours ago. Steele, as well as the hundreds of thousands of spectators in the Square, was probably already infected. He rubbed his weary eyes at the thought and turned to the marksman sharing the rooftop with him.

The man lay flat on his belly with his weapon raised, the long barrel aimed at a disturbance that had erupted behind the grandstands. Beijing police scuffled with a group of brave demonstrators who had smuggled in signs protesting Chinese policy towards Taiwan. Steele watched the scene unfold through his field glasses. Police handcuffed one of the demonstrators and started to escort him away, but not without a fight. An officer struck him on the back of the head with a nightstick. The protester fell forward and knocked an elderly Mao look-alike to the pavement. A father and his young daughter standing near the scuffle stumbled backwards to avoid being hit, and in doing so, plowed into a woman holding a kite string.

Steele and the sharpshooter exchanged quick glances. It was her. It was Gunga.

Steele snapped the binoculars back to his eyes. The little girl was crying. Gunga handed her the kite. The tears disappeared immediately. So did Gunga.

Steele panned the crowd. For several agonizing seconds, he thought he lost her. Then he caught a glimpse of her pushing her way against the throng of revelers towards Dongchan'an Jie Avenue. Steele alerted the sharpshooter, but the latter was unable to get off a clean shot.

Steele said into his radio. "We've got her. She's headed towards the Forbidden City. Maggie, are you there? Where are you?"

"Directly in front of you, by the street," she said.

"She's coming right at you and in a major hurry."

Steele rushed to the ladder. His radio suddenly came to life again.

"I see her, Brazos. She's crossing Dongchan'an Jie Avenue. Headed north along the eastern wall of the Forbidden City."

An ear-splitting report from a rifle caused Steele to flinch. He heard the sniper bitching in Chinese.

"Did he get her?" Steele asked.

"No. She's still moving. Tell your friend to be careful. There are too many people around here. He's going to hit one of them."

"Stay with her," Steele said. "How many of Wuhang's men are with you?"

"None right now. We split up a few minutes ago."

Steele's handset crackled and the voice of Wuhang broke in. "Don't worry, Dr. Steele. My men have been alerted. We just received confirmation on that rental car license plate. The car has been identified parked outside the Beihai Hotel across from Jiongshan Park. I sent my people over to intercept her. She will not get away."

After a brief pause, his voice came back over the radio. "Was she able to release the agent?"

"I don't know," Steele said. "But I'm fixing to find out."

Steele scurried down the ladder and jumped to the concrete below to search for the little girl. Using the grandstand as his landmark, he methodically traversed the area he had marked like a hunter searching for a fallen bird. He found her in less than two minutes.

Steele snatched the kite away from the girl. He reeled in the line. The youngster's lower lip quivered and tears welled up in her eyes once again. Her father advanced on Steele like a grizzly bear defending its cub. With a shrill yell, he rammed a fist into Steele's side. Steele doubled over, but kept bringing in the kite, his eyes focused on the metal canister affixed to the kite's cross supports. The father reared back again to strike, but Steele's rooftop companion appeared on the scene and snagged the father's arm in mid-air.

The kite finally came within arm's reach. Steele ripped the canister from it. Thankfully, it was still intact. He recognized the make and model. It was a commonly-used mode of bioweapon dispersal that utilized a radio-controlled detonation device, a "soft" detonator, which would punch a hole in the container without harming the inner contents. He also knew that at any moment, he could hear that sickening "click," followed by the "hiss" of particle-filled pressurized air. He had to move and move now. Get far away from Tiananmen Square and bury the damn thing as deep into the ground as possible.

The sharpshooter loosened his grip on the girl's father and apologized. Steele stuffed the canister and his radio into the back pocket of his jeans. The little girl was still watching him with glistening eyes. Steele knelt down and wiped her tears away with his thumb.

He handed the kite to her. "I'm sorry I took your kite."

Happiness magically returned to her face. Then without saying another word, Steele sprinted through the crowd.

Chapter 48

THE ROYAL GUARD melted into the woods farther up the ravine while the main body of Tsek's troops continued their slow uphill advance on foot behind the cover of the two remaining BMP-2s. Tsek's sharpshooters secured strategic positions among the rocks high up the ridge. One by one, their precise enfilading fire thinned the enemy ranks.

Petrokov could feel the warm Havana sands cooling beneath his feet. Yet he couldn't give up now. Not after finally finding that damn treasure after all those years. No, he must make a move and make it fast before the Royal Guard surrendered or was overwhelmed by Tsek's forces.

He left his position behind the sarcophagus and crawled on his belly to his jeep. The hood and grill were riddled with bullet holes, and Petrokov had no doubts about the condition of the engine. He reached inside and retrieved his duffle bag and phone, then crawled uphill to the first abandoned vehicle he came to, a dump truck laden with crates. Other than two bullet holes in the windshield, it survived the initial assault unscathed. Petrokov tossed his carry-on through an open window. He dropped to his knees when he heard the squeaky grind of mechanized tracks and the excited voices of Tsek's fighters approaching from the opposite side of the truck. He put his pistol on the ground, lay face down on top of it, and feigned death.

An armored vehicle rolled within three meters of the dump truck's front bumper and continued uphill, followed by a squad of Tsek's men. The squad leader ordered two of the soldiers to stay behind with the truck and secure its load while the others continued the advance. One of the men noticed Petrokov on the ground next to the truck and, with his gun in ready position, slowly approached. Petrokov held his breath. The soldier took one step back, then kicked him hard in the ribs. The impact knocked what little air Petrokov had left out of his lungs and the pain was excruciating. He bit the corner of his buried lip, yet managed to suppress any further outward reaction. Satisfied that he had kicked a corpse, the soldier rejoined his colleague on the opposite side of the truck.

Petrokov maintained his ruse to allow time for the main assault force to distance itself. Suddenly, he heard the door of the truck open, followed by animated chatter. Now was the time to make a move. His hand slid beneath his belly and retrieved the pistol. Petrokov took a deep breath, then scrambled to his feet and pointed his pistol through the passenger side window at the two soldiers. They were too busy admiring his sword to even notice him. He fired four times. Both fighters dropped. Petrokov then stuffed the pistol under his belt, climbed into the cab using one of the bodies as a step, and fired up the truck.

The gunfire up the ravine diminished significantly. Petrokov watched the members of Bagaryn's Guard emerge from the distant tree line with hands held high in the air. The fight was all but over.

Petrokov spit out of his window in disgust. Even though it was Bagaryn's enemies who brought ruin to his venture, he still held Bagaryn accountable for the misfortune. He wondered if the son-of-a-bitch had taken a bullet yet. Just the thought of it gave Petrokov a sense of satisfaction, if only for a fleeting moment. If Bagaryn wasn't dead, then Petrokov resolved to make that his next mission in life, even before Havana. But right now he had to get the hell out of there. With the crates in the back of the dump truck, he still had his hands on enough treasure to live life like a king, assuming he didn't have to share any of it with Komvich. That would be another matter to contend with. He must get to the Russian border, which, from previous calculations, was a ninety minute drive north.

Petrokov put on his seatbelt and jammed the truck into gear. The truck pitched forward, then bounced and skipped down the side of the hill at an accelerating pace. Up ahead, a smoldering army vehicle partially blocked his route. Next to it, a soldier with a wicked leg wound crawled along the ground. He waved his arm in the air, wanting Petrokov to stop and help him.

He couldn't tell if it was one of Bagaryn's men or not. It didn't matter. Petrokov, in a typical display of compassion, punched the accelerator. The front bumper of the dump truck struck the vehicle and spun it to one side, while its tires mashed the helpless combatant into the ground without so much as a bump.

Petrokov glanced in his side mirror and smiled. He reached into his jacket pocket and pulled out his phone. If he could reach his buddy Vladimir Tuchin in Naryn, he could get him started on securing a location to temporarily stash the treasure. Petrokov balanced the phone on the steering wheel and used his thumbs to punch in the number.

His attention diverted, he never saw it coming.

Chapter 49

SHELTERED BEHIND A tuft of pine trees along the edge of the ravine, Jeb watched Tsek's forces continue their advance without him. Unable to locate a weapon, he wisely decided to stay put, in direct disobedience to the gnawing anxiety within him that told him to dive into the thick of the action, weapon or no weapon. However, he knew his services weren't needed. Tsek's forces proceeded forward virtually without interruption. It was only a matter of time until they overwhelmed the resistance.

He was about to go back and check on Nagi when suddenly, farther up the ravine, he saw a dump truck turn the corner and start down the hill. The speed at which the truck was traveling aroused his suspicions. Moments later, observing the same truck mow over a wounded, helpless man aroused his anger. It wasn't difficult to decide that whoever was behind the wheel was not one of the good guys and that he needed to be stopped. Jeb took a quick inventory of everything around him. It was the CAT 936E wheeled front-end loader parked off to the side at the base of the ravine that caught his eye. He took off at a sprint and arrived at the machine's foot ladder in thirty seconds. After taking note that the right front tire was flat, he climbed inside and inspected the controls. Just like home. Growing up on a Texas ranch, clearing land and digging tanks for livestock did have its advantages.

Jeb coaxed the diesel engine to life. He knew right away that he misjudged the speed of the truck. It was traveling too fast. He would never have time to maneuver the loader into position to block its path, especially with a flat tire. That left him with only one option.

A puff of smoke shot out of the rear stack and the crippled loader limped forward at a ninety degree angle to the path of the truck. The timing had to be perfect. Jeb yanked on the lever in his hand and raised the loader's hydraulic arms. The truck was less than ten meters away and hadn't altered its course. Jeb cursed the loader, trying to shame it into moving faster. Five meters. "C'mon baby, you can do it," he prodded.

The timing was indeed perfect. A mere nanosecond after the massive frame of the dump truck filled Jeb's windshield, the teeth of the big bucket dug into the passenger side door and ripped it off its hinges with a metallic howl. The glancing blow knocked the dump truck sideways and lifted the loader off the ground, spinning it like a top. The loader crashed to earth and settled on its side amidst a cloud of dust and smoke.

The wounded dump truck rocked back and forth, its crated cargo spewing across the ground like confetti. A stunned Petrokov battled the steering wheel. He caught a glimpse of his duffel bag of goodies and prized sword sliding towards the open gap where the passenger door had once been. He reached across the seat to grab them and in doing so, surrendered control of his vehicle.

The big truck levitated momentarily, then flipped on its side with a thunderous crash. It bounced twice and somersaulted down the hill before coming to rest next to the smashed helicopter.

Petrokov was dazed. Blood streamed from his disfigured nose and from a comma-shaped gash on his forehead. His left shoulder was shattered.

He managed to unbuckle his seat belt and free himself. Gritting his teeth to counter the waves of stinging pain, he used his legs and one good arm to shimmy out of the collapsed cab through the missing front windshield. Then he rose to his feet and started up the hill. His left arm hung limp at his side and one leg lagged slightly behind the other like a zombie from some cheap horror flick.

Petrokov continued his slow, measured ascent up the hill, sloshing through pieces of wood, scattered treasure, and shattered dreams. He eventually arrived at his intended destination. His eyes glowed with an unquenchable hatred as he stood in front of the disabled CAT936's front window and leered at Jeb, who had escaped serious injury but was trapped like a bird in a cage.

Petrokov put a finger to one nostril and snorted. A blood clot landed with a splat on the glass. He then removed the pistol from his belt with his good hand. With a malevolent smirk, he aimed at Jeb. Jeb could only brace himself for the Reaper's deadly swipe.

It never came. Petrokov's pistol fell and bewilderment replaced the hatred on his face. He lowered his head and stared in disbelief at the steel blade protruding from his abdomen. He gripped it with his right hand and cast his eyes on Jeb, who looked back at him with equal surprise. Petrokov opened his mouth to speak, but nothing save a trickle of blood came out. Suddenly, his body lurched forward and hit the loader's windshield. The blade disappeared into Petrokov's body, slicing through the tendons in his palm as it went.

Petrokov slid off the glass, leaving behind a nutmeg-colored smear. Through the white haze that filled his eyes, he strained to make out the image standing over him. The narrowed eyes and noble facial features, the black mustache and goatee, the sardonic sneer - they all bore a strange resemblance to ...

The terror on Petrokov's face was evident. "It can't be," he mumbled through blood-matted teeth. "It can't be," he repeated, much softer this time. He tried to raise his arm, but couldn't.

The Russian let out a sigh and the light of his soul flickered, wavered and then died out completely; he descended into the darkness. However, his last image on earth was one he would carry with him throughout eternity. Standing there, looking into his eyes, sword in hand. The image of ultimate requital. It was him.

It was Genghis Khan.

Chapter 50

GUNGA MADE IT to her rental car and plunged inside, slamming the door behind her. She leaned back in her seat and exhaled deeply. She did it. Her father would be pleased. So would the restless spirit of her mother.

She removed the tiny transmitter from her pocket. It was equipped with two indicator lights, one red and one green. Depress the transmitter button and hold it and the red indicator light would glow. Once the detonator received the signal the green light would flash, an indication of a successful release.

Gunga rolled down her window, stuck her arm out, and held the transmitter high into the air. Time to complete the mission. She pressed the button. The red indicator light came alive. She waited for the green light to follow. And waited. Nothing. She pressed on the button again. The red light lit up again, but still the green light refused to follow suit.

A flurry of Mongolian expletives exploded from Gunga's mouth. She couldn't believe it. She must have traveled out of the transmitter's range. Or else something interfered with the signal. She pulled her arm into the car and tossed the transmitter on the seat beside her. She had to get closer to the Square and try again. But the risk was enormous. They were on to her. They had even taken a shot at her. But visions of a father's disappointment rapidly overshadowed her hesitation. If she failed to carry out the mission, especially this close, how would she be able to look her father in the eyes again?

Gunga pounded her hands against the steering wheel, then turned the key to the ignition. She would detonate that canister, even if she had to go back and bust it open by hand.

Her rental car was parallel parked between two delivery trucks. She looked over her shoulder to back up, but then stiffened in disbelief. It was her. The woman doctor from the palace prison. It couldn't be. She was dead.

The "dead" doctor and a slew of policemen were no more than one hundred meters away from Gunga, held up by the heavy pedestrian traffic that gathered on the streets and sidewalks. Gunga swung her head around just in time to see the squad of soldiers shuffle in double quick time down the middle of the street two hundred meters in front of her.

Gunga screamed with rage and punched the accelerator. The rental car heaved forward and clipped the rear bumper of the delivery truck in front. The impact collapsed the left side of the hood and blew out the left front tire. Gunga's upper body jerked against the steering wheel. Bruised and shaken, but still fully aware of her immediate danger, she grabbed the transmitter off the car's floorboard and spilled into the street.

A series of rifle reports followed. The front windshield of the rental car frosted and imploded. Gunga shielded her head from the airborne chunks of glass, then scrambled on her knees behind a hedge on the hotel lawn. The gunfire created instant panic in the street. People, bicycles, and cars scattered in all directions. Gunga saw that her pursuers were caught waist deep in the general bedlam and barely able to move. Now was her chance.

She sprang to her feet and ran. Police helicopters swooped from the sky. One hovered over the rental car. The other started searching the area.

Another series of shots rang out. Gunga heard a helicopter approach. She took a sour-smelling alley and hid behind a rusted dumpster. She wasn't sure if she had been spotted or not. The helicopter passed overhead. Gunga sprang from behind the dumpster and left the alley. She hurried down a side-street, then headed west on another until she finally reached Beijing's Beihai Park and Gardens, famous as the favorite haunt of Jiang Qing, Gang of Four conspirator and wife of Mao Zedong.

The park was surprisingly vacant for this time of day. Everyone must be at the Square, Gunga surmised. All the more reason for her to return and get the job done. After performing a quick scan for police and troops, she slipped into the park and skirted south along the grassy bank of the park's impressive lake. Gunga heard the faint sound of marching music. The top of the People's Government Building on the west side of Tiananmen Square poked above the distant trees. She was close. A bit farther and she would try the transmitter again.

In front of her, the lake made a sharp bend to the left. Gunga pulled up behind a tree and listened. The helicopters were near. She continued along the lake bank. Just a minute more. She rounded the corner at the bend and almost tripped over him.

There, on his knees directly in front of her, was Steele. The shiny canister lay on the ground beside him. He dug furiously at a hole in the earth he had created with his bare hands.

Gunga's abrupt arrival caught his attention. Both froze and locked eyes on one another, neither knowing exactly what to do next. Gunga figured it out first. She pulled out her transmitter. Steele held up a dirt-covered hand.

"Don't do it, Gunga."

Her lips curled upwards and she extended the tiny antenna. "You're supposed to be dead."

"Sorry to disappoint you," Steele replied. His eyes narrowed. "It's over. Your father has been deposed. There's a new government in Mongolia."

"Liar!" she spat. "I spoke to my father just yesterday."

She pointed the transmitter at the canister.

"Put the transmitter down," Steele said. "If you detonate it, you'll expose yourself as well."

"I'll take my chances," she said. A smile appeared on her face. "Neither you nor anyone else will stop me now."

The words barely left her lips when the tiny raspberry dot magically bloomed on her left breast. Gunga didn't notice it, but the subtle reflection of the afternoon sun off the distant rooftop of the People's Government Building did catch her eye. Steele hit the deck.

Gunga's thumb lashed out for the transmitter button. *Zip.* The sniper's bullet tore into her chest and knocked her off her feet.

She was dead before her body hit the grass.

Chapter 51

THE CROWD INSIDE Ulaanbaatar International Airport thinned by the time China Air Flight 132 pulled up to the gate. It was the first plane to arrive from Beijing since the flight ban was lifted twenty-two hours prior. Steele was the third passenger to step into the terminal, where he was met by Jeb and Enkee. Following brief, ebullient salutations, the three headed for the bar to wait on the boarding call for the outbound flight that would take Steele and Jeb to the United States via Seoul, South Korea. Steele insisted on returning to Ulaanbaatar instead of simply linking up with Jeb in the Korean capital. He didn't want to leave Asia without saying good-bye to Enkee and taking the opportunity to thank him in person.

The men planted themselves at the bar counter atop aged, olive-colored vinyl stools. A wispy bartender sporting an Elvis-like pompadour took their drink orders and promptly got to work. Jeb abandoned his stool and wandered to the nearby jukebox, but after perusing the selections, decided to leave it well enough alone. He returned to his seat disappointed.

"What's wrong?" Steele goaded. "No Justin Timberlake?"

Jeb gave him a high-five with his middle finger. "Very funny."

Enkee smiled. "My country wants me to express its gratitude to the both of you for your part in protecting our national heritage." He paused to allow the bartender to deliver three frosted mugs of beer. Jeb had his half finished before Elvis even left.

"I want to extend my personal thanks as well," Enkee continued. "How can we ever repay you?"

Steele smiled and patted Enkee on the back. "Dr. Enkee, your friendship is reward enough."

Enkee reached into his coat pocket and pulled out two purple boxes. He handed one to each man. "Even so, these are for you."

His curiosity peaked, Steele opened his box. It contained a gold medal affixed to a crimson ribbon with light blue stripes. The raised image on the medal's surface, surrounded by ancient Mongol script, was that of Genghis Khan sitting tall in a saddle.

Enkee pointed to the medal Jeb held in his hand. "It's the Mongolian Freedom Medal, the highest honor awarded to civilians by my country. In the past fifteen years, only three such medals have been awarded. Now there are six."

"Six?" Steele asked.

Enkee reached into his coat again and retrieved another box. He handed it to Steele. "Please give this one to Dr. Townshend when you see her."

"I'll do that," Steele replied. He accepted the box and slipped it into his carry-on bag. "She deserves it more than any of us."

"Here, here," Jeb added. He raised his beer mug and drained the remaining contents.

"She sends her regrets for not saying good-bye to you in person," Steele told Enkee, "but she flew to Geneva this morning to brief the big wigs at the World Health Organization. Then I imagine she'll return to Canada for some well-deserved R&R."

"So what happens now?" Jeb asked. "Who is slated to replace Baggy?"

"The Great Hural will convene on Friday," Enkee said. "The first order of business is to schedule national elections as soon as possible. In the meantime, the deputy prime minister will assume the leadership position within the government."

"Speaking of Bagaryn," Steele broke in. "Do they know where he is?"

Enkee shook his head. "Not yet, but it's only a matter of time. A sizeable reward has been offered for his capture."

"You know we tried that with Bin Laden and it didn't work," Steele said.

"Fortunately, Bagaryn is no Bin Laden," Enkee said. "His network of support dissolved the instant the Mongolian people learned the truth about his plans. Someone will turn him in. That is, if General Natambaa's forces don't find him first. His soldiers have sealed off a nine hundred kilometer stretch of the northern border, and Russian President Molkov has even reinforced his own border patrols to make sure Bagaryn doesn't try to slip into his country. By the way, Moscow has issued a formal apology to Beijing for what has transpired."

"Perhaps this signifies a new era in Russian-Chinese relations," Jeb said.

Steele nodded. "I think when the facts are finally in and all parties involved, including the United States, sit back and reflect on what could have happened here, it will scare the hell out of them. Hopefully this fiasco will prompt a new round of talks to permanently ban genetically –engineered weapons."

Steele turned to Jeb. "By the way, you never did tell me what happened to Petrokov. After all, he was the weapons pimp in this grand scheme."

Jeb's eyes lit up. "Do you remember Nagi, my driver?" He mimicked a thrusting motion with his arm. "He ran that sorry son-of-a-bitch Petrokov through with one of Genghis Khan's swords. Saved my life. It was classic. You should have seen it."

"The FSB arrested his boss in Moscow, along with his merry band of criminals," Steele said. "They also seized the facility where Komvich held his weapons stockpiles."

'Did they get all of it?" Enkee asked.

"All of the cultures and laboratory animals were destroyed by Komvich's scientists before the FSB arrived. A team of UN weapons inspectors have been sent in to verify that. The batch of virus that I recovered from Gunga is on its way to the States. We stuck it aboard a FedEx jet with Brad Jeffries, a special agent with the Defense Department. Colonel Masters assures me that it will be properly destroyed upon arrival."

A voice over the intercom system announced the impending touchdown of their plane. Enkee waved at the bartender. Steele and Jeb reached for the tab at the same time, but Enkee jerked it away.

"Let me get that, Dr. Enkee," Steele said.

"Not a chance," Enkee replied.

Jeb and Steele thanked him. Enkee then walked to the cash register to settle up.

"You look worn out, buddy," Jeb told Steele.

"I am." Steele replied. "It's been a crazy three weeks, hasn't it?"

Jeb agreed. Steele handed his travel bag to him and pointed towards the men's bathroom. "Hold this for me, will you? I'll be right back."

"Don't be too long in there," Jeb replied. "We'll be boarding here pretty quick."

Steele stepped aside at the bathroom door to allow a man and his five year-old son to exit, then he slipped in through the door behind them. The facility was empty. He walked to the nearest sink and shot a quick glance at himself in the mirror. Jeb was right. He did look tired. What could you expect, he reasoned, after weeks of almost continuous adrenaline rushes, of dodging bullets and bad guys, of pushing physical endurance up to and beyond reasonable limits, of dining on a banquet of emotional extremes? All that he wanted right now was to sleep in his own bed, take his two dogs for a jog, kick back with a beer and watch some Monday Night Football. Everything else could wait.

He splashed water on his face and reached for the paper towel dispenser. He didn't hear the stall door creak open. His only warning was the dark reflection that spread across the towel dispenser's stainless steel surface. By then it was too late.

A jackhammer-like blow came hard across his back and a burly arm wrapped itself around his neck. It then cinched down with the force of a python. Steele tried to pry it off. He could feel his trachea bending to the point of collapse. He bulled his neck to counteract the pressure. It didn't help. His brain screamed for oxygen. Through the reflection in the mirror over the sink, Steele recognized the face behind the arm. The filthy mug of Vachir Bagaryn sneered at him, his eyes brimming with murderous intent. The otherwise natty politician was now arrayed in an elephant grey jumpsuit and a faded green baseball cap that covered his newly shorn scalp, a weak attempt at disguise that no doubt fueled a desperate hope of slipping aboard an outbound flight unrecognized.

"Nobody interferes with my plans and lives," Bagaryn hissed into Steele's ear. His humid breath contaminated the nape of Steele's neck.

"You'll die first," the fugitive president continued. "Then I will kill Enkee and your friend. You will all pay for the trouble you have caused me."

Steele's head spun for the third time in two weeks. He was familiar with Bagaryn's wrestling reputation and knew that any time the man chose, he could snap his neck like a rotten twig. Steele wasn't about to wait around for that to happen.

Summoning a burst of strength, he bucked forward in an attempt to flip Bagaryn over his back, but his load didn't budge an inch. Without missing a beat, Steele leaned into his attacker and braced one leg against the wall, then pushed off with as much force as he could muster. This time, Bagaryn's body did move. The pair backpedaled across the floor while Steele pumped his legs like a running back. Bagaryn's back slammed against a stall door with a vicious crunch. But his titanium grip on Steele's neck held firm.

Bagaryn took the offensive. He manhandled Steele into the stall and forced him to his knees in front of a toilet that hadn't been flushed in months. Using his free hand, he pushed Steele's head towards the filth. Steele braced his own hands against the bowl and resisted, but he felt himself losing. With Bagaryn's full weight on his back and the grip around his neck relentless, Steele's arms started to give way. His head inched closer and closer to the stench.

Steele freed a hand and groped into his vest. His Freedom Medal tumbled out of the pocket and clattered to the floor. Steele grabbed it and unlatched the pin with his thumb. He then drove the pin into Bagaryn's wrist, advancing it through the joint as far as it would go.

It certainly wasn't a lethal blow, but it was a painful one. Bagaryn howled and slackened his grip. A healthy flow of precious air returned to Steele's lungs. Steele used his new found freedom of movement to take a hefty bite out of Bagaryn's forearm. Bagaryn bellowed a second time and withdrew his arm entirely from around Steele's neck. He stumbled backwards out of the stall, his hand clamped over his forearm, the Freedom Medal still flopping haphazardly from his wrist.

Steele hopped to his feet and charged Bagaryn. He hit the Mongolian in the chest with his shoulder and drove him against a towel dispenser. Steele then unleashed a swarm of punches to the face. Bagaryn countered with a kick to the groin. Steele doubled-over and stumbled backwards. Bagaryn advanced. He applied a crushing bear hug to Steele. A loud "crack" heralded the demise of two of Steele's ribs.

Steele recalled the only one true wrestling move that he knew. It was time to use it. Despite the knifing pain in his rib cage, he shifted his weight forward and placed his hands on the ground with Bagaryn's leg positioned between both of his. Steele grabbed the heel of Bagaryn's foot and yanked. Bagaryn fell to the floor. Steele then sat hard on the knee. The grotesque "crunch" ended Bagaryn's wrestling career and left him with a leg bent at a forty-five degree angle at the knee. In a pain-fueled rage, Bagaryn kicked out with his good leg and landed a blow to Steele's wounded rib cage. The stabbing pain dropped Steele to his knees.

Both men rose to their feet and squared off. Steele drew first. He lunged at the crippled Bagaryn and drove him into the stall. Bagaryn's head struck the toilet bowl. Steele shoved the face of his stunned adversary into the commode, then braced for the rodeo. It came swiftly. Bagaryn's body convulsed, thrashed, and bucked, but Steele stayed with him like a champion and kept the head submerged.

The show didn't last long. Steele felt the big body start to relax beneath him. He held on a few seconds more, then pulled Bagaryn's dripping face out of the bowl and shoved his limp body to the floor. Steele stood triumphant over his defeated adversary for several moments. Finally, he knelt down, lifted Bagaryn's wrist, and retrieved his Freedom Medal.

The intercom announced general boarding for the flight to Seoul. Jeb said his final goodbyes to Enkee and was about to set out to find Steele when he saw his friend totter out of the bathroom door and head their way. Jeb's head jerked in a quick double-take. Enkee stood speechless, his lower jaw dropped like an anchor.

"What the…" Jeb mumbled. Others standing nearby were obviously thinking the same thing. One mother snatched up her two young children by their collars and spirited them away. A flight attendant in Steele's path took one whiff of him and threw up, nearly triggering a chain reaction within the terminal.

When Steele finally reached them, Jeb held up his hands and took a warning step backwards. "Whoa there, partner," he grimaced. "Would you mind not coming any closer? Thank you."

Steele rubbed his neck. He scoured the terminal with his eyes as if looking for someone.

"Damn, Steele," Jeb complained. "It looks like you just dropped out of a Rottweiler's ass."

Steele nodded in agreement. "You wouldn't happen to know if there's a janitor in the house."

"Why do you ask?" Jeb smirked. "I'd say it's a little late for a plunger, wouldn't you?"

Steele casually pinned his Freedom Medal to his vest. He then patted it and looked Jeb straight in the eye. "Because, my man, there happens to be a piece of shit lying on the floor in there that needs tending to – stat."

Epilogue

OUTSIDE THE DANCE hall in Deets, Texas, the March air still packed a nippy punch; but inside, the Saturday night crowd was turning on the heat. An ever-thickening horde of dancers flowed like lava around the floor to the music of the band on stage. The long tables throughout the hall filled up fast with new arrivals pouring in from surrounding counties. In another hour, the place would be packed to capacity, accepting new patrons only as the old ones left on their own accord or were tossed out by Gus the bouncer. But for now, Steele and Maggie laid claim to two bench seats next to the dance floor, where they shared a beer and studied the dancers.

"It really doesn't look that difficult," Maggie said. She scrutinized a young cowboy and his tight-jeaned partner as they danced by.

"Believe me, it isn't," Steele replied. "Get a few songs under your belt, and you'll be a pro."

Maggie watched the couple disappear to the opposite side of the dance floor. "I don't know," she replied with mild trepidation.

Steele leaned over the table and held out his hand. "C'mon. Let's give it a try."

"Not yet. Let me watch for a little bit longer."

Steele retreated. "Fair enough. Just let me know."

"I will," Maggie replied. She shot him an alluring smile.

"What time does your flight leave tomorrow?" he asked.

"Not until 6 p.m."

"That's nice," Steele replied. "You can sleep in."

Maggie playfully circled the top of her beer bottle with her finger. "Are you implying that tonight is going to be a late night?"

"Maybe," Steele grinned.

She took a sip of beer while peering at him over the top of her bottle. "If that's the case, Dr. Steele, then you better help me monitor my drinking. I wouldn't want to spoil the evening by passing out on you, or worse yet, throwing up all over your boots."

"Lovely," Steele remarked with feigned disgust. "Consider yourself monitored. Besides, it wouldn't be right for Canada's newest Assistant Minister of Health to be caught drunk in public."

"Always watching out for me, aren't you?"

Steele tipped his beer bottle at her. "You bet."

A furious polka erupted on the dance floor. Steele fidgeted in his seat.

"Have you heard from Dr. Enkee lately?" Maggie asked. Steele knew she was trying to keep his mind off dancing. That's okay. He'd get her on that dance floor before the night was through, come hell or high water.

"As a matter of fact, I received an e-mail from him last week. Bagaryn is going on trial before the World Court next month for genocide, extortion, terrorism, and crimes against humanity. The Mongolian populace wants his head on a platter. Enkee tells me that he'll no doubt get the death penalty."

"It couldn't happen to a nicer person," Maggie said.

"Enkee also said that they have just broken ground in Ulaanbaatar on a new National Heritage Museum. Evidently, donations have flooded in from all over the world, including China of all places, to help finance the project. The Khan's treasure will be housed there on a permanent basis, although there are rumors that the museum curators have already organized an exhibition tour for Europe and North America."

"That's one event I'm not going to miss," Maggie replied. "I wonder if they'll bring Genghis along with his treasure."

Steele shook his head. "He won't be making the trip. Tsek and his Darkhad buddies spirited away the remains and reinterred them in an undisclosed location. This time, hopefully, for good."

Maggie nodded. "That's the way it should be."

"Exactly," Steele replied. "The old man deserves to be left alone to rest in peace."

The music stopped, prompting Steele to rise to his feet. "I'll be right back," he told Maggie. Then he walked to the stage and signaled for the band's fiddle player. The musician exchanged pleasantries with Steele for several moments. Steele shook his hand and returned to Maggie.

The band struck up a two-step. Steele turned in his seat and gave the fiddle player a thumbs-up. Then he held out his hand to Maggie. "It's time, Dr. Townshend."

A panicked look shot across Maggie's face. It stuck for several seconds, but slowly gave way to courage. She leaned her head back and drained imaginary beer from her bottle. Then she popped the bottle down and rose to her feet. "Let's do it."

Steele circled the table and wrapped his arm around her shoulders.

"I have to tell you, though," she warned. "When it comes to any type of dancing, I have two left feet."

"No problem," Steele replied. "I'm wearing steel-toed boots."

Maggie slapped him on the butt.

"Just follow my lead and you'll be fine," Steele told her.

They moved to the edge of the dance floor and stopped to yield to the heavy traffic flow. Steele swung Maggie around and drew her close. He kissed her gently. "Ready?" he asked.

"As ready as I'll ever be, Dr. Steele," she replied with a smile. "Lead on."

The End

Chris Pinney is the author of the popular Brazos Steele series of adventure novels. An amateur historian and travel enthusiast, he holds a doctorate in veterinary medicine and has his own practice in San Antonio, Texas.

For previews of upcoming books and more information about the author, visit his website at http://www.brazossteele.com.

To contact Chris Pinney, or to be placed on a mailing list to receive updates about his latest blogs and new releases, go to http://www.brazossteele.com.

www.ingramcontent.com/pod-product-compliance
Lightning Source LLC
Chambersburg PA
CBHW031657170626
46808CB00005B/1484